THE RIG

THE RIG

ROGER LEVY

TITAN BOOKS

The Rig
Paperback edition ISBN: 9781785655630
Electronic edition ISBN: 9781785655647

Published by Titan Books
A division of Titan Publishing Group Ltd
144 Southwark St, London SE1 0UP

First edition: May 2018
2 4 6 8 10 9 7 5 3 1

A CIP catalogue record for this title is available from the British Library.

Printed and bound in Great Britain by CPI Group (UK) Ltd, Croydon CR0 4YY

For Tina, Georgia, Alex

One

ALEF

Welcome to AfterLife
You have selected subject [xx] (restricted access)
Subject name: Alef Selsior
Subject condition: Unspecified. Physical state – *rigor vitae*. Nil significant trauma. Nil significant disease. Conscious state – hypersomnia.
Special Note: This subject is ineligible for ballot. This Life is unfinalised and available for research only. It is not currently accessible via AfterLife random search programs.
Please select review criteria:

Entire Life/Significant Events?
Thank you for selecting Significant Events.
Chronological Order/Random Sequence?
Thank you for selecting Chronological Order.
With Insights/Without Insights?
Thank you for selecting With Insights.
Please confirm review criteria.
Thank you for selecting Alef Selsior's Life, Significant Events in Chronological Order With Insights.

SigEv 1 The arkestra

My name is Alef Selsior. I am an only child.

I was born and brought up in a village in the restricted community of the planet Gehenna. The village was called JerSalem. My father, Saul, was a statistician with a small binary consultancy. Marita, my mother, sang in the church choir and baked cookies.

I struggle to remember much of my life before the arrival of Pellonhorc and his mother. Perhaps it was my age – he arrived when I was eight – but I think it was really that he came to us like a wheelstorm, changing everything and casting the time before himself into deep shade.

One thing I remember from the time before Pellonhorc is when the arkestra came to Gehenna. I've looked back at the event so many times that I feel young and old, wise and naïve, together – though, on reflection, this is how I have always felt.

We travelled to the city cathedral, a day's long journey, to hear the arkestra play. Other than lullabaloos, there wasn't much in the way of music on Gehenna except for hymns and carols, and of course the planet shielded itself from the Song, which it called the pornoverse, so arkestra music was a novelty. The arkestra were only licensed to play godly music while they were on Gehenna, naturally. Hymns and carols.

We travelled to the city by bus. I was so excited that I found it hard to concentrate on the prayers at take-off, mouthing them without heart. Because of this I remember feeling responsible when we hit turbulence, and I also remember a priest in the capsule accusing me with his gaze. I knew it would be my fault if we crashed, but he said nothing, and I spent the rest of the trip praying desperately.

In the city, we went on a flycykle down the river. I'd never been on a flycykle before, or a river, but all I remember was praying that the canopy would hold against the swirling gas, and that we wouldn't sink to hell under the mud.

The cathedral was a vast stadium. Elsewhere in the System, such places were used for sports. I'd seen the cathedral on our screenery at home and in church, of course, but to sit in the stands among the tens of thousands of congregants was like being raised to heaven. Our small church in JerSalem would have sat on the huge central pitch beneath us with a margin of grass so wide that I couldn't have thrown a ball to reach it. This great stadium was open to heaven, and the sky peeled past above us, clouds unscrolling their terrible shapes, the devil tempting us to imagine the worst. As I'd been taught, I kept my eyes down. I could make out where the stakes normally set around the oval pitch had been removed; the circles of scorched earth were clearly visible. While we waited for the arkestra, historic confessions were shown on the pitchside screenery. Confessions of apostasy, idolatry, heresy, and the occasional plain law crime.

I think of that day now and can't quite believe it. It's strange. I think of my early childhood – before Pellonhorc – as a time of innocence. Gehenna called itself an innocent planet, and its priests defended that innocence with rigour.

But what is innocence? Can one hold one's eyes open against the world and remain innocent? Can one close one's eyes against life and call oneself innocent?

Looking back at all that I have seen and done, can I? And who can judge me? No one can judge who cannot understand.

The atmosphere in the cathedral was wonderful. There was an extraordinary sense of comradeship. I sat between my parents in the high stands, holding their hands. My mother's face was rosy. My father's eyes shone. I stared at the pitch, enthralled. It was odd to see anyone other than groups of the condemned on the grass. Notes of music pricked the air as the musicians prepared their instruments. I can, even now, remember the perfect randomness of that sound, the absence of order in the notes and chords. The freedom.

The preacher's stand at one end of the pitch was so far from our seats that we cricked our necks to see him better on the high screenery. Father Sheol was the day's preacher. He stood there and spread his arms.

Father Sheol was legendary, an old man almost in his fifties yet still abrim with hellfire. His voice was separated from the movement of his mouth on the screenery, as if he were calling to us from heaven.

'Welcome,' he boomed.

We roared back, a wave of joy stirring the stadium.

'And welcome, Arkestra of Amadeus.'

He pronounced their name carefully. On Gehenna, names carried great weight, and the similarity of Amadeus to Asmodeus had been debated for a considerable time before the arkestra had been permitted descent rights. The members of the arkestra stopped their preparations to bow to the congregation and acknowledge the priest's greeting.

He announced, 'We are all here to share in the glory of godfear. We are here to be reminded of the temptation above, the retribution below, the suffering here and now, and the reward beyond. We of Gehenna welcome the Arkestra of Amadeus, and we remind them of godfear.'

A few of the arkestra had gone back to prepare their instruments. But they froze as the screenery around them cleared and went hellblack.

Father Sheol continued. 'Today Gehenna welcomes not only the Amadeus Arkestra, but the eyes of the Upper Worlds too.'

I could tell by the reaction around me that this was unexpected. I've since gone back to see the records of the event, such as exist. Father Sheol looks small and his voice is tinny. Each time he repeats the arkestra's name, it seems to sound closer to Asmodeus. Asmodeus, one of the devil's names.

Why would Father Sheol and his Ministry have permitted the Upper Worlds (as we referred to the rest of the System) to peer at us? The Upper Worlds were the devil's agents; yet we were allowing Gehenna to be seen on the pornoverse. What sin, and by whom, was being committed here?

There was murmuring all around the cathedral. Everyone was thinking the same thing. Why would the pornosphere be allowed into the godliest of godlys?

The hellblack of the screenery slowly faded, and new scenes appeared. These were not the usual confessions, though. These images were of retributions.

Odder and odder. These were not the usual burnings at stake of lone sinners, but mass sentencings to the pit. There on the screenery were crowds of shivering men, women and children standing on the pitch over the pits, waiting for them to open beneath their feet.

I thought how off-putting it must be for the arkestra to be sitting on a platform built there. But the images on the screenery only showed the moments before the pits opened, and I now realise that the musicians had no way of understanding the significance of the images, of what came next. All they knew of Gehenna was the opportunity it presented to play before an immense new audience on one of the two closed planets – the other being the obsessively secretive (even to the point of protecting its name) unsaid planet – and simultaneously throughout the System.

On the preacher's stand, a small box was visible, a lead chest edge-laced in gold, and Father Sheol stood tall behind it and paused a moment. Everyone knew what it held. It was opened once a year, and today was not that day.

He bowed his head, briefly put his palms together in prayer, then flexed his fingers and slid a pair of stiff, black gauntlets onto his hands, pulling the long, lead-mailed cuffs up beyond his elbows, and then he leaned forward to rest his hands on the domed lid of the chest. He took a long breath and closed his eyes.

We were silent.

In a single smooth motion of ritual, Father Sheol opened the chest, reached inside, withdrew his hand and let the lid fall closed again.

We cheered as he brandished the book high in both hands. The cathedral trembled with our ecstatic approval. It was the godly Babbel, and Father Sheol was holding the Authorised Version. It shone in his gloved hands, radiating awe. Father Sheol stood in its fierce glow, and as the roar settled, long, deafening seconds later, everyone in the cathedral shrank back in their seats and held their breath. Only the arkestra failed to understand the significance of what they were seeing.

I could hear people murmuring, chanting the seconds

just as I did, although for me, to count was as natural as to breathe.

Three, four...

Even I knew that the light of the godly Babbel was lethal.

'On Gehenna, we *believe*,' Father Sheol roared.

The arkestra were quite still. Now they sensed that something special was happening here. They could see the Babbel's fierce glow reflected on the high priest's cheeks.

Seven, eight, nine...

And still Father Sheol held the book up. The eyes of the pornosphere were on it, and he was preaching with fire. He was showing the Upper Worlds the unquenchable power of our belief.

He lowered the Babbel, and we breathed out. But then, before shutting the book away in its leaded chest, he suddenly brought it to his mouth and kissed it hard with his bare lips, holding it there for a long moment. Only then did he close the book away. He touched a finger to his mouth and blew a silent kiss towards the arkestra. There was a wisp of smoke at his lips. They were already blistering.

What did this mean? On Gehenna, everything had meaning and was to be interpreted. But there was no time now, for the arkestra launched into their music.

I forgot Father Sheol instantly. I thought I was in heaven. The soaring, swooping, gliding of the music enfolded me. The fading and regathering of melody, the subtleties of variation, the – I can't describe it. I'd heard everything they played before, a thousand times, Sinday after Sinday as long as I could remember. But this was more. It was wonderful and terrible. I sat there and tried to hold it in my mind, the simplicity and complexity of it, and then I gave up, closed my eyes and let it bear me away.

As it continued, filling me with something I'd never known before, I found myself staring up, up into the sky. Without thinking what I was doing, I stared at the clouds and saw them as great, beautiful beasts, bounding majestically along, shot through with distant light.

The music filled me and I stared, I don't know for how long, until I was brought to my senses by a violent cuff to the head from behind. It dizzied me for a few seconds. I turned round, startled and hurt. My eyes regained their focus as the man who had struck me hissed, 'Devil-watcher! Keep your eyes down.'

As if the slap had flicked a switch inside me, the music fell flat in my ears. I still listened, but in a different way. I don't think I'd ever been hit before that moment. My parents had never struck me. But they didn't say anything to the man who had just done so. There was a moment when they glanced at each other, but they did nothing else.

Strange. I thought I was accessing a memory of simple life prior to Pellonhorc's arrival, a time without pain and confusion, and yet I find myself disturbed.

The music ended. As we waited for Father Sheol to conclude the service, my mother asked if I'd enjoyed it, and I said yes. My voice sounded new. We locked eyes. Looking back, I realise that my mother had seen that something had changed in me.

My father didn't notice anything. He smiled at the two of us and said, 'Good!' And as Father Sheol returned to his stand, my father added, 'Interesting. The string section made up seventeen point eight per cent of the arkestra.'

That was the type of comment he always made. It was

the way his mind worked. Whenever he came out with such a thing, my mother would always glance at me and roll her eyes. He was not like us, she meant, but this was the first time I fully understood that. At other times, of course, it would be my father and me sharing a similar glance aimed at my mother who was unlike my father and me.

I answered my father, correctly, 'Did you notice that the string section was responsible for thirty-eight point two five per cent of the notes played?'

My father blinked and said, 'Yes,' in mild surprise. And then his attention, and that of everyone in the cathedral, turned to Father Sheol.

The preacher was saying, 'This is a day we shall all remember. Gehenna will remain strong, a beacon of faith unsullied by the polluting gaze of the Upper Worlds.'

It was clear that the arkestra had not expected this. They had been putting their instruments into cases, chattering to each other, but now they hesitated.

'The Arkestra of Asmodeus –' it was certainly not Amadeus that he articulated so precisely, this time, '– has taught us a lesson today. It is a lesson that the Upper Worlds shall do well not to forget.'

Father Sheol held something high. It was not the Babbel this time; the screens closed in on the black orb in his fist. He was holding the Pull.

In the congregation, people began to moan. My mother gasped. The musicians stopped what they were doing, sensing that something was happening that they didn't at all comprehend.

In my head, I made calculations, percentages based on the different manners in which they displayed their panic, approximating my figures to the nearest one per cent. Eighteen per cent were screaming, thirty one per cent were clutching each other, twelve per cent were falling to the ground. No one prayed. Zero per cent.

When I analyse it now, the way the music had freed my mind to think, to imagine, and then the way that logic allowed me to escape my imagination, the way it let me withdraw into numbers; all this was an insight into my father's mind. But now I had the beginnings of my mother's perception too, or at least an early foresight of it.

I was not grateful for that.

Holding the Pull high, Father Sheol walked from his stand towards the pits, to stand at their edge. I wondered whether the pit directly beneath the arkestra was broad enough. I'd seen condemnations on the screenery at home, the calm resignation of the repented sinners as they murmured their prayers before the ground opened. They were always in groups of twenty-five, the largest of the traps five metres in diameter. Father Sheol would stand at their side on solid ground as he operated the Pull. There was a dignity to their going.

There was little dignity here.

Father Sheol smiled at the musicians. They plainly couldn't tell what was going on. Their panic began to subside, but about forty per cent were still wailing. He made a signal and the screenery closed on his face. His Babbel-burnt lips couldn't control his words and we struggled to understand him.

'Here is the lesson.' He could hardly say his esses. His gums were shrouded in blood. He spat blood. 'Let it be seen.' A gob of bloody spittle landed on the Pull. 'Let it be shown.'

He stopped to wipe the Pull on his red robe. 'Let it be known through every world!'

He held the Pull high, his thumb ready on the black orb. A violinist broke away from the arkestra and launched herself at him, screaming, her instrument making a discordant sound that reminded me of the earlier tuning of instruments, but Father Sheol threw her off. The violin bounced on the orange grass.

'We are all of us sinners. All of us, above and below and between. Our only freedom lies beyond.'

His thumb twitched on the Pull, and he drew back his arm and hurled the orb high in the air. As he hurled it clear, he stepped forward and joined the arkestra over the pit.

Now every member of the arkestra screamed and the sound was louder than the sound of their music had been. It drowned even its memory, I'm sure, for most of the congregation, as Father Sheol must have intended.

The air rushed from the cathedral towards the pit as it groaned and gave way, and the air swirled back, swollen with heat. There were flames and a roaring, a sudden rush of air and light that left me gasping and dizzied, and then the pit closed and there was silence.

On the pitch, beside the pit, all that remained were the Pull and a broken violin. Father Sheol was gone too. He had sacrificed himself.

The congregation screamed, whooped and yelled for seventeen minutes as the exits were opened, and the great censers swung across the pitch, trailing ropes of sweet incense. Hymns played us out of the cathedral; 'Heav'n o'erwhelms Hell's awful thunder' and 'We march with fear to Thee our Lord'.

My mother said nothing all the way back. My father muttered to himself. I pretended I was a puter, challenging myself to calculations.

How had such a thing been allowed to happen? Had the Upper Worlds not considered the possible consequences of sending an arkestra to Gehenna?

Now, from a distance of time, it's quite obvious to me. The arkestra were a sacrifice, of course, but they were not merely a sacrifice by Father Sheol.

The System – all but Gehenna and the unsaid planet – was rigorously godless. While the unsaid planet had withdrawn entirely from the System, maintaining its privacy to the point where it monitored and obliterated all reference to itself, Gehenna was a sanctioned aberration. It had suited Gehenna to invite the arkestra. Father Sheol had thought to teach the Upper Worlds a lesson, but the Upper Worlds had known exactly what to expect from him. They had offered up the Amadeus Arkestra as a sacrifice. It was a perfect opportunity for the Upper Worlds to demonstrate what they saw as the insanity of godfear.

In the end, it was a lesson in the ways of humanity. In a secular system, the existence of Gehenna was vital.

But on a day-to-day level, Gehenna wasn't a place of torment. The small community in which we lived was peaceful. There was no crime to speak of. We lived far from the deletium mines. All I knew of the mines was that sinners from the Upper Worlds were sent to work in them.

There was tax, though. As much in Gehenna as elsewhere in the System, tax was a complex burden. Every planet had its own Infratax codes, and System Administration exerted several codes of Ultratax on top of that.

Gehenna was the only haven in the entire System for a tax exemption on grounds, technically, of mental incompetence. As long as you lived there, submitting to godly writ, rejecting the pornosphere and all other trappings of secular confusion, and contributing to the export of deletium, which was unique to Gehenna, you would pay little Ultratax.

Most people employed specialists to calculate their taxes, but my father didn't. He loved the complexity of taxation just as he loved putery with its systems and processes and its promises of certainty. Even on Gehenna, he was unusual. He loved the tax system and the Babbel equally and without question, loved how they pervaded every aspect of human existence, entirely impervious to common sense. Sitting with his friends while he fixed their putery, he would explain how they were taxed. He would advise them to avoid tax by claiming this exemption or that, and advise them how to avoid the wrath of God by this act of kindness or that.

I look back and wonder how someone as logical as he was could accept godly writ. Why was I not able to believe? When did I first realise how strange it was? Was it that slap on the head in the cathedral? Was it the look on my mother's face as she saw me register her failure to defend me? Was it the irresistible tide of her genes? Did *she* ever believe? Or did she simply keep quiet about her disbelief?

Two

TALLEN

It's a border planet, Bleak, and Lookout, the town where I live, is its last outpost. That's if you don't count the rigs, of course. Here in Lookout, people hunch their shoulders and keep their heads down, do their jobs and then take their breaks off-planet. They say monotony causes madness, but we have three seasons, so it can't be monotony that sends people crazy here. Most people think it's the wind that does it. The seasons in Lookout are as eventful as you'd expect considering Bleak was crash-terraformed from methane to nitroxygen inside three centuries.

Our longest season is between winter and summer, when the wind comes in hard off the sea, heading for the mountains, slapping thunder and rolling silverblack cloud in its wake. Anywhere else, they'd call it spring. We call it flux, and it's one grand hell of a sight. Squinting out to sea, you can make out tumbling shapes in those vortices of cloud. Sometimes the shapes remind you of animals you might have seen pictures of, or dreams or faces or maps of worlds, but sometimes it's the shape of a rig, and if it is, no matter how godless you are, you ask that the cloud doesn't drop what's left of it on your head. Lookout's only once seen a falling rig, and that was well before my time, but they still talk of it when the wind's beginning to build and they're drinking brush brandy in Bar/red. Mostly the rigs are well anchored, though – what the riggers call semi-submerged – and they're far enough out to sea to be unlikely to fall here if they do get torn away.

Everything in Lookout is geared around the rigs. There's pretty well nothing here but the rigyards and their support systems.

No, that's not quite true – there's the sarcs, of course, and everybody in the System knows about them, but the sarcs are dropped into the sea a long way from Lookout. They're big enough news elsewhere, but no one here pays them any attention unless once in a while one of them slips the shield and gets itself beached. Oh, there's the Chute, too, but I'm not crazy enough to spend my time there.

During flux, Lookout shuts down so you can't hear a thing outside the complex, and you don't go beyond the shield until the summer, when it's a different story. The wind drops and at the shoreline the sea is easier, smearing itself over the beach. I take my break in the summer. The weather's relatively gentle then, and I find the brief hope it raises too hard to bear, so I pack up and head for the snows of Colder. Colder's a few days away by slowship. I don't sleep on the journey, I just watch Lookout fade away, or else I stare out at the stars. I used to see a woman in Colder, but she got attached to someone and I don't see her any

more. Now I take a hut high in the white hills and go walking by myself.
I come back to Lookout in the winter. Bleak has no fall to speak of. Our winter is the wind flipped around and returning to sea with a freight of rock torn from the mountains. The terraforming of Bleak hasn't taken properly, but it doesn't matter – like I said, the town only exists for the rigs, and they only matter as long as there's core to be drilled, and I guess the core will be exhausted by the time Bleak falls back to shit again.
But I'll be long dead by that time, so what the hell.

Tallen looked over what he'd set down, closed his eyes a moment, then sighed and rechecked the prompt for the third time, looking for the catch.

FINAL REMINDER. YOUR FREE [StarHearts] WELCOME-BACK OFFER IS ONLY VALID FOR TWELVE HOURS. YOU HAVE ONE HOUR REMAINING. TO REDEEM THIS OFFER, PLEASE REGISTER YOUR [HeartStar] PROFILE NOW. THIS OFFER WILL NOT BE REPEATED.

For a month they'd been sending him better and better deals, and he'd ignored them all, but a free offer was unheard of.

He hated the idea of being manipulated, even though he knew everyone was. It was impossible to participate in the Song without losing part of your spirit in the process. This, though, was almost impossible to refuse, even if he wasn't in the mood for company. StarHearts didn't come cheap.

He felt a brief rush of the usual melancholy, and wiped the whole thing from the screen. StarHearts had never done him any good before.

And then he sighed to himself and brought back most of the text he had written, letting it end after the hut in the white hills. He closed his eyes and remembered Lena telling him goodbye, her open hand rising to the screenery, and him, stupidly, touching the glassy interface.

After Lena he'd sworn never to use StarHearts again, and yet here he was, drawn back once more. They knew how he thought. They knew him inside out.

Fine. When they started charging him, as they would soon enough, he'd cancel. They should know that about him too.

There had been no future with her anyway. They'd both known it. It wasn't the fault of the program. He was never going to leave Lookout for anyone and she'd never live anywhere but Colder, and that was all there was to it.

The message to no one glittered on the screen. He restored the whole thing, all the way to 'what the hell'. What the hell, he thought, and yessed it.

The screen glowed instantly.

—Welcome back to [StarHearts], Mr Tallen. [StarHearts] is a ParaSite of AfterLife.

—Subscriber advice follows. You are not being charged for this advice.

—You have not explained your employment. Detailing well-remunerated and/or socially respectable employment statistically raises your chance of a response.

—You have used words or phrases that may be off-putting to some [StarHearts] subscribers. Some of these words or phrases are: Monotony; Madness; Slapping; God(suffix); Hard to bear; Don't sleep; Drinking; Used to see a woman; Got attached; Exhausted; Torn; Shit; Hell.
—Words or phrases that you may find more effective include: Love; Companionship; Warm; Kind; Sense of humour; Funny; Wealth (only in connection with yourself); Genetically stable (only in connection with yourself); Healthy (only in connection with yourself); Home-loving; Good-looking (only in connection with yourself).
—Do you wish to edit your [HeartStar]?

Tallen chose No.

—Your [HeartStar] has been posted to all subscribers for a period of one hundred charge-free hours. After this time your [StarHearts] account will achieve positive charge-status of fifteen dolors per (local calendar) month.
—You will be informed of any responses.

He tried to close the screen, but it wasn't ready to let him do that.

—Please complete this Opportunity String before exiting AfterLife. Failure to do so will clear all details of this session and invalidate the current offer.
—Thank you for agreeing.

—Many [StarHearts] subscribers combine [StarHearts] access with main database access and access to TruTales and other payment-positive ParaSites. Do you wish to take this opportunity now or later?

Later.

—You have not accessed the main AfterLife database for twenty-nine hours and fourteen minutes. You currently have a cache of eighteen votes to cast, of which five expire in nine hours and fourteen minutes. Do you wish to vote now or later?

Later.

—Thank you. This Opportunity String is complete. You may now close –

He closed it. Leaving the screen to itself, and feeling restless and oddly guilty at having yessed the HeartSearch, Tallen shrugged on a jacket and took to the street.

He was regretting it already. What was he doing? It always made him think too much, writing or talking about himself like that. How the hell had he got to a place like this – the woman he'd met the other night in the red bar, the writer, she'd said Lookout was full of sound and fury, saying it like she'd heard the description herself somewhere. Now he had it lodged in his head, along with the way she'd said it. There had been something unusual about her, a sense of life and curiosity, and he'd wanted to carry on talking to her. He'd thought maybe she was interested in him too, but she'd turned away from him as soon as the big Paxer had come in, and that had been the end of that. Razer, that was her name. Maybe he'd see her again. Razer and the Paxer had still been there, drinking hard, when Tallen had left the bar. Most people, even non-crimers, were nervous around law officers, but Razer wasn't.

No, Tallen shouldn't have let himself be suckered into another HeartSearch. Look at the subscriber advice. What did he have to offer anyone? Lena had been right, and the woman before her, and all the others. And look at the insanity of where he lived. Who would live here by choice?

He walked beside the buildings, his thoughts for once extraordinarily clear. At night, Lookout was almost shadowless. The days here were strange enough, but it had taken him a year to get used to how the town was at night. Under the odd glare of the shield, the air gave no sense of depth or distance, everything seeming not distant or near, but just big or small. Your brain had to learn a new visual judgement. The buildings were no problem, but door grips were awkward, and eye-parallax was more important than focus. Getting around Lookout after sundown was like walking through a kids' flicbook.

And there was the shield. During flux, the shield protecting the complex was a booming weave of magnetism and electricity. Tallen thought of it as smoke and mirrors. He believed in the shield's existence, though, unlike the dozen or more drunks and crazies every year who took it into their heads to run through it and were swept away like that girl in the Oz flicbook his mother had read him as a child. Except that they were never seen again.

During the day, the shield was almost invisible, a

troubling blur you could briefly squint at. You'd plant your feet firmly and focus on a wall, the ground, something solid. Nothing could resist that wind, but the soft, graduated shield could deal with it. At its outer edge, it was hardly there at all, merely taking the wind's measure. A few metres in, it was rolling with the punches but starting to blunt and spread them, while a few metres deeper, it was soaking up the assault and making enough energy of it to power the complex and the shield together. The surplus stored energy was sufficient to run Lookout for the rest of the year. Bleak's wind was an inexhaustible source of power and catastrophe.

Tallen wandered on, unable to dispel an odd feeling of being shadowed through the streets. It was just this absurd place, though. Nothing on Bleak made sense.

It was cool now and well past midnight, and the shield hummed. As always, Tallen headed down to the beach, descending close enough to the water that it lapped at his feet. The surf hissed through the stones underfoot. He preferred the shingle at night, when the brilliant sea-washed colours of day were muted to purples and scarlets.

Tonight the calm of the sea didn't dispel his vague feeling of desolation. It was a mistake to have come out. These nightly walks were a bad habit. He should have taken a capsule and at least got himself some chemical rest.

Rocking gently from foot to foot to avoid sinking through the shingle, he wondered where his life was headed. There were more of the nearly-dead here than the living. They say you come to Lookout if you're tired of life, and you go to the rigs when you are ready for death. The bars of Lookout were full of such end-of-everything talk. The trouble was, Tallen was starting to come out with it himself.

He thought of the woman in the bar again. Razer. What was she doing here? Most people let you know what it was that had brought them here after the first drink. Not her, though. There had been a life to her.

He reached down and stirred a finger in the slow water, watching the ripples go out to join the spiking sea beyond the shield and out of sight. Further out, he could see the shield forcing coronas from the wind, reds and blues and iridescent purples, shards of colour hard as rock and gone in an instant. Beyond that there was nothing to see. Space had its stars but the sea had nothing at all. Nothing but the sarcs and the rigs, anyway.

Maybe he'd feel better when he got back to work in a couple of days. Time off in Lookout wasn't a good thing.

He let his thoughts drift, wondering what it was like to be on a rig out there. Crazy and lonely, he guessed, with the machinery thumping day and night, and the wind and the sea. He closed his eyes, trying to imagine the thunder of the drills and the fury of the elements working relentlessly to rip you away.

And then he forgot about the rigs and tipped his head, listening. Something wasn't right. There had been a sound, and there it was again, sharper. He pulled himself upright and started heading for home at a brisk walk.

There were definitely footsteps behind him. Tallen looked quickly back, stumbled, then began awkwardly to run.

Three

RAZER

Razer sat with Bale at a small table under a dead light in a corner of the bar, the pair of them drinking steadily. The late evening was quiet, only a few others around the place, some talking but most of them sitting and screening alone. Looking around, Razer counted fifteen screeners, which meant that, statistically, eight or nine would be on AfterLife or one of its ParaSites. She used to wonder why they didn't stay home and screen from there, until someone had told her that AfterLife's screentime restrictions didn't apply to public-area screenery. It kept people social, gave them a reason to go out. It kept AfterLife popular with bar owners, that was for sure, and it kept the System's Administrata happy.

The screeners here seemed content enough too, nodding to themselves, muttering intently, tapping the air. At least, judging by their demeanours, none of them were on porn sites. Mostly, though not invariably, they stayed home for that. Razer wondered whether any of them were linked to TruTales.

There was something nagging at her, had been since she'd got here, and it took her a moment to work it out: Tallen wasn't in tonight. Not that it mattered, now she had Bale, but even so, there had been a sense of curiosity about him that she seldom found. She was sure he'd have made a good story. She'd thrown out that line from *Macbeth* and he'd jumped on it. And the way he'd described the rigyards, there was definitely something to him. Odd, too, for Cynth to appear undecided, giving her both men at first as material for Razer to tell a TruTale. Bale was way out of the ordinary, of course, and Cynth, with her AI logic, had been right to bring her here, but yes, if it hadn't been for Bale…

She turned her full attention back to the Paxer. Something was off with him tonight, but she couldn't fix the reason. Usually it took a few drinks, a story or two for her to catalogue later, maybe a smile to be raised from him, and the evening was done. But not tonight. Tonight Bale had drunk steadily without showing anything of the alcohol except an unusual reflectiveness. There was nothing relaxed about him, though.

He said, 'You like it here on Bleak, Razer?' Saying it like an accusation.

She made a non-committal gesture.

'Don't just do that. Tell me. What do you like about it?'

'It's peaceful,' she said.

'I'm not in the mood for jokes. What do you like here?'

'Usually I like drinking with you.'

For an instant she could clearly see Bale in a cell with someone who'd given a wrong answer. It made her shiver. She said, 'I like the sea. I like the wind and the noise. It's a good place to think.'

'The eye of a storm. That's what you told me the first time we met.'

She said, 'Did I?' though she remembered it perfectly. 'Has something happened, Bale? You're in an even fouler mood than normal.'

As he stared past her, she noticed how the non-screeners in the bar fell silent at his gaze. The same thing had happened that first night when he'd pushed through the door and let her catch his eye. He'd interviewed her like a suspect for an hour, drinking soft while she drank hard, as much as telling her no one comes to Bleak without a very big reason, and then he'd given up the questioning and started drinking vavodka with her, catching up and then overtaking her within fifteen minutes.

She'd never met anyone like Bale before, anywhere in the System. They'd slept together three times, the second time to see whether the first time was just because they'd been too drunk, and the third time to see if being sober the second time had put too much pressure on them. Razer had known it was never going to work after the first time, but she'd become fond enough of Bale to want to let him work it out for himself. She had to see if he was strong enough to let some kind of friendship surface from the wreckage of their sex. It had taken him a few weeks, but it seemed like he'd made it, though you could never tell with men.

It was an odd sort of friendship. She made sure Bale knew he was being mined for stories, but it didn't seem to bother him. It was obvious to her that he had few other friends on Bleak. And – though it was a pity – he was professional enough to give her nothing identifiable or sensitive. He was good at his job, she was certain. She just wondered why he did it here. He wasn't fit for anything else except soldiery, but there were thousands of better places to live in the System than Bleak. Cynth had sent Razer to most of them and she'd never found anywhere worse.

Thanks to Bale, though, she knew a little more about the

rigs than could be trawled from the Song, and about life on Bleak. Cynth had chosen him well.

'You ever think about life?' Bale said now, a faint slur to his voice.

She bit back a flippant answer. One of the few personal things she knew about Bale was that he didn't think much about anything outside his work. That was one of the things that usually let her relax so well with him. That perfect focus would make him good at his job, but it made him vulnerable too. If everything was black or white to you, you'd be blind to grey. For Razer, everything was a shade of grey.

'I think about life,' she said. 'Why?'

'I've been thinking. The Administrata, the Corps, Pax, it's like they're all in an airlock with a single inrush of air. Too many people, just one source of oxygen from a high corner.'

She nodded, glancing idly round the bar. Still no sign of Tallen.

'By the air, the Generals and the Presidents are standing on everyone else, breathing just fine, pissing and shitting down.' Bale was almost all the way drunk, squinting at the damp rings on the table. 'Below them there's a little piss and shit, but the air's still pretty good. A few bodies lower, the air doesn't taste so fine. Near the bottom, it's all shit, the air's foul, they can't move for the pressure from above, but they're alive.'

Razer started to say something, but Bale held up a hand.

'The thing is,' he said, 'the people at the top need the ones at the bottom in order to get their mouths to the best air, and the ones a bit lower down have their eyes fixed on the breathable air. They don't care about the top, never will, and they don't care about the bottom, never will.'

He dealt himself another drink. One of the barstaff came and scooped a few of their empty glasses away and wiped the table in a single smooth move. Razer tried to acknowledge the service, but the staffer kept his gaze to himself.

She wondered what to say, not sure how to gauge this mood of Bale's. In the end, she said, 'It's simple, but it's a fair metaphor. Most people die at the same level they're born on. Is this your philosophy of life?'

'It's how it is.'

She tried a small laugh. 'Where are you, then?'

Bale blew a long breath of scummy air and said, 'In a goddamn bar with you, as usual. You need another drink and so do I.' He drained his glass and slapped it down on the refill pad, and swore at the sudden bloodcheck warning shining on the pad.

Razer had never seen him quite like this before. As lightly as she could, she said, 'Well. It looks like we're both walking.'

'Hell to that. I look drunk to you?'

'No, Bale. A drunk never looks drunk to a drunk.'

Bale slid his index finger into the table's blood slot, watching the screen light up and reading the result.

MACHINERY PRIVILEGES WITHDRAWN.
PLEASE RETEST IN FOUR HOURS IF CEASING ALCOHOL INTAKE NOW. HAVE A GOOD EVENING, OFFICER BALE.

'Hell to that, too,' Bale said. He held his glass at eye level for a count of ten and then drained it evenly. 'Is that fine motor control or what?'

Razer gave up and grinned. 'It looked fine to me.'

He pulled a new drink and drained it, the empty glass hitting the bar before the bloodcheck display had flicked from four hours to four fifty.

'Maybe we should slow down just a little,' Razer said.

'Doesn't matter to me. I'm not working tomorrow.'

The tone of his voice had changed again. She said, 'No?' Bale stared at the empty glass until she said, 'Day off? When did you last have one of those?'

'Suspended.'

'What?' Razer put her own glass down, suddenly halfway back to sober. Had she missed something? 'Why?'

'Insubordination.'

She relaxed a little. 'So, what? A week? You just have to take it easy, Bale. Didn't you say this happens to you every month, sure as night?'

'Yeah. Maybe I'll go home. Sleep.'

She caught his look and laughed aloud, breaking the mood. 'No. That won't help either of us. Go. Sleep. I'll be seeing you, Bale.'

He stood up and she watched him leave, walking a little too steadily, his thick frame momentarily silhouetted in the watery shimmer of the doorway. Razer counted a few minutes away, then followed him out.

He wasn't waiting for her. She was surprised to find herself vaguely disappointed.

She started to walk home, the alcohol mellowing Lookout's disturbing streets. She was just sober enough to skirt the alleys of the Rut. Every town, city and port had its own version of Lookout's Rut; an enclave of monitored illegality, permitted to exist on the unwritten understanding that the crimers inhabiting it didn't draw too much attention to themselves. The Rut's inhabitants were minor crimers who dealt in drugs but didn't brew anything serious, who only emerged to commit street crime and small theft. Its existence suited Pax perfectly. Razer knew how they all operated, these crime valves. On Spindrift she'd spent a week in the alleys of Darknode for a TruTale, learning to skin IDs and to travel unseen, to misdirect and conceal, to look clean and fight dirty.

It was about time for her to leave Bleak. Bale and the stories she'd work from him were the best things about it. There was little else of real interest to her except, maybe, for the Chute.

Whatever else there might be for her in this place, she'd probably got by now. It all turned around the rigs and the bars. Everything was designed to keep the rig-constructors fit to work and on the edge of sober. The money brought them here, the work kept them busy and the bars kept them quiet. Pax kept them reasonably safe and straight. Ronen, the corporation running the rigs, conducted their industrial espionage in secret, never exercising Pax.

Razer knew a little about the rigs too, now. She'd talked to drinkers who had told her they'd been on the rigs, and she'd taken their stories, and she'd also been told they were liars, that no one who'd ever been on the rigs talked about it. One man she'd certainly believed, but the story had mostly been in his eyes and his silences. She'd offered to pay him, but the only return he'd accepted was a tale in exchange. So she'd told him a story she'd been given by a crimer who claimed to have survived the deletium swamps of Gehenna. Telling that helltale to a dead-eyed rigworker in the sweat of the Neverie bar, Razer had felt like a lost child.

She felt odd at the thought. A story for a story, the rigworker had said, and it had sounded like her kind of transaction. Like her life, even. Some kind of a life.

Back in her room, she fell onto her bed, closed her eyes and tried to sleep. When that failed, as it often did these days, she opened her screenery to AfterLife Live!

Holoman had just started. She left him chattering and made herself caffé, came back to the bed, pulled the covers to her chin and sipped the tasse in front of the display.

'Hi, Razer. Good to see you again. Today's show is a very special two-parter. First, an amazing AfterLife Past Tale, and then, on the Vote-Slot, a brand-new ballot. Hold on while I run quickly through the legal blahdery, and then I'll show you the Past Tale – this one's a real eye-opener.'

Holoman stepped off-screen as words began to scroll.

AFTERLIFE RESPONDS TO ALL ATTEMPTS TO INTERFERE WITH ANY PART OF ITS ARENA AND ASSOCIATED SYSTEMS WITHOUT NOTICE AND WITH ALL MEASURES IT MAY CONSIDER APPROPRIATE...

Eventually Holoman walked back on, smiled and wiped his creaseless brow. 'Nearly done, Razer. Don't go anywhere.'

'Sure,' she murmured. She was a registered worker for one of the ParaSites, and that was about as good as working for AfterLife itself, so couldn't they give her a rest on the legals? She yawned. Maybe she shouldn't have had the caffé. It was bound to kick in just as she was about to doze off in front of the screen. She needed to sleep.

Holoman indicated an image of a brain behind him and said, 'Somewhere in here is the secret of AfterLife. The neurid. It's quite undetectable. It is impossible to locate by knife, scan or scope…'

Razer half-closed her eyes and mouthed the litany along with him. '… Any attempt, or investigation considered by AfterLife to constitute an attempt, to detect the neurid will be subject to immediate response. This includes all neurological scans, investigations and neurosurgery that is not precleared with AfterLife.'

The screen cleared behind him. 'There. That's the boring part over. Now for our very, very special Special! The first part of today's show, Razer, is the story of an ordinary-looking man. You may think you've heard his story before, but never, I promise you, like this.'

A man's face came up on the screen, pock-skinned, a rack of even, discoloured teeth, hooded brown eyes. Razer instantly recognised him, as everyone in the System would recognise him; Ajeenas Rialobon, the AfterLife Killer.

Holoman was talking, but Razer didn't need to listen. Like everyone else in the System, she knew every detail of the story.

Over the course of a decade, Rialobon had murdered more than two thousand drifters across the System. Since most of the victims weren't immediately missed, his activities hadn't been noticed for years. It was only after he'd been caught, when he gave up the location of his cryovault, stacked with skulls and neurosurgical tools, that his motive was discovered. He had been dissecting brains in search of the AfterLife neurid.

'Of course, he failed utterly,' said Holoman cheerfully. 'It's an impossible task. As it develops, the neurid merges with the host's brain, and unless it is activated by trained AfterLife medicians using encrypted AfterLife bioputery, the neurid's function and appearance are totally indistinguishable from normal brain tissue and activity.'

Holoman looked solemn. 'Rialobon's activity was only brought to light by skilled AfterLife daticians who identified a significant but unaccountable fall in the homeless population.'

He turned to a different cam and smiled. 'It was a shocking discovery but a triumph for AfterLife. Our constantly ongoing audit suggested the presence of an active serial killer before a single body part was found. AfterLife gave Pax the data and the programs to pattern-track and eventually to catch the killer.'

The stark Pax symbol came up and fell away again. It made Razer think of Bale. Would he be asleep yet? She checked the time. Nearly four. The violet glow in her window was starting to be touched by daylight. She'd never sleep now. It was stupid to watch this. The Holoman Specials were never new, just old tales endlessly graphically reworked. She only really watched the pre-vote segment out of habit.

She wondered if she should call Bale and decided not to, and then for some reason she thought of Tallen. She'd felt bad about leaving him so abruptly for Bale, but that was sometimes the way of it. And since then, he hadn't been in the bar when she had.

Holoman brushed a lock of shining brown hair from his eyes. 'Allegations are frequently made that AfterLife favours the wealthy in its selectees. It does not. Nor could the ballots be rigged. All randomising programs are openly available.

AfterLife maintains only one totally protected secret, and that is the neurid. Total protection of the neurid allows everything else to be entirely open. AfterLife is fully System-monitored and rigorously controlled.' Holoman began to walk, the cam following him through blocks of pulsing data, murmuring voices fading up and falling away. She heard the clipped consonants of Vegaschrist, the glottals of Heartsease, voices of the old and the young, women and men, and the fragments of text swimming across the screen –

... *The one thing that sustained me...*

... *She never realised...*

... *When he finally died...*

As it all subsided, Holoman said, 'Let's look at the facts. There is a potential AfterLife neurid for every birth on every planet in the System except – of their own choice – Gehenna and the unsaid planet.'

Holoman was, as always, padding the so-called Special. Razer started working out how she was going to fit Bale into a TruTale. She always got good response figures when she put herself into them. A bit of sex didn't hurt, either. And people liked to think they were learning something new on TruTales, just like they did with AfterLife, even if they couldn't register a judgement on a TruTale. Bale's reminiscences were heavy on violence and tech. It wouldn't be hard to wrap a story around him.

Holoman had moved on to neurid-placement. 'Parents may decline to participate on a child's behalf, of course, though the statutory AfterLife tax cannot be revoked. In rare situations where facilities are not immediately available at birth, neurid-implantation can be carried out within the first year of life.'

The caffé was kicking in. She tried to start the Bale story in her head, but found herself thinking about his problems rather than his narrative potential. He lived for Pax. What would he be without it?

Was she worrying about him?

The possibility of that sat her up more than the caffé. She'd met more interesting men, and far more attractive than Bale. His stories were good and his bluntness was appealing, and that was all.

No, her only worry was that she might not gather everything Bale had to say before TruTales moved her on.

'The neurid is pluripotent-cell-based, cheap to produce, and implanted via a simple cranial infiltration. Its production is subsidised by the System. The randomised distribution of placebo neurids is AI-moderated, although the overall use of placebos is diminishing year-on-year as new memory storage facilities are introduced, thus expanding the AfterLife database. The only person in the participating System who cannot be implanted is me.' He passed a hand theatrically through his own torso, demonstrating his unreality, and finally returned to Ajeenas Rialobon.

Razer didn't need to see the detail of Rialobon's killings and capture again. Tonight there were a few brain images she hadn't seen before, some new detail about a couple of the victims and a series of interviews with the suspiciously growing catalogue of people who claimed to have escaped Rialobon's knives. Holoman said, 'For Civil Liberty reasons, remember, AfterLife information is never made available to Pax or Justix. It is not even known whether Rialobon himself had an active neurid.'

She was still thinking about Bale. She was taking too long

over him. So what if she liked his company? It was still work. Or maybe it was a rest she needed at the moment, a bit of conversation instead of her usual questioning and recording. The reason didn't matter, though. She really should have finished with him by now. She'd already spent over a month in Lookout, far longer than she spent in most places.

'Enjoy that? I did! Coming up now, Razer, part two of the show – a new *vote*!'

She drained the last of the caffé, feeling fully alert at last.

'But first, some more facts.'

She slumped. Every time, she thought. She never learnt. But no one ever did. The same need to trust came out, over and again. As much in the small matters as the big.

'It is only on a clinical judgement of your imminent death that AfterLife medicians are authorised to check for an active neurid. If you turn out to be neurid-positive, you are placed in *rigor vitae*, settled into a sarcophagus, or sarc, and dropped into the ocean on Bleak, and your Life is uploaded from your neurid onto the AfterLife database.'

Music swelled. 'And then, Razer, after a year, ten years, perhaps after a pause of a century or more, when a cure or new medical technique becomes available for *your* predicament, it's up to –' he grinned and spread his hands as the camview withdrew to make him a dot in the sudden backcloth of stars. Chords of triumph swelled until, into the abrupt silence of the music's end, he yelled, '– *to all of you*!'

Despite herself, Razer felt her heart thudding.

'At that point of potential return, Razer, *your* threatened life, and the lives of others in precisely the same predicament, will be listed for ballot. And anyone can vote, for anyone. Only I, Holoman, cannot vote. The ballot is not,

I repeat not, a competitive choice. When you vote, you vote *for* a second chance, or *against* one, for as many or as few ballotees as you wish.'

Irritated with herself for continuing to watch, Razer brought up Holoman's current viewing data. Thirty-seven per cent of the available System was watching with her. She scanned the breakdown and extrapolata. Within the next fifty hours, eighty-nine per cent of the System's adult population – with the normal two planetary exceptions, Gehenna and the unsaid planet – were projected to have seen the show and started voting. It never ceased to astonish her. Administrata elections struggled to draw half this much engagement.

'How do you make your voting decisions? It's easy and it's fun. You simply examine their lives. Were they – *are* they – kind or hateful, loving or cruel? Do *you* feel benevolent or not?' And a whispered aside, 'But remember, if your own neurid is a true neurid, you may be judged on your own judgement, one day.'

It was quite extraordinary, Razer thought. AfterLife, the one thing that united the System, was so simple that it was almost banal. It was beyond politics and goddery, and it was the one tax burden that no one resented.

And its existence gave Razer her living. Through her work with TruTales, one of its ParaSites, it paid for her to travel the System, to listen and imagine, to create narrative from chaos. Perhaps that was the most remarkable thing about it, that she could live off the back of it, and by nothing more than telling stories. AfterLives were true, but they were messy. People went to TruTales for comfort after the troubling truths of AfterLife. And thanks to her own skill and to the selections and guidance of her AI, Cynth, Razer was one of the best tellers.

Holoman's tone had become businesslike. His hair was shorter and neater, his expression stern as he said, 'All votes are independently checked. The ballot is completely open and beyond corruption.'

As she listened to people's lives and composed her stories, Razer often wondered what life might have been like back on Earth, when you could expect to live beyond fifty and to enjoy fair health for much of that time. What would their stories have been? Might they have guessed at such a future as this? The irreversible radiation sicknesses, the autoimmune diseases, the constantly shifting metaviruses, neocancers and reaction-toxicities? The savage mortality and general blight? The simple hardness of everything?

Back on Earth, they had imagined that the future would bring cures for everything, that eventually technology would outstrip nature.

She yawned, sleepy at last. How wrong we always were.

Four

ALEF

SigEv 2 My father's tax bill

Shortly after we returned from the cathedral, my father's routine tax demand was mis-delivered and opened by mistake by one of our neighbours, Josip Farlow. The story goes that Josip nearly fainted at the scale of the error. The legend of Saul's tax bill became a folk tale on Gehenna. A parable, even.

The story goes like this.

Josip was convinced that Saul would be quite unable to accept that the Tax Administration could have made such a mistake. He thought Saul would have a breakdown and crash, like putery. Not knowing what to do, he went to Father Grace, and Father Grace went to Marita, who had no idea what to do either.

In the end, they convened the church committee, whose technical advisor was Saul. Father Grace initiated a conversation about printing errors in Babbel translations, and at the end of the meeting, Josip passed the tax bill to Saul with an apology for mistakenly opening it. Josip also made a light comment at the obvious printing error and offered to mediate with the Tax Administration on Saul's behalf, to arrange for the error to be corrected.

Saul examined the bill and said nothing at all.

The table was silent around him.

Father Grace made a joke about Saul's equally vast knowledge of Tax and the Babble, and of the occasional inevitable errors in both.

'Thank you, Josip,' Saul eventually murmured. And he folded the paper and put it into his pocket.

'What will you do?' someone asked, a little anxiously.

'It's a tax bill,' Saul said, shrugging. 'I'll have to pay it, of course.'

This was a response no one expected. As soon as Saul left the meeting, Father Grace called Marita and told her to contact him if she needed help, adding that frankly he wasn't sure what the best thing might be to do.

Marita tried to behave as if nothing was wrong, which was easy, since Saul did the same. A few days later, she asked him what he had done about the tax bill, and he told her he'd paid it.

Everyone in JerSalem waited anxiously for the situation to escalate, as it had to. Tax had made a mistake that hadn't been corrected, and Saul had clearly sent them a payment that, purely by being submitted – as Saul, of all people, would be quite aware – irrevocably validated the mistake. But, of course, he had made the payment without possessing anything within several decimal points of the funds to meet it.

The whole of JerSalem buzzed with concern. Saul must have assumed, with his faith in Tax's certainty, that if they had asked for it, he must have it to give them. The error must be his.

Everyone knew what would happen. Pax would send a prison van to Gehenna and haul him away.

But months passed and no one came for Saul. There was a sense of apprehension for a long while, and then everything settled back, though not quite how it had been before. Saul would fix people's putery and they would insist on giving him something for the work, where in the past they had not. Saul wouldn't take money, so they gave things that could be sold. They didn't give them to Saul, but to Marita. They called Saul to sort out trivial problems, just to give Marita something against the future.

And then, at last, another letter came for Saul, marked TAX. The postman delivered it immediately to Father Grace, who opened it.

It was a receipt for payment, in full, of the tax bill. Father Grace resealed the letter – the preacher saying a prayer of thanks, no doubt – and passed it on to my father.

The general conclusion in the village was that it had been an elegant and logical mechanism for Tax to correct their original error; the idiocy of the demand had only been brought to light when my father's payment didn't clear. In order to save face, Tax had pretended that both correct demand and correct payment had taken place, and in this way balance was restored. For the villagers, Saul had shown up the heretic System for the fools everyone knew them to be.

My father, quite unknowing, became something of a hero. Father Grace made a sermon about turning the blind stupidity of the godless against itself, a sermon whose precise point everyone in JerSalem but Saul understood, and normality returned to our village.

Until the arrival of Pellonhorc.

* * *

SigEv 3 My first puter

After school I often spent my time in my father's shop, helping him with the putery.

Programming was quite effortless for me. Picking it up was not like learning to read, but like learning to talk. My brain, like my father's, was configured ideally for the task. It was as simple as that. The games we played together were not the father/son pastimes of assembling towers of plastic blocks or shoving balls with our feet. We played with screenery and putery. While I was still bellied in my mother, my father devised a system that would model my first sounds as visual symbols, and he surrounded my cot with screenery. I swiftly learnt the sounds that pictured rudimentary faces, and within my first few months I was learning the elaborations that might make the face on the screen smile or wink or blow bubbles. As my language became complex, the symbols became less crude, the programming opportunities more intricate. Before I could walk, I was choreographing simple rivers. My father and I would play with the digital water. He would throw rocks into it and I would predict and calculate the effect on the flow. It made us both laugh.

I soon had a puter of my own, and I'd devise my own programs for it. My father told me about secrecy and privacy, and about the difference between them and the importance of both, and he taught me about codes and encryption. We played memory games, and he was as pleased as I was when, at about six years of age, I started to beat him at them. We devised an encryption routine for my own puter. The primes I used seemed immense at the time. He asked me how I memorised them – his own visual tricks failed at the levels of complexity that my primes demanded – and I told him I thought of them as trees in leaf, great trees blowing in the wind. Each branch and twig had to be read in order of ascent from the ground, and each leaf from trunk to tip was a digit.

I was used to the incomprehension of other children and adults, but when I saw my father trying to imagine my forests, he laughed, although it was a slightly odd laugh.

After that, my father and I agreed a rule for my puter. I gave him an encrypted permit so that he could enter puzzles and games there for me to solve, but he couldn't roam freely on it or interfere with my programs. I, however, had my own, greater level of encryption that allowed me full access to the puter's capabilities.

Of course, I see now that this was simply a tacit agreement through which, in exchange for me restricting myself to my own puter, my father could let me in the shop with him. There was no rule my father could enforce on me. It was as if, in a more normal family, a father suddenly recognised that his son had grown bigger and stronger than he was, and decided that they'd play no more wrestling games.

I never showed him my conclusions regarding the Riemann hypothesis and the Goldbach conjecture. I wish I had. But at that age, I was only thinking he'd use them to break my codes.

SigEv 4 Pellonhorc

Shortly after my eighth birthday, Josip Farlow and his family died in a terrible accident, their flycykle sliding into a methane sink, and a new family was chosen from the list to come and live in the village. The list was long. There were always people wanting to leave the Upper Worlds for the rigorous joy of Gehenna.

Looking back, though I never thought it at the time, there were immediately a number of clues to the strangeness of Pellonhorc's arrival. Most new families were either childless or with a child bellied in its mother, and they arrived together, man and woman. There were never unattached adults and there were never children.

But this odd family arrived, and as was traditional, the priest welcomed the newcomers into our community at a service of celebration and mourning that began, 'In the midst of death, we are in life.'

Avareche, the mother of the new family, sat in the church wearing the tatters of mourning. She cried as if she were a survivor of the accident that had killed Josip Farlow's family, rather than its beneficiary. She sobbed and gasped as if life were not tragedy from dust to dust, as we were taught, but something more unbalanced.

There was no husman. Instead, to Avareche's either side sat her cousins, the two men Garrel and Traile. We'd seen no one like them in JerSalem. They were dressed in dark, weaveless clothes and they sat on the hard pews with extraordinary stillness, as if they were cracked out of rock. Even then I thought how they looked like soldiers with their eyelenses glittering in the gloomy church, their hands resting palms down on their broad thighs, glove knuckles worn to silver, and their thick jackets hinting at concealed weaponry.

And then there was the boy, Avareche's son. Pellonhorc.

It's hard now to think of Pellonhorc as a boy, after all this time. He was eight years old, as was I, and he was running around the church, wild as the wind.

No one did a thing about him. It was up to Father Grace to ask his mother to deal with her boy, but he didn't. I wonder now how much he knew, but perhaps he was just bewildered by the extraordinary newcomers.

Avareche sat and sobbed. It was incomprehensible to me. Her cousins sat impassive at her either side, and my mother quietly stood up and went to her. Garrel – he was the taller cousin, his earlobes fat with sensors, his waxed hair in tightly gridded bunches like the casing of a grenade – showed no sign of letting her past him, but my mother waited. Avareche made a quick gesture to her cousin, and he let my mother sit with her, though he waited long enough for the pause to be evident to everyone in the church. Everyone except Pellonhorc, who was building a tower of prayer books in the lancing light from the high window.

Father Grace continued the service. 'We mourn Josip and Neisha, and their children Jonie and Jess, and we give thanks for the arrival of Avareche and Pellonhorc and Garrel and Traile.' There was silence, even momentarily from Pellonhorc at the back of the church, who stood back and squinted at his perilously tall architecture of books. Buttressed with knee-cushions, the tower was as high as his head. I watched him balance a silver censer carefully at its summit, where it caught a brilliant beam of light.

The priest moved towards the conclusion of the service with a prayer for the unsaid planet. 'We pray for the souls of those whose terrible faith has taken them from the possibility of salvation, that one day they may return to us.'

Everyone knew the stories of the unsaid planet, how they

had cut themselves away from the System and had destroyed the ships of any who tried to approach, and sent squads of assassins to slaughter any who mentioned their name. It didn't seem likely, but on Gehenna little was ever questioned.

Finally, Father Grace gestured again to the new family and said with quiet authority, 'We hope that Avareche and her family will soon be joined by her husman –'

Crash. Everyone jerked round at the clatter of Pellonhorc's tower of prayer books falling and the metal-on-stone smash of the incense holder. Garrel and Traile were on their feet, I thought fleetingly, but no, they were the only ones in the church sitting down. In my memory, later, this was not true. They *had* stood up and turned, their fists gun-filled and aimed; they had assessed and eased back and withdrawn even before anyone else in the church had reacted in the first place.

That marked the end of the ceremony. We all filtered out of the church, through the beams of light now choked with sweet incense. Avareche continued to sob. Everyone else – except Garrel and Traile, who must have had laryngeal air filters – coughed their way through the arched doors. Pellonhorc swung his arms about and danced.

That was their arrival. It was a while before anyone in the village learned the name of Avareche's husman. By the time we did find out, it was no real surprise. Even on Gehenna, we had heard of Ethan Drame.

But it took a long time for this to come out. There was always a reason why Pellonhorc's father couldn't join them. It was work, transport problems, or just 'complications'. Avareche shrugged. Garrel and Traile said nothing.

On Pellonhorc's first day at the school, one of the boys in

our class asked him about his father. Pellonhorc beat the boy so badly that he was off school for a month.

Avareche and my mother became best friends. There were inevitably things Avareche needed, and my parents helped her. It never struck me that this was more than kindness and coincidence.

They were an odd household. There were five of them; Avareche, Pellonhorc, the two cousins and a green cheekicheep. The cheekicheep was Pellonhorc's pet, and he kept it in a hutch. Its wings had been clipped, and it strutted awkwardly about the hutch. Pellonhorc didn't take very good care of it, according to my mother, so it had fallen to Avareche to look after it. The creature had taken against Pellonhorc for some reason. His mother often had the cheekicheep in her arms, cradling it and idly stroking its soft plumage.

And I became friendly with Pellonhorc. He had a wild, extraordinary charisma. When the boy he'd beaten returned to school, Pellonhorc was the first to greet him, and with genuine enthusiasm. Pellonhorc didn't mention the beating. As far as Pellonhorc was concerned, it was as if it hadn't happened. The boy was oddly grateful, though he was forever cautious after that.

It was an interesting lesson for me. I think we all knew that we were in the presence of someone unique. He immediately became our leader. We took risks, climbed and swam where it was dangerous. Of course, none of us ever said no to him, and he was always the first to climb, to dive, to fight. He was without fear. We thought he was brave. He was, of course, psychopathic.

The only people who had any control over him were

Garrel and Traile. He taunted them all the time, and they ignored his taunts.

But one day I saw Traile hit him.

It was like this. Pellonhorc came over to our house in the afternoon, unannounced, saying he wanted to play with me. We went up to my room. He was agitated at first, and then subdued. I'd never seen him like this before. After a while, my mother answered the comms and it was obviously Avareche. My mother left, and a few minutes later Traile arrived and was knocking at our door.

I shouldn't have let him in. I wasn't supposed to let anyone in if there was no adult in the house, and Pellonhorc was screaming at me not to, screaming like I'd never heard anyone scream before. And he swore, too; he swore he'd do things to me that I didn't even understand.

You have to imagine my fear. I'd seen Pellonhorc beat a boy unconscious for no reason and still carry on beating him, calmly and steadily, until he was sure the rest of us got his message. He never lost control. And at the same time I could hear Traile's voice through the door, steady and slow and carrying more threat than anything I could imagine.

I listened to Pellonhorc screaming, but Traile's quiet voice drowned his screams. I reached up and opened the door to him. The man's eyeshades shone as he flowed past me and up the stairs. I followed him. I saw Pellonhorc's expression through the crack of my bedroom door for an instant before he slammed the door in Traile's face. I thought at the same time how scared Pellonhorc would have to be to think of closing the door in Traile's face.

But he would be safe in there until Traile calmed down. Because of the prison labourers in the deletium swamp, every door in the village, internal or external, was entry-secure. My bedroom door was no different. Anyone inside could get out, but you could only get in if you were print-registered. A rhinoceroo with a hundred metre run-up couldn't have broken that door down.

Except that Traile put his hand on the door handle and leaned on it, and after a moment the door made a strange screeching sound, bent, and creaked, and then burst inward. Traile rubbed his fist and glanced back at me. What he meant me to understand by that look, I have no idea. The glitter of his lenses was the same as always. I watched him go into my room and I watched his arm come back and swing casually forward. I heard a dead, flat noise, and Pellonhorc's scream abruptly stopped.

After an odd, still moment, Traile turned sideways, facing neither me nor Pellonhorc, and his head was bowed. I heard him swear. He brought up a cupped hand and muttered into it. His face was white and his hand was shaking. He carried on talking, then stopped and waited and talked again, this time a little more calmly. The colour returned to his face. He breathed a long breath and bent to pick Pellonhorc up, gently, in his arms, and left with him, the boy not meeting my eyes.

Pellonhorc wasn't in school for a week, and we never saw his cheekicheep again. I asked my mother about it, and she said it would be best not to mention it to Pellonhorc or his mother. My father arranged for my bedroom door to be replaced. I looked forward to the workmen asking how it had come to be smashed like that, so that I could tell them, but they didn't say a thing about it. They were very polite to me, though.

* * *

SigEv 5 The pornoverse

'Let's go to your dad's shop,' Pellonhorc said, one day.

'Okay. I'll ask him.'

'No. I mean by ourselves.'

'We can't do that. Anyway, why do you want to do that? He won't mind us being there. I often go and help him.'

'No. I want to show you something.'

'What can you show me?'

'You'll see.' That was one of his things, *You'll see*. He used the phrase equally as a threat and a temptation. I could tell he would scorn me if I didn't agree, but there was a way around it. I said, 'Anyway, it's locked. We can't get in.'

'I can get us in. Don't worry about that.'

I had to say okay. I told my parents I was going out to play, and I met Pellonhorc at the shop. The day was fading and our reflected faces gleamed in the window.

'So, how do we get in, then?' I said reluctantly.

He showed me a small device that he told me he'd taken from Traile. I wasn't surprised. I'd long ago stopped thinking of Garrel and Traile as being in any way ordinary. I wasn't even sure they were Avareche's cousins.

Pellonhorc held the device to the lockplate of the door and put his hand to the palmreader.

'How does it work?' I said.

'It gives us a permit. Here.' He held my hand to the plate. 'There. We're both listed. We can go in any time we want, now.'

I shook my head, looking for a way out of this. 'My dad'll find out.'

'Only if he checks the list, and no one ever does that. Not on Gehenna.'

I stared at him. 'You don't know my dad.'

He grinned back at me and said, '*You* don't know your dad.'

And before I could react to that, he added, 'Come on, then. Or are you chickyfrit?'

We went into the shop and through the banks of putery and screenery with their flickering programs, the calculations that never stopped running, the probability counts and option strategies for fuel economy and speed and oxygen expenditure, and risk factors for this route and that between one planet and another. I'd understood most of it by the age of about ten, and was tweaking the programs with my dad a year later.

I went to my own puter and started to bring the screenery up, but Pellonhorc wasn't interested.

'Here,' he said, standing at the door to the back of the shop.

'That's just the workroom. He keeps the old putery there. It's slow junk. Most of it doesn't work at all.'

'You think?'

I shrugged. Pellonhorc palmed us in and I reluctantly followed him. He sat down at the front screen.

'That one's totally busted,' I told him.

Pellonhorc ignored me. The screen was tilted to the side and he straightened it, made himself comfortable and pressed it to go.

'See?' I told him.

He pressed it again, then keyed a few riffs of code at the keyplate. Still nothing, of course, no point in keying dead putery, but he keyed it again, concentrating, and the screen abruptly glowed and its voice murmured, 'Connecting.'

'Hah,' Pellonhorc said.

That it worked at all didn't make sense, but that Pellonhorc could bring it up made less. It wasn't encrypted in any serious way, which was unlike my father, and Pellonhorc knew the code, which was crazy. But all I could say was, 'What are you doing?'

He settled himself on the stool. 'Checking up on my dad.'

He had never mentioned his father before, and since the time he'd beaten up the kid who had asked about him, no one else had mentioned the subject. I didn't know what to say, so I said nothing. Like most of the kids, I'd begun to assume his father was dead. I started to wonder about him now, though. What did he look like? How old was he? *Where* was he?

I almost asked, but I held back. I was afraid the delicate friendship we had would vanish. It was possible that he would swing round and hit me. With Pellonhorc, that was always a possibility.

The screen showed to an interior, a featureless wall of grey and nothing more. 'He isn't there,' Pellonhorc said, disappointed. 'Let's try something else.' He keyed again, and the screen changed to the graphic of an open gate, black and high-barred.

'You can't do that,' I said.

Silver words faded up, floating over the gate.

Please register for entry to the Song. You are identified as Gehennan. Please enter personal registration passcode to continue.

Pellonhorc keyed something, his fingers too fast for me to follow.

Please confirm registration by plain voice.

Confirm? Had he actually, successfully, registered to the Song? I wondered how he could have done that. But now he was stuck. His fingers hovered. I knew Pellonhorc wouldn't fall for the lure of voice-key. As soon as you used your unscrambled voice, you became individually identifiable and permanently traceable. That was one of the reasons everyone still keyed whenever possible. Even within Gehenna's small version of the Song, Babblepool, no one ever voiced, and we were – somehow – already way beyond Babblepool. And we'd managed it on a puter that wasn't supposed to work at all, let alone be connected to the Song. The Song!

I reached past him and thumbed an audio code. 'Now tell it we're frequency-disrupted. Electric weather. My dad rigs all his putery to mimic that.'

Pellonhorc keyed what I'd told him to, and after a moment the gate slowly opened and faded away, leaving the screen brilliant blue and pixelled with options. This was the Song. I'd heard of it, but never seen it and never expected to.

As I gasped, Pellonhorc smiled in triumph. He held a hand high, and I shrieked and slapped it hard. The sharp clap and sting of our palms was like the sealing of a bond between us.

We spent about an hour there, looking at all the sex sites we could wriggle into. I was impressed by his navigation, and he was clearly impressed by my ability to trick the sites into letting us in.

Pellonhorc controlled the screen. He lingered on certain types of image, asking what I thought of them, of the participants. Many seemed about our own age, though they were far more practised than I was, or – I assumed – Pellonhorc. My comments of admiration and disgust apparently pleased him and I came home exhilarated, not so much by the great swathes of flesh and friction as by the freedom we'd had to roam. And also by the unexpected switch in the relationship I shared with Pellonhorc.

Five

RAZER

Razer dozed and dreamed. The leaving of Earth had been chaotic. It had started in desperation and concluded in near despair. Razer had a sense that no one on Earth had truly believed anywhere viable would be found, and that the resources pumped into terraforming and transport were simply to provide people with a purpose through the final decades. Those who had departed had not expected to arrive, and those who had arrived had had to devote themselves to immediate survival. And so the System had begun to establish itself in an unstructured way, each planet with its own problems. Every planet had spent the first century or so looking inward in the way that Gehenna and the unsaid planet still did. Gehenna had turned to one faith, and the unsaid planet had turned to another; the unsaid planet had also retreated into such a fiercely protected seclusion that it might as well not exist. Every unexplained disaster drew rumours and suspicions that the unsaid planet had had a hand in it.

For decades the System had possessed no structure other than what was necessary to maintain the mechanisms of trade, while Earth's Internet had developed into the Song. There was lawlessness and corruption. The System sprawled like Earth had never sprawled.

Her head ached, and she sat at the edge of the bed and drank water, imagining how much worse Bale must be feeling.

Holoman was gesturing animatedly as he talked. No one in the System, other than on the usual two planets, would fail to recognise that face.

Into this chaos, nearly a century ago, AfterLife had burst abruptly into existence, almost fully formed, and in a few years it had changed the System utterly. It struck her that the calendar should acknowledge this, that the year should be marked 'Before AfterLife' or…

Maybe not. More water. And caffé.

Nevertheless, life was still hard. There was a ruthless pragmatism now. While an Earther might marvel at some aspects of current technology, they'd find others in everyday use that had been discarded long before the Earth's end. In the System, reliability was valued more than innovation.

Holoman had moved on to TruTales and StarHearts and some of the other ParaSites.

Some features of Earth life had faded. Goddery had been one of the main casualties of Earth's end, other than on Gehenna and the unsaid planet. But goddery continued to work for those two – for Gehenna, anyway, since no one had any idea what life was like on the other place.

And then, just as the System had been starting to disintegrate, riven by disease, despair and internal conflict, as Holoman was telling Razer again now, the neurid had been discovered. It had been a consequence of a failed pluripotent cell experiment for which some anonymous technician had accidentally discovered an almost miraculous application.

And from the neurid had come AfterLife.

Holoman brushed a lick of unruly hair from his forehead. 'In just a moment, a vote! But first, today's medical technology. A significant new advance in gene-specific heart-lung regenerative treatment means that AfterLife can offer a second chance to up to a thousand genetically appropriate sleeping subscribers who have succumbed to the N23XN meta-prion.'

Razer was still thinking about how an Earther might look at the System. Keystrikes and caffé were the rulers of Razer's life, and they hadn't changed much since humanity had migrated to the System. There were other priorities.

And people always wanted to read. It was cheap, quicker than listening and resistant to accent. Even now, the System's formal languages remained close to those of Earth. As for caffé, everyone wanted to stay awake with the warmth of a drink.

She finished the cold tasse and took it back to the kitchen, wiping it clean under the tap with a finger. How many caffés had she drunk, over the years? How many stories had she told?

When she got back to the screenery, it was to a simmed view of the sea, blotblack rigs fixed in the swirling foam, sarcophagi glittering around them like sequins.

It fully struck her that she was actually here, on the planet of the sarcs. There was little money, no comfort, not a single moment's ease, and yet Bleak had become the most important place in the System.

Holoman's voice was telling her, 'Among these are today's potential lucky chancers. Let's look at one. His name is Larren Gamliel.'

The AfterLife theme played, and Bleak's oceans crashed across the screen. Razer started to pay closer attention.

Here it was at last. These were the lives. This was the stuff of AfterLife.

The sarc-strewn sea glowed as the sim of a single dark sarcophagus rose into the air and opened a crack, leaking words:

LIFE SUMMARY

LARREN GAMLIEL

> WARNING – recollections of certain experiences may be traumatic. Especially traumatic experiences are marked in the summary with a {grgrgrgr} sound, or a ** if you choose to text-read.

Razer chose voice, fell back on the bed again and closed her eyes. The voice was low and slurred. Razer imagined a pocked face and skinny arms. Larren began to speak the bones of his life.

> My name is Larren Gamliel. Lar. I was born some place I don't recall, didn't stay there long enough. Don't remember my parents at all. Brought up in a drifthome, remember mostly stars, looking out my little window and the stars endless as bedlice.
>
> Had a friend in the drifthome, boy called Bude, straggly red hair, taller than me, always blinking. We was playing hide'n'find, nine years old, I remember, and he was hid all morning. I didn't find him, got bored and it was middlemeal. I went to middlemeal; it was meatcakes. I ate his. He was late. Actually he didn't turn up for it.
>
> So after middlemeal, the alarms was going. Long

story short, there he was in a voidlock, sort'v floating. {grgrgrgr} He looked sort'v sucked out. Like one of those dried fish. His eyes gone squinty.

That about totals my childhood, I guess. I don't think about it much.

I got to fifteen, had to leave the home, went down planetside. {grgrgrgr} Can't remember which planet, didn't stay on it long anyway.

{grgrgrgr} Didn't stay on any of them long.

What I liked most was the trips one to the next. That's where I felt most comfortable, on those ferries. I guess they was like the home again. Got work as a steward once, but not for long. Stared at the stars, got reprimanded too many times.

Planetside, I was generally in trouble, which I guess was the total of my life, really. {grgrgrgr} Stealing and drifting. What Pax call sad. That was me. I never had nothing of my own, never held onto anyone else.

Never felt sorry for myself, though, not much anyway. I guess I was happiest in the jails, drifting up there like I was a kid all over again, in that little cell surrounded by stars. I told them not to let me go, that last time. Maybe if they'd'v listened I'd'v had more of a story now. {grgrgrgr} Killing that woman was a mistake, or an accident. The Justix explained the difference, but I never worked it out. All I know is I didn't mean it and I was sorry for it. I was not responsible. The drugs was responsible.

It's strange, and maybe you can work it out for me, 'cos I sure as shame can't. Why is it that everyone said it wasn't my fault about Bude, and I still can't help blaming myself, couldn't all my life, and everyone says that woman was my fault, and I know she wasn't? Can you tell me why is that?

I done my time for her, in any case. Two days out, and then I got this disease. Is that justice?

I know there's nothing else, but I'd like to'v met my parents one time, my mum anyway. And I'd like to see Bude again. Maybe he's here too, somewhere. This disease that's eaten me up, maybe it's not forever.

I don't think I had a good life so far.

END OF LIFE SUMMARY

Razer froze the screen.

That was weird, she thought. Had she known this man? The name was different, of course, all the databased names were anonyms, and of course the voice was putery, but she'd once taken a story from a man almost the same as this early life – the drifthome childhood, the hide-and-find death in the voidlock – and used it in a TruTale. It had been one of her first, years back.

Maybe it was him, though that would be a hell of a coincidence.

No. More likely it was a common way for a kid to die. Still, it was weird.

She restarted the screen. A NewsAlert flash was pulsing in the corner, but she stayed with the ballot.

AFTERLIFE CHOICES.

Please touch or interrupt at any time.

Open Larren Gamliel's whole Life?

Vote on Larren Gamliel's Life?

Please touch or interrupt for further information.

She wondered whether to open the life, but knew herself well enough to recognise that that would be the entire day gone. She thought a moment more, then yes-voted him. It troubled her that she still couldn't remember the name of that TruTale source. She could see his face, though, a high forehead and deepset brown eyes, always squinting. An engineer, that was it. And not a crimer, but on the edge of it.

Holoman was speaking again. 'All other candidates are available on your VoteNow page. I'll be looking at them all, over the next weeks. The decision, though, is always yours. You can view further scenes, or review these, on AfterLife.'

The screen went to ash as Holoman's voice swelled and echoed.

'And remember – AfterLife begins at birth.'

Razer nilled the display, but the NewsAlert flash still held its position. Razer told it, 'Later,' and let the flash dull and slow until it was barely paraliminal. She couldn't sleep. She brought up TruTales and signed herself in.

'Hey, Cynth,' she said.

GREETING LOGGED, KESTREL DUST. THIS PROGRAM IS WAITING. PLEASE COMMENCE.

Yawning, Razer started sending down the day's notes and the contents of her augmem. It was always odd to imagine her experiences loaded onto a memory device, without her having any awareness or chance of accessing them herself. But really, it was little different from a neurid except the vast difference in scale, and that the augmem was putery.

THIS PROGRAM OBSERVES THAT KESTREL DUST HAS ACCESSED THE DAY'S VOTING OPPORTUNITY. WILL KESTREL DUST VOTE FOR LARREN GAMLIEL?

'Hey, what's this? Are you making conversation?'

THIS PROGRAM IS PRESENTLY UPLOADING YOUR AUGMEM RECORD. PROCEDURE ALMOST COMPLETE. CHITTLECHATTLE CONFIRMS BILATERAL CONNECTION ACTIVITY, BUT THIS PROGRAM CAN MAINTAIN SILENCE IF KESTREL DUST PREFERS.

'No, I don't prefer silence. Not tonight. Can't you call yourself Cynth for me? Or even *I*? Use the first person, just once?'

YOU CAN CALL THIS PROGRAM WHATEVER YOU WANT, KESTREL DUST. REFER TO PREVIOUS CHITTLECHATTLES.

Razer wondered if the program could tell she was a little drunk. Yeah, it probably could.

'At least call me Razer?'

YOUR CONTRACTED ACTIVITY PERMITS YOU TO THINK OF YOURSELF AS WHOEVER YOU CHOOSE.

Razer tried to clear her thoughts. 'Kestrel Dust can't vote, Cynth. I got you there, huh?'

THIS PROGRAM UNDERSTANDS THE SIGNIFICANCE OF NAMES. THIS PROGRAM APPRECIATES KESTREL DUST'S HUMOUR TRAIT AND ACKNOWLEDGES HER NEED TO ATTEMPT MISCHIEF. THIS PROGRAM COMMUNICATES CONCISELY FOR PURPOSES OF CLARITY AND EFFICIENCY. RAZER AND KESTREL DUST ARE COTERMINOUS FOR CONTRACTUAL PURPOSES. KESTREL DUST HAS EXHIBITED A LEGALLY VERIFIABLE AWARENESS OF THIS.

'No one's called me legally verifiable before. Exhibitionist, yes.'

THIS PROGRAM UNDERSTANDS THAT KESTREL DUST DERIVES PLEASURE FROM TREATING THIS PROGRAM AS IF THIS PROGRAM WERE A HUMAN RESPONDENT VOID OF SELF-AWARENESS AND HUMOUR TRAIT. DATA UPLOADED, AUGMEM ERASED AND RESET. PROCEDURE COMPLETE. CHITTLECHATTLE CONCLUDED. CONTACT TERMINATED.

Razer felt the brief vertigo of the augmem re-engaging. 'I love you, too,' she murmured. The display reverted to the TruTales gate. Razer coded herself past the laugh/cry/gasp/scream site entry and entered the teller gate.

Thank you. Please enter teller's name.
Thank you. Kestrel Dust is presently number 12 of 2578 top tellers.

She spent a few minutes checking her tale-hits and all their paradata, the seeker come-froms and go-tos, linger-times, skip-zones and boredom locations, and it all depressed her as much as it always did. One day her paradata would no longer be acceptable to Cynth, and what would she do then?

She lay her head back and sighed, the sigh morphing to a yawn. What was the name of the man she'd written of, with his drifthome childhood? That was a paradata seekset that ought to exist, linking AfterLives with similar TruTales. Such an obvious idea. Maybe she'd suggest it to Cynth. *THIS PROGRAM IS NOT SO PERFECT AFTER ALL.*

She was almost asleep when the Gamliel link started to come back to her. His business was in reverse logistics. It had made a good TruTale, and she wondered, not for the first time, how Cynth chose Razer's subjects.

What was his name? She remembered well enough what

he did. When defective tech was returned to the seller under guarantee, he bought it at component value and reworked it. Then he resold it, tagged *My triple promise – high value, low price, no guarantee*. She sat straight, the name at the tip of her tongue. It wasn't *My* promise. It was his name that began with an em. Mordle's promise, something like that.

The reverse logistics was the story Razer had told for TruTales. She'd kept the other side of his business to herself. He also handled defective military hardware, not merely fixing it but disassembling the hardware and fixing the putery, and then adapting and improving on it. At that, he was a genius. At everything else in life, thanks to that childhood, he was a mess.

But what *was* his name? She fell on her bed and closed her eyes. There was a fragment of metal he used to play with when he was thinking, it used to catch the light.

At least she had enough detail to find it on TruTales now. That would surely trigger his real name for her.

Not tonight, though. Thinking about Larren Gamliel – Mardle? Mardley? – and with the NewsAlert still pulsing on the screen, and for some reason with Tallen on her mind, she finally fell asleep. She dreamt of a shard of shiny metal tossed into the air and caught, and tossed again, again.

Six

ALEF

SigEv 6 Ethan Drame

'*You* don't know your dad.'

In the thrill of the pornosphere I'd forgotten him saying that, but it came back to me later. It was like a riddle. He knew my dad had putery that would get him beyond the BabblePool, but how had he known?

He'd also known exactly how to use Traile's device to get into my dad's shop. I suddenly realised that Pellonhorc had *already* been registered at the door; it was just me that he'd needed to add to the list. He just hadn't wanted me to know he had a registered key. And now I thought of it, it didn't seem likely that Traile would let such a device be stolen by Pellonhorc. Traile was far too careful.

And Pellonhorc had known where in the shop the putery was to get us access to his dad. That meant he didn't just know the slow junk putery was fast, and its location. He also knew it would take him to his dad.

I didn't like the idea of Pellonhorc knowing more than I did about my dad's putery, but far more than that, I didn't like him knowing more about my dad than I did. So I set out to rectify the situation.

On Sindays, everyone went to church. Even Pellonhorc was taken to church. It had had an extraordinary effect on him. What we Gehennans took for granted, Pellonhorc struggled with. He had no fear of anything in life (other than the episode with Traile), but he hadn't begun to consider the idea of death until now. And here on Gehenna he had been taken straight from considering death to the prospect of the Damnations, Eternal and Internal.

I knew he would be in church, then, learning with his extraordinary concentration of the terrors to come. On Fireday I feigned stomach ache and made myself puke enough to be allowed to stay at home on Sinday while everyone else went to church.

I went to the shop and let myself in. I went through the main shop to the slow junk room and shut the door behind me. I tried to crack Pellonhorc's father's portal and found it blocked, which didn't surprise me at all. I looked at the blocking pattern, and then I went into my father's own portal. I knew his codes.

There had to be a code I'd never seen before. Pellonhorc had coded himself to his dad's portal, and I knew my dad's putery well enough to know Pellonhorc hadn't done it from void. My dad had to have the same code. What I didn't know was why my dad should be connected to Pellonhorc's dad.

I memorised the blocking pattern – a few hundred digits with some slick traps and reverses, but my short-term memory was good enough to hold a sapling like that, and I certainly wasn't going to send or hardprint it – and went to the front of the shop, to the fast putery. There was one screen that my dad never linked to anything else. It was a simple rack. Everything was kept on it in case of disaster. I keyed myself into it and entered the blocking pattern from the back room, and waited.

ERROR. INVALID INSTRUCTION. PLEASE REKEY.

I waited.

The message repeated, pulsing red and mauve. I waited. The error note blinked again and disappeared. I still waited.

A brief number sequence appeared, with no label or other instruction. It vanished almost instantly, but I was sure I had it. Ten digits.

I closed my eyes and saw Pellonhorc's fingers dancing across the keypad, eleven times. He'd concealed his fingertips, but I'd counted the strikes he'd made.

I nilled the screen and returned to the back room, and entered the code, all ten digits. I stared at the grey screen for a long moment before making the eleventh keystrike, knowing I only had that one chance. Not 'Enter'; that would be the trap. And none of the other laterals or punctuations, numerals or directives.

I held my breath and punched 'Erase'.

The screen went to the same room I'd seen when Pellonhorc had keyed in. Only this time Pellonhorc's father was sitting facing me.

It wasn't really him, of course, and at the same time it was. I could tell that by the shape of his mouth, the flatness of his gaze. The image had been sent encrypted, and my father's supposedly slow junk putery was decrypting and reassembling it. Between there (wherever *there* was) and here, was a babel of white noise in black space.

As I was thinking this, I realised how stupid I was to

be doing this. Pellonhorc's dad was sitting back in his chair, clearly alert to my presence. He frowned. His lips began to part.

I shut the whole thing down, cutting him off as he started to speak.

But the image simply flickered momentarily, and the room on the screen reasserted itself.

'Well,' Pellonhorc's father drawled. His voice was as flat as his gaze. 'Little boy.' He looked away and said to someone I couldn't see, 'Saul's kid's a smart one, huh, Sol?' He looked at me again. 'All by yourself, eh.'

I shook my head. I was already working the puter again to try to cut him off, using a different escape protocol, but again it didn't have the slightest effect. I pushed my chair back and ran for the door to the main shop. I was tugging uselessly at it when he called, 'Sit down again, boy. The door will unseal when *we* are done and *I* am ready. So sit back down and don't touch anything. You'll only irritate me, which would be unwise. Nothing will work for you in here unless I want it to.'

I returned to the screen and sat down again.

'Good. Are you scared, Alef?'

'Yes.' I was, but not very. Not yet.

'Good again. You were curious. You took a risk. It didn't pay off.'

I said nothing. While he was frightening me, he didn't know how accustomed I was to fear. I'd grown up on Gehenna, and my true fears were of greater things. Up until then, anyway.

He bent his head closer towards me. His chin was rough with stubble, though I could see a thin scar beneath it. He stared at me. His eyes were as brilliant a blue as Pellonhorc's, but their hearts were burnt-black needlepoints. He said, 'I can see you, Alef. I know what you look like. Do you know what that means?'

'No.'

'It means that I can reach you. It means that I can always reach you.'

He was watching me intently, his voice soft and laconic, his gaze terrifying. I felt myself shake. The word 'reach' held a meaning entirely new, the way he said it. Father Grace used a similar tone when he was preaching hellfire, but Pellonhorc's dad spoke of *reaching* me in a way that made the prospect of hellfire fade away totally. This was real fear.

'Your father's told me about you, Alef. You know what he says?'

I reacted without thought. 'Your son doesn't say anything at all about you.' I don't know why I said it, but I knew it was the wrong thing, instantly.

A delay. He said nothing. I thought the screen had frozen, he was so still and for so long.

'My son…' he murmured.

His chest rose and fell. The wall behind him was not as smooth as I'd thought. It was creased and pocked, washed with some sort of plaster and painted roughly, like a bunker. Where might he be?

'You will look after each other, I know. Your father is the one I trust, and now I know the line will continue.' He relaxed, or at least he sagged in his chair. 'Family is more important than anything else, Alef. My son doesn't understand that, but he knows what is safe. He also knows you're to be safe. He knows if he were ever to harm you, it would be as if he had killed his own brother. It would be worse than that. You don't need to fear him. You have Ethan Drame's word on it.'

I had heard of Ethan Drame, but Pellonhorc and I were on Gehenna and Ethan Drame was not. What Drame said meant nothing to me.

He looked weary, suddenly. Emboldened by this, I said, 'Where are you?'

His gaze sharpened again. 'I'm always at hand.' He glanced to the side, then back at me. 'Now. Your father will know of this conversation but he need not know any more than that. He knows well enough not to ask me, nor you. Don't discuss it with your mother and it can't ever harm her.' He paused, then added, 'Pellonhorc's mother is not to be told. But tell Pellonhorc we've spoken. Only that. It will do.' He rattled this off, not waiting for acknowledgement. He was more comfortable now, giving orders. I thought of my father and what we had in common, the two of us bonded by codes and numbers, by the deep abstract, and I wondered what bonded Pellonhorc to his dad.

'Don't contact me again. Speak to Garrel or Traile if there's a problem.'

And that was it. He was, for the moment, gone. As the screen cleared and the door unsealed, I wondered what problem there might possibly be.

SigEv 7 Hell

When he and I searched the pornoverse together that first time, Pellonhorc had been recruiting me. He was alone until then, but now I shared his guilt.

I didn't feel too guilty, though. I knew I was damned in the eyes of the church, but I had an idea of what it should feel like to be damned – fire in my dreams, God's voice in my skull condemning me, physical agonies – and none of that had happened. I was analysing and in the early stages of shedding my faith.

But as far as Pellonhorc was concerned, I was now as guilty as he was, and that cemented our friendship. I became the only person he could talk to about his guilt and damnation. And damnation, I soon realised, meant a great deal to him.

Sin wasn't all we talked about, of course. When he was in a particularly easy mood, I took the risk of asking him what his father did.

'He doesn't do anything. Other people do it. He just tells them to.'

'Like a priest,' I said. We were walking out of the village. It was a Sinday afternoon and the morning's sermon was in my head, the usual mix of piety and threat that was beginning to wash over me. Pellonhorc and I were heading for the wasteland below the purple hills where there were antmounds to poke with sticks, and the village's cesspits to hurl things into.

'Not like that. He's a crimer. He sometimes tells people to kill people. He's the best crimer in the System. You know the pornoverse? He runs it.' Pellonhorc broke into a trot, swinging his arms, jumping high and being a bird.

I caught up with him. 'He *runs* it?'

'Maybe not the whole pornoverse,' he said, 'but other stuff too. Your dad works for him.'

'My dad doesn't kill people.'

'My dad said your dad's in too deep to quit, whatever your mum imagines. I heard him say it. Look, there's one.' He picked up a stick as we walked up to the tall mound, pulling a small knife from his pocket to carve a point to the stick. It took him just three swift jerks of the blade. Even at that age, he was strong and focused. 'Here, take it,' he said.

'What do you mean, he's in too deep?'

'I don't know. I just heard it. Take the stick, Alef.'

I took it. He picked up another stick and worked it to a point.

'He said your dad's useful, too. And he trusts him. That's good. He doesn't trust many of them. I think that's why we came here. It isn't safe anywhere else right now.' He gave me my stick. 'I'm safer here, even though I love my dad. And so does my mum.' He looked at me as if I was going to challenge him on that.

We stopped talking, saving our breath. The mound's peak was higher than our heads. We began digging into the hard spit-and-earth cone. It soon started to hum as the ants shivered out their alarm call. Pellonhorc was working at a distinct bulge in the side of the mound while I was reaching up and scoring a circumference, intending to knock the top off. I lost myself in the labour.

'Alef!' Pellonhorc shrieked.

I stopped what I was doing, and saw that his stick had plunged abruptly into the swelling and he'd lost balance and fallen against the mound. He staggered wildly away with the stick. There were ants on his arm, biting and stinging. I began to help brush them off and they were on me, too. The pain was instant and terrible and I screamed. We were scratching and flailing at each other for I don't know how long, and then the last of the ants were gone.

Pellonhorc sat down, laughing out loud.

'What's funny?' I said.

'You.' He mimicked my scream.

'It hurt like hell,' I said.

His face cleared. He stabbed his stick into the ground. 'That wasn't hell,' he said quietly. 'Don't you listen to Father Grace? *No* pain's like the pain of hell.'

'Maybe not, but you shouldn't laugh at me. It hurt. It isn't funny.'

'It may as well be. That's what I think. Anyway, you don't know anything about pain.'

'And you do?'

He sat crosslegged and picked up his stick, and put it to his palm, in the soft centre of it, the point dimpling the flesh. 'Let's see.' He rocked the stick, started to lean over it, gathering his shoulders. 'Let's find out about pain. Shall I do this to you or to myself, Alef? Which of us?'

His voice had gained a deeper edge. I stepped back and said, trying to be jokey, 'That's crazy.'

Immediately he was on his feet, hurling me over, and my face was in the earth. I tried to push back, get up, but he knocked my elbow away and twisted my right arm hard, locking it straight and almost dislocating my shoulder. I screamed.

'Shut up, that's nothing.' He didn't release me but adjusted his position until he was steady and comfortable behind me, holding me down, keeping my arm locked straight. Along with the pain, I could feel his calmness. It was terrifying. 'Open your fist, Alef. Open it or I'll break your fingers. I will.'

He was sitting across my shoulder blades, keeping my

trapped arm along the ground, his boot on the point of my elbow. I could hardly breathe. My head was wrenched to the side so that I could only see my left hand, which was quite free, though there was nothing I could do with it but scratch at the earth.

'Open it, Alef.'

I did so. I didn't say anything. I felt the point of the stick settle itchily in my palm.

'You or me, Alef. You think you know about pain? Who gets it, then? Choose.'

As I tried to get the breath to speak, his weight adjusted and he pushed the stick into my palm. The pain was instantly unbearable.

I screamed, 'You. You!'

He let me go, jumping to his feet. I rolled over and cradled my hand. My shoulder throbbed. Sitting crosslegged, Pellonhorc put his left hand on the ground, palm up, and the stick back in the heart of his palm, as if we had simply erased the events of a few moments ago. He was completely calm. He just looked at me and said, 'I don't think I can push it all the way through with one hand. I'll hold it. You get a stone to bang it with.'

I said, 'This is really stupid. No.' I was shivering. I had no idea what to do.

'Then you hold the stick and I'll get a stone and bang it. You decided, remember. Or do you want me to put it through your hand?'

I shook my head. A thought came to me and I just let it out. 'Anyway, we can't. It's blasphemy. Like Our Lord crucifixed.' I had forgotten how all this had started, how it had got to here.

He frowned at this and after a moment said, 'You're right.' He examined me carefully, as if he suspected I might have been trying to trick him, then continued to look at me with a kind of respect. His face abruptly cleared. 'Yes,' he cried out, 'it is!' And then he leapt to his feet and punched the air and yelled, 'It's gone!'

I couldn't work that out. I had no idea what had gone, but something certainly had come and gone inside Pellonhorc's head. Something terrible had surfaced and submerged again, and somehow I felt responsible for both.

He yelled, 'Come on!'

He was at the mound again and furiously working his stick into the deep hole he'd made. I sat hugging my knees, watching him. He was concentrating utterly, as if nothing had happened. Maybe nothing had, I thought. But my palm was stinging, and threads of blood beaded its lines when I clenched and opened my fist.

For a long time he stabbed and scraped with all his strength. I didn't join him. Usually we scratched a few centimetres off the surface and that was the best we could do, enough to draw a hissing trail of ants out of the mound. We'd provoke them and lead them to a stream if we could, and then we'd leap across it and watch them mill around at the water's edge. After that we'd wander off to one of the cesspits.

'Hey, Alef! Here!'

He'd broken deep into the bulge in the mound, and opened it wide. It was quite hollow, and inside the umber cavity lay the motionless body of a small bird. The creature was in perfect condition. Its wings were vivid red and yellow, its beak bright orange, and its eyes even glittered in the sudden light.

'How did that get there?' Pellonhorc said.

'The ants are scavengers. Maybe they swarmed into its nest and dragged it back here and walled it in. A bird's unusual, but they can overcome mousels as big as your fist.'

He stared. 'How could they do that?'

I was often astonished at what he didn't know. But he could never believe I was quite so ignorant of anything beyond Gehenna.

'Scout ants locate a prey for the colony,' I told him. 'If it's a mousel den, they summon an army of stinger ants who climb over each other and block the entrance with their bodies. Then they swarm inside, filling the den like whamfoam, ground to roof, wall to wall. The animal can't escape. The ants paralyse it with stings, thousands of stings, and ferry it back to the mound where workers carry it up the wall and encase it.'

'But this is a bird. It could have flown away from the nest.'

'It could have been protecting its young.'

'Stupid bird.' He kept looking at it, and said, 'It's dead anyway.'

'No, it isn't. Look.' Its beak was open, faintly quivering as, every few seconds, an ant crawled inside the mouth and disappeared.

He leaned in closer. 'What are they doing?'

'They're being eaten by the bird. The bird can't feed itself, so they work their way down into its stomach to be digested.'

'That's stupid. Why?'

'When they first get it here, they lay an egg under the bird's skin, deep in its thorax. The pupa of a new antrix will be developing there, growing. The body of the living bird keeps it warm and fed and protected.'

'Like a mother.'

I looked at Pellonhorc, not sure if he was joking. He didn't seem to be. I said, 'Not exactly.' I leaned forward and held my stick up close to the bird's head. Its bright eye followed the point of the stick. The head twitched fractionally. I said, 'It's being eaten from the inside out by the pupa. As the pupa grows, it nibbles space around itself. The bird's heart is beating and its brain's still functioning. There's no motor response from the head down, but it retains full sensory function. It's still in this world.'

School lessons. Biology and theology. Pellonhorc was learning both here on Gehenna. 'As far as a bird can,' I told him, 'it knows and it feels.' I pulled away and said, 'Horrible way to die. You think hell's worse than that?'

Pellonhorc leant in close and squinted at the bird. 'It has to be. It's worse than anything, isn't it? Father Grace says whatever you see, whatever you can imagine, God makes hell a thousand thousand times worse. So it's best not to imagine, isn't it?' He took his own stick and twisted it hard into the bird's body, skewering the creature and lifting it out of the mound. He shook the stick and dropped the paralysed thing. A few ants, thrown clear of the mound, scurried back towards it, but Pellonhorc trod them into the ground. He knelt to peer closely at the bird. I knew he was going to kill it. He was fascinated by the deaths of small creatures.

But he just stared. I wanted him to kill it quickly. Normally I was just relieved when he was done with his little experiments. I found them hard to watch. There was no method in them and I could see no purpose. I wanted the bird dead. Its wings shivered in the air, though that might just have been the breeze.

He rolled it over and murmured, 'You think animals go to hell? Birds? Ants?'

'No –' I thought again. 'I don't know. They're innocent, aren't they? They just do what they're designed to do. They can't choose. Can't be bad.'

'But we can, can't we?'

'Of course.'

He poked the bird. 'Will we go to hell if we kill it, or if we don't kill it?'

'It's just a bird. You won't go to hell over a bird.' I wanted it dead now. Its head was trembling, its feathers lifting in the breeze. Ants were coming from the mound, summoned by the drones returning from the bird.

He poked the bird again, rolling it to and fro. 'My dad said some people don't deserve to die in their sleep. What if you kill someone who's going to hell anyway?'

'Forget about it,' I told him. 'Who knows what's going to happen? God forgives us when we die.'

'Who told you that?'

No one had told me. I was guessing. I wasn't sure about God any more. It was fine in church, when the chanting stopped me from thinking and the music was good, but when I thought about it, the idea of goddery was plainly illogical. As soon as you spotted the first false assumption, the whole thing unravelled like faulty puter code. Only you didn't discuss it, not even with your parents. Not on Gehenna. But I always followed the rules in what I said, even with Pellonhorc. It was safer. While I no longer quite believed in hell or heaven, I believed in death, and I'd certainly seen that before. I was pretty sure Pellonhorc had, too, before he'd arrived on Gehenna.

Pellonhorc knelt down beside the twitching bird and whispered, 'Where are you going, little one?' He stared into the bird's open eye and held the stick there, almost scratching the gleaming surface. The pupil oscillated between the stick's point and Pellonhorc's squinting eye.

Pellonhorc whispered, 'Where are you going? And where will I go?'

I wanted to look away but couldn't as Pellonhorc leaned down and drove the stick hard into the eye and on through the thin skull of the bird.

He sat back. He had done it, yet the bird was still moving. I realised before Pellonhorc what this had to mean. I drew the knife from its notch in his belt and cracked the bird's breastbone open, and let the wriggling, plump, white-jawed new antrix out onto the ground. As it began to stretch and uncoil its wet palps, I set the flat of the blade over its abdomen and pushed down, squirting the thin viscera across the earth.

I looked at Pellonhorc. He was bent over, vomiting. That surprised me.

'There,' I said, when he was done puking and wiping his mouth. 'The bird was going to die anyway. You ended its suffering. But I killed the antrix's brood, potentially a whole colony. So I'll be the one going to hell, not you.'

I was joking, but he said, quite seriously, 'No. That isn't how it works.'

Seven

BALE

Bale woke at three a.m. with a migraine that shined up his skull like a furnace. He stumbled to the toilet and puked himself dry, washed a handful of pills down his throat with a mug of water and puked it all straight back out again. He changed tactics, chasing the rest of the pills down with visky, and this time as the puke rose he swallowed it back down. After that he sat in the dark, riding the blistering novas until about four, when at last he spun down into a black hole of sleep.

The crashcall woke him at five. He thought it was still the migraine and tried to ignore it, but the shriek grew too loud. Half-conscious, he screened in and almost choked at the image filling the wall.

The projection was split into eight frames, each rectangle colour-coded and featuring a corpse sprawled or folded on the street. Bale cracked open a vodkaffeiner and flushed it down his raw throat. It tasted mostly of bile. His teeth felt sticky.

He concentrated on the screenery, where a translucent flatmap of Lookout floated like scum over the images of corpses, incident locations colour-matched to each body.

They were all males. The images were stills, clipped

mostly from Pax cams, but a few were injury-mapped images where the paramedics had arrived first. These images of the dead were overwritten with 'TO MORGUE AFTER FORENSIC'. Every few seconds a line of text snapped across the screen and vanished: '*NOT* repeat *NOT* AN EXERCISE. ALL SOCS ACTIVE. INCIDENT ONGOING.'

A ninth body appeared, indigo-framed, a matching locater blinking on the map. Bale pulled his trousers on, tripping and swearing. He yelled, 'Chronology,' and the screen flashed a row of colours: red, yellow, green, blue, purple, brown, orange, black, indigo. Then pink, and the screen put up a new pink-framed corpse and a further location.

Still swearing, Bale shrugged himself into the long jacket. The gun's weight sobered him a little. He swung the visor over his head but held off the eyeware. The earpiece slid home and Vox was howling.

'—OPERATIVE IMMEDIATELY. ONE MALE SUSPECT SIGHTED WITH UNCONFIRMED MANUAL SHARP WEAPON, RIDING BLACK AND GOLD JIGUMI ZIPRIDER. NO OTHER DETAILS AT PRESENT. SUSPECT UNIDENTIFIED, DISMOUNTING AND ATTACKING AT RANDOM. ALL REPEAT ALL UNITS OPERATIVE IMMEDIATELY. INCIDENT ONGOING. THIS IS NOT AN EXERCISE. ALL REPEAT ALL UNITS OPERATIVE IMME—'

Bale was stumbling through the door, the map branded in his head. Pax was just getting everyone on the streets, which meant there was no clear pattern ident.

On the street, he stopped. There was no point running anywhere. He leant back against the wall and waited there, gathering himself. Still half-drunk, he couldn't drive. He shouldn't have drunk the vodkaff, but it wouldn't be registered for a while, and he needed the jolt. It didn't matter

– he'd be stood down well before it hit his blood titre. Hell, he was suspended anyway.

Feeling good now, the vodkaff unfuzzing his thoughts, he considered the kill sequence. Maybe it wasn't premeditated, but there had to be some sense to be made of the spree. It couldn't be seen from the flatmap, though. A ziprider could take the K anywhere. Oneways and gridlocks wouldn't give him pause.

Bale touched his throat and murmured, 'Desk? Who's up? Any connection yet? Anything?'

'Nothing, Bale. The K's stopping, hitting, moving on. Just keep your eyes open. Someone's got to get lucky.'

'Delta?' Bale said. 'That you?'

'Yes, this is Officer Kerlew.' She emphasised it. 'We've got nothing else. It's a mess. Everything we've got's coming through on Vox, and it's all nilnegative. First male was found half an hour ago, knifesliced at least twenty times.'

Even on duty, Delta never used her surname with Bale. Someone must be at her shoulder, or else Delta was thinking ahead to the debriefing, to blame and discipline. That was the difference between them. She was good, though.

She was still talking. 'The SOC officer assumed a mugging gone sour. Then two more, same and same, at ten and twelve minutes later, and someone at each SOC mentioned seeing a ziprider. The others started to come in at about five minute intervals. And –'

Delta cut out and the comms flipped to Vox's puterised monotone.

'SUSPECT K POSSIBLY RIDING ZIPRIDER PLATE 264FRR4587, REPORTED STOLEN TWO HOURS AGO.' A pause. **'NEW VICTIM ONE MINUTE AGO. JUNCTION OF**

GARNET AND MISTRAL. CODE MAROON. ALL PAXERS IN VICINITY APPROACH WEAPONREADY WITH EXTREME CARE.'

Then silence.

'Delta?'

A quick sigh, then, 'I hear you, Bale.'

'I'm near Garnet and I'm on foot. How about I go there and start processing it?'

'Sure. I have no other orders.' She checked herself and said in a sharper tone, 'Wait. Aren't you suspended?'

'Crashcall, Delta. You know that.'

'Yeah, but –'

He lost her voice for a moment, and when she was back, her tone was slightly different again, almost strained. She said, '– You won't get paid's what I meant.'

Bale pulled his visor down all the way, finally engaging the eyeware and wincing in anticipation. He closed his eyes. His hangovers reacted badly to the abrupt starkness of the Pax worldview.

The overlay cut in. Sounds ebbed and returned, filtered and changed. He squeezed his eyes open, gently, breathed deeply and swore.

The visor was fully engaged. He was on duty, now. Street detail had been largely erased, his world turned to a cartoon of pure line; the edges of buildings and kerbs, the outlines of stationary vehicles were just grey lines thinning and paling into the distance. In this sketched city, only what the system considered worth attention was drawn to Bale's notice. Moving vehicles took on colour that brightened with speed and proximity, and stick-drawn pedestrians only flickered into solidity as they approached Bale or if he held his attention on them for more than a second.

He took that setting down to half a second.

His skull still thumped. The eyeware was bad enough when he was fully sober. He pulled up the visor's recognition facilities and nulled most of the list. No use flagging the usual thugs and thieves. He pulled up the vehicle options and hi-lit *Ziprider, Jigumi*, colour-selecting *black and/or gold*. From a weapon catalogue he picked *knife*, and out of forensic he chose *visible bloodspatter*. From gait he chose *running, limping* and *other*. That done, he started to trot through the cartoon city. Street sounds were distant and unreal, and the steady thump of his feet on the hard ground fed the residual thud of his headache.

He increased speed slightly, thinking maybe he could damp the hangover that way. Loping too quickly round a corner and stumbling, he swore at the visor as his shoulder scraped the sudden edge of brick.

'You okay out there, Bale?'

'Fine,' he mumbled. 'Don't babysit me, Officer Kerlew.'

'I'm not babysitting, Bale. You flagged an adrenaline surge.' She broke away again.

'I tripped.' He wondered what was up with her. He steadied himself and trotted round the next corner, this time more smoothly. A paramedic siren flared close, *woe-woe*, maybe a street away. He heard Delta start to speak, but her voice cut out. Unlike her to be anything but focused, he thought. He'd never heard her cross-comm before. But then this was something fast and getting faster.

His visor flashed up an oncoming ziprider, black and red. Bale started to go for the gun, but it wasn't a Jigumi, the rider was a girl and there was no forensic. He trotted on, heading for the siren, which was steadying, the parameds coming to a halt not far away.

'You don't trip sober, Bale. We can cope.' Delta was whispering now, her voice coming and going. This wasn't like her at all. She was like Bale, ice in a crisis, thriving on the fast stuff. 'Want me to stand you down?'

He ignored her, optioning an arrowmap, the program footstepping him round the cartoon corner and past a gaggle of sketched pedestrians. His visor snatched flagwords from their conversations. *Killed*, *stabbed*, *knife* and *blood*. It was just chatter, though.

Delta's voice came through again, low-toned still, but this time penetrating, pure business. 'Bale –'

'I've got it.' He was at the head of an alley. There was blood here, the visor rendering it jewel green, but Bale was overloaded by the visor, everything in his sight and hearing registering max. After the simple view of the unaffected streets, the alley's maxed sound and colour overwhelmed him. Beside the central dense green wellspring with its radial spatter and spraymarks, a fat-tyred yellow paramed bodyrider was kerbed with its rear doors wide. The vehicle's system readers were bleeping and keening, tubes and wires everywhere, and the screams of the man on the ground cut through everything but the rapid rocksteady conversation of the parameds at his side. *Clamp this, get me that, shit I've lost –*

Bale tuned the visor down until he could bear the levels, and focused on the paramed who seemed in charge. He was leaning close to the wounded man, muttering calmly.

'Nonotyou, sir, don't you worry, you're going to be fine, what's your name, I'm Limmy and this is Harket here, can you feel this at all? No? This? Don't worry. Can you see my hand here? My face? I'm the good-looking one. Yes, that's better. Stay with us, you're going to be fine.'

Bale put himself at the edge of the parameds' field of view, waiting for one of them to switch away from the vic and acknowledge him. Neither did, so he said, 'Did you see the K?'

Limmy murmured, 'He's not a K yet. This one's still alive.'

'Whatever you do here, my target's already a K. You see anything?'

Harket gestured towards the closed end of the alley. 'That way. Tall, skinny, wearing a brown onepiece, blue surgical gloves like ours. Didn't see a blade, but –' he gestured at the victim, '– it's a sharp one, serrated, maybe ten cents long.'

Bale looked at the alley's end. 'Over that?' It was a mess of rubbish, and above the rubbish a wall maybe ten metres high, blade-topped.

'Not over it,' Harket muttered, his eyes fully on his work again. 'Through it.'

Bale looked again, using the visor, and swore. The gap was tiny. He would have missed it. Not concentrating. Hungover. 'He got through there?'

The screaming had settled into an exhausted, lung-bubbling groan. The paramedics didn't answer Bale.

He tried again. 'He's supposed to be on a zip.'

'Didn't see one. Frankly, we were happy to see him go.'

The parameds lost interest in Bale. Bale never understood how they kept so calm. He could see the vic was going to die, and they'd have seen even more of the dying than Bale had. What was the point? Bale knew it just by all the spreading green. But they kept going.

Limmy said, 'Harket, can you go to the rider and get me

some eph and morph. Sir, can you hear me? We're going to give you something for the pain now.'

Bale wished he could be like the parameds, calm and steady. Razer had said maybe he needed the adrenaline.

Limmy raised his voice a fraction. 'Harket? We got more saline back there?'

'Not enough. Ain't enough in the sea, the speed he's losing it.' As Harket came back, Limmy's blue-gloved hand slipped and a breathtakingly bright green fountain fizzed from the body and slapped Limmy's visor. Limmy leaned over the vic, putting his weight down, swearing, then jerked up and down like he was riding something. Bale saw this motion was the body convulsing, out of control, the paramed only trying to hold it down. Harket was back with him now, his fist punching something into the arching chest. The body locked momentarily, then fell still.

Harket leant back and quietly said, 'Limmy?'

Gently and unhurriedly, Limmy put his hand to the man's neck, his fingers searching for the carotid. Bale found himself touching his own neck, checking the racing pulse there.

Harket said it again. 'Limmy?'

Limmy murmured something back, but the atmosphere in the alley had changed and what he said didn't break through Bale's visor filters. It was too calm. Bale could lipread it, though, the gentle, 'Shit.'

Bale raised his visor. The alley looked drab and dirty, the blood like blood, the corpse as meaningless as every corpse he'd ever seen. Bale's skull thudded, the hangover reasserting itself. Limmy looked up at Bale, wiping a muddy smear of blood from his mask. For the first time there was emotion in his voice. Irritation. He said to Bale, 'So? You going after this K or giving him a chance to ruin our whole day?'

Bale walked to the alley's end and saw where the junk had been partly pushed aside. The gap was shoulder-wide at best. Metal packaging, plaswrap and bundle-wire mostly blocked it. He stood back, breathing hard, his head thumping solidly.

He pulled the visor back down over his eyes. His map told him he was staring at a refuse access shaft shared between the sleepotel behind him and a go-food stall. That was all it told him.

'Delta, where does the shaft exit? I don't seem to have that loaded.'

'Wait.'

Bale tried to pull the packaging and bundle-wire further aside to expand the opening but the whole mess threatened to topple and close the shaft off entirely. There were threads of blood, bright green, on the wire. The K had cut himself.

Delta came back, talking fast. 'It's a sewage access point, Bale. You go down there and you're off-comm. I can load you a map but it'll take a minute. It tracks all the way down to Central Recycle, then it pipes out undersea. I'm getting officers to every access point I can, but we can't cover them all. Can you follow? No one else is near and the K can't be more than a few minutes ahead of you. Hold it while I load the map.'

'Forget that. I'm following now. He's on foot and he's cut, so there should be a good trail.' He pulled at the bundle-wire and held it back with a boot, and said, 'Access is poor. I'll just get through.' He started to shrug off the thick jacket. 'I'll have to leave my jacket and visor this side. I'll be out of contact, just carrying my gun. Don't get me shot by one of us, Delta.'

'Bale –'

'That wasn't a joke.'

'It wasn't funny. Listen, Bale, the gun –'

'I'll warn him, don't worry.'

'No, Bale –'

She started to say something more, but he'd taken the visor off. He had no idea what had got into Delta, but she was tense as hell. Anyway, he'd acknowledged standing orders, and that should be enough, and he'd also justified leaving the visor behind. Whatever happened down there, he wasn't going to get into trouble by leaving evidence of it. He wasn't intending to walk any K out of this.

Dropping his jacket over the visor, retaining only his small seeker torch and the gun, he glanced back at the paramedics. At a second thought he retrieved the light-intensifier from his jacket and slid it over his eyes. The bundle-wire sprung clear of his boot.

Standing up from the body and stretching his arms, Limmy looked straight at Bale and said, 'I wouldn't have your job.'

Bale's heart was speeding. He didn't tell Limmy what he was suddenly thinking, which was that he wouldn't have any other job but this. Odd thought to have. He'd remember to tell Razer that. It was the sort of weird thing that turned on her smile.

Yeah, he thought. Maybe it was his friendship with Razer that was pissing Delta off.

He still had the hangover, but adrenaline was pumping as he forced back the harsh tangle of wire and pushed through into the abrupt gloom of the down-chamber. He stopped there and turned back to the ragged edge of light to pull the rolls of bundle-wire towards him until they toppled. The gap closed to an impenetrable lattice and the gloom became darkness. He pushed hard until he was satisfied it was meshed securely. No exit for him or the K, and no one to come after them and get in the way.

Limmy's voice came back at him again. 'And I hope we don't get to see you later.'

The down-chamber stank, and Bale almost wished he'd taken the visor, just to be able to nil the stench. He stepped onto the narrow pole platform, held his breath and punched the GO button. Five seconds of smooth drop, half a second's decel and a muddy slap as the platform hit the floor. Bale stepped off and sent the platform back up.

Moving off, he wished Limmy hadn't said that last thing. It was too much like the bad luck of wishing good luck. He set the visor to register recent blood, and followed its click-prompts.

The surface underfoot was rough, and the warren stank of vomit and mould, of stale piss and the sea. He broke into a slow trot. He thought he could hear the sea crack and roar distantly. It was like something breathing, something primitive. The air down here sucked and blew at his face, and the rock trembled beneath him. Lookout's shield only worked overhead, not beneath the city's foundations. The crash and smell of the sea scoured the recycling tunnels.

Rats chittered as he walked on, the visor registering the blood left by the killer, clicking at every splash.

His head was still thumping. At the first fork with an exit option, the killer had stopped, judging by the cli-cli-clicking in his ears. 'What did you do, K?' Bale murmured to himself. He knelt and touched the blood, then looked towards the exit. 'No. You didn't go straight out here. But you did pause. So, you were thinking of it.' He looked the other way, into darkness. 'But you didn't just keep on running, either. Why did you hesitate?'

Bale went on, more slowly. The tunnels twisted, and then they began to narrow until he was ducking through headhigh pipe, rough with seashell clusters and splattered joint weld. Sewage ran at his feet like clotted jelly. Bale tried to keep his feet to the sides, running skewed, but after he'd fallen twice into the caustic waste, he gave that up and ran through the stuff. He didn't need the clicks any more. The K's boots had left a trail of shit splashed up the sides of the pipe. It was impossible to miss it.

Why had the K hesitated back there? It didn't make sense. He was definitely a runner, not a hider. He'd ditched the ziprider somewhere before the alley, when he hadn't needed to. When the parameds had arrived, he'd panicked, run into the dead end of the waste shafts when most people would have known parameds would throw themselves out of anyone's way, that they were trained to avoid confrontation.

But Bale's head was thumping again. He was losing time. Anyway, the K wasn't a thinker; he killed someone in what he must have thought would be a blind alley. He was just stupidly lucky.

And there he was, the K. Blue gloves, just like the parameds had said.

Bale stopped, puddled sewage splashing at his feet. The grain of Bale's heightened vision separated the K from the dull grey side of the pipe where he'd tried to flatten himself, and Bale winced at the brightness of the knife he held at his side. Harket had been right about the blade. Even without the visor to identify it, Bale recognised it as a military killing blade. He couldn't tell whether the K had the training to go with it until the K moved fluidly forward, spinning the knife across his palm. He had the training.

Something was wrong about all this, though. What?

Bale pulled his gun and said, 'Drop the blade right now. That was your warning.'

The K raised his arm carefully, high and at his side, keeping his line of sight clear, then opened his hand and flicked the knife outward and away from him.

Such a shining blade, Bale thought. He'll have cleaned it after each kill, but military ceramic turns dark in low light, doesn't give you away. Which means he's drawing me to it.

Nevertheless, the knife fell, and Bale instinctively eased up.

No. Something about the drop was as wrong as the knife.

Bale sucked a sharp breath, starting to move. The knife wasn't spinning. This was a drop-and-catch.

Bale pulled the gun up again as the K launched himself sideways to pick the knife out of the air by its tip, picking and throwing it at Bale in a single liquid move that Bale remembered learning years back. He'd never been this good at it, though.

Bale fell back, feeling warmth on his cheek, and fired the gun, conscious of the slowness in his reaction, knowing it was the hangover. But his aim was good enough, the K not expecting a Pax officer to have had military training. Bale saw the barrel centred perfectly on the K's chest as he fired.

Only the gun didn't kick, hadn't fired, and the K kept

moving, rolling to his feet and running away down the pipe, his footsteps echoing. Bale swore, the word thumping down the pipe, knowing immediately but way too late why the gun had failed. That was what Delta had been trying to tell him. The gun wouldn't let Bale use it. He was still too drunk.

He threw the weapon aside. At least the K was unarmed now. Bale picked the K's knife up, retuned the visor to register sound, and ran.

The K had hi-lit vision. That would be military, too. Finding the alley hadn't been a lucky chance. He'd planned it, ditched the ziprider nearby but not too close. Finding someone in the alley had been bad luck, otherwise he'd have disappeared totally. He hadn't expected anyone to be in the alley. He'd known how Pax worked.

The other thing Bale was sure of was that the K had no gun, or he'd have used it.

The visor clicked away evenly, still registering blood spatter. Bale was behind the K, keeping pace. The K was younger, but Bale was just as fit. And the hangover was fading as he ran.

A few more minutes and it struck Bale that the K still wasn't going for any of the exits. He was going deeper, heading seaward. Why? He must know Pax would have the exits blocked. Was that it?

No. He wanted Bale. He was going to ambush Bale somewhere up ahead. Bale was the only one who might identify him.

They were deep below Lookout now, far from RECYCLE and entering WASTE. The stench was different, a more heavily acrid ammonia smell with an underscent of the ocean. What couldn't be recycled was broken down here to be taken far out to sea by the banks of wave pumps. Bale could hear the pumps groaning far ahead. A corroded sign on the pipe wall told him: WARNING. THIRTY MINUTE AIR SAFETY BEYOND THIS POINT. CHECK YOUR SUIT AND START YOUR TIMER NOW!

Bale went on. Ten minutes should be enough. Anyway, if it said thirty, it meant an hour. A stutter from the visor, and Bale slowed before a fork in the pipe. The passage to the left was dark and narrow, a dead-end feed to the main tube. A moment's silence from the visor, then *cli-cli-clik*.

Bale knelt to pick up a dead rat by the tail. He felt light-headed and had to lean against the side for a moment. The K must be just round the corner, crouched in the feed tube, waiting for him. The rat was largely a skinbag of bacterial froth, but there was enough weight left for Bale's purpose. He took a long, throat-stinging breath and lobbed the corpse across the mouth of the feed tube, bringing up his arm a fraction of a second after the rat thumped and splashed. The K had to straighten awkwardly to come out of the narrow feed tube, but Bale didn't give him the time. With all the strength he had left, he stiff-armed the K in the throat and watched him drop, and that was it.

Bale put his hands to his knees, exhausted and breathing hard. Another *cli-clik* made him look up sharply. He stared at the corpse, uncomprehending.

Clik-lik.

The slumped body was dressed in a sewer suit. His gloves and boots were heavy duty, green. Bale hadn't dropped the K at all. This was a wasteworker. He'd been shoved out of the tube for Bale. Bale had made nothing more than a distraction kill.

'Nice move,' the thin man whispered, standing straight,

his blue fists flexing. 'But it takes more than that.'

It was over for Bale. He could see it in the K's eyes. The man had known it wouldn't be just Bale down here, that there would be wasteworkers. As he'd been running, he'd been looking for one. Bale had fallen for the oldest trick, and now every move he could make was covered. The K was just waiting for Bale to choose one.

'Why?' Bale said, though he didn't care. He just wanted time.

'Good question,' the K said, and lifted his arm. 'That's one more thing you'll never know. Make your last move. At least try to surprise me.'

Bale threw the knife at him. The K ducked easily and followed Bale's drop and roll like it was a planned exercise. Bale glanced towards where the knife had fallen, but couldn't see it. Only the visor responded to the direction of his glance beyond the K with a final *cli-cli-clik*.

The K stood over Bale and said, 'Is that all? Disappointing,' and swept into a kill move.

Bale blocked the flat hand with his forearm, feeling his arm crack. Out of the corner of his eye he saw the K's foot coming for the point of his jaw, to splinter it and drive through, into his skull. Not good enough, he thought dismally, and that was all.

Eight

ALEF

SigEv 8 My last day starts

I've probably given the impression that Gehenna was generally isolated from the rest of the System, but Gehenna did have a routine connection with the Upper Worlds. It had its deletium swamps. Gehenna had its faith to fire its soul, but the sustenance of its body was founded on the value of the deletium that the Lord had sown in our Eden.

Deletium was a radioactive substance used as a nuclear fuel potentiator. It could be synthesised, but the process was neither safe nor cost-effective. In the entire System, deletium was naturally present only on Gehenna. It was unstable in contact with air and dangerous to extract from the swamps, and Gehenna's strict restrictions over the use of machinery meant that human workers had to be used to harvest it.

This was not a job that anyone willingly volunteered for, but Upper World crimers often chose to work in Gehenna's deletium swamps, to reduce a fraction of their Upper World sentence. Hard as the killers and thieves and pirates thought they were, they never anticipated the horror of the swamps. Gehenna's own crimers knew better, preferring the second chance that they believed execution by fire offered.

Work in the swamps was unimaginably dreadful; there was blood-boiling heat and bone-eating radiation, and while the swamp was like thin mud at the surface, it was as thick as molasses at its floor.

Moreover, the swamps could not be approached from their banks, due to the toxic gases that churned above, so the workers were dressed in full-body atmosuits and swung out over the mire on long-arm cranes before being lowered a hundred or more metres to the swamp's floor.

Once down and footfirm, they were effectively blind. Their only hope of return was the harness connecting them to the winch above.

Since the laws of Gehenna prohibited almost every device that might have helped them move with less effort, or to see, or to locate deletium vents more efficiently, the workers were forced to bump and stumble along the swamp floor, searching for faintly luminescent filaments of deletium dripping up through the heavy, sulphurous swamp. If they found one, they stopped and signalled along the winch cable, and an extraction pipe was lowered to them down the cable. Still virtually blind, they had to seal the awkward, thickly shielded pipe to the mouth of the vent, trapping the deletium stream.

This was body-breaking labour. Miners spent no more than an hour a day trudging the swamp floor, unless they located a deletium source. If they did – and the average location rate was one source for every three point eight hours spent searching – they were not winched out of the swamp until the source was in flow. This alone could take three hours.

Many workers died down there, or shortly after surfacing,

of heat exhaustion or dehydration or atmosuit failure or acute radiation sickness. Workers with low location rates were suspected of deliberately failing to flag vents. Such workers sometimes failed to surface alive at the end of their shifts, or else fell back into the swamps or onto hard land while being winched back up. These were logged as suicides, and some of them perhaps were.

The average sentence crimers received for the swamps was a year, and the average survival rate there was just over five months. You didn't need putery to calculate the chances of completing a sentence. And yet they kept coming to the swamps of Gehenna. They died and kept coming.

The reason they kept coming was that the many workers who vanished forever in the swamps without being declared suicides were recorded as missing, and the crimers celebrated them as escapees. By comparison, there was no possibility at all of escape from an eight-decade sentence served in a sealed, high-orbit prison hulk. So to many convicts, the swamps of Gehenna represented some insane form of hope.

We were constantly warned to beware of escaped crimers. There were even reports of sightings. Escaped crimers were one of the Lord's most potent weapons against sinners. These sightings of escapees, reported eagerly in the System, only encouraged more crimers to volunteer for the swamps. They also very effectively encouraged Gehennans to obey the strictures of the Lord. It was another twin-win situation.

On my last day, warnings of escaped deletium workers issued from the kitchen comms as we were eating our breakfast. My father and mother exchanged looks as the

News Preacher said, 'A group of five armed and extremely dangerous crimers have escaped from the deletium swamp and are believed to be making their way towards JerSalem. They have thus far successfully evaded all attempts to apprehend them. All JerSalemites in the area are advised to be vigilant and to examine their consciences until the crimers have been recaptured.'

There was something more forceful than usual about the News, and it was particularly odd that a location should be specified. I wondered why crimers would head this way. The rocket station they would need to reach to escape Gehenna was far from JerSalem in the other direction. Had one of our community sinned so terribly that the Lord had to target us this way?

I discounted this, as it was without logic; if they were the Lord's instruments of punishment, why were we being warned, rather than told to submit to them?

Considering the minuscule statistical likelihood of our encountering the escapees, my parents were unaccountably agitated. My father opened the screenery he kept in the main room and hunched down in front of it. He swore, which was unlike him, and closed it again, and glanced at my mother, shaking his head.

My mother visibly trembled. She said, 'What, Saul?'

I remember her tone. It wasn't confusion, or surprise, or even shock. It was simple despair. She knew instantly what had happened, what was going to happen, just as if she were a sinner awaiting the Lord's righteous vengeance. I felt sick at her helplessness. I'd never seen her like this before.

He said, 'Compromised. I'm going to the shop.'

'Maybe it's nothing.'

He hesitated, then said, 'I'm sorry,' and was on his feet and gone.

My mother kissed me, hugging me close and for a long time. We both pretended she wasn't crying. I didn't know what to do, so I waved goodbye and left for school. There was an image in my head of the pit opening beneath the arkestra, and the looks on the musicians' faces as the ground was taken from beneath their feet.

School began as normal, with prayers and confessions. There was no mention of the crimers. Shortly after the morning break, Garrel slipped into our classroom and whispered something to the teacher, who glanced in irritation at Pellonhorc. Garrel made a beckoning gesture to Pellonhorc, and then, to my surprise, also to me. Pellonhorc went straight to the front of the room, while I began to close my screenery. Garrel said, 'Don't worry about that, Alef. Leave it and move.'

I started to say something, but the levelness in his voice silenced me. The three of us left the school. Pellonhorc and I had to trot to keep up with Garrel's long stride.

This is a hard memory to hold. Since that day, I have seen some terrible things. I have been part of them. One of the things I have observed since leaving Gehenna is that when we sit with someone who is going swiftly and certainly to die and nothing at all to be done about it, what we say is always the same thing. We tell them, firmly, 'You're going to be all right,' and we tell them not to worry.

And that day, as Pellonhorc and Garrel and I walked away from the school, I knew in my head and heart that something unimaginably terrible was unfolding. As we left school behind us, I cracked the brittle silence and said to Garrel, 'What about my mother and father?'

Garrel glanced at me and away, and said, 'Don't worry, Alef. They'll be fine.'

I said nothing more, and Pellonhorc didn't ask Garrel about his mother. At the school gate, Garrel had a flycykle I hadn't seen before. It was sleek and dark and glassy, not like anything on Gehenna. The morning's bright sky reflected off it like thundercloud. I reminded myself that Garrel wasn't like anyone on Gehenna, and nor was Traile, nor Pellonhorc. I thought of the look that had passed between my father and my mother earlier, and tried to fit everything together, but couldn't. I decided not to think about them.

Garrel pushed us inside the flycykle and lifted us away. Once we were in the air, he relaxed slightly.

'Where are we going now?' Pellonhorc asked him. I thought, from the way he said it, that this – whatever *this* was – had happened to him before. I added that possibility to my data, in brackets.

Looking down, I could see the school, and the church, and the rows of streets. I'd never seen JerSalem from above, but it was easy for me to synchronise my knowledge of it with this new perspective and immediately locate our house. It was on fire, as was Pellonhorc's house opposite. Garrel brought the flycykle round in a tight circle. We were as high as the church steeple.

People were beginning to gather at the fire, and as I watched, a man standing in the street brought something long and ponderous to his shoulder. It didn't look like a quellfire canister, and in any case the device was aiming towards us rather than at the fire, the man staring straight along the thick barrel at us. His eyes were black ovals. I wondered where Traile was.

A wisp of smoke spread from the heel of the device, and at the same time a light flashed red on the screen in front of Garrel, who swore and wheeled the flycykle round dizzyingly as the missile (I concluded) straightened its arc and closed on us. I heard a whistle and shriek as it passed by, and the flycykle shuddered in the air and accelerated alarmingly. We were now out of sight of where I had lived all my life.

'Is my mother dead?' Pellonhorc said in an odd, flat voice, as if referring to something that had happened a long time back.

'Unless I hear otherwise,' Garrel said.

'Where are we going?' I asked, though I suddenly knew exactly where we were going. The logic wasn't hard to work out. The flycykle dropped down as if following my lines of thought and sight, and whispered to stillness on the ground, just out of view of my father's shop.

Garrel locked down the flycykle's drive and dulled the lights, leaving only the console bright. He brought a threedy grid to the screen and hunched forward as the contours of the grid realigned to the dimensions of my father's shop. I watched over his shoulder. I'd seen this in games, the determination of vulnerabilities, the consideration of options for swift or subtle strike. Garrel overlaid and discarded a variety of views in quick succession. Most of the data I could have told him. Entrance/exit modes – just the two doors, front and one internal, no windows. He checked the thicknesses of walls, their physical make-up, and I noted him briefly register and disregard a weakness in the flat roof at the front of the shop. It leaked in heavy rain. He checked heat sources, and there were two fixed points; one of them was muted, more orange than red. Both people, I thought, were probably seated. There were others, too, moving about, merging and parting confusingly. Garrel held this view momentarily, trying to make a body count, but was unable to and gave up. They were all in the small room at the rear of the shop where Pellonhorc and I had roamed the Song, and where I had encountered Pellonhorc's father.

It was thrilling to watch Garrel gathering information. I was almost in his head, only with him it was automatic routine, while with me it was from games, my brain processing and leaping. I knew what was coming, what all this signified. I knew it all except the end. I knew how games always ended, though.

'Get out, Alef,' Garrel told me, closing the screen decisively. 'I need you. Pellonhorc, you stay here.'

'I'm coming with you,' Pellonhorc said.

But I was already out and Garrel too, and Pellonhorc was pushing at the door without result, his mouth opening and closing silently at us from behind the black reflected sky in the glass of the flycykle's cockpit.

At the shop door, Garrel stopped me. 'You wait here. I'll come for you when it's time. Understand? You wait. Your parents' lives depend on it. All our lives. You must believe me.'

I nodded.

As he let himself in, he glanced at me and disabled the door's keypad.

So he knew I'd been entry-listed. I noticed that his chest and thighs were slightly puffed up. He pushed the door closed behind him, but I trapped it with my foot just as it was about to click. I thought he might notice, but he was entirely focused ahead. I heard him walking quickly past the shelves of putery in the front of the shop to the door to the back room where all the heat was. He didn't hesitate on the way and I heard nothing, so I guessed the main shop must have been as empty as the screen had told him it was. He simply knocked on the far door, like an appointed guest. I held my breath. After a moment, I heard the door open and close. Odd, I thought.

I could have run away. No, that's not true. I wanted to, but I couldn't. It was like standing at the top of a cliff-high dive board and being momentarily unable to choose between the long spindly ladder behind and the quick helpless fall ahead.

I couldn't wait. Not with those choices. I wasn't sure Garrel could be trusted. I took a breath. Ahead, then.

SigEv 9 Spetkin Ligate

As quietly as I could, I slipped into the outer shop, leaving the door cracked barely open behind me. I felt oddly shaky and a little sick.

My father had security cams in the rear office, of course, their feed accessible from the shop. I crouched down behind the counter and activated the small screenery there, to see what was happening.

What I saw in the fisheye view of the back room made me stop breathing. In two chairs facing each other were my father and my mother. My mother's head was down, her chin on her chest, and she wasn't moving. Hers, then, had been the weaker of the two fixed heat sources. She was already badly hurt.

I started to calculate from there, or tried to. I don't know how far I had got with that when I fell apart inside and simply charged, screaming, into the back room, crashing the door open and running to her. If I had been more like my father, perhaps I wouldn't have done that.

Someone, probably Garrel, yelled, '*Wait!*' and everyone froze. I was on my knees, hugging my mother. From the warmth of her cheeks against mine, I thought she was crying, but the tears were sticky and not tears at all, but blood.

'He's a child,' my father said from the other chair, his voice thick. I heard the creaking of wood.

Someone took my shoulders and lifted me to my feet. I looked around. Along with Garrel and my parents, there were three other men in the room. One of them was injured, his arm slung against his chest, strapped there by a reddened gauze web. Traile was not there, nor was Pellonhorc's mother.

'Well,' said someone, 'it's the boy.'

I knew the voice, and turned to see the face of Pellonhorc's father on one of the screens. He was leaning forward, but now he leaned back again. His face was a little drawn, as if he'd slept badly, but no more than that. His voice was easy.

The injured man said slowly, 'Never mind the boy. How are we going to make this right? Are you going to give me Saul?'

'It looks as though you have him already.'

'You know what I mean, Drame. I want what he knows. What he can do.'

'I don't think that's up to me, Ligate,' Pellonhorc's father said mildly. 'Why don't you ask Saul himself?'

The man called Ligate turned. His voice came out awkwardly, and I assumed his wound was making it hard for him to concentrate. He was slow-moving, too. He said, 'Ask Saul? Saul knows what you'd do to him if he deserted you. No, Drame, you have to agree to it. I get Saul, you get your wife back, and your child.'

My father glanced at me. I could see the muscles in his neck straining. I thought he wanted to say something, but he didn't. I wanted to have him hug me, to be able to cry into his chest. He looked so helpless, his hands out of sight behind his back. He was otherwise unhurt, though, and that told me of his importance here. I looked at my mother again. Only the tension of her arms yanked back at her shoulders kept her from collapsing to the floor. Her head was slumped on her chest. She was not conscious.

Pellonhorc's father said, 'Our families are outside this, Ligate. That was always understood.'

Ligate's face showed nothing. 'I always thought so. You broke the rule.'

'Really, Ligate. Do you believe that? You have evidence?'

'Then tell me why you sent them here.'

'I knew you'd jump to conclusions. I wanted you to have time to consider before you acted stupidly.'

'I've had time. I've considered. I'm offering you your family. I only want Saul. I think I'm being generous, here. My family –' he took a breath, '– are all gone.'

Drame said, 'Leaving that aside. Can I trust you, Ligate?'

'Trust *me*?' Ligate turned lethargically to Saul and said, 'Do you trust your boss? If he tells you to come with me, will you come? Will he send his soldiers after you, to kill you?' It was odd, the way he moved and spoke. Everything he said was sharp and precise, but the man himself seemed drugged. Perhaps the wound was worse than it seemed.

My father didn't answer. There was nothing for him to give but wrong answers. I can see that now. This was a conversation without logic, just threat and parry. Whatever was going to happen would happen, and I can see that Drame and Ligate already knew what that was going to be. At the time it seemed like a Babbel tale, its end inevitable, full of doom.

Garrel was standing quietly. The other two men were standing to his left and right, as if the three of them were comrades.

Ligate said, 'Give me Saul, Ethan. Give me Saul and you can keep your wife and your child.'

'Saul knows everything, Ligate. If I give you him, you take everything.'

'Then you should have taken better care of him.'

Pellonhorc's father said nothing.

Ligate went on. 'You know, Ethan, if you hadn't murdered my family, I'd never have found Saul. I searched and searched. And all along, he was on Gehenna, of all places. Gehenna! Why would anyone choose to live on this ball of shit? Someone like Saul, with all that he could have had.' Ligate shook his head slowly, the expression on his face not accompanying his words. 'And I'd never, ever have thought of looking for your wife and child here. Why would you send *them* to such a place?'

Garrel was Ligate's agent. That was the only way it made sense. Ligate had had a spy in Drame's organisation, and the spy had located Saul. Drame, in sending his wife and child to Gehenna, had given away Saul's location. Garrel or Traile were the only possibilities.

This fitted the data. One of them had been Ligate's agent all along. He'd told Ligate that Drame's family were here, and revealed that Saul was here too. Garrel and Traile had fought, and one had been killed. Whichever had been Ligate's agent would have had the advantage of surprise there. And Ligate's agent would have brought Pellonhorc to him. Whoever had fired the missile at the flycykle simply hadn't realised who was in it.

Garrel shifted his feet and glanced at me with open contempt. That reaction was enough for me to dismiss the possibility that the spy had been Traile.

Drame repeated, 'Saul knows everything.'

'Indeed,' Ligate said, vaguely rubbing his wounded arm. 'Your right hand is Saul.'

'How do I know my wife and child are alive?'

'Yes.' Ligate nodded. 'Let's establish trust.' He put a hand to his ear and muttered something, and the rear door opened. I saw Pellonhorc's mother standing against the light, trembling slightly, a new man gripping her upper arm, forcing her to stoop and stumble forward a few steps. Her hands were behind her and there was no expression at all on her face, but her blonde hair was crusted thickly with blood. Ligate said, 'She's alive, then. You see her?'

Drame said, 'If she's hurt –'

'I said she's alive. She's alive. Don't make threats, you aren't in that position.' Ligate nodded to Garrel, who glanced at the screen before saying, 'Pellonhorc's locked in the flycykle outside.'

'Then let's speak to him,' Ligate said.

Garrel pulled the flycykle's comms device slowly from his pocket. He was watched closely by Ligate's other men, as if Drame might not have grasped that Garrel had to be the spy. Maybe Drame hadn't, though. Ligate clumsily snatched the device from Garrel and tossed it towards me. It fell to the floor and I picked it up.

'You talk to him, boy,' Ligate said.

I put the unit to my mouth and said, observing that my voice was shaking, 'Pellonhorc?'

He answered instantly. 'What's happening?'

'We're talking to your father, on the screen, like before. He wants to know you're okay.'

Pellonhorc's voice cracked. 'Alef? What about my mother?'

'Quickly, boy,' Ligate said, slurring the words. 'Tell him to confirm he's okay. Nothing else.'

I held the device tight, the controls pricking my palm. As clearly as I could, I said, 'Communication's open just for a moment. You have to tell him you're okay. Do you understand? It'll close again in a moment.' I squeezed the device, keeping the words as steady as I could. 'It's open now. You only have a moment before I have to close it. Do you understand me? You have to confirm what I'm telling you.'

There was silence, and I couldn't tell if he'd understood. But then he said, firmly, 'Yes. I understand, Alef. I'm okay.'

'That's enough.' Ligate gestured at me. 'Close it.' I flicked the device closed and tossed it to him. He didn't attempt to catch it, and it bounced from his arm to the ground. He lifted a foot, nearly losing his balance as he did so, and stepped hard on the unit, shattering it.

'Alef,' my father murmured. He raised his head. I could see the effort it cost him.

'You realise that if I say yes, Ligate,' Drame said, a new sharpness in his voice, 'Saul will never believe I mean it. You'll never be able to trust him. He isn't like you and me. I didn't put him there on Gehenna. It's where he wants to be. Put him anywhere else, he'll be lost to me and no use to you. You know that.' His voice dropped. 'And one day, Ligate, I will reach you.'

Ligate only smiled.

My father was staring at me. He was hardly able to hold his head up. He said, 'Alef, I –' and I looked away.

I looked away.

My throat catches even to think of it, that I took away from him his last chance to speak to me, and at the same time I rejected my last opportunity to listen to him.

So, I looked away from my father for the last time. I looked instead at Drame, who was still talking.

'... And if I say no to you, you'll kill them all.' On the screen, Drame's face hardened. 'But if you do that, Ligate, there will be nothing to stop me.' He said, slowly, 'It is no choice. Do you understand? Do you fully understand the consequences of this, Ligate? I will have nothing left.'

Then, suddenly and for the first time, Drame's voice faltered and all expression in his face emptied away. At last he had seen what I had seen and my father had seen. This, for Ligate, had not at any stage been a negotiation. It was all intended to end here, for Drame to watch them all die. Ligate only wanted to see hope swell and fail in Drame's eyes.

Drame sat straight again, though it was clear that he was having to exert great effort to speak at all. His voice was thin. 'I will come after you, Ligate,' he said. He swallowed and added, 'I *will* reach you.'

Ligate shrugged. He spoke slowly and clearly, as if exhausted. 'I already have nothing left, Ethan. This is all that matters to me now. Do you see what you have done, finally? We could have lived alongside each other, but you ended that. When you killed my family, you ended everything. Are you watching? Everything...'

Nine

RAZER

'Just do your work,' Razer told herself, but all she could think of was TEN PEOPLE AND ONE PAX OFFICER BELIEVED DEAD.

She knew it was going to be Bale. She wasn't going to check the updates, though. Not until the story was done. She started writing.

'Tell me about the Chute,' I asked Bale in our aftersex. My head was resting comfortably in the crook of his elbow. His bed was little more than a cot, and Bale [need to change name, something active, sense of menace. Risc?] took up most of it, but it didn't matter to me.

'It was discovered by accident. Imagine an immense underground cave system, like a natural burrowmite warren, only this has been scoured out by the wind. Five hundred kils of tunnels splitting and relinking, winding and doubling back, narrowing and widening. Imagine the wind in it like water in endless flood, only this is Bleak's wind and it's like a whirlwind forced through a drinking straw.

'It was used for research at first,' he said. 'Lookout was its dormitory. This was before they discovered core here. But the Chute came first.'

I was surprised at how he lit up as he said it, this man of such fierce mood, but he did. The blue in his eyes could seem electric. There was nothing concealed in him, and maybe that was what I had fallen for, here on the planet Bleak. Over the clock years and light years of these journals, as I've roamed the System and met humanity in all its masks, I've had more adventure and found deeper passion, but Bale touched me as few others had. Bale was a rare find; a good man.

He said, 'They used it as a testbed, on the principle of a wind tunnel. Everything you see here on Bleak was tested in the Chute. If it couldn't survive the Chute, it couldn't survive Bleak.'

I said, 'But most of Bleak's under shield, isn't it?'

'The rigs aren't. Thrummers aren't. There's fixed stuff, too, outside the shield. All the environment monitors, shuttles, tracks –'

Outside his room, the day was mostly gone, purple evening light filtering through the window. I fell back in the sheets. Two weeks we'd been together now, and I was still happy to be with him, to talk or to be quiet. Simply to look at him. Bale was special. [His name – Stele? Possible. Steal my heart. And steel, a hint of crimer too. Definitely possible.] Bleak suited him and it didn't, at the same time. He was fiery and flawed, a soul adrift.

And at this moment he was a man with a child's light in his eyes, telling me of the games he played. 'So they dropped stuff into the Chute, watched how far it got before it was ripped apart. They redesigned, remade, watched it get ripped apart again, but each time it lasted a few seconds longer. Vehicles, buildings, bits of rig – the Chute took anything. Even deepspace ships got impact-tested here. If there was a fault, the Chute'd rip a billion-dolor hull to nanoshreds in zero point no-time.'

His enthusiasm was endless. How like a small boy he always was in our aftersex, a boy who'd done something forbidden and not been caught. His bedroom was not a boy's, though. It was clean and lifeless. Metal furniture, wallscreenery facing the small bed. The only untidiness – the only personality – was the clot of our clothes on the floor.

I stroked the hair of his arm as he said, 'The channels aren't uniform but the wind is, so there's fast and slow curves, high and low g-grades, and there's debris and...' He sighed almost mournfully. 'I can't explain.'

It wasn't that he lacked the words. He just wanted to say it all at once. As if I knew nothing. He had no idea what I had seen, where I had been, though I'd made no secret of it, as I never do. You can't tell the stories of women and men on the edge unless you live there with them for a while. You learn to fix and to fight, to shoot and to pilot almost anything. And I had learnt it all.

I'd thought his ignorance of me strange at first, but then I realised why Bale hadn't sought me out on the Song. It wasn't out of any lack of interest in me, but because his Pax life was full enough of searching and checking. With me, it was enough for him simply to be. The ignorance was born of trust.

I twined my fingers in his and asked him, 'Why don't the Chute's walls get shredded?'

'They do. It's like a river eroding its banks.'

'And you deliberately drop yourself into this?'

'People who work on Bleak, they're of a type,' he said.

I smiled at him and said, 'I've noticed that. But who was first to think of it as a ride? Or did someone fall in and survive? That's usually the way with these freak discoveries.'

He reached across me to take a drink from the glass by the bed. I enjoyed the press of his weight, the added gravity. 'Not this time,' he said. 'Someone was curious, designed some sort of a suit and jumped in. Just one man on a whim.'

He offered me the glass. The visky tasted of him. We'd finished half the bottle before stumbling, undressing, towards the bed, and now a swirl of gritty lees was all that remained to be finished. Licking the roughness from my lips, I said, 'What happened to the first man?'

'He lasted fifty metres. The next man lasted longer, and it was about a year before someone looped the circuit and climbed out half alive. After that, it was just technique and bringing down the record. Sport. You've seen the exos we wear? They're unique to the Chute.'

'No, I haven't. What do you need from them?'

'You're flying, so it's protection plus clips and cutters, fins and lines. They all modify your speed and trajectory some way or another. Some flyers carry streamers. Some flyers like to go soft, some hard.'

I reached and put my hand between his legs, wanting him again. 'Like this?'

'Not like that.' He grinned at me.

She stopped writing. It hadn't been a grin on his face. By then, the sex had gone wrong between them. But she left the words there. This was part of why she wrote, so that the story she wove around the truth could take root. The present might last a moment, but its memory, well-prepared, could remain a comfort. Razer was a master of such adjustment.

Yes, she was being good to Bale, and she was being good for her readers, but it was only important, in the end, to be good to herself. To create a good past from a harsh present.

She carried on writing, trying not to think of him dead.

Afterwards, when his breath was running even again, he continued our conversation as if nothing had interrupted it. 'Soft means you fly safe and central, with less risk. Hard means you take a bit more control. Are you getting all this?'

'Fins, I think I can guess,' I told him. 'And streamers, maybe. The rest, no. Are you going to tell me?'

'They can't be told. Not by me, anyway.' He leaned back and looked at me. His hair was tousled and I brushed it away from his eyes. The blue of them had paled, and I remembered a sky that colour above Vegaschrist, the black-haired girl at my side laughing as her yellow kite disappeared into the blue. [link here]

'Tell me something else, then,' I said.

I wondered how much I really knew of Bale. Of the stories he wore on his body. Of the small scars that were a pitted constellation on his right cheek, of the shadowed hub of a collarbone healed without care. Yes, I knew those stories, and I knew what they told of him. But otherwise, what did I know?

He said, 'Okay. Here's one for you. You ever heard the word darkspeed?'

I thought a moment. Darkspeed *was the name of a ship I'd once been on. It was drug jargon on some planets too, darkspeed an imprecise memory bleach. The clumsier kidnappers veined their victims with it before returning them amnesiac. Not just amnesiac, though. Families discovered they'd paid for the return of twenty-year-old mewling infants. I had used the idea once [link here], following a long day on Further talking to a woman whose gaze never settled and never would again.*

I was sure Bale didn't mean this, though. There were several other usages of the word, all of them less intriguing. Darkspeed was an interesting word, but it was an obvious enough reverse-construction out of lightspeed, a term just looking for a use. It was always the usage that interested me more.

'No,' I told him. 'I've never heard it.'

'Okay,' he said. 'It's a fuckdrug too, but not here on Bleak. Listen.'

He moved slightly and I could feel the acceleration of his heart. He brushed the heel of a hand across his overnight stubble and said, 'You go fast down the Chute, the g-grades rise, so you get heavy.' It was always action that excited him. The talk of it and the thought of it were enough. And that was what we had between us, this adrenaline-soaked talk and restlessness, and that was why it couldn't last. It was a constant moving forward that was simply a prelude to moving on.

He said, 'This isn't the even compression that rocketeers get, though. Straight rocket suits won't do for this. If you want to manoeuvre at Chute-speed, you have to wear a special exo. This suit needs as much g-damping as it can get, but you're not sitting in a cabin here. Efficient damping like in a rocket suit wouldn't be any use. You ever worn one?'

'Yes.'

'Well, it's like wearing a pair of mattresses front and back.' He caught himself and stared at me and said, 'You've worn one?'

I smiled at his astonishment. 'I've done lots of things, Bale. Some of them even real.' How much of me he didn't know. Lost souls both of us, brief companions in the dark, dark night.

'If it ain't real, it ain't real,' he said, then paused and added, 'You're always a surprise, Kes, you know that?'

It was almost as if Bale had said he loved me. Just close

enough and no more. Just right. This man.

He chewed on the dregs of the visky, the grit cracking in his teeth, then went on. 'Okay, you get the idea. You need fins to bring your lines tight, but fins also cut your speed. Clips, cutters, streamers, all the rest, they give you a bit of refinement, take away some of the raw. You also need good visor screenery to read the Chute upwind and check the laterals, but most flyers think that's cheating, they only like to use available signs –'

'And you?'

'Me?' He grinned. 'I use what's available. I got no shame. If tech's available, yes, I'll take it.' He raised the glass and held it up to the window, squinting at the pale late afternoon light lensing through it.

'You were telling me about darkspeed,' I reminded him.

'I was getting there. What I was trying to say, it's all a trade-off. Speed and control. Like being alive and staying alive. The one's speed, the other's control.'

I noted that for later. I hadn't heard it before. He'd made a little frown before saying it, and I was certain it was a phrase all his own. Yes, Bale was special.

'At some stage, the point comes when the suit can't carry the gs. Usually you don't quite black out, because, like I said, the gs are uneven. You blubber and cramp, but you can take that, so you go faster. Now…' His blue eyes were glittering. 'Faster still. Going into a curve, you're blurring and losing peripheral focus, but as you straighten and lock steady, your head comes back again, sharp and clear.'

He closed his eyes and then opened them, and I could see he was on the brink of tearing up. 'It feels better than ever. Your focus is incredibly clean. This is the edge.' He emphasised it, repeating it so I would know it was something important.

'The edge,' I said back to him, almost as hooked by now as he was. My heart was thumping. 'Go on.'

'Right.' He pushed me off him and sat up straight, and I could see that this man was somewhere else altogether, somewhere alone.

Dreamily, as if suddenly hit by the visky, he said, 'You're fine but going even faster now, and here comes another curve.' He swayed slightly. 'Your fins are perfect, the cut's perfect, you hear the Chute around you and you're part of it. You watch yourself making exact and infinitesimal adjustments. This is perfect. You cannot imagine it being otherwise. *Nothing else exists but you and the Chute and the sweet, beautiful curve approaching. And you have a choice to make.'*

He stopped and sat back, slightly flushed.

'And?' My heart was pounding.

'Your choice is this. You can take a shallow line, taking slightly lower gs at this speed, coming back from the edge, or –'

'Yes?'

'Or you can go midline and try to hold it, to stay on the edge –'

He blinked, the tiny movement making me catch my breath.

'Or else you can force it.'

'Yes,' I said, far too sharply. It was just a story, after all. I folded myself back into the warmth of him, trembling, waiting for him to continue. Bale always said he wasn't interested in stories, but he was a born teller.

'You decide to force it because out of the curve there's half a second of straight and wide and that's long enough to recover.' He was leaning to the side and I was leaning into him, the sheets caught around us and taut. 'You go tight into the

curve and immediately *you're halfway down the straight at the far side.'*

He suddenly held me. It felt like he had caught me in a fall. I gasped.

'You understand, Kes? There was no sensory pause. It was just a seamless that/this. Done. You lock and carry on.' He looked straight at me and said, 'You see? The curve never happened, it was so fast.'

I tried to collect myself. 'But it wasn't. It couldn't have been.'

'Of course. Yes. What really happened, you blacked out into the curve and recovered the other side of it. And that's darkspeed. You hit darkspeed.'

'Risky,' I said. My mouth was dry.

'Yes. Another term usually goes with it: You fell into a black hole.'

'Dead. I can guess that one.'

He said, 'Flyers say no one ever really sees the edge because no one ever stays there. They come back or they go over.'

'How many times have you gone over, Bale?'

He looked at me slyly. 'What edge are we talking about?'

I laughed at him. 'Every one of them, Bale. Every edge you've ever seen, you've jumped, haven't you?'

'I hadn't thought about it.' He paused, then he said, 'What about you, Kes?'

'Come on, Bale. Me? What do you think? You really think I'd jump?'

'No.' He looked serious. 'You'd be the one.'

'The one?' I tried to laugh again, but I couldn't do it. 'What do you mean?'

'You'd be the one who gets to the edge and holds it there.

You'd be the one who stops, looks down and looks back. And then looks along the edge too, both ways. You want to see it all. That's you. The storymaker.'

I felt more naked and exposed than I'd been with him inside me, earlier, and somehow I felt him even deeper within me now as he added, 'You can't stay on the edge forever, though.'

I tried to look away, but he cupped my face in his hands and turned me towards him and said, 'Let me take you, when there's time. I'll show you what the words mean. Not darkspeed, of course. Not even close to the edge. But I'll show you the Chute.'

'I'd really like that, Bale.'

And I nestled closer and kissed this reckless, wonderful, crazy man.

There. She'd been true to the core of his story, as she was always true, since stories were all that mattered. But the rest of it… the sex hadn't been like that at all, and in truth, the trigger for the story of the Chute and of darkspeed, for Bale, had been his need to distract himself from the sexual failure. But writing it like this, now, already seemed true enough for her.

No. She was fooling herself.

She closed her eyes and remembered it. The talk of darkspeed – *that* had been the sex, the intimacy, not just for Bale but for them both. The failure of the sex wasn't only his, of course. She could never let herself truly loose any more than Bale could. She never had, never would. Darkspeed was Bale's real sex, and the story of it – no, the *telling* of the story of it – was hers.

Was that so bad? She'd met crazier people. She'd had

worse sex. And every time, she'd written a memory and moved on.

She'd move on now, as she'd moved on before. Maybe she could tell the story of the other man in the red bar. Tallen. It was odd for Cynth to be indecisive, offering her two stories before fixing on one. And then to ask questions about the vote for Gamliel as the AI had – Razer still couldn't remember the man's name. Madrow, Manler? The image of that knot of metal tossed up and caught wouldn't leave her. Moncrell?

She glanced at the screenery. Yes, she'd move on.

TEN PEOPLE AND ONE PAX OFFICER BELIEVED DEAD

So why was she crying?

Ten
ALEF

SigEv 10 The first deaths

Something in Ligate's eyes changed, as if a jolt had passed through him, and for the first time he moved sharply and with decision.

If you're searching this record for an explanation, this would be its heart, I imagine. At the time, part of me was possibly even aware of the fact. I watched my parents die and I saw the effect it was going to have on me. I saw my mind conducting this analysis of the experience of seeing my parents killed. I saw myself examining this phenomenon too, and at a greater remove observing *this*. I examined each stage of self-observation and analysis like the intellectual scrutiny of a logic cascade.

Bodily, though, I froze. I couldn't breathe. The next events unfolded like a series of fixed images with sluggish, blurrily linked scenes. I felt a curious cold flush as Ligate slipped behind my father and made a slow but graceful swirling movement with his hand, as if drawing a halo in the air above his head. My father jerked upright and started to groan and stopped again. A line of blood appeared at his neck, fine at first and then thickening, like the rim of a cup overflowing. His tongue came out. His eyes widened and stayed wide.

It sounds dramatic, a death described like this, but in reality it wasn't, since there was little sound or movement. We need flailing and screams if we are to appreciate a tragedy in its fullness.

Ligate let my father go. He went to my mother and did the same thing: the halo and then the blooming red line. The wire was thin and effectively invisible; I deduced it from the line of blood and a calculation of angles.

There it was. I see that scene now like a smashed hologram, each shard – some big, some small, but infinite in number, and all of them jagged – containing the whole, the pieces scattered not in place but in time, so that I see one at the corner of my eye everywhere I look, at every moment in my life. And they are scattered not only from that point forward, but they have spread backwards, into my memories too.

This, this is the core of me, this shattering, and nothing before or beyond it was ever again quite as it might have been. It's a curious thing.

The events continued, and now there was a proper screaming and flailing. The man at the rear door, holding Pellonhorc's mother, sawed her throat across with a knife as she began to screech, curtaining blood down her front and winding her cry down to a mewl and then nothing as he let her body coil to the ground.

Garrel and the men to his sides were moving too, but as Ligate – a shooting weapon in his good hand – took aim at me, a shrill, piercing scream came from the other door, the door that opened to the main part of the shop.

Pellonhorc was standing there with a pipgun braced unsteadily in both hands, whipping a silent stream of pips across the room. Garrel and the two men beside him dropped to the floor quickly enough to avoid the arc of pips, but the man who had killed Pellonhorc's mother was snagged and fell dead on her body. For an instant, Pellonhorc let his gun hand falter, and stared at his mother's body. Then he raised the pipgun again.

Ligate was moving his own gun towards Pellonhorc but the pip stream from Pellonhorc's weapon was faster and Ligate's needles only stitched across some screenery up on the wall, the glass screeching and blowing in. Ligate crumpled.

Garrel swung an elbow up hard into the chin of the man on his left, the man's jaw cracking, an eyeshield detaching and spinning brightly across the room. He lay clutching his face. The other man had a blade, but Pellonhorc's gun removed the arm that held it.

Garrel yelled, 'Out!' and pushed us through the door and closed it behind us. One of his eyeshields was cracked. He said, 'Wait there. Do not move. This time you listen to me. Do you understand? *Do you understand?* Wait for me. I have to work out what we do. Trust me. I'm trying to save us. All right?'

Pellonhorc was shaking. I was vomiting. Neither of us was going anywhere.

Garrel went back into the office and closed the door again.

Coughing bile, I told Pellonhorc, 'I don't think we can trust Garrel.'

Pellonhorc didn't answer.

I said, 'Who was Ligate?'

Pellonhorc didn't move. I wiped the back of my hand across my mouth and went to the counter. I brought the screenery up and watched Garrel in the back room. He was nodding at some screenery, but I couldn't see the image, and the audio was down so I couldn't hear anything. Garrel then went to all the bodies and checked them methodically. He took a ring from Pellonhorc's mother's finger and held the ring up to the screen, then pocketed it. If it wasn't Drame he was talking to, who was it?

As Garrel came back towards the door, I returned to Pellonhorc's side. I didn't know what to do.

'We have to be quick,' Garrel said. He looked at Pellonhorc, who showed no sign of having heard anything, and then at me. 'Alef, you have to get the data.'

I waited for him to tell me what data he was talking about, but he was waiting too, and I saw he expected me to know.

'Come on, boy,' he said. 'Quickly. We need to take your father's work.'

I said, as if I believed Garrel was loyal to Drame, 'Ligate's dead. We're okay.'

'Ligate?' He was astonished at the idea of it. 'That wasn't Ligate in there. It was a dummy. Ligate would never risk himself in flesh, any more than Drame would.' He broke off and said, more softly, 'You've never seen Ligate, have you? He doesn't look anything like that. It was just his voice. He was no more in that room than Drame was.'

I felt stupid. Of course. The slowness of reaction. He'd dummied one of his men, and only relinquished motor control at the very end, leaving his soldier, the dummy, to do the killing. But he'd have been there behind the man's eyes.

Until the soldier died, Ligate would have seen everything.

I put my hand to my mouth again, as if I was going to vomit, but I was thinking. Garrel was trying to confuse me. What he'd said made sense, but he was still almost certainly Ligate's spy.

And another thing; whoever Garrel was loyal to, if I were no use to him, he'd probably kill me. It made sense for me to cooperate.

Why, though, would he imagine I knew my father had worked for Drame?

'Come on, boy.' Garrel looked at me, then knelt down and took my hands in his thick armoured gloves. The gloves were sticky with blood, but they were warm, too, and the enfolding and unexpected warmth made me start to cry. He didn't know what to do now, and swore. 'Didn't you know *anything* of what your father did? You must have known something.'

I shook my head, wiping my eyes.

Garrel took a long breath and his forehead closed into wrinkles. The fractured eyeshield fell like a black tear and clicked once on the stone floor. I'd never really wondered what was behind those shades. Where his eye should have been was a ball of puckered pink scar tissue stitched with sensors.

I glanced at Pellonhorc to see his reaction. It was the kind of thing he'd have been fascinated by. But he was sitting like Henro the God-touched, rocking gently in his limbo. Henro had been like that for twenty years, they said. I hoped Pellonhorc hadn't been touched as thoroughly as Henro.

Garrel picked at his eye, flicking away the last of the glass. I stared and he stared back at me, the sensors drawing in and out, adjusting. Eventually Garrel said, 'Your father ran it all, Alef. Everything must be here, and we have to take it with us. If we don't, he'll kill me and he'll kill you. Do you understand?'

I said, 'Who will?'

Garrel frowned. 'Ethan Drame. Who else?' He paused, and his face changed. 'You think –?'

I realised I should have kept quiet, but Garrel just sighed. 'This has to be quick and you have to believe me. This is what happened. They got to the house. You heard about the escapees from the deletium mines? They were Ligate's men. They came down in a prison detail. Traile and I went to intercept them, but it turned out that Traile was Ligate's man too. He tried to incapacitate me. He should have killed me when he had the chance. I killed him. I came to collect you, but the rest of Ligate's team were faster than I expected. They got to your parents and Pellonhorc's mother before we got back from the school. Well, you saw that.'

Pellonhorc moaned and rocked more rapidly for a moment, then settled back to his previous rhythm.

'Why did you go in by yourself like that?'

'Alef, we haven't time.'

'Tell me.'

'Ligate wouldn't kill me unless he had to. I'm worth more alive. My instructions are to protect what is Drame's. If I can't safeguard Drame by keeping them alive –'

'You do it by killing them,' I said. 'You would have killed my parents.'

'I would have tried not to, and in the end I didn't. We really haven't time for this, boy.' Garrel looked at Pellonhorc and at me again. I could see him reviewing the fragility of his story. 'You've no way of telling, have you?' he said. 'You just have to trust me.'

It was like the choice Ligate had given Drame. It was no choice at all. So I said, 'Yes.'

'Good.' He waited. 'So. The data, Alef.'

I smiled and shrugged. It was all crazy. Garrel said, slowly, 'Oh. Oh, hell. You didn't know a thing, did you?'

'No.'

Garrel sat down heavily on the floor. 'Then we're all dead. Drame trusted Saul because Saul didn't trust anyone at all. But he assumed that you –'

'Wait.' I realised I did know something. I had to know it. My father had never told me anything, I suppose in an attempt to protect me from his life as long as he could, but if the data were that important, he would still somehow have given it to me. It was his nature to have thought of every possibility, and this was one; the possibility that possession of the data might one day keep me alive.

'In the office,' I said. I moved towards the door, but Garrel said, 'No. You've seen enough of that. I'll get it. Where is it?'

I told him where to find it: my own puter. The data held where only I could reach it, within the programs my father set there for me. From death, he was safeguarding me.

Garrel came out with the puter in his arms, the small, sea-grey, heavy ribbed box with its edgeless screenery. 'Is this all?'

'It's all I need.'

He hefted it and said, 'Can we lighten it?'

I put it on the counter and pulled the screenery away, and cracked off all the conns and comms junk. The puter was now two thirds the depth and width, but its weight was almost the same.

Garrel turned it over in his hands. What remained was smaller than the copy of the Babble we had at home. He said, 'That's all we can strip? There's nothing else we can dump?'

'Other than the shell I stripped away, there's just the information sled and its cocoon.'

'What's the cocoon for?'

'Armour. Against invasion and corruption, hammer and blade, intentional or environmental.' I tapped it with my fingernail. 'Most of this is cocoon. I can strip it all off, and what's left, what really matters, I could just about swallow with a gulp of water. You want me to?'

For the first time, Garrel looked uncertain. 'What do you think?'

I wondered fleetingly whether he was clever enough to understand what he was offering me; if I swallowed it, I could slip away and run. But where could I run to? Was he dangling bait, or was the question honest?

'Keep the cocoon,' I said. 'Safer.'

The overhead light flickered across Garrel's remaining eyeshade. He picked up the puter and said, 'Okay. Pellonhorc? You hear me? We have to go.'

Pellonhorc shuddered and stood up. He looked at Garrel and then at me. The look he sent me made me scared. He stopped shaking and became peculiarly still, and his eyes set hard until they were no more readable than Garrel's. He was not at all like Henro the God-touched, I realised. He was not overwhelmed by godfear, was not brimful of mystery. Something had been removed from Pellonhorc forever. I wondered why I was not like him, what the difference was between us.

I don't know whether Garrel saw what had happened to

Pellonhorc. Maybe his odd obedience was enough. Garrel pushed us in front of him to the door, checking carefully that I didn't try to pick up any of the discarded elements of my puter. Smart of him, I thought, and smarter still that he caught me registering his check and nodded approvingly. Almost as if we were covering each other's back, instead of each watching his own.

We went out of the shop. In the sharp sunlight I was suddenly aware that hardly any time had passed since Garrel and I had gone in.

A crowd had gathered in the street, though, Father Grace among them. He raised a hand, but Garrel simply told him, 'We're going,' and pushed through to reach the flycykle. I heard Father Grace mutter something about donations and reparations. Over his shoulder, Garrel said, 'You've seen the end of them, Father. Back you go to God, now.'

As Garrel closed the flycykle door against the crowd and sat down at the console, he murmured to me, 'That was very smart, the way you let Pellonhorc out of the flycykle.'

I wondered whether he'd worked it out at the time, or only as Pellonhorc had appeared in the doorway shooting pips. The answer might help tell me whether he was Ligate's agent or not. If he'd guessed instantly but kept quiet to let Pellonhorc in, he was Drame's man.

And as we lifted away from JerSalem, heading for Pellonhorc's father or for Ligate's camp, it struck me that while I would be equally unsafe at either destination, Pellonhorc would live or die by it.

Pellonhorc was sitting beside me, neither speaking nor moving. He had saved my life. I was letting Garrel take us to this coin's toss of a fate, either to Ligate or to Drame, from the flycykle to a shuttle, to a ship, the stars and then the Upper Worlds, and I sat hugging my puter and could do nothing but stare into the chaos of the future.

SigEv 11 A journey

I wouldn't hear Pellonhorc speak for days. The transfer from vessel to vessel might have been familiar to him, but for me it was astonishing. I'd never even seen a ferry station before, with its tiers of trucking vessels, let alone the silver-pocked blackness of space.

The journey began simply enough, as we moved innocuously from the shop to the ferry station, keeping to speed limits along the flycykle lanes. At a small, closed hangar, we were ushered to a dark-windowed cart and taken directly to a transfer vessel – three of us choosing wherever we wanted to sit from a thousand empty seats, and opting to sit crammed together, our thin shoulders to either side of Garrel's bonehard forearms – that shipped us up to a midspace platform. The platform seemed deserted, though I noticed that where there were shutters, they were down; where there was dimglass, it was set to dark; and where there were doors we didn't need to pass through, they were closed.

We went directly from the platform to the shuttle bay, jogging clunk-footed and breathless in Garrel's wake through twists of booming metal corridors. There were health warnings everywhere. Each time we passed one, I read a few lines, and by the time we reached the shuttle bay I had memorised the vaccination requirements for every planet in the System, with the exception of the unsaid planet.

I had never left Gehenna before, so I assumed the process we followed was routine, that anyone could transfer from ground to exitspace within hours, without need for registration, security or a moment's pause other than for the opening of doorlocks.

From the time Garrel touched the flycykle down at the ferry station to the time we squeezed into the shuttle for the brief sweeping upglide to the fastship, we saw maybe a dozen people. (Actually, thirteen. Seven were women. I'm trying to simplify this account, but I am what I am.) Those few people we encountered were present, it seemed, merely to roll us forward, through the right door, along the right path. The speed and smoothness of it was both soothing and numbing. There was no time to think until we reached the shuttle, and even there, although we were just sitting for an hour or so (seventy-eight minutes), the whine and roar, the slow slams of acceleration and braking, all denied the possibility of reflection. Not that, at that time of my life, I even understood the concept of reflection.

But I did notice that of the dozen and one people we saw, not one glanced at us. They looked away, or ahead, or aside.

I grew used to the reaction later. I became conditioned to it. Eventually I expected their fear to the degree that the rare ordinary glance, or incurious flicker of eye contact, tensed me with anxiety. It's a pathologic logic path.

The shuttle locked to the fastship, we stepped out onto the great floor of the transit deck, and there were people again. They paid us no attention, but this time it was because they were occupied with preparations to leave. There was bustle and chatter and, if not a wealth of colour, at least shine and shadow, the grime of machinery and the primary colours of alert and alarm. I looked at Pellonhorc and put my palm on his arm. He was rigid but breathing almost evenly, and he answered my look with a thin smile that disappeared instantly. I mouthed, 'Are you okay?' and he shook his head.

Garrel said, 'Captain. Thank you for picking us up. I'm Garrel.'

I hadn't noticed the captain until then, but he must already have been standing there as we stepped from the shuttle. He glanced briefly at the three of us. He must have been wondering what to say. What had he expected? We stood there; a soldier with one cracked eye and one exposed retinal implant, and at his sides a virtually catatonic child and a runt clutching the carcass of a puter as if his life were held in it.

The officer pulled himself together quickly enough. 'Yes,' he said. 'I'm Captain Janquile.' He was a hardweathered man, the skin of his face broken and blackened, and his eyes set as if everything he had ever encountered had surprised him, but none of it for more than an instant. Whoever he was, whether he was Drame's or Ligate's ferryman, I imagined that to be trusted with Drame's son, he must be one of the best.

'We've got five minutes to be clear,' Janquile said. 'I'm bodystopping you all for the trip. We'll be two weeks, and you might as well bank the time.'

People were in motion around us, like a torrent flowing past a boulder. A few of them glanced at us, though only if they were out of Janquile's eyesight. Garrel started to say something, but the captain didn't even raise his voice, continuing, 'Save your breath, soldier. You take my orders or I don't take you anywhere.'

'I can't let the boy out of my sight,' Garrel said.

Janquile gestured at Pellonhorc. 'What's wrong with him?'

'Not for you to worry about.'

'I'm not worried. I just need to know he's safe for *rv*.'

'He is. No drugs or 'plants.' Garrel put a hand on Pellonhorc's shoulder. 'He's just in shock. Shut him down totally – as long as you don't leave him exposed to his thoughts, he'll be okay. Might even do him some good.' He glanced at me and added, 'You can sleep this one whichever way he wants it. I have to stay awake, Captain. I'll keep out of your way, but I don't sleep. Not ever.'

Janquile's face didn't change. 'You go into *rv*. Those are my direct instructions.'

The two men stared at each other for a short, electric moment, and then Garrel grinned abruptly as if it were all in jest, and glanced up into the dust that ghosted the deck's high canopy. 'He doesn't trust me! After all this, he still doesn't trust me?'

He looked at Janquile again and waited, and I realised that Garrel, cold-headed and hard-handed in battle, was quite out of his depth here, and close to panic.

Who didn't trust him, I wondered. Whose name were they avoiding? Ligate or Drame?

The captain didn't respond. I stared from one to the other, trying to work out the balance between them.

An officer came up to the captain and murmured in his ear. Janquile said, 'Acknowledge it, then lock all comms. I'll be with you in eight.'

The officer left, and Janquile turned back to Garrel.

'How do I know I'll wake up?' Garrel grinned again, less convincingly, and it was plain that he'd given up.

The captain turned on his heel. Garrel hesitated only a moment, then followed him, with me and Pellonhorc moving alongside. Janquile halted, waiting for us at a low oval doorway, and motioned us ahead. The corridor beyond was too narrow for more than two to walk side by side. I went first into the ship's belly with Pellonhorc. I could hear the captain talking to Garrel behind us.

'In this business,' Janquile was saying, 'how do any of us ever close our eyes and know we'll open them again? You've just got it set out plainer, Garrel.' There was only the crack of our feet for a while, then the captain added, 'I was told your arrival wasn't certain. I was told you had to have the boy. That if you didn't –' The sound of our feet again. I calculated the differing beats at our various stride-lengths, how long it might be before we were all planting our left feet in precise synchrony – one hour and twelve minutes. The few crewmembers we passed flattened themselves against the walls and saluted the captain.

Eventually Janquile broke stride, raised his voice and said, 'Turn left here.' He tapped Pellonhorc's shoulder. I steered the two of us into the next corridor. The booming, squeaking and and ticking noises of the ship were muted here.

We walked on. The captain lowered his voice and said to Garrel, for the first time gently, 'You got this far, soldier, so maybe the odds are still good for you.'

'That's not reassuring,' Garrel said.

'I wouldn't insult you. The truth is, my instructions are to get you there safe, all of you. I've got a narrow course to chart and the possibility of action along the way, and I don't want any extra shit, so I want you asleep, just like my orders say.'

A tap on Pellonhorc's shoulder again, and Janquile's voice rose. 'Stop here, boys.'

The door opened and there were the *rv* beds with their canopies and streamlined hulls, and their flanks inset with instruments and dials. The units were larger than coffins and smaller than shuttles, but they could have been either thing. You could wake up somewhere else, or never.

The captain stood in the doorway and said, 'You got the boy here safely, Garrel. If you were good only for that, you wouldn't have walked off the deck you arrived on. You may be a good soldier, but you're just one, and I've got shipboard weaponry. I'm telling you this out of respect. At present, I've no orders to kill you. I can't say it plainer than this. I want you asleep on orders and for my convenience. That's all there is to it and no more.' There was no inflection in his voice. He was unreadable.

I looked at Garrel and at Janquile; the one with cracked machine vision, the other dead-eyed and drawn. I looked at Pellonhorc, whose eyes had been filled with horror and now held nothing at all.

And in my eyes there remained everything I had ever seen, nothing lost or forgotten. It was a tide ever rising.

We stood there, all of us alone, each quite different, but all cursed by our vision.

Janquile was still waiting for Garrel to accept the open bed. He made a small gesture to indicate that time was passing and nothing done, and then he told Garrel, curtly, 'I need to be on my bridge in two minutes. I've said what there is to say. You can believe me or not, as you like, but you are going to be asleep, soldier, and that's the close of it.'

Garrel moved forward and touched the cool metal of the

unit with a finger. 'Then switch my head off too. I don't want to be thinking about it.'

The captain nodded. He murmured with sudden gentleness, 'Yes. That's what I'd do, too.'

He turned to me. 'You, boy?'

I climbed into the cushioned cocoon and said, 'I want to know everything.'

The tomb closed over me.

Darkness.

SigEv 12 Hyperlepsy

And with the darkness, light. On Gehenna I had never been bodystopped. The technology of *rigor vitae* was heretical. But I was so very curious. Not knowing where we were going, I spent those millions of kils on my own journey, connected to what Gehenna called the pornoverse, and what the rest of the System called the Song.

For days I simply drifted through it all; through the currents of conversation, the truths and assertions and facts; the fogs and mists of hope and desire, and I started to understand the workings of the Song.

And then I began to search. I caught and released filaments of suggestion, I picked apart some of the rumours and diversions, unravelled codes; I dissected and discarded, and eventually I started to identify the most reliable data strings.

And so it was that, in my first hyperlepsy, I began to search for Drame and Ligate.

And I began to learn about my father.

What I learnt about him was difficult to accept. He was my father, after all. I told myself that he'd killed no one, and in a way that was true. But I had been brought up on Gehenna, and in addition I had my own directness of thought, and the combination of those structures made the truth harder to handle. My parents were dead. I was alone. And it had been my father's actions that had brought this upon us all.

In Janquile's ship, threading its passage through the System, with my body seized in its physiological stasis and my mind wheeling through the Song, I couldn't sob or scream. I could have turned my brain to sleep, of course, but I was Gehennan and trained to scourge myself.

I also needed to prepare myself for either of the fates ahead, at the hands of Ligate or Drame, and I needed to work out which it was more likely to be.

Searching for information on Ligate and Drame was not straightforward, but I hauled myself on. The Song was awash with rumour and counter-rumour. The only certainties surrounding the two men were legal investigations, and no charges were ever pursued. There were pictures of the two men, but in such vast variety that I realised images were not to be trusted.

However, what I learned about Drame and Ligate gained meaning from what I discovered about the System. It was the System that had created them.

On Gehenna, we were told little about the System's origin. The Earth was discussed purely in terms of comparisons with Sodamned and Gloccamoral from the Babbel. We were told that the Earth had been destroyed by God in the Final Adjustment, that He had chosen us to survive, and He had permitted others to escape along with us for two reasons: as a continuing warning to us that while we had been chosen, that decision was no more than provisional; and as a message to those heretical others that they might yet repent. This, we were told, was why Gehenna – unlike the unsaid planet – maintained such contact with the System as we did.

Now, swimming in the Song, I learnt more.

It's hard for me to tell this from the perspective of my childhood mind. Child and adult – I am both at once, and neither. These nightless days I first spent in *rv*, learning about the System and about so much else, changed me forever in as dramatic a way as I had been changed by the events hours earlier. The deaths of my parents changed my emotional self. This hyperlepsy changed my intellectual self.

SigEv 13 The System

When the System was discovered by Earth, the terraforming of its planets had to be funded, and worlds within the System had to be allocated to the States and Equities that could afford it or else raise the money by contract and promise. It was little different, except in scale, from the type of project that governments, corporations and Equities carried out all the time: undersea tunnels, sub-sea mining, off-planetary exploration and exploitation.

After all the negotiation and funding arrangements were complete, two primarily religious funds remained; that which bought the rights to Gehenna, and another, the name of whose observance was protected, which bought rights to the unsaid planet. The other States and Equities were secular. They acknowledged the right of Gehenna to allow contact on its own terms and to remain exempt from contributory taxes other than by agreement, and they acknowledged the right of the unsaid planet to withdraw from all contact except such as it determined necessary to pursue the legal protection of its name and observance.

I spent hours in *rv* reading the records of the contracts and the negotiations over clause and subclause.

There was a great deal of risk involved in the leaving, I learned, but the risk was comparative. The Earth, ecologically and financially, was in desperate, terminal decline, and one of the reasons for that was the inability of Earth's population, despite the knowledge of disastrous ecological consequence, to look farther ahead than the closing of the banking day.

It was extraordinary. I read the histories and reread them, unable to believe it at first. I had been taught on Gehenna that the Lord had visited doom on the Earth as He had created Gehenna for the godfearing, but the real tale was almost equally ludicrous. If what I was reading were true, what had destroyed the Earth was not any unforeseeable disaster at all, nor any sudden and irreversible calamity. No. Predictions were made and justified and proved to be valid, and then simply ignored for commercial reasons.

Of course I was aware that this was the pornoverse – I would come to use its real name, the Song, but never quite got used to it – and that nothing there could, or can, entirely be believed.

But eventually, when the banks failed and they had to accept the Earth's end, they acted. They tooled up and they shipped out. They came to the System.

There were seven major planets in the System and a few minor ones. It was easier to terraform these, all advantageously distributed as they were, than to attempt to work further on the planets of Earth's own system upon which the technology had been fine-tuned.

There was, briefly, unprecedented cooperation, all driven by contract and debt and the chance of advantage and profit. The science was shared and the ships built, but it was plain to me that the crucial thing, the engine of it all, was money.

It was the money that fascinated me; no, not that, but the negotiations and the deals. The science I found bewildering and uninteresting, as I almost always have.

The resources located on the various planets were different, to begin with, and on top of this, the geological consequences of terraforming were imperfectly predictable with the analytical resources of old Earth. For example, no one predicted that Gehenna would be found to have deposits of deletium, or that such a unique resource would later be discovered on Bleak.

So, money and labour and technical expertise were lent at various rates of interest, and with various conditions attached. Financial blocs of Asia, Greater Europe and America negotiated the best choices, and had to borrow little and accept few contractual penalties. Each bloc took one or two of the main planets, Heartsease, Spindrift, Magnificence, and the twin-mooned Vegaschrist that lay at one end of the asteroid belt called the Eden String. As well as the continental blocs, there were two independent Wealths-of-Faith, one of which claimed Gehenna and the other an especially harsh planet that no other bidder wanted. The Wealth-of-Faith that claimed that planet declined to give it a name, and it became known as the unsaid planet, existing under a self-imposed and vigorously maintained isolation.

It lay beyond even Vegaschrist, at the farthest limit of the Eden String, and at the very edge of the System.

I was not interested in the unsaid planet. Even if anyone survived there, it was a planet of goddery, like Gehenna.

I turned my attention back to what interested me.

In addition to the three continental blocs and the two Wealths-of-Faith, there were a number of small unaffiliated Equities. One of these took the planet Bleak, and others leased the two moons of Vegaschrist, calling them Brightness and New Hope. Finally, there were a number of asteroids, the largest of which were Peco and Gutter.

I lay there, fixed in almost precisely the same *rigor vitae* that had been endured by the first colonists in their long journey to the System, travelling also to an unknown destination, and I was entranced by the funding of the original adventure.

The contracts were complex and elegant. By their trails, the offers made and the counter-offers tabled, I understood the negotiators and their skills, and even the way society had worked at that time. There were provisions for problems over repayments, for actual defaults; taxes and interest rates were agreed and fixed in advance, and while the criminal and civil laws that would be introduced for each planet were no more than sketched out, the tax systems and economic protocols, both intraplanetarily and System-wide, were defined as immutably as the laws of physics.

While the scientists and manufacturers calculated and created, built ships and reconfigured worlds, the politicians, the bankers and the brokers sat and haggled over their percentages and their rates, and made it all contractually feasible.

And so it was, I learnt, that the Earth fled its failing home and embarked upon its greatest adventure, up into the wild black yonder, each colonising entity confident in the knowledge that its investment, its profits and its losses were adequately ringfenced against all foreseeable risks of fraud and default. Only the unsaid planet existed extracontractually, in physical and financial isolation.

Of course, with such a degree of risk involved, and so much that was unforeseeable, it was obvious that nothing could be guaranteed. While the ships were still in space, thousands of sleep-years away, the terraforming of one of the worlds, Magnificence, failed utterly, with the loss of hundreds of trillions of dolors along with the collapse of banks and the obliteration of fortunes, not to mention the human tragedies on considerable scales. But this led to consolidation and imaginative restructuring of debt; humanity is almost infinitely resourceful.

I trawled the Song, and as I started to examine the recent history, I discovered the unsaid planet to have vanished progressively from all record. It appeared that any attempt at contact resulted in silence and any mention was brief. They were rumoured to be fiercely protective of their privacy. Indeed, for all that the System knew of it now, the unsaid planet might no longer be inhabited, everyone dead of war perhaps, or disease or starvation. It did not matter which, but its likely fate served as a warning to the rest of the System; cooperate or perish.

All this was engrossing beyond anything I had ever experienced. I had no sense of the passage of time. I plunged ever deeper into the Song, absorbing its secrets and filing them away in my mind.

Along with the first footfall in the System, there came crime. Synthesised drugs were imaginative and various, and theft was commonplace. Along with the first assembly of the earliest Administration, there came organised crime. Gangs came and went, merged, fought and collapsed, reformed and grew, just as the political parties of the Administrata did. And over the years of growth, as the Administrata became more structured, organised crime became more significant. Finally only two great and farsighted organisations were left. Those organisations were headed, now, five generations post-arrival, by Ethan Drame and Spetkin Ligate.

I searched and searched. It wasn't easy. The Song was full of voids and lies. I meta-analysed the existing data, extrapolated and refined until, a few days later, I had what I confidently felt was a fair summary of the current status quo.

Drame, I concluded, operated banks, while Ligate controlled transport systems. The full story was naturally far more complex than this, but this was the core of it.

Ligate, then, was a pirate and a smuggler, while Drame, through his banks, owned and controlled debt. He was clever, acting almost legitimately much of the time, manipulating the confusions and eddies of interplanetary tax law to his advantage.

Both Ligate and Drame used leverage to secure and expand their ground: the leverage of money, and of threat and its consequence. They were cold killers. But while both had proved themselves personally untouchable by the law, and enormously commercially successful, Ethan Drame had accelerated away from Ligate in the last few years, and the Song was flooded with rumours of a vendetta between them – that Ligate was determined to murder Drame, who had some brilliant financial strategist orchestrating his moves, and that Drame wanted Ligate finally disposed of.

In the voids and silences of the Song, his name wasn't anywhere to be found, but my father, without the slightest doubt, had been Drame's strategist.

I lay in the *rv* unit and could only think, and I drifted through the Song and thought for three hundred and thirty-eight hours and forty-five minutes. I had the option of switching my thoughts off and sleeping a dreamless *rv* sleep, and I couldn't, I didn't do it.

The Song was clear. Spetkin Ligate had killed my father, and I was carrying the puter with every scrap of information that Drame needed and that Ligate was probably desperate to get his hands on. And I was the only one who could access it.

There was only one question remaining, and the Song did not hold the answer to it. To which of the two terrible enemies, in this agitated sleep, was I headed?

Eleven
BALE

The times he woke up, he couldn't turn his head too well. His head ached worse than any hangover. Now and then he opened his dry lips and said, 'Hey. Can you hear me?' without getting any answer, and occasionally he glimpsed medics walk past him, heading for the next bed, where there was a guy in what looked like some sort of skull-fracture scaffolding. Sometimes the passing medics glanced at Bale and sometimes they didn't. There weren't just medics, either. There were people wearing Paxtags, though he recognised none of them, and there were others. He was sure the others weren't friends of the guy. They had the look of the type of people whose stories Bale enjoyed taking apart, eye-shifting deskers unused to being streetside.

But these deskers were looking happy. Maybe they were legals, he thought. He'd never seen an unhappy legal.

Bale slept, half-woke, slept again, woke up.

He knew he wasn't in a good state. He ran through his memory of the whole thing. He knew he should be dead. Every time he closed his eyes he saw the flat of that hand coming at the bridge of his nose like the end of a training sim just before it tells you, *'Incorrect option. You're dead. Retry?'*

Maybe he'd been through AfterLife. Was this what it was

like, coming out the other side? Maybe decades had passed.

No. No one would vote to bring back a Paxer. Not one with Bale's history, anyway.

He dozed, woke again, dozed again.

In the end, it was the guy in the headcage who opened the conversation. Having rolled carefully to his right so he could face the next bed, Bale was examining the peculiar rig more closely. He hadn't seen anything like it before. Neck or spine injury, he guessed. The man hadn't moved. He could have been a corpse, though for a corpse he had a lot of visitors.

The corpse said, 'Hey. You hear me?'

He sounded like his sinuses were blocked. Bale said, 'I hear you. You've been asleep a long time.'

The reply came, low and unsteady, 'I wouldn't exactly call it sleep.'

Bale said, 'Well, it's better than the alternative.'

'I'm not complaining. You're Marus Bale, right? The Paxer? I'm Tallen. Herrel Tallen. You saved my life, you know that?'

'How was that?' Bale's head was throbbing.

'In the waste tunnels. Don't you know?'

'No.'

'Apparently, if you hadn't kept him running, he'd have had time to finish me.' A pause, which Bale wasn't sure how to read, then the man added, 'I thought maybe you were going to die.'

'Ah.' Now it made sense, the two of them being put side-by-side. 'So did I, Tallen. Listen. I didn't know anything about you, didn't even see you. If you think I saved you, you're wrong. Medics do this, put people together like there's some bond. The idea is we're more likely to pull through if we're bonded. Like I'm so proud of what I've done, and…' He let it go, knowing he shouldn't say it. He'd gone too far already. The guy didn't deserve it.

But the man completed it, flatly. 'And I'm too grateful and guilty to let myself die after you almost got yourself killed for me.'

'Something like that,' Bale said. 'But like I told you, I didn't know you were down there. I don't even know how I'm alive.'

'How about I say thanks anyway?'

'That'd do it.' Bale tried to say it like it was meant. He didn't like being here with the man next to him. He wasn't going to let himself get involved. He knew better than to pick up guilt for the man getting left like this, worse than dead.

Later, after a few more driftaways and sleeps, Bale observed, 'You've got lots of friends, Tallen.'

'No. I've got interested parties.'

'How do you mean?'

'Seems I didn't have enough medical cover for what happened. They could have let me die. I was an opportunity. I cost them a fortune. Don't exactly feel it, though.'

Razer stood for a few minutes just looking at him asleep before whispering, 'Bale?' And then she saw him hurt himself with a smile.

She said, 'You're a sight, you know that? I thought you were dead.'

'I thought so too.'

'Are you in pain?'

'Less now. How long have I been here?'

'A while. A week and a few days. They weren't allowing you ordinary visitors. They didn't believe I was your sister or your wife.'

'Now I'm allowed visitors?'

'No. I told them I'm your legal.'

'They believed that?'

She smiled. 'I can be very convincing.'

'Tell them to let me out, then.'

'As your legal, I'd advise against that. You don't look good enough to me.' She glanced at the bed beyond Bale's. 'He looks a lot worse. What happened to him?'

'Apparently I saved his life. You wouldn't believe it to look at him, would you?'

She stared at the motionless body for a while. 'You're sure he's alive? He doesn't look like he's breathing. What is that?'

'Ask him.'

She raised her voice and said, 'Are you in pain?'

The man murmured, 'I recognise your voice. I can't turn my head.'

She moved across and bent over him, and let out a sharp breath. 'Tallen.' She took a step away and looked at him again. Why hadn't she realised? 'The red bar,' she said. 'We spoke there. You remember that? These last nights, I've been looking for you there. No one knew where you were. I should have guessed. Don't you have any friends, Tallen? Anyone? Are you in pain? Can I get someone?' Her heart was thumping crazily and she didn't quite know why. She remembered the words they'd exchanged and the expression on his face. Her questions had somehow energised him. He had done more than answer them. He had considered his answers and asked his own questions and been fascinated by the way she thought. He had surprised her, and it had been a long time since Razer had been surprised by anything. There was something about him, similar to Bale, but also the opposite. An odd tenderness.

'I remember you. Tired. Going to sleep now.'

Bale reached out, wincing, and touched her arm. She looked back at him and said, '*I'd* believe you saved his life. You're quite something, Bale.'

He didn't seem to have any idea what to say to that, and she didn't know why it made her choke up. Was it Bale's bravery, or the shock of seeing Tallen here?

After a moment she said, 'They told you what happened?'

'I don't think so. I can't remember it all.'

'He killed ten people. You saved the eleventh.' She glanced back at Tallen. Weird coincidence. Life was full of them, though. Her life, anyway. She touched Bale's cheek and said, 'But then, you nearly were the eleventh. He was a crazy. He's dead.'

She gently disengaged herself from him and stood up, looking along the aisle. 'I think they just discovered I'm not a legal. I'll see you when you're out.'

Bale watched her go, then closed his eyes and fixed her there, in profile, as she'd looked when she was talking to Tallen. The expression on her face as she looked at Tallen – that had been more than surprise.

When he next woke up, Bale eased himself to the side of his bed, rested his feet flat on the cold floor and just breathed there, looking at Tallen with a bit more interest. There were several days of scrawny beard over the man's jaws, and Bale examined the metal cage enclosing his head. The bedcovers drawn up to his neck were held entirely clear of his body by some kind of concealed armature that ran all the way down the bed, covering his entire body. Bale had seen that part of the procedure before, the protection of a body's damaged, fragile flesh from contact and pressure, but he'd never seen a headcage like this. Tallen's eyes were wide.

Bale said, 'You got burnt?'

'I don't think so. Why?'

'Your bedding. That's what they do if you're burnt, keep it clear to let you heal. And what is that, on your head?'

'You want the full term or the nickname?'

'Whatever.'

'It's a stereotactic neurosurgical targeting frame.'

Bale shrugged. It took him a moment to realise Tallen wouldn't have seen the gesture. He said, 'You've lost me. *Targeting* I understand, and *frame*, but the rest of it, no.'

Tallen smiled, the movement pulling ripples of skin up against a pair of silver struts securing the frame to his cheeks. The frame wasn't on his skin at all, Bale realised. It was sunk right through it, down into the bone. There were two struts entering his temples and four more at the back of his skull. Tallen's head, Bale now saw, was suspended within the gleaming exoskeleton. Its angles and joints were knotted with docks and sockets. He also noticed that Tallen had no pillow, and supposed there was no point in having one. It was eerie. Only the bottom jaw was free. 'That's a hell of a thing,' he said.

'It's a surgical rig. I've been neurologically mapped and

tapped and fixed up fine. I can do anything but move. Do you mind if we change the subject?'

'Sure. Do you remember any of it, what happened to you?'

'Some, yes. Are we allowed to talk about it?'

Bale said, 'You mean legally? Your guy's dead. We can talk.'

'Why did he do it?'

'It wasn't just you. He killed ten people.' Bale reflected on what Razer had told him. 'Maybe more. I guess he was a crazy, but he must have been a well-organised one. Anyhow, since he's dead, there's no case and no legals, so there's no reason why we can't talk. As long as you don't mind.'

'I remember some of it. Look, I can't see you. Can you come round in front of me?'

Bale limped over and hauled the chair to the foot of Tallen's bed so he could face him. The shape of the frame under the bedclothes was reminiscent of a coffin. Bale said, 'How far down does that thing go?'

'To my hips. Every vertebra has its own dock.' As Tallen frowned, the skin of his forehead scalloped deeply against the struts at his temples. 'Actually, every vertebra has two docks. Every muscle has a myoelectric implant.'

'You had nerve damage?'

'I had brain injuries,' Tallen said. 'Neuromuscular consequences. Can't move spine or head, can't feel.'

'And this is to repair it?'

'If it works.'

Bale nodded. 'When will you know?'

'When they decide to tell me.'

Bale snorted. 'Medics?'

'Legals.'

'You can't move at all?'

'This cage is too heavy. I'm like a bug on its back.'

'What about your arms?'

'They're pinned to the cage. And my legs. They say it's for my own safety. Only real movement I've got is my jaw. So I can moan.' He took a long, shallow breath and let it go, then said, 'You ever been hurt, Bale? I mean hurt bad?'

'Apart from this time? Sure. Stabbed, shot, smashed up. But not like you.'

In that flat, echoless voice of his, Tallen said, 'Does it change you, getting hurt?'

For a moment, Bale marvelled at what a stupid question that was, asked by a man who was never going to be the same again. 'Inside? I don't know. I don't know how I was before the first time I got hurt. I'm not even sure I remember it any more. Working in Pax, it's like being a soldier, you develop a shell after a while, a way of not thinking. It holds you together.' Bale didn't know what else to say. He wasn't sure how to talk to Tallen. He could talk to Paxers and to crimers, but Tallen's world, where people were complicated in different ways, was out of his reach. Struggling for a way through to him, Bale thought of Razer. Her world was closer to Tallen's, and Bale could talk to her. In a moment of inspiration, he wondered what she might say to Tallen if she were here, and said that. 'Do you feel changed?'

'Yes. I do. But I'm not sure how. I mean, I think back, and there are gaps. I have memories, and they're returning, but they don't seem real. And what it is –' a long, long pause, '– is that the *me* remembering them is not the me who experienced them. I look at things and they don't seem real. I mean they seem real, but differently real. Does that make any sense?'

Bale didn't say anything, looking up and down the bare aisle lined with empty beds and curtain rails. Machinery beeped and cheeped, lumes twinkled. It was like a party long over but the lights were still on.

'Well, you asked,' Tallen said.

'So tell me what you do remember. Of the attack, I mean.' He felt easier asking Pax questions, and Tallen didn't seem to mind.

'I remember seeing the knife. It was blurred. I see it like a still, like it's frozen in his hand. I looked from his face to the knife, and as I was looking, I was feeling the pain of the first blow. Like a delay, light and sound, you know?'

'Flash and bang. I know.' Bale looked at Tallen's eyes. Tallen couldn't shift his head or give himself away with a crossing of the legs, a scratching of the chin, so all Bale had were the eyes, but he could see the trouble there. Tallen obviously remembered some of it. Just enough to foul him up but not enough to make sense of it.

'Maybe you shouldn't think about it,' Bale said. 'It isn't always good to know. They say it's worse to imagine than to know, but that's not always true. Believe me.'

'No. I have to know as much as I can,' Tallen said. 'Look at me. I lie here and I can't move, and even the past isn't right any more, either it's gone or it isn't quite mine. If I know, at least I have control over it.' His voice rose, and for the first time Bale felt the damage there, the helpless, raw, too-late panic.

Bale said, 'Do you get flashbacks?' Stupid question, he thought instantly, but Tallen was opening his mouth to answer it.

'Footsteps,' Tallen murmured. 'I don't remember where. I was walking back from the beach, I think. I remember deserted streets, but I'm not sure when. The footsteps, the knife. I start to turn, then a thump in my side. The thump makes me gasp aloud. I actually feel it, every time. If I weren't wearing this thing, I'd fold over with it.' The skin of his face tightened around the struts and relaxed again. 'Do you remember, Bale?'

'We're trained to. And usually we're linked up to Vox, though I wasn't this time.' He saw in Tallen's eyes that Vox meant nothing to him. 'Vox is Pax's central command and record puter. It logs everything and advises us. But we're trained to remember. Colours, positions, movements –'

'I mean *you*, Bale. Do *you* remember *me*?'

'Like I said, I never saw you. I didn't even know you were down there. All I was interested in was the K.'

'The what?'

'We call a killer a *K*. Pax-speak. I had no idea about you. You know that, don't you? Not at any stage. Didn't they tell you?'

A long slow breath left Tallen. A sigh, Bale realised. Without physical movement, everything was harder to read.

Tallen said, 'I just wondered.'

Bale thought he could change the subject now. 'You asked me about remembering. I'll tell you something. You remember people mostly by their walk, not their profile or their height.' He remembered telling Razer that, and the way she filed it away. 'You recognise gait at a distance. It's usually quite distinctive. People don't realise that.'

Tallen said, 'I never saw anyone coming or going. Just *there*. I remember pain. At least I think I was feeling it. I can't be sure of anything. Not even the order of it. Or else I remember it in the wrong order. Even the street didn't sound like a street.' He paused. Bale was getting used to the pauses now. Tallen was like a driver stopping at every intersection to check it was clear. And Tallen was off again. 'They say nothing you remember is true. As you remember it, you change it. You add, you filter, you lie to yourself through time.'

'That's not something we like Justix to know, Tallen.' Bale forced a grin. 'Let a Justix know that, you'll drop our jail-take right down.'

Tallen said, 'My mother told me no woman would have a second child if they remembered the pain of birth.' Another pause. 'After he'd stabbed me the first time, I looked from his face to the knife. Neither was anything much. He had a few days' stubble. His hair needed a wash. I think he was tall, but I was probably falling back and looking up. The shield must have been behind him, giving him a huge halo. It seemed incredibly bright. The knife looked small and skinny, but they say it was long, what they call a boning knife, judging by the wounds. Deep. I've seen the surgical graphics, the reconstructions –'

'Are you sure you want to talk about this, Tallen? All this headstuff?'

'The headstuff helps me.'

'You know you're crying,' Bale said. 'Is that helping?'

'Actually, it's itchy on my neck and I can't wipe it. Can you –?'

'There's an isolation warning above your bed. You want me to call someone?'

'Wipe my cheek, Bale. It's not going to kill either of us if you do that.'

Bale hobbled to Tallen's side. Close up he could see a hash of broad scars already turning pale, puckering his right cheek, and a long track of stitches running like a sickle from his left eyebrow to the top of his ear and around the back of it, reappearing at the angle of his jaw and heading down his neck. At Tallen's collarbone the tidy stitches stopped and the staples began. Where the staples hadn't quite pulled Tallen's body closed, there were browning curds of blood and the dull gleam of metal beneath.

Before Bale could get anywhere near Tallen's face with the wipe, a beeper sounded and a nurse was there, snatching the tissue from Bale's hand, shouting at him. 'The hell do you think you're at?'

'Wiping his face.'

'You don't go anywhere *near* him. This sign not big enough? You certainly don't *touch* him.' The nurse turned to Tallen, professionally furious. 'And you. You have no rights here. You get any of these ports infected, you're personally liable. I know you understand that, so don't you look at me, Mr Tallen. I'm not losing my job for you, no matter how much you want to die. And you, Mr Bale, you see this line on the floor? This line means do not cross. This sign means do not touch this patient. You are only here because the medics feel it would help you both, but one more time like this and you're both isolated. You hear me?' She wiped the skin of Tallen's face, navigating around the struts, then used another wipe to clean the framework with equal care.

Bale watched her leave. 'That's a nurse?'

'That's a company nurse. She's looking after their investment.'

'What was that about you wanting to kill yourself?'

'Her manner of speaking.'

Twelve

ALEF

SigEv 14 Arrival

Coming out of hypersomnia was not like emerging from true sleep. I sat up, instantly alert, to see the captain's ridge-browed eyes inches from mine, which startled me. I pulled back from him and looked round to see that the other beds were still down. He had roused me first.

He was staring at me. 'Are you all right?' he said.

I nodded.

'I've never had anyone remain brain-up in *rv* more than half a day. You stayed the whole time. You sure you're okay?'

'I'm fine.' The technician at his side handed me my clothes, and I pulled them on as Janquile went to raise Pellonhorc, who sat up shivering and dressed himself quickly.

Janquile arranged us at the side of Garrel's unit as its canopy rose, the polished convex shell slinging arcs of light across the ceiling. The captain seemed tense. The shell finally locked open, and a few seconds passed, and a few more. There was no movement at all from Garrel.

Janquile stepped nervously back from the unit, and I took half a step towards the door, and then another. No one was looking at me. The *rv* technician leaned over Garrel's motionless body, paused, and then tipped abruptly forward. I was concentrating more on the door I was about to dive through, but the technician's scream froze me. I saw Garrel, half-rising, yank the man down and lock an arm around his neck. The technician's legs danced in the air. He tried to heave Garrel's forearm away from his throat, but his neck was lodged in the crook of the soldier's elbow.

With the technician's scream cut harshly off, there was no sound in the room except the thrum of aircon. Now Garrel slowly and carefully came fully upright, holding the silently choking tech between himself and Janquile. Keeping his eyes on Janquile, Garrel stepped carefully out of the unit. The technician was not struggling any longer. His slack arms and legs slid awkwardly over the lip of the unit and his feet slapped on the floor. Garrel held the body between himself and Janquile.

Janquile found his voice. 'It's okay, Garrel,' he said. 'Look, they're both alive. And so are you.'

Garrel let the tech's body slide to the ground. It seemed by chance that the man's head, instead of cracking on the metal floor, had its fall cushioned by Garrel's foot.

The captain released a long, quiet breath. Garrel flexed his shoulders and came around the unit to stand before us, examining Pellonhorc and me as if checking cargo. He was naked, but his nakedness was extraordinary. As he shifted his weight, the warp and weft of exomuscle played under his skin like the mesh of a kite in a hurricane. He was breathtaking to look at, so beautiful that it took me a moment to notice that the smoothness of the exomuscle extended down to his hips and beyond. At the top of his legs, at the crotch, he had no root. He had nothing.

This may sound strange – it does to me from this odd vantage – but I wasn't shocked or horrified. I was young, and at the age when I found the idea of sex disturbing. Pellonhorc and I had seen images of sex on the pornoverse, but mostly they had been of women parading together. We'd found images of men, too. Gehenna had attitudes to women, but its attitudes to men were far more explicit. Only a man's wife could touch his root. In school and in church, we were shown pictures of men's roots standing up, and taught how vile they were. We were taught how the touch of a man's seed is lethal to any other man and that only marriage neutralises its poison to a single woman, his wife.

Pellonhorc and I had watched actual sex on the pornoverse, men with women, and what I had liked about it was that the man's root disappeared from view while he was having sex. During that time they were, man and woman, quite smooth. Garrel's body was smooth like that.

An explosion of coughing and choking, and then the sound of dry vomiting, broke the moment, and the technician got unsteadily to his hands and knees.

In a cool voice, Garrel said to Janquile, 'You should have raised me first. Not the boys.'

'I felt safer letting you see them as soon as you opened your eyes. Before you could do something stupid.' His gaze flicked across to the tech, and he added, 'And I felt a lot happier knowing they were okay before I let you loose.'

I looked at the captain's face and I saw that the burden of Pellonhorc's and my safety had been just as terrible for him to bear as it had for Garrel.

'We're an hour from the port. We've all survived. Get

something to eat. I'll say goodbye here.' And with that, Janquile nodded and was gone along with his technician. I never saw him again.

SigEv 15 Peco

The trip from the fastship to the platform and from there down to the planet was as simple as the trip up and out had been. At the hangar, a sleek grey flycykle met us, and climbing inside, Garrel said to the driver, 'Maxy, you're a great sight.'

Maxy looked a little like Garrel had looked before everything had gone wrong. His gaze ranged from Pellonhorc to me and back to Garrel again, and he said, 'Strap yourselves in,' and then, grinning, added, 'You're some sort of a sight yourself, man.'

Garrel gave a long, exhausted sigh. '*He* going to think so?'

'Well, you got the boy. Not your fault what you were handling turned into a fallback op. You want to give me what happened?'

The flycykle nudged easily into the air, making hardly a sound. It rose swiftly and wheeled left. I looked out and gasped at our speed and at the drop.

Garrel said, 'Hadn't I better save that till I see him?'

Maxy shrugged. 'He's probably watching us now.'

They fell silent. The flycykle sped on.

I was starting to relax. We had to be on the small world Peco. I'd guessed it from its off-white caul of a stratosphere as we'd descended, and the climate – the wisps of windborne slime-algae greening the air – had confirmed my theory as soon as our flycykle had exited the hangar. And now we were hurtling above its capital, Pecovin, which I recognised from Song images. We were over its industrial quarter and approaching the financial sector.

I found all the information in my head just as it had been in the Song. Everything I had seen in my sleep I recalled in every detail, in the sequence I had accessed it. I could shift through it at immense speed, or jump, or reverse. I could carry out several runs at the same time, as if side by side, to compare contradictory information or draw conclusions. It seemed an awesome amount of information, but of course what I held in my head was a fraction of a fraction of a percentage point of all the information contained at that time on the Song.

Peco had originally been an Equity planet, really a large asteroid. It had mineral deposits and a manufacturing industry based on those. I knew Peco's Gross Planetary Product and its Planetary Debt status. I knew that the building with the tall arched doors, beside which we were drifting gently to the ground, was the headquarters of the Planetary Bank of Peco. I knew the declared assets of the bank and I knew where the sums didn't make sense. The anomalies were like lights in my head.

The reason I relaxed was that I knew PBP was the centre of Ethan Drame's empire. And so I knew Pellonhorc was safe. And I figured that as far as I was concerned, Drame, whether as my saviour or kidnapper, was a better option than Ligate.

Garrel slapped palms with Maxy and got out of the flycykle first with Pellonhorc. It took me a few moments to gather my puter, and by the time my feet were on the ground,

Garrel and Pellonhorc were gone. A woman was standing in the arched doorway, watching me. She was tall, and dressed in a perfectly fitted ash-grey suit that looked like she'd never be able to sit down without it ripping.

There was no one else. I adjusted my grip on the puter. She glanced at it, then at me.

'I'm Madelene,' she said. She reminded me of the women I'd seen on the Song, her smile taut and functional, more like a twitch than a smile. 'You must be Alef.' She made a gesture I didn't understand, and we walked through the atrium of the bank.

The atrium was as high as I could see, rising in clouds of foliage from the ferns and ivies that snaked up the walls and across the ceiling. There was birdsong and the scent of something sweet and pure. It was green and wonderful. I stumbled, unable to take my eyes away.

'It isn't real,' Madelene said crisply.

I knew that, of course, but I had wanted it to be real. For a few moments, at least, I wanted something impossible to be as it seemed. I had a sense that I would never have that opportunity again, to believe against fact. I already had too many facts. On the Song I'd only seen images of the outer shell of the bank. Every internal dimension and detail was security-protected, so the atrium had briefly been an unknown.

We stepped through the illusory Eden towards an elevator. I said, as we waited at the elevator door, 'What about Pellonhorc? Where is he?'

Madelene said, 'He isn't ready for his father yet.'

The elevator doors opened. As we started to ascend, I checked the timer on my chronom. It took us twenty-three point two seconds to reach the ninety-fourth floor. Madelene looked at her nails as we rose, and rolled her lips across her white teeth. I watched the numbers on the destination display, calculating acceleration and deceleration rates, figuring speeds. I wasn't sure how tall the building was, but I knew Pecovin had eighty-two buildings with this many storeys.

'How high are we?' I asked Madelene as the doors opened.

She looked curiously at me. 'Didn't you see? Ninety-four. Top floor. I thought you were supposed to be clever.'

'I didn't *say* that. I said what *height*? How many *metres*?'

She raised her eyes and sighed. 'To the floor we're standing on, or to the top of the building?' She glanced past me, and I turned to see what had caught her attention.

In the flesh, Ethan Drame was striking. His shaved skull had a single broad indented scar stretching back from his forehead, and his eyes were extraordinary, close set and deep-browed, the irises small and intensely blue. He hardly blinked. He was a great deal taller than my father and I could see Pellonhorc in one of his mannerisms, the unconscious loose clenching of a fist. His smile, though, was easy and wide. This was one of the things that I found hard to comprehend, that he could always be as the moment demanded, no matter what else might be happening. His ability to concentrate on the necessary, to dismiss distraction, was extraordinary.

'Alef,' he said. 'The boy Alef. Good.' He turned and led us into an office. One of the walls was glass. The view was over the financial district. As the light caught his moving skull and fell on it from different angles, the scar seemed to deepen or to disappear.

He sat down at the vast desk, then he put on a voice and mimicked me. 'How many *metres*?' He gestured for me to sit down across the desk from him. 'Your father asked questions like that.' I realised at that moment, as he looked hard at me – *the boy* – that all of this concern had not been for his son at all, but for me.

'Madelene, get him some… what would you like, boy? Water? Juice?'

'To the *floor*,' I said. 'Floor to floor.'

I still occasionally do that, even now, so many years later. When I'm stressed or anxious, I go statistic. But at that time I wasn't simply anxious. In hyperlepsy I'd absorbed more raw information at once, uninterrupted, than I ever had before or ever would again, and it had just hit me that I was never going to see my parents again, and that this man who was in some way responsible for their deaths was all I had to take care of me.

Now, I find this first encounter with Drame mildly embarrassing to recall. But it fixed Drame's and Madelene's impressions of me as a machine-child, with no more than a machine's predictability, its simple strengths and weaknesses.

'I don't know,' Drame said. 'Get him the answer and some juice. Hurry up.'

Madelene didn't move. She pulled her vivid pink lips tight and stared at Drame.

His tone eased. 'Madly, please.'

She swivelled and left. We waited in silence for her to return.

'Two hundred and sixty-three point nine four metres,' she said, holding the glass of red ham juice. Her fingertips were as round and unused as the fingers of a child, but her knuckles were white. She glanced at me and smiled. As before, it wasn't anything like a real smile, though, not even a pornosphere smile. 'Not including the carpet,' she added, as if helpfully, but not in a helpful voice.

'There's no carpet in the elevator,' I said.

Drame laughed. 'You won't mock him,' he said. 'He's like putery. He can't be mocked.'

'What's the point of the stupid question?' she snapped.

Drame looked at me.

'To get the answer,' I said.

Madelene put the glass down hard in front of me, causing the juice to jump out and slop onto the table, pooling thickly. I ran my finger through it like parting the Red Sea, and licked it. Madelene stared at me again and I decided not to think about her any more.

How foolish of me. I'd imagined her a sort of waitress. I had no idea what a mistress was, no idea how powerful she was. But I know I'm blaming myself too much. After two weeks in the Song, the limited skills of perception that my mother had bequeathed me were not at the forefront of my mind. Usually I would have been able, if awkwardly, to comprehend Madelene. My mother had started to teach me the techniques I needed. I would have examined the tone of voice Madelene had used, and the words and their context, and I would have decided she was being sarcastic, and I would have reacted appropriately, and perhaps not made such an enemy.

But maybe she was already determined to be my enemy. Our relationship predetermined. Like fate, if you believe in that. Though I don't believe in anything.

'Alef,' Drame said, as soon as she was gone. 'I'm sorry about your parents. Your father and I were very close.'

'He never talked about you. He never mentioned you at all.'

'That was out of respect, Alef. You won't believe me, but

I will miss him as much as you will.'

'I have the puter.'

He wasn't expecting that. He was probably wondering how, and how quickly, he could coax me to it; I analyse it like that now, but at the time I didn't see it so clearly. Even within the AfterLife program, you cannot truly look back, because facts, if you were involved in them in any way, are not facts at all. Perhaps the insights I have as I review the past become confused with perceptions of the actual time. Looking back at events changes them in your memory, and the looking back changes you *now*. This is another logic path. Or a logic loop. Everything here must be entirely true – the nature of the AfterLife program and the neurid is such that I couldn't lie or invent anything – and yet…

'Your father was always direct with me. I hope you and I can have the same relationship, Alef. You're friendly with my son, as I was with your father. Did your father ever tell you how he and I first met?'

I wanted to repeat what I'd said, that my father had never even mentioned Drame's existence, so how could he have told me how they'd met, but I didn't. I said, 'No.'

Drame ran his finger through the juice on the table, making my minus sign into a multiplier, and said, 'We were at school. He was being bullied. I wasn't good at schoolwork.'

I wasn't interested. Anyway, my father was dead, so it would have been better if he hadn't ever met Drame in the first place. Why would I want to know about a bad thing? I put my hands on the puter and said, 'Do you want me to open this for you?'

My mind was starting to clear, now. The need to cloud it with a soothing clatter of fact and calculation was starting to fade, and I was thinking clearly again.

Drame sat back and looked at me as if there were a trick in the question. 'Yes.'

'I need something to handle it. Something bigger.'

He called people in. I told them what I needed, the screenery and putery, and they set it up. They didn't look at me or seem surprised at a boy giving them orders. They left, but I had a sense of someone remaining, standing directly behind me. I didn't turn round to look, though.

I displayed the data on the wall. There were vast quantities of it. It was the first time I'd seen it, so it took me a while to take it in and organise it to my satisfaction. Out of the corner of my eye, I saw Drame watching me, and I saw his gaze flick over my shoulder. There was definitely someone else. I was sure it wasn't Madelene.

I moved the numbers around the screen, connecting them carefully with transaction-chronology and remembering the tax implications of interplanetary transfer. I saw what my father had done, how he had moved money around and set up contracts to take advantage of differing laws. All the laws and regulations were in my head, and I saw how clever my father had been, and I also saw mistakes he had made, opportunities he had missed.

'This is boring for you, boy,' Drame said, eventually. He took control of the puter himself, laboriously shifting its information around, peering at it. He understood some of it, I could tell. I read this by the pattern of his movement around the data, just like I read expression and tone from voices and faces. The analytic principle is the same for me. He was quite unable to read me, though. I'm certain he thought my stillness meant I was puzzled or bored.

I pointed and made a suggestion. He stopped and frowned, and said, 'Are you sure?' Again, he glanced over my shoulder, this time for a longer moment.

'Look,' I said, and I explained it to him. It was little more than a comparative calculation of interest rates, advantages of transfer against certain penalties.

His frown deepened. 'Your father never suggested this. Are you sure about it?'

I didn't reply.

'Of course you are,' he muttered. 'So why didn't your father see it?'

'Did you ask him?'

He looked at me sharply. 'Are you trying to be –?' He stopped. His voice dropped. 'No. No, of course you aren't. It isn't in you, any more than it was in him.'

It had been a risky thing for me to provoke him, but I learnt something from it. I realised that while my ability to empathise, limited and hard-learned though it still was, might keep me alive just as effectively as the usefulness of my brain, if I allowed Drame to see this ability within me, it would not be to my advantage.

There was a definite movement behind me. It took all my willpower not to turn round. I heard the door open and close, and a moment later Drame said, 'That's all, boy.'

SigEv 16 Solaman

I didn't see Pellonhorc again for some time, or his father. I was given a small room, in which I slept and ate. And I roamed the Song.

On the second day, a man ambled into my room and stood squinting at me as if he thought I couldn't see him doing it. He was odd, a short, barrel-gutted man, and his black hair was so oiled that it could have been moulded from clay. After about a minute of being stared at, I said, 'Hello,' to him and waited for an answer. There was none.

'Hello,' I said again, uncomfortably. 'I'm Alef.'

'Alef, yes, yeees,' he muttered, still squinting at me. 'What's in a name, what's in that one, an alphabet name, symbol of a name, name of a symbol, but they're all symbols, names are, signifiers of the named, mine's Solaman and what's in that, I wonder, hmm?'

I didn't know if I was expected to answer. He tipped his head, seemingly lost in thought. I noticed a mark on his right cheek, rough-edged and slightly raised, just beneath the eye. Otherwise his face was smooth and creaseless, like a child's.

'There's a Solaman in the Babble,' I said eventually.

'Wise man, wise enough but not enough, hmm?' He hopped from one foot to the other, like a bird. 'Not enough, hmm? Any more, I wonder?'

I guessed he was talking to me, but I was lost.

'Solaman,' he said. 'Might he be *only* a man? Do you see that?'

I had nothing to say. What was going on? Was he talking to himself, or about himself?

'Doesn't see it, but might he be taught? See this, perhaps – could Solaman be the only man, could he be a man of light, a man of stars?' His finger wandered to the mark on his cheek and he rubbed it, then caught himself and pulled his hand back.

I was still quite lost. I could have given him thousands of

names, of Solamans I'd discovered in the pornosphere, but I sensed he didn't mean that.

Solaman murmured, 'Doesn't see it, not at all,' then raised his voice again. 'What about this? Reverse it, almost *nameless*, hmm?' He tutted to himself and frowned. 'Namalos, nameless? Does he see that? Is there enough there, is there anything for Solaman to stretch? Is it just a databank standing there in a boy, and an index and a calculator? That's not enough, no. Solaman can't work with this. A dictionary isn't the bones of a symphony.'

'Solaman is a man as well,' I said.

'As well?' He stopped fidgeting and became slyly alert. 'As *well*, did you say? You meant what? A man as well as a symbol? How do you mean?'

'I meant as well like also. *Also* man. Sola makes also.'

Solaman beamed. 'Aaah. Yes indeed. Left, right, left, right, off we go, after all,' he sang to himself, jiggling his head from side to side. 'Good. Hah. Perhaps we can march in time, then, you and I.' He tapped my head gently and stood back to examine me again. 'More than a dictionary here, perhaps more than a juggler. Are we together, hmm?'

I thought I could see dimly what he meant. 'Riddles. Logic paths,' I said. 'I like logic paths.'

'Logic, yes, but logic's just a springboard, Alef, like Alef is the springboard of the alphabet.' His hands were fluttering. 'We will march, and then we might leap. Solaman will be Alef's springboard, and what somersaults there shall be!'

And so my true education began.

Weeks and months passed. I felt increasingly comfortable with Solaman, and soaked up everything that he told me. I learnt how to think. I learnt how to formulate my thoughts and to test ideas, to examine data and to apply theory. I began to understand the difference between data and knowledge, between theory and fact.

In many ways, he was like my father. The difference was that Solaman was less able to extrapolate and calculate numbers. But where systems were concerned, where logic and language were involved, he could make connections between seemingly quite unrelated pieces of information. Learning this wordlogic from Solaman was like learning puterlogic from my father. It was as exciting as that. I'd find myself grinning and interrupting him, shouting, 'Yes! And that means –'

Solaman would sit back and smile and let me finish, just as my father had. And I'd feel as connected to Solaman as I'd felt at those moments with Saul, my father.

It was odd. Sometimes when I was sitting with Solaman, my head burning with the heat of all this understanding, I'd sense my father standing at one side of me and my mother at the other, her hand almost touching my shoulder, and I'd know they were both smiling. Solaman would say, 'Alef?'

And I'd say, 'I'm sorry. I was just thinking.'

And we'd carry on.

Solaman also taught me law. I learned the logic and the illogic of it, of how it was a hammer and a blade. I learned how it could be turned to say whatever was needed of it. I learned about accountancy, too, and the way that the law was subservient to accountancy, that money controlled law, and that both were necessary to maintain the illusory stability of the System and the actual stability of power.

He would test me.

'Here's a situation, Alef. You have a distillery on Peco.

You're a manufacturer of coconut brandy. Fine stuff.' He stroked his chin. 'There's a demand for it on Bleak, a pointless place but a fine market for sweet oblivion. Tell me, Alef, at what time of the year would you export your sweet oblivion from Peco to Bleak?' He waited for me to reply. The mark on his cheek was smaller than it had been when I'd first met him, and paler than the surrounding skin that seemed to be pinched in. I wondered what it was.

I answered his question. 'In Bleak's flux, but only every third year.'

'Interesting. Why in the flux?'

'Atmospheric descent's hard then, and you'll lose thirty-three per cent of your cargo, but Bleak drops its import tax by eighty per cent during flux to encourage trade.'

'But why every third year? Why not every year?'

There was a note of surprise in his voice, and I wondered if I'd made a mistake. I said, 'I'd only send my surplus to Bleak. Coconut brandy sells well throughout the System. Despite the tax incentive, it isn't worth diverting easily saleable product to Bleak.'

'Nevertheless, there's still surplus, as you say. If you took it to Bleak every year, you'd avoid warehousing costs here on Peco.'

'Peco is still only twenty-three per cent habitable. Warehousing costs would be negligible if you used the outland.'

He shook his head in disappointment. 'The outland's insecure. It's toxic and unpatrolled. No regulations apply in the outland. That's why no one warehouses there.' He said this as though it ended the matter.

I said, 'Maybe, Solaman, but Pecovin's city limit is

constantly creeping outwards. You build your warehouse reasonably close by, and you take the risks. You'll lose some product to the planet and some to theft, but as Pecovin extends, the land you're on will be incorporated and be worth much more.' I checked that I had his attention. The warehousing idea had struck me as soon as he had set the problem, and the detail was coming to me as I spoke. I could still be wrong, though. There were other variables arriving in my head and I had to dispose of them or use them. 'If you're using land outside the current environmental limit, you get development tax benefit, and if you've built on that outland and been using it for ten years prior to its incorporation into Pecovin, the land's yours without windfall tax.'

Solaman nodded slowly. 'You know this?'

The figures glittered in my head as I quoted them. 'The last ten years, Pecovin pushed out at an average of ten point one metres a year. The last five years, it averaged ten point eight metres. Allow for exponential acceleration of this growth, and look ten years ahead for the tax relief, and it tells you that you need to be warehousing one point eight kils from the current limit in order to maximise tax breaks and mitigate the most significant loss factors. It's an investment.'

Solaman winked at me with his right eye.

No. It wasn't a wink. The tautening of his lips flexed the mark on his cheek and pulled his right eye down a fraction. I hadn't noticed this before.

He said, 'It's a lot more complex than that, Alef, but your basic thinking is good. You've touched on about eight per cent of the variables, and you have no real grasp of the tax implications yet, but you're trying. Go back to your three-yearly export protocol and explain that to me.'

I didn't feel scolded by him. It had been like this with my father; each time I felt I had leapt a few steps up his schedule of learning, he had given me a glimpse of how much further there was to go. The idea of more, the vision of it, always thrilled me. I concentrated now, and said, 'The market's stronger on Bleak if they know it only reaches them every three years. That boosts the price. Each year, you build up more surplus in your warehouse, and every three years the accumulated surplus will be sufficient to fill a StarCargo.'

'Why would you want to use a StarCargo?'

'It's the biggest freighter available. It's cheaper to use one StarCargo than ten smaller ships. Bigger profit margin.'

Solaman shook his head. 'Not to Bleak, and certainly not in flux. You lose that one StarCargo to the wind, that's your entire shipment gone. And you're uninsured. No insurer touches anything Bleak-bound during flux. The percentages are better with small ships.' He was unhappy with me and showed it. 'Look at the statistical risk, Alef. You're the numbers man.'

He was scolding me, but nevertheless, it was the first time he'd ever called me a man. After I'd taken that in, I said, 'No. Look at it in the long term. Over ten years, losing only one StarCargo, you're in greater profit. And look at another factor. It's not only what you'd lose to the wind. Ligate's pirates pick off one in ten of the smaller freighters.' I thought of Janquile, remembered the tension in his voice, and I wondered what he might have seen over the years. 'Ligate leaves the StarCargos alone. They're too big and well-armed, not worth the risk to him.'

Solaman looked hard at me. 'This is a theoretical test, Alef. We're just examining tax and commerce. If we were putting Ligate into the equation, you'd have to take in the fact that he'd see you're using a StarCargo and trace it back to Peco. His soldiers would simply visit your warehouse here. Your stock wouldn't reach the ship. He'd take his ten per cent directly, and if you were lucky he'd only break your arms as interest. You missed that, Alef.'

'No, I didn't. Anyway, Solaman, it isn't theoretical. It's impossible to look at tax and commerce in the System without looking at Ligate and Drame. I'm aligned with Ethan Drame. Ligate wouldn't ever dare hit his home.'

Solaman chuckled. 'Ligate's unpredictable. Don't ever try to guess what he'd do. And anyway, Alef, the problem didn't specify you were with Drame.'

'It's a constant,' I told him. 'I never forget it.'

Thirteen

RAZER

DATA UPLOADED, AUGMEM ERASED AND RESET. PROCEDURE COMPLETE. YOU DID NOT INITIATE CHITTLECHATTLE, KESTREL DUST. WOULD YOU LIKE CHITTLECHATTLE?

Razer said, 'I'm not in the mood.'

THE BALE STORY CONTAINS EIGHTY-SEVEN PER CENT POSITIVE FACTORS. IS IT COMPLETE?

'No.'

TALLEN WOULD BE A GOOD SUBJECT.

For a moment, she froze. 'I haven't finished with Bale. I haven't even named him.'

THIS PROGRAM CAN NAME HIM. THIS PROGRAM'S NAME SELECTIONS RAISE APPRECIATION RATES BY THREE PER CENT BY COMPARISON WITH KESTREL DUST'S.

'No.' She caught herself. 'Tell me, Cynth, I meet Tallen and Bale, both through you, and then they both nearly get killed. That's a hell of a coincidence, don't you think?'

NO.

'You don't think it's odd?'

NO, THIS PROGRAM DOES NOT THINK. IT CALCULATES OPTIONS AND MAKES SELECTIONS. YOU ARE NOT THINKING LOGICALLY. YOU ARE A WRITER. YOUR COMMISSIONED SUBJECTS ARE SELECTED FOR CRITERIA INCLUDING

SUBSTANTIAL RISK OF TRAUMA OR DEATH. BALE'S LIFE INVOLVES EXTREME RISK.

'Tallen's life doesn't involve any risk. He has no one. He just fixes things.' Razer had a sudden vivid picture of him standing with her in the red bar, and she remembered the rare experience of having a conversation with someone that wasn't simply for a story. How open his smile had been, how curious about her; she'd been momentarily excited at their – she grinned to herself – their chittlechattle. When had she last had a moment like that? The light flickering magenta and lilac above them, the languid music, the screeners nodding and muttering all around them, and a moment of purely emotional connection with someone.

And then Bale had come in, and she was working. Enjoying her work, yes, but working.

YOUR COMPREHENSION OF STATISTICS IS NOT ADEQUATE TO FURTHER DISCUSSION. WOULD YOU LIKE CHITTLECHATTLE NOW?

'Hell with you, Cynth.'

She rescreened to her TruTales locus where Cynth had pulled out a list of reader questions for her to respond to.

—Hi, Jellezebelle. Yes, I missed her for a while, but it wore off. Such emotional intensity [link *here*] can't be maintained. Not by me, at least.

—That's a good question, OneTwoMany [link *here*]. No, I never wonder about the past. I don't have the time. Once a story is done, I'm thinking of the next.

—Hi, Roarshack. It's hard to pick the most scary. I've come close to death a few times. But that time in the slimpipe [link *here*] sometimes pops into my thoughts, even after

all these years. That certainly taught me a few tricks.
—Thank you, Seemless, yes, that one [link *here*] was a lot of fun. I'm glad you enjoyed it too. Flying anything blind is always a kick, and when it's something as big as that, it's special. Writing it was a challenge, too, and the fact that it's one of my highest raters means a lot to me.
—Hi, Timezup. Thanks for the offer. I'm afraid I can't write about anyone I want to, though you do sound amazing. TruTales employs me, and of course I have an AI that sends me on assignments. -Yes, I call it Cynth. I'm lucky my AI knows me so well. But then we've been working together for almost ten years. -Of course, Cynth will certainly be aware of you, so you never know!
—Hey there, Vortic. Two questions? Okay, just this time. And I see you're new to Kestrel Dust. So, here goes. How did I get this job? Well, if you think this life's for you, you can check the advice [link *here*] but if you mean me in particular, I was just lucky. I didn't apply. Cynth found me. No link to anything there, I'm afraid, since it's a time in my life I don't really like thinking about. Maybe one day I'll go back to it, and I suppose it might all be out there if I turn out to have a neurid and I end up in a sarc. And your other question: why do I write? Two words: curiosity and dissatisfaction. Of course, if you look in my archive, you'll find I've given a lot of answers to that question over the years. It depends on how I feel when someone asks me. And that's your lot for now, but please keep reading Kestrel Dust!
—Hi, Rift/drifter. What can I say to that? I suppose all of you are my family. You, and Cynth. Though that's a love-hate thing!

Enough. She signed off, suddenly exhausted.

Bale and Tallen. Maybe Cynth was right, it was just coincidence. She'd never known Cynth to be wrong.

Delta

From this distance, Delta thought, the bay was like a roughly simmed sea. It was so thick with sarcs that the water was little more than a frothy webbing about them, and their slow heaving was unsettling to observe. These were the sleepers summoned in by vote, waiting to be picked up by drones and loaded into containers and shipped on to the hospitals where they would be restored and returned to the System with new identities, since their old lives were known in every detail.

Delta and Bale were standing high above the town, just within and below the arc of the shield, looking down and seaward. The wind bullied them. Delta said, 'You could have been somewhere out there, Bale.'

He didn't answer.

'What's wrong, Bale. You're alive.'

'You know what I thought for a moment when I first woke up in the hospital? I thought I'd been through AfterLife.'

She laughed. 'Hundreds of years gone and you in the future.' Her face changed, mock-upset. 'And me dead.'

'Not just you. Everyone.'

At the dock, rows of cranes nodded slowly up and down, lifting the tide of arriving sarcs from the water and swinging them into great containers. The breeze carried the muted noise of engines and the occasional tang of metal on metal.

The containers moved on railed sleds to and from the ferry station, endlessly arriving and departing.

'Anyway, who'd vote for you to come back, Bale?'

'When I die, there's going to be nothing to pour into a sarc, and that's fine with me.'

Delta shook her head. 'I came to see you in the hospital. I was there when you were brought in. You and Tallen, you had a whole floor to yourselves. It was quite a thing. He had a squad of medicians all of his own. You should have seen them arrive, all gloved and gowned and putered up. But whatever they did for that guy, you're the one who saved his life.'

'If you say so. I don't remember. There was a lot of screenery in the hospital. Racks of it. That's why there were no more beds. His medicians looked more like techs.'

'What do you expect? They were neuromeds.' She closed her eyes and let the breeze play on her face.

'I can't work it out. What happened down there, Delta? He was about to kill me. There was nothing to stop him. So why am I alive?'

'Why are you alive? I don't believe this, Bale!' She groaned. Why did he always have to be like this? 'You killed the K. The case is closed. You go home and take a month's leave, then you come back to work. Is that so hard?' She stared furiously at him. 'It was slippery and he lost balance. You were lucky. Your reflexes must have been good, too. You managed to stab him before you lost consciousness.'

'How do you know that?'

'Forensics reconstructed it.' She tried to stay patient. He *had* to listen. 'They had a hard job of it though. It was a mess down there. Shit everywhere, and the sea backing up. But it all made sense in the end.'

Delta had no idea whether Bale was taking in anything she said. He was impossible. He'd always been impossible. And she was stupid for caring. Did she really imagine that this experience might have changed him?

He said, 'And Tallen?'

'He was really ripped up. Lucky as you, Bale. Even luckier with that neuromed team carrying out research here on Bleak.'

'Why would the K take him down there? Razer said he didn't take anyone else.'

'He was crazy. Who knows? Case is closed. Please, Bale.'

Vast cloud shadows stroked the bay of sarcs below them. The cranes rose and fell, the containers rolled, and in the distance was the sea.

'Yeah.' Bale sighed.

Delta relaxed. 'Yeah,' she said. She couldn't make out any of the rigs from here. They were far away, where the sea and the wind fought. Everything on Bleak was conflict.

'Hell, I was drunk,' Bale said, eventually.

She grinned. 'You were indeed.'

'That was bad luck. Don't you think?'

'Yeah, it was.' She caught herself, adding sharply, 'What do you mean? How?'

'I don't know, I'm not sure. Something about it. It was like he wanted me down there, wanted to be followed. Like –' He paused. The breeze brought a screech of metal up from the bay. The sound trailed mournfully away. He said, 'I'll check it.'

'It's closed. Didn't you hear me? You keep screwing up, Bale, and this time you screwed up again, but you were lucky. You had some good luck, Bale. Take it. The K slipped in the shit and you're a hero, and now it's closed.' She took a deep breath, the ammoniac air up here, close to the shield, burning her throat. 'Hell. I knew this would happen.'

'What?' he said.

'Okay. I wanted to be nice. Why can't you ever be? You scared the hell out of me, you know that? You know how worried I was?' She stared out at the sea. 'I don't know why I should give a damn about you if you don't give a damn about yourself.'

He stood up, restless. Delta wondered whether he was going to walk away. 'We're friends, Bale. I didn't want to be saying this, but you'll be hearing it from Navid anyway. Your suspension ended a month ago. You're currently on unpaid leave pending investigation for being drunk on duty.'

The bright sky was behind him and she couldn't make out his expression. She added, 'It's bad. But just go home, take a break and it will all go away. Navid said so. Please, Bale.'

He rolled his shoulders, stretched his back and his legs. When he was done, he said, 'I see it, fine. You're just here to pass on a threat, Delta. Well, listen. I wasn't on duty. It was a crashcall. Vox could have decided to leave me out of the link but didn't. Then you could have stood me down, but you didn't do that either. I had no choice and you know it. If I hadn't responded to the crashcall, I'd have been suspended for that.'

'You took your gun, knowing you were drunk.'

'It was disabled, remember? Useless. If I'd known I was that drunk, I wouldn't have taken it.'

'But you didn't know, which makes it worse. You see what I'm getting at?'

'Yeah, I see. Clear as words.'

'Please don't be like this.'

'Is this an official conversation?'

'No. Bale, please –'

'Fine. Just tell me what you're not here to tell me.'

She turned her back on him. Inland was the ferry station where the container sleds came from and returned to. One of the hospital barges was ready to leave and she watched it start to rise on its stalk of flame. She almost turned to face Bale again, to tell him about that night at her end of the crashcall, but what would that have achieved? It had been odd, but there was nothing suspicious about it.

Below, the barge continued to rise. The rumble came a moment later and lasted well after the barge had diminished to a sliver of grey and then vanished altogether. There was water in the wind, and she wiped it from her cheeks. 'Hell, Bale. I'm not being subtle. The case is over, so forget it. We all did what we did. We were all lucky. Just be a hero, take your break, and come back to work. Please.'

'One last question.'

'As long as it is that.'

'You know about Razer.'

'That isn't a question.' Yes, Delta knew about Razer. Since Razer had turned up, Bale had spent all his time off with her, when he wasn't in the Chute. This was the first time Delta had had Bale to herself for… how long?

Bale said, 'Razer turned up in Lookout just before all this sparked. And she was with me the night before the K-event. And you haven't mentioned her. Every time she comes up, you go quiet.'

'Still not a question.'

'Something's going on here, Delta. Is she a Paxer?'

For the first time since the crashcall had kicked in, Delta smiled. 'Sometimes, Bale, you get it so totally wrong.' And the sound of her empty laugh echoed as she walked away down the mountainside.

Fourteen

ALEF

SigEv 17 A past and a future

I was gradually introduced to Drame's business practices. The process of transfer was delicately done. Solaman kept setting me tests, and the tests became increasingly complex, each problem containing more factors and variables. Occasionally the extra information I asked for, or my solution, surprised even Solaman, and I had to wait while he left to clarify the 'detail' with someone else.

Months of teaching and conversation passed, and the day came when Solaman said I was to be moving on.

'I've enjoyed teaching you, Alef, more than you realise. Far more than you can know.' I thought he was going to stop there, but he nodded to himself and said, 'Your father was very proud of you. He told me about you. He –'

Solaman paused and looked at me. He was weeping a little and I had no idea why. The tears from his left eye followed the contours of his face and he licked them from the corner of his lip, but the tears from his right eye skirted the mark beneath it – the mark was raised again – and disappeared, never reaching his lip. I was fascinated by this, and a little scared. The salt water sank away into a deep fissure in the cheek that I had thought was just a crease.

I asked Solaman, 'Did you know my father well?'

He took a while to collect himself. On the screenery in the corner of the room were the programs we used when we were problem-solving. I played with them while I waited. My eyes were tuned to them so that once I enabled screenery with three steady blinks, I could summon and shift information by a series of protocols; left or right eye winking, long-blinking, wide-eyeing. When the screenery was not enabled, it trawled the Song randomly. Solaman thought the stimulus it provided to be invaluable.

'You remind me very much of him, Alef,' he said, startling me out of a financial datafield. I blinked it off and found him still crying, though he seemed unaware of it. His right eye and the fissure seemed part of a self-contained circuit of tears.

'Tell me something about him,' I said.

'What do you want to know?'

'Why did he go to Gehenna?'

There was a long pause, and then he sighed. 'You ought to know it all, Alef. Or maybe you do know it already.'

I said, firmly and stupidly, 'I know that Ethan Drame is a criminal and my father was working for him. Why was he doing that?'

I had never asked Solaman this before, just as I'd never asked him about the terrifying mark on his cheek. I didn't want to know the answers. I had lain in my bed at night, night after night, until I had invented and polished a flawless story. In this story, my father and mother had tried to escape Drame's clutches and nearly succeeded, but he had hunted them down and blackmailed them, threatening their lives and mine; and my father had been steadily building a dossier against Drame to take to Pax. But now I thought I was ready for the truth.

Solaman said, 'Yes.'

He seldom sat down, preferring to pace, but now he did. 'I'll start at the beginning. You were born here on Peco, Alef. Not on Gehenna. But the story really begins before that.

'Your father was very special,' Solaman began.

He spoke slowly, as if the words coming out were on delay; it was like he was formulating them very carefully, a few sentences ahead. 'He didn't fully understand people. Your mother understood him, though, and they both loved you, Alef. Saul wasn't anything like Ethan. He was never interested in the consequences of the work he did for him.' Solaman paused and examined me carefully. 'It wasn't that he didn't care. You have to remember that he couldn't project what emotional capacity he had beyond his immediate environment. Do you understand, Alef?'

I didn't, fully. I'd never heard Solaman talk like this, about emotions. He didn't seem to be saying my father was a bad man, or that he was a good man. It was that he had been a straightforward man, which I knew, but Solaman was making it complicated, saying my father was neither bad nor good. I wanted him to be good.

'Ligate and Ethan were always rivals, but they cooperated from time to time. On one such occasion, before you were born, when your parents still lived here on Peco, Ethan took advantage of Ligate, and Ligate responded forcefully and then went into hiding. Everything was disrupted for a while, and it took a long time for the business to recover.'

He waited to see if I was following. I said, 'Then?'

'Ethan – well, Ethan Drame is tenacious. He told your father that he wanted to mend the damage between himself and Ligate, so your father developed a scheme that would benefit both Ligate and Ethan. Saul couldn't locate Ligate, but by using financial transfer patterns he managed eventually to track Ligate's family down. He had a wife and five children.'

I nodded for him to go on.

'Saul imagined that Ethan would simply contact Ligate through his wife and children, and make peace. Instead, Ethan killed them all.'

I had a sudden vision of my parents in my father's workshop, about to die. I closed my eyes against it and grew a tree of prime numbers, but its leaves withered. Solaman waited until I opened my eyes again, and he said, 'Well. Your father was suddenly confronted by the consequences of his work.'

He looked at me until I nodded for him to go on.

'Ligate declared war. Ethan was forced to retrench and fight. Saul had a breakdown. I had to take over from him, alone, but it was hopeless. We needed Saul, but Saul couldn't do anything. He was no use to Ethan.'

'You?' I said. I had thought Solaman was just my teacher.

'I was your father's aide, Alef. I'm quick, but beside him I was like your father beside what you could become. I don't know precisely what it was that shattered Saul, the deaths or the putery of war or the scale of the rebuilding, but Saul was shattered, that was for certain.' He took a breath, looking away from me. 'Ethan was focused on his empire, and your mother took the opportunity to tell him she was leaving Peco with her husman and child. You were almost a year old, Alef. She made a deal with Ethan. The deal was that if

Saul recovered, he would work for Ethan again, but that they would never return to Peco. She told him that if Saul didn't get away from here, he'd never recover.'

'I don't see the difference. Here or on Gehenna, what's the difference? And why Gehenna?'

'Your mother thought Gehenna would be a safe haven from both Ligate and Ethan. And it would be a place where no one would point you out, Alef.' Solaman almost smiled. 'You were already obviously special. She chose Gehenna carefully, Alef. While Saul might be able to stay unnoticed in his putery anywhere in the System, you were another matter. It was clear that you'd swiftly draw attention wherever you grew up. She wanted the best chance for you to be normal and unnoticed, and that led her to Gehenna. And Gehenna would teach you about good and bad. That was important to her.'

'Evil,' I said instantly, surprising myself as much as Solaman with my sharpness. 'Good and *evil*.'

'Evil. Your mother didn't quite appreciate how… how raw life would be on Gehenna. She imagined simplicity. It was hard for her. But Saul adapted well, and you thrived, so she accepted it.'

'You know her as well as you know Saul,' I said.

'I should do, yes.' The loop of tears began again. 'Tell me, Alef. Why do you think someone like your mother might fall in love with a man like Saul?'

Love! The idea of this puzzled me. And the word coming from Solaman, a man in many ways similar to my father. I shrugged.

He leaned forward, though. 'Can't you see it, Alef? Can't you see it?'

I realised it was a real question, a test he was setting me, like those other tests, but quite different. And I guessed the clue was in the question.

I stared at him. *Can't you see it?*

I went back to the beginning, to first principles. How would she have met Saul in the first place? Saul had spent his life here, with Drame, so she must have met him here. And she had understood him, and how could you understand a man like Saul?

It was to do with looking.

I began to get there. It was in front of me; you would understand a man like Saul because you are like him yourself, or else because you know people, or someone, like him. And since she wasn't like Saul –

Can't you see it?

I looked at Solaman, who was still weeping with his right eye, though his left was dry. I saw Solaman crying, and I could see my mother crying. That same tilt of the corner of the mouth as they sobbed.

I said, 'She was your sister, Solaman.'

He nodded.

A minute passed until I could say, 'Why didn't you tell me before?'

He put his hand on my shoulder. This was the first time he had ever touched me. My uncle. My family.

It had been Solaman standing behind me that first day here in Peco, in Drame's office. My uncle.

He kept his hand on my shoulder, softly, as he said, 'I couldn't tell how you'd react, Alef. You might have ignored it or you could have broken down altogether. I didn't want to risk that. Until very recently, I've found it easy to say nothing. You showed no interest. You never asked about any of it.'

I saw how the pieces fitted – no, I *understood*. The feeling was like the feeling I had when Solaman had taught me to analyse, to think. It was extraordinary, overwhelming. It was as though my mother's legacy to me had finally fully arrived, without warning and thunderously. Saul had been her brother's best friend; of course she had fallen for him. She had understood the best and the worst of him, and accepted it all. She had even been able to tolerate the terrible rigidity of Gehenna because she was already accustomed to such unwithering certainty.

Everything made sense. And with my Gehennan need for self-punishment, for following the logic path, I made myself take this further. 'Why are you telling me now?'

But I knew the answer. I hated this terrible capacity for human understanding that my mother had bequeathed me. I didn't want it at all. It was easier to go statistic, and I wanted to do that now. I brought up lists of numbers, only for the digits to shred away. All I could hold there were terrible, unflinching words like melanoma, sarcoma, metastasis. The Song was full of them, and of the wailings that chorused around them.

I said, 'What is it on your cheek, Solaman?'

My uncle squeezed my shoulder gently, then took his hand away. I still felt the phantom of its touch. Eventually he put the hand to his cheek and said, 'It's my death, Alef.'

And his tears poured endlessly over it.

SigEv 18 The Floor

After the revelation of his disease, I didn't see Solaman for a while. The overwhelming surge of human comprehension that I had suffered faded after that episode, though for weeks afterwards I was plagued by dreams of my father and my mother.

I had no one to talk to about the dreams. Without Solaman or Pellonhorc, I had no one to talk to at all.

Solaman's illness catapulted me towards the life he had been grooming me for. I was to be my father's replacement and my job was to help maximise Drame's profits. I sat with the data until it was part of me.

Perhaps I could have walked away. I could have told Ethan Drame I would work for him from another base, like my father had, only unlike my father, I could have disappeared entirely.

Though could I have? I had my skills and knowledge, but they were mind-skills. I was not practical. While I could plan meticulously, I was clumsy where the *actual*, the physical, was concerned.

In any case, I had no one. There were only two people alive I cared about: Solaman and Pellonhorc.

And I wanted revenge. I wanted my vengeance to fall on Spetkin Ligate. I was too scared of Ethan Drame to consider acting against him at present. If I had been older, I might have thought otherwise, but I was still in my teens, and my thoughts were raw. I would have to bide my time.

When I next saw Solaman, he said the time had come to begin work, and took me in the elevator to the place he said I'd be based. There was a slight slur to his voice. His cheek was sinking in and it was drawing his eye down and his lip up. The thing was rooted in the hollow of his maxillary sinus, and it was like a quicksand into which his face was falling. Neither of us mentioned it. I didn't ask if he was having treatment for it. If he wasn't, there would be a reason, and if he was, the treatment clearly wasn't working.

Perhaps he wanted me to talk to him about it, but I couldn't. My new empathy wasn't up to it. I knew about death – I had spent my childhood carrying a small coffin about with me, after all, as did every child in Gehenna, and I had seen my parents slaughtered in front of me – but I couldn't talk to Solaman about his.

'Are you ready?' he asked me at the door. He had to strain in order to speak. The muscles of his face had started to fail and he couldn't maintain lip-seal, just as he couldn't blink his right eye. The thing growing in his sinus made him sound like he was speaking in the teeth of a terrible wind.

'Yes,' I said.

He pushed the door open.

They all stopped whatever they were doing. No one looked at me. They stared at Solaman.

Speaking slowly and as clearly as he could, he introduced me to the team I was to work with. He introduced me by my name and also as Saul's son. He introduced the twenty-eight of them to me by name, one by one, and I remembered every single name, and not one of them, it turned out, remembered mine. All we had in common at that moment was that we knew Solaman was saying goodbye.

He didn't say it, of course. He made his introductions, and then he said, 'I'll be gone for a few days. I'm due a break from all of you,' and they nodded.

As he turned to go, I turned after him, but he whispered, 'Later, Alef.' The door closed itself silently behind him, leaving me inside and him out there.

I can't remember the rest of that day. I got to know them,

though. The room in which we worked took up an entire level of the building. They – we – called it The Floor.

It took a while to get used to. Some of us would sit down as we worked, some paced constantly. There was little talk. Threedy screenery hung in the air like wisps of soft dark glass, pale numbers and words briefly glowing and fading again as information changed. There were charts and maps, exchange rates, share prices, margins of profit and loss. Only the changes mattered to the twenty-nine of us; the rest of the data we held in our heads, to varying degrees. Some specialised in planetary industry, some in law, others in accountancy and tax and business infrastructure. All the skills and specialities overlapped so that none of us was isolated or indispensable, and someone with specialised knowledge was always at hand.

No one on The Floor had ever met my father. They had communicated with him by screenery from his little shop on Gehenna (though they had never known where the shop was). By their initial reaction to me, I knew how special my father had been. Solaman had been more loved, perhaps, if that's the word, but Saul had been the leader of the team, and it took me little time to see how much they missed him.

SigEv 19 The weave

It took me about a week to assimilate the overall situation. I visualised Drame's interests as a funnel-shaped four-dimensional weave that reflected through itself repeatedly. It was interestingly complex, the dimensions in which it existed including regulatory parameters that varied from planet to planet, and with time.

The weave needed constant repair and reweaving, and we twenty-nine were at its heart, feeling the vibrations of tax law and economic judder and even natural disaster transmit from one strand of the weave to another. Our job was to anticipate what might be anticipated, to adjust to the disruption and to repair the weave and extend and even strengthen it.

At no point did I take charge of The Floor, but it was simply accepted, over a period of a few weeks, that prime authority had been passed to me.

I didn't question the origin of Drame's business opportunities. I noticed, of course, that he bought into hugely profitable businesses with minimal investment, and that the markets for businesses in which he had an interest became, at the point of his entry, suddenly keen to buy their product and uninterested in negotiating on price. If you knew nothing about Ethan Drame, you'd think he had the golden touch. If you knew enough, you'd know he had the touch of death.

Nevertheless, on the whole, Drame's empire functioned legitimately. Laws were used where it was advantageous to the business to use them. Solaman once told me about this – he said that for most businesses, the laws were the roads on the map, while for us they were roughnesses in the terrain.

I didn't notice the passage of time. What seemed like hours were days, and what I thought were weeks turned out to have been months. In that way, two years passed. I had a room in a nearby building where I slept. It was all I needed. Sometimes I had to be reminded to eat, and sometimes I was so tired that I had to be accompanied back to my room to sleep.

I started to shave. I ate and slept. I worked on The Floor. I had no time to think for myself, or at least I gave myself none.

Of course it was a criminal enterprise. I had never thought otherwise. But I replaced some of Drame's excessively direct methods with tools of finance and law. He even encouraged this, where it reduced business risk. Directness, though, was one of Drame's favourite words. He liked such euphemisms. They made him feel like a businessman or a politician. I would stand in his office while he was – as he called it – *negotiating*, with – as he called them – *colleagues*. He had a voice that could carry enormous meaning. It was low and vibrant, almost a monotone, and he would pause between words so that their weight would hang. *I shall take direct action. I can reach you. I am tenacious.* The threats enclosed in these phrases carried a greater force, somehow, than if he were simply to have said, 'I shall kill your family,' or, 'You will never be safe from me,' or, 'I shall not stop until you are dead.'

He realised, though, that action within the law was more profitable to him. Direct action carried a small risk of failure, and to minimise that, such action had to be excessive and extreme, which was expensive in terms both of manpower and of the ongoing procedures needed to ensure the consequences were never investigated.

Still, direct action was taken from time to time. Drame's empire was extensive enough, thanks to my father's and Solaman's efforts, that it could have carried on expanding quite legitimately, but Ligate took every opportunity to attack Drame, and vice versa, and Drame got bored if legal routes of expansion were too slow for his liking. So the business continued to expand, and rapidly, through the routes of business, bribery, extortion, murder and ruthless competition with Spetkin Ligate.

Fifteen

TALLEN

'Why would you want to work on a rig, Mr Tallen?'

Hoob spun a pen evenly through his fingers as he talked. The pen looked sharp-tipped, which Tallen thought was a good thing, and its barrel was lightly ribbed.

Looking at the pen comforted Tallen. You could get a good grip on that barrel, drive it down firmly, he thought. And he found himself fingering the notch of the sternum at the base of his throat. He pushed the tip of his finger down inside the sternum. Drive the pen down, hard, just there, behind the notch, and he'd probably get it close to the heart. He'd have to change grip as he drove it down, use his thumb to drive it the last few centimetres…

Hoob was looking at him strangely.

Tallen dropped his hand to his lap and made himself concentrate.

'I'll put it another way,' Hoob said. 'Why would Ronen take you?'

'I heard you take anyone who wants to go.'

'No,' Hoob said. 'What you heard was that hardly anyone wants to go. You heard it's a dead job applied for by crazies, and you think you're not really crazy, so we'd leap at the chance to take you.' The pen clicked on the table. 'That's partly true. Crazies do apply.' He eyed Tallen speculatively. 'We don't take them. There are a few people who are suited for it, though, and there are many more who imagine they're suited. Some of each are certainly crazy, to a greater or lesser degree. We filter the crazy from the not-so-crazy. So, you think you're suited?'

'Yes.'

'You believe in any sort of goddery?'

Tallen shook his head.

'Some people still do. It isn't illegal.' He gave Tallen a moment. 'Not even maybe?'

'Not even interested.'

Hoob nodded slowly. Tallen knew Hoob was waiting for him to break the silence with a truth, but Tallen had none to offer. Eventually Hoob said, 'And you're not in any way crazy? You think that?' He put his pen away, inside his jacket, still staring at Tallen.

Tallen tried to meet his eyes. They'd taken his own pen at the street entrance, and Tallen hadn't tried to smuggle in any of his other sharps, but there was a desk ornament between them, a scaled-down drill rig with a spike that he was sure he'd be able to drive across a wrist. It wouldn't really do the trick, not swift enough or certain, but the possibility was enough.

'I have a small problem,' he said. 'You know about that.'

'Yes.' Hoob nodded again. 'I have a note here.' He tapped the desktop without taking his eyes from Tallen. 'A reference from a psych. It doesn't mean much to me, but you have to get past me before our own psych gets to trigger your twitches, so why don't you explain it to me?'

Tallen said, 'May I?' and took the ornament from the

desk. It felt good in his hand. Hoob pushed his chair back and glanced pointedly up at the ceiling behind Tallen. Tallen wondered how quickly someone would be in the room if Hoob gave the signal. He guessed there would be decisive, maybe deadly force from behind, and that he wouldn't know a thing about it. He rolled the little rig around his hand, fingering the sharp drill bit, and relaxed at the reassuring thought.

'I was attacked. He attacked ten people. I was the only survivor.'

'I know about that. I saw the reports. You were lucky,' Hoob said.

'That's a way to look at it. I suffered neurological as well as physical damage. You know all this. You really want me to go through it again?'

'This won't be the last time. You'd better get used to it.'

Tallen touched the spike to his palm. 'The physical damage has been fixed, but as I had insufficient insurance, I was only accepted for treatment as an experimental subject, on a mutual consent basis.' He smiled at Hoob. 'That means I consented *in absentia* to unmonitored treatment that MedTech agreed to provide me with at no charge and at no risk of litigation. As a result, I am alive and I have a considerable range of augmentations. I have considerably revised proprioceptory receptors and analytics extending to most industrially useful wavelengths including ionising radiation, and various other adjustments including neuromuscular ports – I can show you them, if you like –' he slowed, but Hoob shook his head, '– which makes me ideal for neurodynamic machinery operations. I imagine you use neurodynamic systems on your rigs.'

'It doesn't give you a walk-in here at Ronen, Mr Tallen.

Our workers get external systems fitted at the rig. You simply have internals, that's all. You're convenient but you aren't so special.'

'I'm told I'm faster. But once I'm engaged, I can't disengage. I have no control. It's a problem for me, an advantage for you. I have to trust whoever's using me.'

Hoob nodded. 'You chose to trust us.'

Tallen closed his hand around the model and opened it. There was a small pool of blood in his palm. He put the model back on the desk, leaving a smear of red beside it.

Hoob stared at the blood as Tallen wiped his hand with a kerchief. 'Okay. MedTech gave you all this and then let you go. Why would they do that? They invested a lot of money in you. They're throwing it all away because you have a, a small problem?'

Tallen shrugged. Hoob would know how unlikely that was. People like Tallen, the *consent in absentia* cases, carrying fortunes of experimental tech, spent their lives paying it all off in research labs or else rented out by MedTech on day-rates to companies like Ronen. Only not to Ronen itself, as MedTech's contractual monitoring requirements weren't exactly to Ronen's secretive taste. Tallen had done his research.

'You know what it is, my problem. It's in the notes in front of you.'

'Let's pretend I don't understand it.'

'You don't need to worry,' he told Hoob. 'Everything works. This is just something they hadn't anticipated. A compulsion.'

Hoob sat back and rocked in the chair, and Tallen realised Hoob didn't understand it at all.

Tallen gave Hoob a moment to try and work out why

MedTech would let such an investment walk away. They hadn't seemed that disappointed. They'd told him no experiment fails – it just gives more valuable data.

And then he leaned forward and inked his finger with the blood on the desk, and rolled it across Hoob's notepad, leaving a perfect print, and said, 'I have a death compulsion.'

He hadn't yet found a good way to say it. No one reacted well to it, though he'd discovered the word death went down better than suicide. It was always the same. They were fascinated, wanting details – what was he thinking *right now*, what sort of *detail* did he consider, had he ever actually *tried* something – or else they were disgusted. It stopped every form of interaction. Once anyone knew about it, everything else was swept away. Tallen had walked out of the hospital after signing away any rights to compensation from MedTech and tried to go back to his work, but found he couldn't concentrate on anything. He couldn't talk to anyone without thinking about –

'What are you thinking now?' Hoob said. 'Right now.'

'A close second is this job,' Tallen said. 'It's perfect for me. I came out of hospital, and I'd changed. I searched around and I knew this was what I needed. You don't know how much I –'

'But right now?'

'I could pick up that rig again and go for you with it.' He made himself lean back, uncontrollably trembling with the excitement of it, the possibility, the adrenaline thrill. 'I wouldn't make it, I wouldn't even get close –' Tallen glanced at the ceiling monitors. 'You'd make your move, I'd be shot in the back, or more likely a head shot. They wouldn't take chances with me, no matter how safe that reference says I am.' He felt a shiver of anticipation. 'Suicide, not murder. That's my compulsion. I could be dead in a moment. I could do it.' He leant fractionally forward once more and came onto his toes, couldn't help himself, watching Hoob tense. 'That's what I'm thinking right now.'

'But you won't do it.'

Tallen thought, does he seriously expect me to say no, to undo the possibility?

It took Hoob a moment to realise that. 'Okay,' he said. 'Let's move on. What do you know about the rigs?'

'I didn't think I needed to know that much.'

'No. What do you do, exactly?' He was holding the application in his free hand.

'I'm a fixer. Stuff that's too expensive or difficult to replace, sometimes I can fix it. Though I don't seem to have the concentration for it any more. Since what happened.'

Hoob said, 'Okay. You know why we ask for handwritten applications?'

'Graphology. Filtering crazies like me.'

'Graphology?' He laughed. 'No. It gives us DNA. We trawl your experiential history and your genetic and epigenetic imperatives. Of course a few forms come back to us machine-clean, but we don't interview those applicants. You know what we got from your application?'

'That I'm applying for a job working on a rig.'

'A history of this attitude, yes. We know your life, everything. You think it was that attitude got you assaulted?'

'*It* didn't get me – assaulted, as you call it.' Tallen closed his mouth, realising how badly he wanted this job, even though he didn't exactly know why, then said, 'I need some time to think. Being alone doesn't concern me, never has, but after that, I find I need… I don't know. Maybe it's time to change.'

'Not goddery, though. You don't need that?' Hoob looked at the ceiling. 'One of our filters is for theistic tendencies. The sea has an effect on people. Disorientation, scale, isolation. These things make some people want to believe in something. It's simply too much. Sometimes they try to destroy the rig. Sometimes they jump.'

'Not me. I nearly died, Hoob. It made me… it made me think.'

'It made you think what?'

'I don't want to die.'

Hoob sat back and laughed. 'You don't want to die? You, Tallen? You want me to have you shot in the head, and you *don't* want to die?'

'That's right,' Tallen said as evenly as he could. 'It's the idea of it. The knowledge that I can have it, that it's under my control.'

'Right.' Hoob chuckled. 'And you want to work on a rig because, actually *because* you don't want to die? Have I got that straight?'

'Yes.' Though in truth, Tallen didn't really know why he wanted to work on a rig. It had just struck him that this was the only thing he was suited for, any more.

'Hell,' Hoob said, wiping a tear away. 'Hell, Tallen, you are just perfect.'

'Once you've got me set up, I can't pull out, like I told you. I think this thing, this problem, gives me a sense of control over myself. That's how I see it.'

Tallen picked up the little rig again, which seemed to sober Hoob.

'Okay,' Hoob said, and raised an image of a rig onto the wall, and swivelled his chair so they were both facing the image. 'That's a rig on the Southern Sea. Tell me what you think you know about the rigs. You want a tasse?'

'Please.'

'Sweetener?' Hoob grinned. 'Maybe a lethal toxin? Or do you just imagine the possibility of that?'

'I've been out a while. I've heard all the jokes.'

'Don't be so sensitive. Or maybe you're goading me into…' He ran a finger across his throat, lolling his tongue. Tallen closed his eyes, opened them to Hoob muttering sourly, 'Your tasse is on the way. The rigs, then. What do you know?'

'Under the sea, there are faultlines. At some of those, core's close to the surface. The rigs locate, drill and extract it.'

A knock on the door, and steam looped into the airconned room as Hoob's assistant put the tray down, keeping his eyes professionally away from Tallen. Tallen wondered reflexively how much of a burn he could give himself. Not enough. He wasn't interested in pain.

'Go on,' Hoob said.

'The core gets piped to the shore stations. That's it.'

'That's it, Tallen?'

'You want me to tell you about the rig processors?'

'Everything you think you know.'

'I don't. The rest is rumour.'

'So tell me the rumours.'

'They say the sea acts as a preservative. That's why people want to be cast there in death, even the unregistered, and why AfterLife drops the sarcs there. One story is that the source of the preservative is core leaching from the bottom of the sea. The rumour is that the rigs don't just extract core, they separate and purify the preservative element. The rumour is that Ronen's discovered the secret of eternal life.'

Hoob sipped delicately at his tasse. 'And what do you think of the rumours, Mr Tallen?'

'I'm not a scientist.'

'You'll have an opinion.'

'The Song's full of stories. Even if there's any truth, the solution won't be simple. There won't be an end to death. Money will be involved. It won't make any difference to me.'

'You're a cynical man. Maybe you'll be closer to the secret of eternal life on a rig. Have you thought of that?'

'First you say I'm unsuitable because I'm trying to kill myself, and now I'm unsuitable because I'm looking for eternal life. I don't want either, Hoob.'

'There are people who would pay a lot of money for the secret, if someone could get it for them.'

'I expect your security is effective.'

'That isn't an answer, Mr Tallen.'

'You didn't ask me a question, Hoob. But I have no interest in money. I'm not an industrial spy. You can check on me.'

'We have checked on you, Mr Tallen, as I have already told you, and I am checking your responses as we speak, and our psych will be looking at this interview and checking further on you. We'll talk to MedTech. Presumably one of their concerns was that you might kill yourself on their premises and incur legal costs. Mine would be that you might want to sabotage a rig. Do you want to sabotage a rig?'

'I thought we'd established I don't want to die.'

'You might still want to sabotage a rig. Someone once

had that idea, setting explosives, casting herself into the sea and imagining she'd be preserved and become immortal. Crazy logic.'

Tallen smiled. 'Your security failed, then.'

'I should have phrased that differently. That was her intention. It was extracted by Dr Veale at the next stage of the interview process. The applicant got past me. Very few people have ever reached a rig and succeeded in carrying out anything unexpected.'

'I thought many of your workers die on the rigs.'

'Not unexpectedly.'

'You expect some to die, then?'

'We expect everyone to die, Mr Tallen. A few don't, and that is a bonus. Every applicant – every successful applicant – imagines they will be the exception. You, of course, might not, with your, ah, condition. Do you have any more questions?'

'Not right now.'

'You only get now.'

'Then no,' Tallen said.

'Okay. You have no relatives? Next of kin?'

'No. No one.'

'That's always easier. Minimum tour's five years, with no return in that period for any reason. Our investment in you is too much. The whole rig and its support system has to be configured to your neural and psych statuses.' Hoob swivelled his chair and said, 'Before you go, let me show you something. This happened recently.'

Tallen realised the image on the wall wasn't a snapture at all, as it began to move. The weather around the structure looked as hard as the rig itself. Sleeting rain, and thundercloud like clods of hammered iron. The rig was slightly off horizontal, but the only fixed point was the frame of the image, so it was impossible to be sure; the sea had no visible surface, whipping and crashing into black-shadowed troughs and grinding slabs of ice-white foam.

The rig shifted abruptly, settling back towards horizontal but then continuing to move. The clouds began to surge and the sea came up and down.

Hoob said, 'This was shot from the nearest rig. The image has been cleaned as much as possible, but it was across fifty kils of sea and hard weather. At this point the storm's about two days high.'

The storm carried on. After a while, the rig started to tilt more, and then it lurched. Around it were black dots – sarcs, Tallen realised – tossed high. In another ten seconds the rig tipped over, splintering, and was gone. *Sound and fury*, Tallen thought, and wondered where the words had come from. Had there been a woman?

'We lose about two every year like this,' Hoob said. 'It's seldom the structure that initiates failure. It's the software, and that would be you, Mr Tallen. You still want to work on a rig?'

'Yes.'

He nodded. 'Okay. You're a long way from an offer, but I'm prepared to put you forward for the pre-acceptance psychs. Before you say yes, you must understand that there's a significant morbidity rate to the investigations, morbidity meaning permanent disability and/or death, of three point eight per cent. This risk is entirely yours and uninsurable. Do you understand and accept this?'

'I'm already uninsurable.'

'Please answer.'

'Yes.'

'Your acceptance is recorded and confirmed. This is now a contractual arrangement, Mr Tallen. Should you be, at the end of the investigations and induction, undamaged and able to carry out the job of rig maintenance, you will be given one day's accompanied leave before being taken to the rig. Once on the rig, for security reasons, there will be no communication externally other than via the company's links and by company agreement. Do you have any questions, or anything to say?'

Tallen told him, 'Just that I won't need the day.'

Sixteen

ALEF

SigEv 20 A return

Other than a few times in passing, I hadn't seen Pellonhorc since we had arrived on his father's world. I had sunk myself into Solaman's lessons. Ethan Drame had not mentioned Pellonhorc, nor had anyone else.

And then I saw him again. I'd had a long day, almost nineteen hours working, and I was tired.

I was sitting at the small table in my kitchen when he arrived. I knew immediately that it was him. Three raps of equal weight and at exact intervals on my door, as he had always announced himself at my parents' house on Gehenna. My heart was pounding by the third rap.

He looked pale and I could see he'd lost weight, too. I felt uncomfortable with him looking at me with such intensity, so I visualised the comforting, shivering glitter of my weave. I could see him through it, though, standing there. I realised with a shock that he was and had always been there in my head, that he was an irremovable part of me.

'Come inside,' I said, and then, when he didn't speak, I added, 'Where have you been?'

Inside, he didn't sit down. 'You've been helping my

father, haven't you?' he said. 'Like your father did. And you're doing well.'

I felt I was missing something. I often felt that, though, except when I was thinking of the weave.

'Yes,' I said, trying to remain safe. It was harder, now. Pellonhorc was a sudden reminder of my parents, and I felt churned. 'I have putery that can carry out as many calculations in a second as –'

'Shut up, Alef. You haven't changed at all. I need to talk to you.'

I looked away. 'Guess which is the larger number: the number of calculations per second that my putery can make, or the number –'

An odd sound was coming from Pellonhorc. I looked at him and I shut up. I'd never seen him cry before. It snapped me out of the maths.

'Oh, you poor child,' I said, instinctively remembering what to do. 'Come here.' I opened my arms, as my mother had done for me so many times. Pellonhorc stood rigid for an instant – what on Earth did he think, I wonder, at my attempt to mothercomfort him? – and then he collapsed into my arms.

I didn't kiss his forehead as my mother had kissed mine – he was too tall, in any case – but we held each other, and I felt his tears on my cheek. I felt an odd sense of completeness. I know exactly how long we stood there.

We stepped away from each other.

'I want to talk to you, Alef. Not here.'

Other than to The Floor, I hadn't been out with any purpose for months. If I wanted anything, someone would get it for me. I'd walk, though, from time to time, just wander through the streets and watch the day come and go around me, counting the people, the windows, vehicles, calculating and comparing.

It was late evening and the streetlumes were bright as we walked together. Pellonhorc kept glancing back, and stopped frequently to let store displays wash over him, and made us backtrack a few times, though it was clear he wasn't lost or interested in what might be bought. I asked if something was the matter, and he just said, 'Nothing. Habit.'

Eventually we went into a small bar, the Drinkery. The music was loud and the owner seemed to know Pellonhorc, showing us to a table in the corner. Pellonhorc sat with his back to the wall, drumming a finger on the table.

'Have you ever wondered why we came to Gehenna, Alef? My mother and I?'

A memory suddenly returned to me, triggered by the question. I, who forgot nothing, had almost forgotten this. I said, 'I asked you once. Just after you arrived.' There was music playing in the café. The rhythm was urgent, almost a hum. 'You wouldn't say.' He'd beaten me for even asking. I said, 'Don't you remember?'

Without looking at me, he said, 'No.'

I said, 'After Ligate… well, after that, I just assumed your father had been trying to keep you both safe from him.'

'We'd have been safer from Ligate here.' He was constantly looking around. I was feeling nervous.

Pellonhorc went on, 'My father did things to me. You can imagine, I expect.'

Images from the pornosphere flicked through my mind. I remembered the first time Pellonhorc and I had plunged into it, in my father's office, and the sites he had exposed me to. Did he mean that?

'He used to hit my mother, too.' His voice was extraordinarily steady, telling me this. I recognised in it the way that I spoke. It startled me to realise he had modelled his veneer of control on my own.

'My mother said she'd take me from him,' Pellonhorc said. 'She was the only one he ever paid attention to, Alef. He needed her. He let her take me to Gehenna just to keep from losing her forever.' His voice broke. 'But now she's dead and I'm back with him.'

'Can Madelene do anything?'

He shot me a look of scorn. 'Madelene always wanted my father to herself. But with my mother dead, she has what she deserves. He needs someone to beat as well as someone to fuck and spend money on. Now she's everything to him.'

He said this as if it was natural, as if I'd understand it. 'She blames me for it. She shouts at him, and he –' Pellonhorc looked directly at me. 'He doesn't always take it out on her. He knows she'd walk out.' In the sharp light of the café he looked hollow-eyed and ill. He said, 'We have to do something.'

'It isn't so simple.'

He laughed so loudly that a few people turned to look, though they turned away again quickly enough. In an instant Pellonhorc had gone from terror to laughter, and I was confused. I'd forgotten how swiftly his mood could change.

'What?' I said.

'Of course it isn't simple. My father is who he is.'

I realised at last why we were here. Pellonhorc had arranged that it was safe to talk here.

'What are you thinking of doing?' I said.

He looked at me carefully, leaning towards me so that

the music cocooned us. 'He killed your parents, as good as. You think we should kill him?'

I felt sick. I hadn't realised how scared I was of Drame until now. I saw how ludicrous all my thoughts of biding my time had been. I knew I'd never dare do anything to hurt him. As a child I'd been scared of Pellonhorc, but that fear was nothing compared to my terror of Ethan Drame. And the bizarre thing about it was that Drame had done nothing personally to me. The threat was just there. It was the memory of his face on that tiny screen in my father's office, and my failure to turn the screen off or flee, and Ethan Drame's voice telling me, 'I can *reach* you.'

'No,' said Pellonhorc after a moment, with a sigh. 'We'll never do that, Alef. Don't worry. But one day I'll prove myself. I'll prove to him that I'm worth more than he thinks. Then his attitude will change.' He smiled at me. 'I'll be his son again, and in time, in good time, I'll inherit his empire. What about that? Will you help me?'

My heart was returning to normal. 'Yes. Yes. I will.'

'Good. I knew I could rely on you. You know something, Alef?'

'What?'

'We have a special bond, you and I. My father had it with your father, and I have it with you.'

I remembered what my father's bond with Ethan Drame had done for him, and for me, though I knew Pellonhorc hadn't meant that.

He ordered drinks. When they came, the waiter slopping them onto the table, we raised the glasses to each other and we drank.

'I have no one else, Alef. You and I, we have to stick tight.'

I nodded, flushed with the alcohol and this renewal of our bond. For a few minutes we sat together and let the music thump around us.

'So. What have you been doing?' I asked him when the beat slackened.

'I check the businesses. I keep people in line.'

'I'm sure you're good at that,' I said, meaning nothing by it.

'Yes, I am,' he said, glancing around. He swiped his payflake over the reader and waited for it to clear, then said, 'I'm sure you're good, too.' He drained his drink and stood up. 'It was good to see you again, Alef. We'll talk again soon. I wouldn't mention this to my father. But if he says anything, don't deny you saw me, and say we talked of old times. Drop by here a few times a month. Establish a routine.'

And he was gone.

SigEv 21 The weave catches me

The weave shivered and grew. I spent my days watching it, and my nights thinking of it, trying to avoid sleep and the dreams that came. When a few strands of the weave broke, I thought only of how to mend, or cross-connect.

I no longer dwelt on how my suggestions might be implemented. If I ever started to consider the hard consequences, the coercion and the extortion, I imagined Ligate killing my father and my mother. Everything I suspected Ethan Drame might be doing to anyone, I visualised happening simply to Ligate.

It wasn't hard for me to shift my gaze in this way. Without Solaman around, I could, to a great degree, subdue the empathy that my mother had bequeathed me.

I was alone, and it didn't seem to matter. The friendship I had with Pellonhorc was replaced by my relationship with the weave. I thought of Pellonhorc occasionally, but his absence didn't matter. That strange conversation we'd had in the Drinkery stayed in my mind, though. I walked there now and then, late at night, as he'd suggested, and sat in the corner and sipped a drink and left. There was never a message for me, and the talk we'd had became an odd, inexplicable but warm memory. The first few times I sat there, bargirls and boys flirted with me, but I waved them away and the attention stopped. I tried not to think of Solaman.

The periphery of the weave interested me more than its core. This was its unsteadiest section. These strands frequently snapped, and with consequences that I found hardest to fix. I'd sometimes make recommendations that Drame would tell me were not viable, and it was rare for Ethan Drame to say this.

But at the same time, new outer anchors would suddenly appear without my consultation, and I'd be told to incorporate them into my plans. These new anchors were often on the outer, minor planets and moons.

I began to notice, however, an increase in the frequency of anchor-establishment in the Eden String, on the Vegaschrist cluster. I extended the business generally in that direction, and since it was an entirely new area of the web, and of uncertain stability, I proposed that when we brought new businesses into the organisation, we give them a limited degree of autonomy, and allow them access to a limited range of the markets we also controlled. In that way we allowed them to build their own businesses, and both they and we profited. Despite arguing that it exhibited weakness, Ethan Drame agreed to it. Now and then one of these businesses took advantage, or tried to, and we closed them down. It didn't happen often.

It all seemed to be going very well.

SigEv 22 Pireve

There was one person on The Floor to whom I spoke more than anyone else. She had arrived there a few months after me, and her name was Pireve. She, like me, was interested in expanding the weave more than in its general stability and fabric. We exchanged ideas and smiles. I found myself searching her out. In some odd way, I felt comfortable with her. Others on The Floor began to glance at the two of us.

Once a week I had a meeting with Ethan Drame. Generally there were three of us: myself, Drame and Madelene, who just stood at Drame's shoulder looking bored. Occasionally, one of the specialists from The Floor joined us, but Solaman was no longer there. Mostly we discussed minor issues and their solutions, though occasionally there were real problems. One of these surfaced while we were working on the Eden String. Pireve brought it to my attention, wondering if it was a simple anomaly. It took me ten minutes to realise it was not. I messaged Drame from The Floor to ask for an emergency meeting.

'How much of an emergency is it?' he said.

'I don't know yet,' I said. 'Maybe I'm wrong, and maybe it's a big one. I don't want to make that choice.'

He leaned forward sharply, the screen already greying as he said, 'I'm waiting.'

I told Pireve to come with me.

Drame said, 'Who is this?' The light from the window fell in such a way across his head that the scar tissue glittered.

'Her name's Pireve. She spotted it first. I want her to stay.'

There was a heavy silence, and I realised I'd overstepped. 'Please,' I said.

Drame said nothing, and I took it for assent. His gaze slid over my shoulder and I heard the door slide open. I turned as Solaman came in. He was in a chair and he looked awful. He was wearing some kind of plastic mask on the right side of his face, and his left was deeply puckered towards the mask's edge. He tried to smile at me, but the smile didn't work at all. His chair was a full medical unit with overhead monitors and tubes feeding into the heavy base. Everyone could see the monitors except Solaman. It was clear that Solaman wouldn't outride his death much longer. For some reason, what most upset me was that his black hair was almost gone. His skull looked as pale and soft as cheese.

His chair came to rest at Drame's side.

'Go on,' Drame said.

'We have a problem on a small site in the Eden String. A few of our partner businesses there have been having problems we've been unable to make sense of.'

Drame sat back. '*This* is your red call?'

'What problems?'

It took me a moment to realise that this was Solaman speaking, his slurred voice leaking from the edge of the mask.

'Profits are reduced. I won't go into detail, unless you want me to.'

'No. Get on.' Drame never wanted detail. Just solutions.

'What we observed is illogical.'

Pireve said, 'Yes,' and I felt the touch of her fingers on my arm.

Drame ignored her and carried on looking at me, still without obvious interest.

I said, 'We checked the figures to make sure there was no mistake. There could have been reasons we hadn't considered.'

Drame said, 'And were there? Are you wasting my time?'

'There were none.'

'Have you approached the businesses? How many are we talking about?'

'At present, twenty. There may be more. It's complex.'

Solaman cleared his throat – it began as a human sound, but ended as the suck of a machine – and said, weakly, 'When Alef says it's complex, he means –'

'Shut up, Solaman. I know what he means. Alef. Have you asked any of these businesses for an explanation?'

'No,' I said.

Solaman tried to break in. 'It's –'

'I'm talking to Alef. Go on.'

Solaman was trying to protect me, but it wasn't necessary. He was dying and he couldn't let go of his sense of responsibility to me. I wanted him to know it was okay, but I couldn't say anything here. And maybe it wasn't okay. The touch of Pireve's hand felt electric.

I said, 'It's a pattern. It's a long way from Peco. I'm sorry, but you need a little detail. The businesses we're talking about are all within a few days' travel from Vegaschrist.'

Drame sat back against the chair and laughed. That surprised me. Vegaschrist was Ligate's stronghold, just as

Peco was Drame's.

I said, 'Someone is taking our business, and they're doing it in an extremely subtle and structured way.'

Drame nodded. 'And no one has come to us.'

'That's right.'

He leaned fractionally forward and said, 'How exactly is that?'

He wasn't stupid. He didn't ask who was doing it, but *how*. It was obviously Ligate. No one else was as powerful, and it was too close to Ligate's home. But the businesses were linked to each other – it was the nature of Drame's empire that every business he controlled had to feed and be fed by others – and these links simultaneously maximised profit and made treachery harder. For this to have happened without it being immediately obvious meant that another huge organisation was involved, with its own infrastructure and means of coercion. This could only be Ligate.

I said, 'Either they're more scared of him than they are of you, or they see more security with him. Probably both.'

Solaman whispered, 'Alef doesn't mean that, Ethan.'

'Be quiet, Solaman. Of course he means it.' Drame stared at the window, where it was late evening or nearly dawn, the sky purple-streaked black and quite starless. Twenty-five sleepdays away was Spetkin Ligate. Drame said, 'Get me Belleger.'

Solaman twitched a finger and his chair jerked forward and headed for the door. From his desk, Drame delayed opening it so that Solaman almost crashed into it. After he had left, Drame gave Pireve an odd look that I failed entirely to understand, and said, 'You, woman, get out.'

Pireve ran to the still-open door and was gone.

'It's not her fault,' I said. 'It's not Solaman's, either.'

Drame dropped his voice and said, 'Do you want the blame, Alef? You're asking me for that?'

I was suddenly aware of the full force of his character. I remembered Pellonhorc with the stick pricking my palm, offering to push it through. I couldn't speak.

Once again, I was reminded that Ethan Drame's empire had been created out of this extraordinary power to intimidate, this power to promise death, and if necessary – or even if it wasn't necessary – to carry it out without consideration of risk or consequence.

But this was only part of his strength, because as soon as he had shown me this side of him, he said mildly, 'You did exactly the right thing, not contacting the renegades. From you, it's good. I expect it of you. But the woman wouldn't have known that. Why didn't she contact anyone herself before telling you? Is she witless? Should I dispose of her?'

'No. She's good.' It was true. The only reason she hadn't alerted the suspect businesses was because she hadn't been sure enough. It was lucky she'd come to me first, but spotting the signs had shown a perception and intelligence I'd never suspected in her. I might not even have noticed it myself so swiftly, had she not alerted me.

'She's very good,' I said. 'Keep her.'

Solaman would have said to dispose of her, simply to protect me, but he was out of the room.

Madelene smirked.

I realised that Drame had deliberately asked me the question while Solaman was gone.

As I was thinking of Pireve in this new light, and for some reason also remembering the shine of her blonde hair as she moved, Belleger came in.

Seventeen

BALE

Bale pulled on his flysuit after balling up his clothes and stuffing them into a wallbox. He still felt sore. It was good to be here at the Chute for the first time since leaving hospital. He could always think best when he was here, and he needed to sort out in his head what had happened down in the sewers.

Only eight other boxes were taken. It wasn't surprising, given the conditions today. Even here in the changing room, fifty metres from the go gate, the buffeting was coming through. He pulled down the visor and drew a clean breath, then checked the readouts of airspeeds along the main curves. He checked the fins on his forearms and pulled the gauntlets on. Rolling his arms, he stepped into the lightshower to check for rips in the suit and found one at a knuckle, the tiny fault picked out as a black spike. It took ten minutes to have the rip sealed to his satisfaction and then he showered again. This time the suit pressure held.

He walked down the corridor. Air was thudding now, and the turbulence warning was up.

Maybe he should have brought Razer. He'd promised her a ride in the Chute. But since he'd come out of the hospital a week ago, she hadn't contacted him. Maybe she hadn't known he was out. Maybe he should have called her.

At the entry gate, he felt his adrenaline pumping hot. He glanced briefly into the dizzying void, slipped across the lip and dropped into a dive, letting out the hip-to-ankle fins as the airdrive pre-accelerated him into a long soft glide, first down and then slowly up towards the go gate and the free wind.

He finned steady, checked left and right and visored the track beyond the go gate. The few other riders today were black tears in the wind. No onetimers today. No slowdowns or look-at-mes to cloud the ride. This was going to be good.

In the last few moments of the entry glide he warmed up, slaloming smoothly and tucking himself into a few easy rolls. The visor read the windspeed for him, hi-lit its currents, its eddies and fluxes. His eyescreenery was set to give him only the relatives. It didn't matter to him that the low was three hundred kph, the high adding an upfactor of twenty-eight. It was only the spread that mattered to Bale, and today was almost the best he'd ever ridden.

It struck him that he might not have been here. Might have died. For an instant he wobbled.

A message hung in the air in letters of light. LAST CHANCE TO ABORT AHEAD.

Bale steadied, put his head neatly through the O of TO, rolled again, straightened out of the hoop. He finned past the abort tube and was through the go gate's glittering ring.

A muscle pulled in his left thigh and he flexed it without thinking, and pitched too sharply into the open pipe. He was in the main Chute.

The entry turbulence was heavy and he took the first few kils slow, swinging dreamily from side to side, easing the sore muscle and settling into the ride. This was the best time, when the whole ride was ahead of him with its currents never the same, the track of hundreds of kils with its forks and turns and careening winds.

Another rider swung past, more impatient for speed, and Bale recognised him by the distinctive yaw, the slight undercontrol of a hipfin. Ghraith, Bale thought the guy's name was. He watched Ghraith bullseye down the pipe, fast enough but taking no real risks.

There was no one coming up behind Bale, so he let the wind carry him a while, then made some hard fin-turns and a few twists and screws until he was sure his leg wasn't a problem.

The visor's blood detector had registered spatter beyond the K. *Cli-cli-clik*. Tallen's blood? But Tallen had been found down the sidepipe, and the source was down the main outflow. Maybe the visor had malfed. It wouldn't be the first time. But that wasn't the only odd thing.

His leg seemed fine now. The manoeuvres lost him some speed, and another rider screamed past him, faster than Ghraith. Very fast. Curious, Bale switched the visor to actual and noted the green racing fins and the gold NTG soles of the rider's boots.

Bale hadn't seen anyone wearing NTGs for a long time. He relaxed again, slaloming smoothly. The Chute was a good place to think.

Something about Tallen's story hadn't made sense. Bale would probably have let it go if it hadn't been for Delta warning him off. And she'd been holding something back too, he was sure. Tallen had said his attacker had been in front, but then behind. And the pattern of attacks was odd, too. Tallen was an anomaly in the spree. The others were clean kill/runs. From what Bale had managed to get out of hospital records before they'd checked his authority and blocked him, the K had been playing with Tallen for a while down there before heading out of the sewers and starting his spree. If the K hadn't decided to return to Tallen, with Bale tracking him, Tallen would have bled to death down there, or been eaten by vermin or outflow acids and all trace of him gone.

Either way, Tallen was a lucky man.

Bale screwed into a shelf of slow air, intending to ride it until he found an interference wave to jump, but the slush eddying there must have held some magnetic rubbish, and by the time he found a good wave and thumped off the shelf he didn't have the velocity to clear the turbulence cleanly. He tumbled a few times and threw out the wrong fin and went into a tightening spin.

Pipe vermin. Of course. That would explain the perverse *cliklik*.

He shuffled fins and reset himself. He wasn't Chute-fit. And the visor was showing him an error, which looked like a rider at his side except that the rider didn't shift relative to Bale as Bale shifted. Nothing magnetic, then. He checked everything else, but the eyetech was intact otherwise. As Bale waggled, the error, a black tear, waggled.

Bale went sharply towards the wall and rolled. The tear did the same. Only this time it was a fraction late. Some fool.

'I don't want to play,' Bale said.

'I do,' came back, distorted.

The rider was good. Maybe it was the NTG guy again. He slowed back along the wall until Bale had passed him.

He had to be using mimic settings to copy Bale's ride and to try and confuse Bale, or else goad him into a smear, and Bale knew how to deal with that. He made some simple moves to keep the guy busy. There was an upcoming fifty-k straightline ending in a two-way fork.

As soon as they hit the straightline Bale finned away from the shadow rider and towards the wall. The shadow held steady with him. Bale accelerated at the wall and held close to it, fighting the drag, holding straight and fast in the thudding air. The visor threw him a proximity warning, then added an alarm for the failing integrity of his fins at excessive pressure. He counted a few seconds and then finned sharply away from the wall, firing himself directly at his shadow, at the same time slowing at max with all his spoilers out, arms and legs and hips. The other rider did the same thing and for an instant managed to hold position with Bale, but Bale was using the wall's drag as well as his fins, and he was closer to the wall.

He felt a surge of nausea at the deceleration. The visor darkened and cleared as the suit pumped hard and gave him a surge of blood and gravity, bringing him back from the near-faint. He straightened into a cruise position and checked the eyescreen.

The other rider was way ahead, down the left channel of the fork Bale had marked for his move. Yes, it was the NTG guy, gold heels glittering. Idiot.

Bale finned right.

He tried to think back to Tallen, but his concentration was gone. Maybe Bale himself was the problem after all.

The rest of the ride was uneventful. Bale half-expected the NTG rider to be waiting for him at dismount, but the only one there was Ghraith. They shared the long trip on the shuttle back to Lookout in silence except when Bale said, 'Hey, Ghraith. You see anyone else at the Chute today?'

'A few. Why?'

'Anyone wearing NTGs? Gold ones?'

'No. Why?'

Bale watched as Bleak shot past. He could see the docks and their cranes rising and falling, bringing in the chosen sarcs. 'Tried to tumble me,' Bale said.

Ghraith shrugged and looked out the other side where the shuttle was passing the rigworks. Bale stared too. The spiky architecture of the rising rigs was a scribble against the sky, redrawing itself as he watched; it wasn't simply the changing perspective from the shuttle, but the microvanes of the fine struts constantly adjusting to the wind, presenting nothing to be battered and whipped. They say each single rig costs more than it costs to build a fleet of freighters, but then a single reservoir of core was enough to justify the whole thing.

Ghraith chuckled at the window, and Bale said, 'What?'

'You're an off-duty Paxer, Bale, with a history of trouble. All of Lookout knows it now. Not everyone thinks you're a hero. I heard you were drunk. People are saying you could have saved that guy before he even got sliced if you'd been sober. You imagine you're not going to get attention?'

The shuttle jolted on and eventually sieved through the shield into Lookout. Ghraith left with a last glance, and Bale stood a moment on the platform, thinking back to the Chute. NTGs and a flysuit. He wouldn't be hard to trace. Even seemed vaguely familiar, the way he flew, though Bale couldn't place him.

Bale was still considering it an hour later as he arrived at Pax for his appointment with Navid. He could check the Chute-shops… and then what? Ghraith had said it; Bale was off-duty and a fair target.

No. For now, the wind could take him. If Bale saw him again, that was fine.

And he had a more immediate concern. Navid was going to be snitty with him, but for now he was a hero. Navid wasn't about to discipline a hero.

He took a breath before pushing the door open. He hadn't been in the Chief's office since the last time he'd been suspended. It was almost a ritual between them, Navid suspending him with a warning, then taking him back with another. This time, Bale was sure, he had to be in the green lane.

Navid sat back in the chair and linked his hands at the nape of his neck. It was impossible to read his face. 'Good to see you. Welcome back, Bale.'

'Thank you, sir.'

Navid let the back of the chair drop forward. 'Did you just call me sir?'

'Yes, sir. May I sit down, sir?'

'What is this? You never call me sir.'

'You never welcome me back, sir.'

'Drop it. You're fit and well? You got out of hospital when?'

'A week ago.'

Navid nodded. 'Been relaxing?'

'I've been working out. Loosening up.'

Navid was still nodding evenly. 'In the Fit Room here? I hadn't heard.'

'In the Chute.'

Navid glanced at him. 'Ah, yes. I never got that. What is it with the Chute? Not enough shit in your life?'

'It clears my head.'

'Right. I hope it's clear now. Sit. Just to get this out of the way, I take it you've read the report.'

Bale sat down. 'I just have a few questions.'

Navid wiped the back of his hand across his lips. 'Have you read the report?'

'That's why –'

'Everything's in the report. We've identified the K. He was a loner. Nothing more to it. Pax is not prepared to waste any more time on it. Do you understand this?'

This was a bit harsher than Bale had expected. He said, cautiously, 'Tallen doesn't fit.'

'Life's like that, Bale. It isn't today's puzzle with a solution next week. It's a mess.'

'I always thought our job was to clear up some of the mess.'

'Clear it up or keep it tidy, yes. And we've done that. Although it's starting to seem like you're part of the mess, Bale. What are you doing? Didn't Officer Kerlew see you? Did she talk to you at all? Did you listen?'

'Yes. Don't worry about her. She ticked all your boxes. I still have a few questions.'

Navid sighed. 'I've done my best here. It's closed. Vox is happy, which means we're all happy. Except for you. What do you want, Bale? A day? Will that do it? A week? Or maybe I should let you use your own time for it. Oh, but you have, haven't you? Despite what Officer Kerlew told you.' He started to stand up, changed his mind and sat again. 'You know what, Officer Bale? I think there's just one way to deal with it. You got your ID there? Let me see it.'

Suddenly knowing it was too late, Bale pushed his chair back and said, 'Sir. One day should do it. I just need access to the archive, to check a few things and I'll be done.'

'I know what you've been doing, Officer Bale. You understand the meaning of "leave"?'

'Yes, sir. My own time. I just thought –'

'It means leave it alone. Forget it. Don't you know a warning when you get one? You've had your warning. You don't know anything. You think this is a chat we're having? Give me that.'

Bale passed his Paxflake across the desk to Navid. Navid took a small niller from the desk and ran it twice over the flake. The first time it brightened, the second time it went dark. Navid snapped the flake in half.

'Now your wrist.'

'Sir?'

'You don't need to call me that any more. Not ever.' Navid held the niller to the skinscreen on the inside of Bale's wrist, lit it up and watched the small reader register and then start to kill the embedded Paxpack. He tilted it so Bale could see his job, which meant his whole life, seep away.

PAX LICENCE VOIDED

VOX ACCESS CANCELLED

PAX RANK REMOVED

As the program wore down, Navid said, 'You have the right to challenge this, Mr Bale. I think you know how far you'll get, though.'

PERSONAL CONTACT DATAFILE CLEARED

'You want to challenge it, Mr Bale?'

'No.'

PROCEDURE COMPLETE. PAXPACK DELETED

The letters faded. Navid said, 'Not quite done yet, Mr Bale. Watch the screen, please.'

THIS PACK MAY NOW BE USED AS A PERSONAL DATASTORAGE DEVICE. THIS DEVICE CANNOT BE REVERTED OR RECONFIGURED. ANY ATTEMPT TO DO SO WILL INSTANTLY ALERT PAX AND IS A CAPITAL CRIME

The small screen greyed. Bale cleared his throat and started to pull his wrist away, but Navid said, 'Wait. One last thing.'

SALARY – FULL DISCRETIONARY FINAL PAYMENTS AUTHORISED

The screen faded until all Bale could see was his bare wrist.

'Now we're done, Mr Bale. You can return your uniform and weaponry tomorrow. The weaponry is of course already disabled, and in the meantime you may not use the uniform or any material in your possession to pass yourself off as a Pax officer. Do you understand, sir?'

'Please. I –'

'Do you understand, sir?'

'Yes, sir.'

'Yes, *officer*, Mr Bale.'

Eighteen

ALEF

SigEv 23 Belleger

Drame said, 'Belleger, we have a small problem.'

Belleger was a soldier. He was the man who enabled what Drame called his reach. He stood in front of Drame like heavy shadow. The rumour in the building was that his speech modulator was broken, and if it could be fixed, people might talk to him, or at least be able to get into an elevator with him.

I said, 'I don't think Belleger is the answer to this.'

'Why not?'

'Because it's what Ligate wants.'

Drame said, 'Belleger, you can relax. This isn't a parade.'

Belleger shifted his stance. He didn't look any calmer.

I said, 'Ligate wants you to see it. He wants you to react.'

'He doesn't realise I know yet. I can't leave it. If I leave it, he'll continue. If I act now, I have surprise.'

Belleger said, 'Do you need me here, Mr Drame?' The timbre of his voice made me tremble. Even Drame seemed to wince momentarily.

Madelene swallowed and said, 'You don't need me,' and slipped quickly from the room.

Drame watched her go, then said, 'Tell him, Alef.'

So I told Belleger.

When I was done, Belleger took about half a second before rumbling, 'It's straightforward, Mr Drame. The first choice is whether we act at all. Can we use words? Will that be enough?'

'Alef?'

'No. This is a provocation. He's prepared his position. I don't know how, but he'll be ready to act.'

Drame said, 'How will he act, Belleger?'

The soldier didn't move or hesitate. I felt an odd sense of identification with him. He knew exactly how it lay. 'Ligate has options. He's set up a situation in which our options will be limited. He has a huge advantage in that the situation is of his making, and it is close to his home ground. In addition to this, he has more control of space, both locally and generally. If we attack, we can only come from one direction, since the unsaid planet is to his rear.'

The presence of the unsaid planet was to Ligate's advantage. No one risked entering their territorial space. Belleger certainly would not risk his forces being attacked on two fronts. Ligate had chosen his base well.

'So the arena is Ligate's, and he will be ready.' The room seemed to resonate with Belleger's speech. My eyes blurred. I'd never heard Belleger say so much, and he was still talking. 'I imagine he will have been ready for a long time, Mr Drame.'

'Will he, Belleger? That's interesting.' Drame turned his gaze back to me. 'Alef, is he ready?'

I wasn't prepared for this. I hadn't thought of it. My role was to monitor Drame's businesses and no more. 'I don't know. I could find out.'

Drame said nothing. The atmosphere in the room thickened. Outside, it was growing darker, the black overpowering the purple. Night.

I cleared my throat. 'I could carry out an analysis of factors associated with the arms markets. But any active searches I initiate might warn him that we're aware. Up to now I've done nothing unusual. We could lose the element of surprise. It's all we have.' And we only had that thanks to Pireve. I didn't say it.

The room slowly settled. The silence and stillness seemed especially deep. Drame nodded. 'Our options, Belleger. You've had time?'

'Enough. There are two options. In the first, you back down and accept the loss of Vegaschrist and consolidate your positions elsewhere. You set boundaries and make them strong. You would have to create a buffer zone and burn everything in it. In the second option, you prepare a physical response.'

Both men glanced at me. I nodded agreement.

'Outline a physical response, Belleger,' Drame said.

'He's ready for the fight. You might win, but if you do, almost everything will be lost in the process. You can only take this option if you are prepared to lose and you think he is not, that he's bluffing with everything he has, that he's not prepared to risk it all.'

I was feeling nauseous. I didn't know if it was Belleger's voice or the direction of his words. Neither disturbed Drame. I wanted to sit down, but I didn't want to draw Drame's notice.

Belleger said, 'Do you have any evidence that this is a bluff?' He waited, then when Drame didn't answer, he continued. 'Ligate has begun this. He knows the conversation we are having. He knows we are asking ourselves whether we believe he is prepared to lose everything. He knows you are asking yourself whether you are prepared to lose everything.'

'That isn't quite true,' I said.

Belleger turned to me. His eyes were quite empty.

'Go on,' Drame told me.

'We do have one thing. Ligate doesn't know we're having this conversation *now*. We're lucky that Pireve had her eyes on Vegaschrist just as the situation shifted. Because of that, I think we've identified the situation earlier than he expects. If I analyse the rate of activity, I think we have three weeks, maybe four, before he'd expect us to spot it.'

I had Drame's attention. I went on. 'At that point, when we can expect him to be entirely ready, he'll reveal his position. That means he's not quite ready yet. But he's close. When he is fully ready, he'll do something we can't ignore and he'll be prepared to deal with any response.'

Belleger was nodding now. A rumble came from his throat.

I said, 'He'll expect you to try to take them back instantly and straightforwardly and fail, and that you won't understand why. He'll want you to try harder and still fail, and eventually, only eventually, to become aware that something is significantly wrong. He'll want you then, too late, to try and withdraw and to realise that he's out-thought and broken you.'

Belleger grunted. It was a terrifying sound.

Drame nodded. 'I would stretch out for him to cut off my fingers. And then he would grasp my arm and chop off my hand at the wrist…' For almost a minute he looked out of the window, at the high unsilvered sky there, and then he said, 'But I shall destroy him first. Belleger, prepare it.'

Belleger stood straight, but didn't move. 'Mr Drame,' the soldier said, the room shivering with his voice. It seemed to me that Belleger was about to continue.

'Enough,' Drame said. 'Thank you, Belleger. Go.'

The soldier left.

As Drame slumped back in his chair, I wondered what Belleger might have been ready to say. Drame watched the depthless sky and said, 'This is it, Alef. This was what he meant.'

I knew exactly what he was talking about. I remembered Ligate's words precisely. *This is the start of it.* When I had been watching him murder my parents, he had been planning this. I looked at Drame's face. It was hard and without colour. His hands were set flat on the desk. Without thinking of the consequences, I said, 'What exactly did you do to Ligate's family?'

Still staring at the window, he murmured, 'I slapped him down, that's all. I had a big contract about to be signed with a third party, and he was trying to break into it. It was pure business. I meant a warning, but –' He wiped the back of a hand across his mouth. 'But perhaps I overshot. The deaths were an error. Ligate is no businessman. He's less than nothing.' He fell silent.

Maybe it was true. It didn't matter. 'And now?'

Drame roused himself. 'Ligate knows I won't back down. There is no such thing as consolidation in this, Alef. There is just death.'

I saw that this was exactly what Ligate wanted. In that

room of slaughter, with my dead mother and father, back on Gehenna, he had said he had nothing left. 'You'll be doing just what he wants. Don't you see?' My voice was shrill.

'Of course.' Drame was calm. 'We have no choice, Alef. It's the way of it. This had to happen, and I should have known it. It doesn't matter. I have never lost anything in my life, Alef. I shall destroy him and everything he has. I shall eliminate every memory of him until he never was.'

That determination was terrifying. Drame was telling me he had never lost anything. Did he believe that? I saw the two of them face to face, Ligate and Drame, and the answer came to me.

I said, 'There is another way.'

'Belleger told us the choices.'

'He told us his choices. There is another. And it's better.'

Drame drummed his fingers on the desk. 'Go on.'

'Remember, Ligate doesn't know he's exposed yet. If we can locate him, locate Ligate himself, and kill him, all this is over. It's a war between the two of you, not the businesses. If he's dead, it's over. After that, don't destroy what he had, but take it intact. Don't eliminate his memory, but rewrite it instead. There's more humiliation for him, more victory for you, in that.'

There was a long silence. I replayed my words in my mind. I went back over the last hour. All of this had happened in a single hour, from all being well to the end of everything. And I thought of Pireve with an aching sense of simultaneous discovery and loss. Oh, Pireve.

Drame frowned. 'How do we do that?'

He looked at me. Had I drifted away for a moment? Was the sky darker?

'Alef!'

'First, pull Belleger back. We must keep Ligate from realising we know anything. There must be no buildup. Just send people to try and persuade the businesses to come back to us, as we normally would, and when they fail, send more. Act like it's routine local resistance we think we can deal with. As Ligate expects. Let him think he's drawing you in, that he still has time.'

'We're giving him that time.'

'We'll be preparing, too, only he won't realise it.'

I was telling Ethan Drame to throw people to their deaths. It was like any one of my calculations. Like leaves falling from the number trees in my mind. I said, 'You have spies in his organisation?'

'Oh, yes,' Drame said softly, and for the first time, he smiled at me. 'Oh yes, my boy.'

'They need to know, in advance, where Ligate will be on a certain day. Just that. It has to be a location we can reach. You need Belleger to prepare a team to be there to kill him.'

'*That's* it?' His face began to colour. 'That's your plan? That's shit. Ligate squats on his planet. He moves around all the time, but he never moves offworld. Nothing brings him out, nothing of ours can infiltrate it.' He sat back, breathing heavily. 'Your plan's no better than Belleger's. To kill Ligate, we have to extinguish the planet.' He inspected me to see if I understood this, then said, 'The entire planet. Do you have any idea what that will cost me?'

I tried to keep calm. Talking to him was like being in freefall. 'We bring Ligate out. We bring him off-planet.'

'*I* hardly ever go off-planet. He *never* does.' Drame was losing patience.

'He would if he knew he'd capture you. If he were sure Ethan Drame would be there for the taking, unprotected.'

He opened his mouth, then closed it again and waited.

'Send Belleger ahead with his assassination team. That must be in total secrecy. It should be straightforward, since Ligate doesn't know we're already aware of his intentions.'

Belleger nodded.

I said, 'Now you tell your spies to let Ligate know that things are going so badly that you're coming out in person, secretly, to see what's going on. To change a few minds. You've done that before, haven't you?'

'Never as far.' His voice had steadied, but I could feel the suspicion. 'Never as close to Ligate as that.'

'You won't be on your ship, so there's no risk to you.'

Drame said, 'Go on.'

'Ligate won't be able to resist it. He'll get there ahead of you, and Belleger will be there ahead of him, waiting.'

He pushed back in his chair. 'Ligate might resist it,' he said, slowly. 'Or he might send a dummy, like last time.'

I tried to put the last time from my mind. 'You think he will?'

He smiled, considering it. 'No. He knows I never use dummies. And his dummy failed. He'll want to kill me face to face.'

'I think so, too. And he knows you take risks.' I returned his smile, but carefully, adding, 'You're even considering this one.'

His expression faded. 'Still, he might not bite. What if he doesn't?'

'We have your spies to tell us. But I think he'll bite. I think it's in his nature.'

'Yes,' Drame said with abrupt certainty. 'It is.'

'And if, after all, he doesn't head for the trap, we leak that you're aborting your trip and giving up on the area's businesses altogether. And you *do* that; you let it go completely. By then, Belleger and his team will be in place, remember. As war gets closer, Ligate will be developing a long focus. He'll forget what's close to home.'

'And Belleger will be sitting behind his front line,' Drame whispered, half to himself.

'Exactly –'

'– And goodbye, Spetkin Ligate.' Drame laughed, an extraordinary sound. I had never heard him laugh like that before. 'You are more than your father, Alef. Oh, you are so very much more.' The joy in his face was like some kind of lust momentarily satisfied. I had a glimpse, in that expression, of what drove him. I thought sharply at that moment of my mother, of what she might think to hear her husman and son spoken of in that way, and what I saw on her face was despair.

I shook away that image and said, 'It could fail.'

'Oh, no. I see Spetkin Ligate as well as I see myself.' Drame turned his face to the window. I couldn't tell if he was staring at the stars or at himself. He said, 'Ligate and I know each other so perfectly that his death will be in every mirror I ever look into.'

He inspected his fist as if it were made of gold. 'No. It won't fail, Alef.'

* * *

SigEv 24 The mission

A few weeks passed. Now that I was aware of Ligate's intentions, his preparations were easier to identify. I never made any actual enquiries and made sure no one else did, but I monitored the movements of his transport fleets, noted the additional fuel he bought and where he stockpiled it, and recorded the weaponry his companies bought as middlemen but failed to find a seller for. I noted where he stored it. I began to be able to guess where Ligate himself might be, and then, as my data accumulated, I began to be able to predict his movements.

In order not to alert Ligate, we had to send our people to their deaths, but we did so judiciously. I was careful to display mistakes not only in the Eden String but elsewhere too. Everyone knew Solaman was ill, and I let them think his replacement was proving inadequate.

Ligate grew more and more confident.

Belleger was not keen on my plan. He called it our alpha option, but I knew he was prepared for my plan to be his beta.

Belleger and I considered options for a large-scale physical response in the event that my plan failed. His military strategies were impressive and detailed. It was strange to see the unsaid planet's space mapped at all, let alone as a solid barrier. Not for the first time, I wondered how they lived. I went over the plans with Belleger, adjusting them where necessary to facilitate supply and other problems. I also made plans to adjust Drame's business structures in preparation for war. No action was taken, nothing discussed or documented, but I readied myself to free money and call in debts of allegiance.

The situation was not yet as bad as I had initially feared. While Ligate had already built up considerable reserves of transport and weaponry, at this point he had far less infrastructure than he'd need to mount an overwhelming attack that might carry him swiftly here to Peco. If it started now, the most likely outcome would be a huge initial loss on our part, followed by a slow attritional battle from which we would be slightly more likely to emerge victorious after the forced involvement of neutral planets. Ligate's real hope would be that his primary surge would be sufficient to gain sudden victory. Right now, he had a forty-eight per cent chance of this succeeding, but I was sure I'd be able to predict the launch of his attack with a few days' notice, and that would cut a few per cent off the probability. And while Ligate waited and prepared, we'd soon have Belleger in place.

It was a risk, of course: in order to give Belleger a chance of reaching his destination in secret and assassinating Ligate, we had to give Ligate more time to prepare. And Belleger might fail.

There was a brief exchange of views between Drame and Belleger. The soldier didn't want to lead the assassination team in person. He felt he was needed here, preparing for the beta option. Drame said it had to be Belleger leading the kill team. That way, there were only three of us, Drame, Belleger and myself, who knew precisely what was happening. And Drame trusted Belleger.

In the end, Belleger agreed. He could see the beauty of my plan, that Ligate would imagine he couldn't lose, that there was little risk and huge advantage in his leaving the security of Vegaschrist.

Belleger was a professional commander of soldiers, and

what he dealt in were not deaths but statistics. He and I were not so very different. He and his three-man team quietly departed Peco. Only Belleger knew precisely where they were going. Even I and Ethan Drame were unaware of the detail.

We waited two weeks for Belleger to be in place, then prepared for Drame's 'departure'. I began to organise the logistics of it on The Floor, stating the destination but not the passenger's name. It was clear enough that such security could only mean that it was Ethan Drame.

Drame's spies reported no leak reaching Ligate. I went on to arrange Drame's fastship along with a fiercely armed escort that Belleger himself had assembled, and I organised security on the ferry station.

After five days, coded word came back from Drame's spies that Ligate was aware of Drame's trip and was making his own preparations.

Drame and I were jubilant.

On the day of his 'departure', a small, armed convoy left the building as the sun rose, sweeping away into the pale sky. Even I didn't know how or at what point Drame was smuggled secretly onto it and then – far more secretly – off it again. Everyone was told he was uncontactable. I carried on working on The Floor, as usual, where everything was a little subdued. This was partly because Drame wasn't around and partly because Madelene wasn't either.

Madelene. There were, of course, not three, but four of us who knew.

Nineteen

TALLEN

There was nothing in the anteroom but a high green counter. As Tallen came through the door, a tinted glass safety screen slid up from the front of the counter to meet the ceiling, barring the secretary from him.

'I'm here to see Veale,' Tallen said. He glanced at the notices. RONEN – ARE YOU READY FOR THE ULTIMATE TEST?

The man behind the grey glass looked down. 'You're Tallen?'

'Yes.'

'I heard you looked bad, but not this bad. Go through.'

The room wasn't anything like Hoob's office. It looked like a cross between a medician's surgery and a physics laboratory. The man surveying him from behind a dull grey metal desk wasn't anything like Hoob either. He was short and fat-faced, his hands plump, fingers nailbitten.

'I'm Doctor Veale, Mr Tallen. Director Hoob's cleared you through to me, which usually means you're effectively a Ronen employee. But not always.' Veale scribbled something, then looked up at Tallen and said, 'I'll take the blade in your right palm, please, and the other one in your pocket. Thank you. Do you feel anxious without them?'

'No. I adapt.'

Veale closed the blades into a drawer and said, 'We like that, Mr Tallen. We can also adapt.' He wiped a slick of hair from his forehead. There was something shadowy at the edge of the high hairline that his palm bumped over. Tallen wondered whether it was tech or tumour.

'I understand you've got some implants,' Veale said. 'I'll need to check there's nothing untoward been slipped inside you. Sit, would you?'

Veale came round the desk and held a scanner up to Tallen's eyes. 'Look at the light, please. Thank you. And now the other eye. Good.'

He indicated a bank of screenery and said, 'Follow what happens carefully. Say anything you feel like saying, please, at any time. Ignore me.'

Veale's voice was so empty of emphasis that the man himself seemed to have disappeared from the room. Tallen concentrated on the main screenery, which was split by a thick horizontal line. After a moment, the line swayed and separated into two lines, one travelling up and one down, so that he had to choose which to follow. He followed the upper. This also split in two.

Veale's voice continued. 'You'll be remotejacked into the rig's putery. No, don't look at me. I don't like your implants, Mr Tallen. Hoob does, but he's thinking of his budget.'

'I have no motive –'

'Your implants may have some element of recording or memory function. I'm checking they're no more than they seem and that they aren't pre-loaded. I'm going to take you through a series of repeats and prompts to check your reactions. See how you react and how much you assimilate, consciously, unconsciously and maybe otherwise.'

Tallen grew aware of his eyes flicking up and down, from line to line. Had the line split this way a moment ago? Had he then looked at the upper or the lower? 'Why would you tell me that while I'm doing it?' He took his eye from the line, focused on a blank area. Was he anticipating something? The blank area remained empty. He felt hot. 'You want me to screw it up. You want me out. Is that it?'

'If you're tainted, yes, Mr Tallen. Are you tainted?'

There were words on the lower screen. Tallen's attention went straight to them.

IGNORE ANY WORDS. JUST CONCENTRATE ON THE LINES

He went back to the lines, aware of the words fading and returning at the periphery of his vision. He couldn't prevent himself from glancing at them again.

DO NOT READ THIS OR WHAT FOLLOWS

'This is stupid, Veale. You're making me fail.'

'Keep going, Mr Tallen. Now, everything I tell you in here is confidential. It will be scrubbed from your memory should you fail the assessment. You may lose other brain function along with it. If necessary, I will also disable your implants. Do you know how we get to the core? How we process it?'

The lines changed colour, from black to blue and yellow. Tallen said, 'Do I need to?' The colours switched round. Tallen stuck with blue.

'For practical purposes, no. For psychological, yes. As you know, there are reservoirs of gas beneath the sea floor. At the base of these reservoirs is often a stratum of rheotite. Have you heard of rheotite?'

'Everyone's heard of rheotite, Veale.'

THE YELLOW LINE REPRESENTS RHEOTITE. DO NOT FOLLOW RHEOTITE

The line he was following disappeared. He flicked his eyes to the other line, which seemed to elude him, jumping and weaving. He said, 'What do you want from me?'

'Reactions. Do you know more than I might expect, or less? Tell me, are the lines on repeat-patterns? Are you following them identically at each repeat? Tell me about rheotite.'

'The hell with you. Rheotite's peculiar to Bleak. It's a thermal insulator. It's used to line furnace walls. Firefighters have suits of rheotite alloys. The newest spaceship engines rely on it.'

FOLLOW THE BLUE LINE

'Indeed, Mr Tallen. The thermal conductivity of rheotite is extraordinarily low. Rheotite is the reason why a cool reservoir of gas, barely beneath the sea floor, can be a matter of a hundred metres from liquid core. A temperature difference of about seven thousand degrees. Follow the line, Mr Tallen. Am I telling you something you ought already to know? *Did* you know this?'

YOU ARE NOT FOLLOWING THE CORRECT LINE

'Do you follow me, Mr Tallen?'

Veale's monotone seemed to have merged with the words on the screenery.

REMEMBER TO IGNORE THE WRITING

'Go to hell.' The line became seven threads, crossing and swelling at random. Tallen let his eyes lose their focus.

'What about this? The floor of a gas reservoir is often very close to the upper boundary of an upflux of core. The presence of rheotite is diagnostic of this.'

Tallen couldn't remember whether he'd known any of this.

'What we've found is that if we drill through a gas reservoir and find rheotite, we will almost certainly go on to access core.'

'Isn't that dangerous, once the rheotite is penetrated?'

'Don't you know, Mr Tallen?'

YOU KNOW, DON'T YOU?

'No.'

'Really? The core would cool very rapidly and self-seal. The problem is actually not so much that the core would flood out, as that it would cool swiftly in the reservoir cavity to leave a thick and impenetrable mantle. Solid core is not what we want.'

'Then why doesn't that happen when you penetrate the rheotite with your drill?'

'Because we line our casings with rheotite.' Veale leaned forward. 'Core is our aim, but rheotite is the key. The pipes still occasionally blow.'

'But surely the temperature drop when they blow simply makes them set solid, like you just said.'

'Not instantly, Mr Tallen. There's a significant discharge of back pressure before this happens. Dense, superheated material at high velocity. In a gas reservoir, it usually gets absorbed. Not in a casing. It rarely happens, though. If it should happen, there's nothing you can do. You'd be dead and the rig would cease to exist. In an extreme case, depending on where along its length the pipe blows, the sea would be vaporised in the area. We have satellite images of such an event. A localised, point-focused inrushing tidal wave, like a plug being pulled. I won't show you. What Hoob impressed you with was nothing to this. The coriolis effect was interesting.'

Tallen followed the line. Just the one, now, and flickering black to green along its length.

'So. The core fills the tanks – rheotite-lined – and is processed for temperature stability. The process is designed to be efficient. Should we have a problem with the tank, there are emergency disconnect systems.'

'Don't the tanks change the rig's stability once they start to fill?'

'The tanks are initially filled with a special mud, an inert material precisely as dense as core. As the core fills the tank, it displaces the mud to the sea bed. The stability of the rig never changes. Once the rig is running, the fresh core displaces the processed material. This is, of course, before the destabilising effect of the sea is taken into account.'

'And what happens to the processed core?'

'It's piped back along the sea bed to shore-based shipping plants. Contrary to common knowledge, it's never used to power the rigs. It would be too dangerous to release exposed core. Are you going to ask me how we power the rigs, or do you know?'

There were words somewhere on the screen. Tallen looked away from them. There was an image of snow in his mind. Snow and… It was gone.

He said, 'I don't know. I can't remember.'

'I'll remind you. When we take core through the reservoir, it comes up with a gas cap. The gas is diverted and used to power the rig and all the processes. It's an elegant system, no waste. That's how and why rigs are self-sufficient. Except for food, but there's only one human to cater for.'

The screenery went abruptly grey.

'You can relax, now, Mr Tallen.'

'Is that it?'

'I'll tell you when that is. You know what can go wrong on a rig?'

'Remotejack failure?'

'Secondarily, yes. Try again.'

'Rig hardware failure.'

'Secondarily. Try again.'

'Overwhelming weather. Drill fault.'

'All secondarily. Human error is the main primary problem. Mood, Mr Tallen. You get depressed, you don't think so efficiently. That's no good to us. We need stable people on rigs, and we need to keep them stable. We favoured the high-functioning autistic spectrum personality, but some couldn't sift the minor from the major, couldn't prioritise effectively.'

'You put someone alone on a rig for five years and more, how do they not get mood swings?'

'There are two specialised humechs on the rig. These humechs aren't just the rig's fault gauges. They're for you, too. They are loaded with theraputery, and will monitor and assess your neurological state. They will examine your mood and correct you.'

'How do they do that?'

'If you get to the rig, you'll find out.' Veale sat down. 'This is a closed room, Tallen. That means it's entirely private and unmonitored.' He stretched out his arms and yawned. The sudden modulation in his voice surprised Tallen. 'Nearly done. Listen to me. Everything isn't quite as I've told you. You still may not get to a rig, but you can't get out of Ronen now.'

'I don't want to.'

'No.' Veale linked his hands behind his head. 'You aren't typical, Mr Tallen. Ronen have taken you, but I don't know why you're here. I don't know why you want to be, and I don't know why Hoob's let you get through to me. I know about the suicide impulse. I can't work that out.'

'Nor could the people who left me with it.'

'You know how long most people last on a rig?'

'If they survive their first tour, they don't ask to go back, do they? They have enough money.'

'We've never let one back on a rig. That's the truth. If they come back, they come back close enough to crazy. Now and then, someone stays out there beyond their first five. No one's ever lasted more than seven. You still want to go? I'm just curious.'

'Yes.'

Veale shrugged. 'Okay. You've got it. You're through.'

'And?'

'That's it. We're done.'

'That's it? But you know all this, how it drives people crazy. You've checked I'm right for it. You have to prepare me for it now. Isn't that your job, once you've accepted me?'

'No, Mr Tallen. You can't be prepared for a rig. You can be out there a year, day up, day over, and think you know it all, and the next day, *every* next day, will show you something new, something worse. All I can do is warn you. So if you want to be prepared, listen to me.' He flicked a finger on the edge of his desk and said, 'Three things. Number one, you are not prepared for it.'

'Your job is to prepare me.'

'No. You will never be prepared, and the last part of my job, if you're accepted, is to make you understand that. We used to try to prepare people, but it was worse than hopeless. If you ever get to a point where you think you're ready for the rig, you're only ready to die.'

He flicked the desk again. 'Which is number two. As soon as you get to the rig, you are about to be dead.'

Tallen said, 'I think that's clear.'

'Don't be smart with me, Mr Tallen. You're not the first and you're not clever. Shall I tell you how I know you're not clever?'

'Tell me.'

'You came here in the first place, knowing what everyone says about rigwork, and you're still here now. If you were in any way clever, you'd be somewhere else. It isn't smart to want to work on a rig, and it isn't brave. On top of all that, you're not scared. So you're dumb too.'

Tallen shrugged.

'But you still think you're clever. What's number one?'

'I am not prepared.'

'Yes. And number two is that you are about to be dead.'

Tallen leaned forward and flicked the desk with his own finger. 'And number three is?'

'You don't need to worry about number three. It's the easiest one of all. We're doing it now. Number three is why you're sitting here. You're someone else's number three.' He waited for Tallen to show he got the point. 'You're only here, Mr Tallen, because someone else got killed. So that's number three; because of you, someone else *after* you is also going to get killed. So you just worry about the first two.'

Tallen said, soberly, 'So I'm not prepared and I'm going to die.'

'You're starting to hear me.' Veale sat back. 'Now. You want to say something?'

'I'm not prepared and I'm going to a rig to be killed. What's the point of me saying anything at all?'

'That's good. Don't talk. Listen.'

Tallen tried to concentrate on the pen the psych was turning in his fingers, wondering if he could lunge for it. Veale had been ahead of him all along. He reckoned Veale would be prepared for anything he might try. He felt himself starting to shake.

As if confirming Tallen's thoughts, the psych closed his hand on the pen and said, 'Your rig allocation is in one of the worst sea regions. I don't know what you did to him, but Hoob must have taken against you. He pushed you through and ticked you for this one. I'll be honest with you, Mr Tallen, you test at the edge. My gut feeling is there's something I couldn't reach, but –' He sighed. 'Anyway, with an attitude like yours, you won't last long enough for me to find your replacement. Are you still listening?'

'You're full of shit, Veale.'

'Mr Tallen, you have no idea what you're going out to. I'm trying to help you. Your rig's seen rogue waves topping fifty metres, and it regularly sees sucking ebbs of more than twenty. In a bad sea, the topside architecture only rises to one-thirty, so you'll occasionally be overwhelmed.'

'Why don't they extend it higher?'

Veale nodded. 'You're listening. Stability. And it's designed to take direct hits from icebergs. You're armed with shatter beams – they operate automatically, you'll only be aware of them if the settings fail. The sarcs are a different matter. The current draws them into the area. They're legally protected, so you can't destroy them even if they threaten the integrity of the rig. In a bad sea, they can hit like torpedos.'

'What keeps the rig in place?'

'The rig's a semi-submerged, which means it floats, more

or less. Think of it as a balloon tethered to the sea floor. It's anchored to a base by a circumferential set of sixty chains. The base weighs close to a million tons. It won't shift. Rarely, at least. Distance from the lowest point on the rig's structure to the base is about five hundred em. The chains won't break. Rarely, at least. At the centre of the base is the wellhead. You with me? Too much information?'

'Go on.'

'The rig's a very simple thing. Other than structural stuff, there's just pipes and tanks. Pipes take gas and core from the well. Subsurface tanks around the rig hold core and gas piped from the well. Core is heavy, gas is light. Core acts as ballast, gas as a buoyancy agent. You shift them around, you keep the rig stable. You deballast and re-ballast, pump or void gas to keep the rig at the right depth. The engineers call it elegant. No one else who's seen a rig ever has.'

'Sounds straightforward. Will I feel it move?'

'You shouldn't. Part of your function is maintenance of the stability putery, so if you do feel it, something's not right. You'll find out precisely how your job works when you get there. No training needed. The rig's self-sufficient in energy and water, and you don't need to worry about food. There'll be more than enough for you.'

Veale stood up and put his hand out, which took Tallen by surprise. 'I still don't understand you, and I know there's something I'm missing. I really don't know why Hoob let you through.' It seemed to Tallen that there was something more that Veale might have been about to say instead of what he did end with. 'We're done here.'

* * *

Razer

'Hey, hero,' Razer said when Bale's face came up on the screenery. Then when he failed to smile, she added, 'Are you okay?'

'No. You feel like some air? Where are you now?'

'The red bar. What's happened?'

'They've pushed me.'

'They're always doing that.' She wrapped her hands around the thick white tasse, letting the heat fade a moment before swallowing the caffé straight down. There was a swift rush but it wasn't enough. On the screen, Bale's eyes had the brightness of a focused drunk and Razer was unprepared for it. Bale wasn't a day-drinker.

He said, 'This isn't that.'

'Has something happened you haven't told me? Have you done something?'

'Nothing special. My job.'

'I thought you were on leave.'

'I was using my own time. I wanted one day of theirs. One day.'

'Hell, Bale. I thought they told you not even to use your own time.' Then, 'Are you sure?'

'I told you. I'm finished.'

She could feel the eyes of the few others in the bar on her, and dropped her voice. 'You can't be. Not for this. Someone's just passing shit down the line and you're the nearest bucket. As usual, Bale. Don't take it personally.' She tried to grin, feeling it not quite work, and said, 'That's your trouble, you take it all personally. And you take it too far. Give it a week.'

'Navid called me in this afternoon. I get two months full

pay, six months half pay, but I'm already gone. They've cut my links.'

By now the caffé was waking her up enough to know she wasn't helping at all. 'That's crazy. You can appeal. They can't do this.'

'They can. This isn't the usual shit. Navid'll give me a dead reference if I look for a job here on Bleak, but if I look offworld he'll give me a perfect one. They don't want me out. They want me gone.'

'Is this to do with –?'

He cut her off. 'You can be at the promenade in ten minutes?'

'Yes. I'll see you there.'

She paid for the drinks and left the bar.

This had been inevitable. Bale was a fighter of lost causes and a lost cause himself. She'd imagined she would have left Bleak before it happened.

Now that she was thinking of leaving, she found herself as acutely conscious of the place as when she'd arrived. Odd how you got used to anything, in time. Even Lookout, an impossible town on an impossible planet. Flick off the shield and it would be gone in a moment, without trace. Bleak was more harsh and unyielding than any other planet she'd seen, and she'd seen most of them. Second by second, nowhere else in the System cost a fraction of what Bleak cost to keep going. If not for the rigs and the sarcs, it would have been abandoned to darkness and chaos. All the other planets were slowly becoming more habitable, but Bleak remained as it had first, reflexively, been named. No attempt had ever been made to fool anyone with a bright new label for Bleak.

She moved through the streets, heading for the

promenade and Bale. The daylight here was always at precisely the same level. Maybe it was to give some illusion of security, of the predictability of a next moment. And the buildings – away from the sea – were uniform. That way, anything that failed was immediately apparent and instantly made safe.

Made safe. The thought reminded her of the killings and took her back to Bale again.

She felt too closely connected with it. Of course she was interested, how could she not be? She'd been drinking with Bale the night before. She felt involved, even a little responsible, which was crazy. And it hadn't helped to see Tallen lying there in the hospital bed in that exoskeleton frame, only his jaw moving like it was gnawing away at him. The frame, so like the ribs of a coffin, had made her shudder. Not for the first time, she'd wondered if they ever returned to consciousness in those sarcs, screaming, hammering at their box like in some old story.

There was Tallen, though. She'd discovered he was out of hospital, but she hadn't seen him again in the red bar and didn't know where else to look. She wanted to see him. Why? Maybe she was slipping. Bale and then Tallen.

She walked on, more quickly. The streets began to gain some character as she approached the shore, qualcrete chipping and cracking, buildings dropping down to twin and then single storey. She could hear the lisping thrum a few streets before its source came into view. As she passed the last dilapidated structure she saw Bale leaning against the low wall of the promenade, his broad, solid back to her, looking out at the sea.

Twenty
ALEF

SigEv 25 Another death

A week passed, and the next. I went out more frequently at night, visiting the bar, but there was nothing from Pellonhorc. I found myself thinking of my parents. Sometimes I missed them so much. I often thought of my mother's cookies, and of playing with the putery in my father's shop. I remembered how we would play with water, generating and calculating the complex movements of water in streams and rivers. I still did that, when I felt especially alone.

It should have taken Drame's convoy two weeks to reach their destination. Drame, of course, would not be on it when it arrived, but he was somewhere in hiding to preserve the secret of that.

Maybe Ligate hadn't taken the hook. Or maybe he'd gone from Vegaschrist but evaded Belleger's team and returned home safely. Success or failure, we should have heard by now; from Belleger if success, or from Drame's spies in the event of failure. But there was only the continuing slow buildup of forces and weaponry around Vegaschrist and the Eden String, the steady increase in Ligate's statistical probability of swift success.

Then Drame reappeared. The first I knew of it was a call for me to come immediately to his office. He was sitting there as if he'd never left, Madelene standing behind him, staring at me with that mix of amusement and disdain that she reserved for me. Her face, with extraordinary precision, matched a stillpic I'd used on Gehenna in order to learn how to read emotion.

Drame's face was drawn and pale. Something had happened, that was for sure.

I said, 'Is he dead?'

Drame nodded, but I wasn't confident that his expression was right for such news. He said, 'You've heard, then.'

'No,' I said. 'Nothing came to The Floor. What about Belleger?'

Madelene cut in. 'He doesn't know, Ethan. He doesn't know what you're talking about. He's a moron. Look at him.'

'You're telling me Ligate's dead,' I said, ignoring her. 'But Belleger? Is he all right?'

Drame shook his head. 'I haven't heard anything from Belleger or our spy. And nothing of Ligate. No, Alef. It's Solaman.'

Everything felt blurry around me. I tried for a moment to understand it. I remembered him tipping his head and saying to me, 'What's in a name?' Oh, Solaman, I thought. Solicitous. Solace.

Madelene snorted. 'He didn't even know, Ethe. Look at him, he's dribbling.'

'Solaman's dead,' I whispered.

I tried to think about numbers, but couldn't. I was crying weirdly, like I had the hiccups at the same time.

'Give him a noserag, Madly,' Drame said, but when she

moved it was to flounce round the desk and out of the office, slamming the door in her wake.

'She's upset,' Drame told me. 'The funeral's tomorrow. You leave The Floor for the day. I'll have you picked up.' He looked at me. He seemed old, suddenly. 'Your father, and now Solaman. Maybe Belleger too. We should have heard something by now. I'm going to have to take good care of you, Alef.'

SigEv 26 A funeral, a mystery, a message

Solaman's funeral was a major event. The coming war didn't enter my thoughts. I kept seeing Solaman in my mind, and he was asking me riddles about his name. But all I could think of was Solitude.

One of Drame's armoured flycykles picked me up at the door of the building. We flew in convoy, Drame and Madelene in the first machine, then me, and then everyone else. There were eighty-four flycykles in all, with two hundred and fifty-five outriders.

I knew how powerful Ethan Drame was in terms of the numbers, but until the day of Solaman's funeral, I had never seen his power manifested. The entire city was closed down. We flew above a world in mourning and fear, everyone standing on the streets and dressed in nova-white. We broke out through the city limits in a wash of pressure that rocked the flycykle, and wheeled over the deadground where Solaman was to be released.

I'd seen burials as a child back on Gehenna, rituals heavy with hymning and celebrations of everlasting life. This was very different. The flycykles landed in a park adjacent to the deadground. Because we were outside the city with its filtered air, a temporary shield had been set up, and it hissed intrusively. The ground was fissured and bouldered, though the fine dust had been blown clear. I, with my memories of Gehenna, saw it as a reminder of how tenuous our grasp of existence was. I imagine Drame saw it as mere fact, and Madelene as a threat to her heels.

And how did Pellonhorc see it?

Yes, Pellonhorc was there. He arrived at the deadground in the flycykle directly behind mine. As he dismounted, we saw each other at the same time, each of us registering the position the other held in the hierarchy. He looked a great deal older, and more than just older. He had had surgery, the sort of augmentations that soldiers had if they could afford them. His forehead was bulked out, the skin stretched and shining, translucent, and he walked awkwardly. He reminded me a little of Garrel, and I wondered whether Garrel would be here today.

'Alef,' Pellonhorc said, striding over to me. 'How long has it been?'

'Two months, five days –'

He laughed, and I stopped. I said, 'Did you know Solaman?'

'A little,' he said, with a wave of his hand. 'Now it's just you and me, Alef.' He squinted at me. 'You don't look right, you know that?'

Madelene was walking towards us. She came to a halt a few metres away, glanced briefly at Pellonhorc and said, 'Alef, Ethan wants you to sit with us for the release.'

I nodded for Pellonhorc to come, but Madelene repeated,

'Alef,' in such a way that it was clear that Pellonhorc wasn't invited.

Pellonhorc's face emptied of all expression. 'I brought some absentee condolences.' He showed her a small message flake.

Madelene raised her eyes, gestured towards the release pit and said, 'Take it to the screenery with all the others. We'll be here all day with them. Find yourself a seat.' Then she smiled at me. It was a real smile, but I knew it wasn't meant for me. It was just for Pellonhorc to observe.

He turned and walked off to join the queue of people waiting to load condolences into the skyscreenery.

The entrance to the deadground was a broad arch framed by the words *Beyond Death, Memory*. Through the arch, we gave our names to the ushers and were guided to our seats in the amphitheatre. Drame, Madelene and I were seated at the front, metres from the release pad, where closest relatives sat. It struck me that I had no idea whether Solaman had any living relatives other than me.

I sat on Ethan Drame's right, Madelene on his left. It took almost an hour for everyone to file in and sit down, and many came up to us – to me as much as to Drame, even though none of them realised Solaman and I were related – and told us how sorry they were, and that life is more in memory than in flesh. The releaser eventually called for silence, and said, 'As we *would* have been, so we *shall* be remembered,' and it was repeated all around the amphitheatre, though I only mouthed the words. On Gehenna they were heresy. Now, even though I believed in nothing at all, I couldn't bring myself to say the words. The releaser waited for the echo to die, then said, 'As we would be remembered, so should we be.' The amphitheatre repeated it. I didn't, but nor did I forget the phrase.

The deadground lay before us, and the officials set about preparing the small rocket for its flight. As they did, the skyscreenery came alive and the flaked messages of condolence hung in the air, trembling and spectral against the makeshift shield. Most were small greetings and reminiscences from people who had known Solaman. There were messages here from people living all over the System (except, of course, from Gehenna or the unsaid planet), and there were a number of mentions of my father as a close friend of Solaman, though none of my mother, Solaman's sister. Twice there was reference to me as having given him joy, which stung and watered my eyes. Some of these messages were in the form of words scrolling across the sky, while others were images of the reader's face, sombre or nervous as they spoke.

And then the amphitheatre was still and entirely soundless; Spetkin Ligate's face was shimmering before us.

I glanced at Drame, who sat like stone. He hissed, 'Get him away. How did he get here?' His voice rose, though only Madelene and I could hear him, as Ligate's image began to speak. And then Drame fell silent and sat back. He was right to. It was better to appear aware that this was going to happen. I glanced down and saw people at the screenery, trying to disengage it.

Ligate said, 'Oh, Ethan, Ethan!'

Ethan sat immobile. Madelene started to move, then winced and held still. I noticed Drame's fist around her wrist, twisting it, holding her. She went pale.

'Oh, Ethan. First Saul, and now Solaman. And of course

you lost your wife, too, Ethan. I almost forgot about her – but then, so have you.' A pause. 'Madelene, it's good to see you.' The image nodded, as if it were something more than a threedy. A brief thrill of muttering ran around the amphitheatre and there was silence again. Ligate was continuing.

'I am grateful for this opportunity to address you all. Ethan, you're well, I trust? I hope you're guarding your remaining loved ones. You can't afford to lose any more, can you?'

I was reminded of Father Grace at a Gehennan funeral, chiding the survivors, warning them of the horrors to come should they not observe the commands of the Babble.

'Who is there to look over Alef's shoulder? And Pellonhorc, your son? Are you watching him closely enough? Whose interests is he looking after?'

Ligate's face swelled as he said, '*As you would be remembered*, Ethan.' His face gleamed like polished copper. 'Remember Saul. Remember Solaman. They are gone and gone. You too will be memory, Ethan, and sooner than you imagine.'

The swollen face turned, side to side, the image distorting against the star-cracked sky. 'All of you here at the deadground are witness to this.' His voice became softer. 'More than one of you is already with me.'

There was a moment's perfect silence, then Ligate carried on. 'Until Drame's own release, I shall accept and absolve any more of you who wish to come to me.' Silence again, and then Ligate's voice stiffened. 'But respond swiftly, for as soon as Ethan Drame has been released into death, that door will be closed and you will be abandoned.'

A dizzying fizz of light, and Ligate's image disappeared.

All around the amphitheatre, people began to chatter.

Drame rose slowly to his feet. The chatter shrank away. As the next message of condolence flared in the sky, Drame unholstered a weapon from within his long mourning coat and took slow aim at the projection tablet, and fired. The tablet cracked and split, and the message vanished.

'Spetkin Ligate,' Drame whispered. He didn't need to speak more loudly. There was no other sound in the deadground but the hiss of the shield above us. Everyone was listening.

'Ligate talks of memory.' Drame scythed his hand through the air. 'But where is he? Is he here? No, he is not.'

Drame tilted his head as if expecting to be contradicted. He spread his arms wide. 'We are here for our friend Solaman. For Solaman.'

A few people nodded.

'Solaman is no longer here. He is memory. But *his* memory will remain. Ligate is not here, is he?' Drame drew a long breath and roared, 'LIGATE!'

He waited. Silence.

'*SPETKIN LIGATE!*'

Silence again.

Drame let his voice fall. 'He isn't here. Of course not. He promises you that I will soon become memory, and that you can join him before that time.'

He waited. There was a perfect silence.

'It's an easy promise, isn't it? It costs nothing and it means nothing. It's a promise that he can keep easily enough. He can keep it all his life, because he will be my memory before I am his.' He looked slowly, steadily, around the amphitheatre, and then said, slowly and steadily, 'Does anyone here doubt that?'

He waited. His calm was extraordinary.

Then he whispered, 'Spetkin Ligate's promise is worth less than his piss. I shall give you Ethan Drame's promise.'

He held up a single finger. 'One person brought this message to Solaman's release. Maybe I might have discovered who that person was, had I not destroyed the projector. Maybe not. Did I destroy it in fury? No. Shall I tell you why I did it?'

No one moved. No one dared. He said, 'I destroyed it to safeguard their identity, so that I could make a promise to them. This is my promise. Against Ligate's piss-promise of safety to all of you, I promise just one person, the person who acts for Ligate, that you may leave now in guaranteed safety. This is Ethan Drame's word.'

He was like a preacher. *Word*, he had said, as if it were an equation or a proof. How could anyone not have believed him?

'Go. Leave in safety and join him.' He paused, then made a great gesture with his arms and said, 'Or *stay*! Only come to me later, privately, and you will have my unconditional pardon. I give my word to this, as everyone here witnesses, and –'

I realised that his voice had gradually been rising, and now it reached a crescendo as he said, '– I have *never* broken my word.'

He was quick and he was cunning, was Ethan Drame. He had turned the attack around. From a challenge on his home ground, following the loss of one of his most precious tacticians, he had confirmed Ligate as an untrustworthy coward and declared himself a man of honour.

Naturally, no one left the amphitheatre, but the

cleverest part had been Drame's final gesture. Of course the agent would not take up the offer of secret confession and forgiveness, but it would appear to everyone else at the deadground that they might. And if more than one person here was an agent of Ligate, they would no longer trust each other.

He let all this sink in, and then he said, mildly, 'So, Ligate? Are you here? No? What was it you said? Hmm?' He put a hand to his ear and waited, then whispered into the emptiness, his words drifting clearly around the arena, 'I can't remember what you said. You are barely in my memory.'

His voice grew once more. 'And after I have destroyed you, Spetkin Ligate, I shall destroy even your memory.' He raised his hands, palms up, then suddenly turned them over and said, 'There will have been – *nothing*.'

The tumultuous applause began as he sat down, and it carried on for some minutes. The ceremony of Solaman's release was a small thing after this drama. The rocket went up with a fizz, its afterburn etched briefly on our retinas as a symbol of his memory in our thoughts, and that was it. For all their ludicrousness, I preferred the pomp of Gehennan funerals.

SigEv 27 Trust

Drame left with Madelene. When I reached my flycykle, Pellonhorc was there, leaning casually against the dark curve of its cockpit. He said, 'My machine's broken down. I'll travel with you. I'll drive. Your driver can wait with mine.' He left me nothing to say, so I sat down and let him lift us into the air. Below us, people were swarming out of the deadground gates.

As we rose above the arena, I said, 'What happened to your flycykle?'

'It was sabotaged. Clever.'

He glanced at me and saw I didn't understand. 'Ligate's making my father think one of us is against him. You or me, Alef. If Ligate makes me travel with you, my father will wonder if we're both in league with him.'

'You didn't have to come with me. You could have waited for your machine to be fixed, or returned with someone else.'

'We're childhood friends. More suspicious if I hadn't done this.'

He was right. Always he was ahead of me. 'Who is it, then?' I said. 'Who brought the message? Who sabotaged your flycykle? Who's the spy?'

'You're the thinker, Alef. Madelene?'

'She has nothing to gain. She already has everything.'

'Ligate could be blackmailing her. If it was Madelene who betrayed my mother's location to Ligate, to get her killed –'

'Her face is unhappy more than fifty per cent of the time,' I told him. 'I think she was happier as a mistress.'

'She may have imagined otherwise.'

The ground spun past. Half-completed roads, exposed pipes and cables, sulphurous pools. 'Maybe there's no one,' I said. 'Ligate could have tricked someone into carrying the message innocently, without even knowing they were doing it.'

'It's possible. My father would never believe that. He'd rather believe it was me. Maybe it was. I didn't check all the messages I was given. If I was Ligate, I'd have used me if I could.'

I could see Pecovin's shield ahead, glittering like the lees of a galaxy. We'd be there soon.

'Your father told me to take the day off,' I said. 'You?'

'I leave again this evening.'

We hit the shield, and he swung the flycykle round as we ground through it, so that we clung to the disturbance for a few seconds and continued to skim the inner edge. I knew we were untrackable in the magnetic flux. The flycykle shuddered. I glanced at the readings, all of them blinking MANUAL OVERRIDE. PLEASE EXIT SHIELD NOW. Pellonhorc was bumping the flycykle steadily along the shield without any of the putery. His voice was even. 'I have an apartment my father doesn't know about,' he said.

I stared rigidly out of the window. I wanted to shout at him, *Come away from the shield*, but I knew how he'd react to that. As steadily as I could, I said, 'This flycykle might be monitored. There might be ears.'

'There's nothing now. I checked while I was waiting for you.'

On my left, through the shield, I could see the deadground shivering, the colours separating and merging. On my right was Pecovin tilting and yawing like a city in a dream. I fixed on the console, which was now rapidly blinking, EXIT SHIELD IMMEDIATELY and beeping in phase with the script. I said, 'He'll be suspicious. This may not be a good idea. And I think I'm going to puke if we don't crash first.'

'You won't puke. You never puke.' We screeched on, losing height.

I had puked at the deaths of my parents, and Pellonhorc

had seen it. As a child, I had puked at some of the things he had done to animals. He only ever remembered what he wanted to, while I remembered everything.

Pellonhorc's hands shuddered with the effort of controlling the handstick. He said, 'My father's always suspicious. He'd be more suspicious if I didn't act suspiciously. I'm a bad influence, Alef. I have to act like one.'

I closed my eyes. I couldn't work him out. This was how it had always been between us. I tried to make simplicity out of complexity, and he turned the simple into the complex. Pellonhorc was the only person who ever baffled me. When we had been children, his complexity had mostly been his own confusion, but now it seemed honed and deliberate.

He took the flycykle low and came away from the shield a few metres from the ground, hard and fast, dropping it to a stop in an apartment block's underpark. It was a cheap premoulded hulk. I could see the advantage for him in a premould. There was nowhere to hide bugs or cams.

His apartment was bare, and we sat on steel chairs at a steel table. He heated some saké and stirred powdercaff into it. It tasted foul.

'It doesn't matter who the traitor is, Alef,' he said. 'If it's you, I'm not interested.'

'It isn't,' I began to say, but he waved me to silence.

'Forget it,' he said. 'It doesn't matter. Though if it were Madelene and I find out she had my mother killed...' He squeezed the saké glass and looked at me seriously. 'We're in danger, you and I, Alef. My father might behave stupidly again.'

'Again?'

'He murdered Ligate's family. You know that, don't you?'

'That was an accident.'

'Apparently not. Ligate and my father used to do business. Ligate did a small stupid thing, and my father found out and did a very big stupid thing. And now we have this.'

He sipped the black drink, watching me.

'What do we do?' I said.

'You wait for me. Keep going to the bar. I'll be in touch.' He stood up. 'This is a big game, Alef. The biggest. You might think you're a player, but you're not. You and I, we're just part of the stakes. Don't ever think otherwise.' He waited for me to nod, then said, 'I've heard stories of people being killed in the Eden String near Vegaschrist, businesses going down, my father making mistakes. You know anything about that?'

'How do you know about it?'

'Don't try to play with me, Alef. Do you know what I do? Where I've been?'

I shook my head. 'No one will say.'

'I'm out in the Eden String. That's where my father sent me. I keep everything running smoothly there. Try to.' He drained the black drink and said, 'I know what you do, Alef; you're the one who decides what I do.'

'I didn't know that. Didn't know it's you out there.'

'Why would my father tell you? You might worry about me. It might enter your calculations.'

I looked to see if he was joking, but there was no sign of it.

He said, 'Is there anything I should know?'

'There may be a localised revolt in the String near Vegaschrist,' I said carefully. 'Perhaps you should stay away from there.'

'No more than that?'

Something in his voice cautioned me. I said, 'Is there more?'

'There's rumour all across the String that Ligate's taking control, city by city. I'm losing influence and I'm losing men. If you hear anything – if you know anything – you'll tell me, won't you, Alef?'

I said nothing. I was trembling and he surely saw it.

He said, 'My father must know what's going on. If anything happens, you have to give me warning. I'm his son, Alef, and everyone in the String knows that. My life is at stake. I have to go back there as soon as I leave Peco. You can't imagine how it is. I survive on my weaponry and my wits. I hardly sleep. I am my father's reach, Alef. Out there I'm strong because of him. As soon as he stops being strong, I'm dead.'

I knew, as certainly as I was holding the truth from him, that he was holding something from me. But at the same time I trusted him more than I had ever trusted anyone except my parents. And I knew that he trusted no one more than he trusted me.

And yet with all that trust between us, we said nothing further, and parted.

Twenty-one

RAZER

What could she say to Bale? What was there to say?

'Tallen,' he said, looking out at the sea. 'It doesn't make sense.'

The promenade carried on to their left and right. Every few metres were signs warning of the sea, of immediate danger and longterm risk.

'You're crazy, Bale. I thought you'd been fired.'

He half-turned to face her. 'Tallen doesn't fit the pattern.'

'Just because he isn't dead?'

'No. We've identified the K. His name was Emel Fleschik. His other kills that morning still don't fit with Tallen. It all stinks of shit.'

'It was the sewers, Bale. What else is it going to stink of? You need to think about something else. Your job's lost and you have to accept it.' She rested her arms on the warm promenade wall. It was a fine day, the high shield glittering and the cloud beyond it moving fast. There was a faint tang of ammonia but nothing more. 'You saved Tallen. You'd rather he was dead so the pattern can fit?'

He started walking. They passed a few other people leaning on the wall, staring out at the brilliant colours of the sea and sky. Razer automatically examined their expressions.

They looked as if stunned. Bleak did that to you.

She followed Bale down the worn steps onto the stony beach. The heat instantly came up through her boots. Where the pebbles were dry, up by the steps, their colour was muted, a range of browns and steel-greys, but further down the shore where the surf washed over them, the water made them glorious. Sulphur yellows, cobalt blues and more, elemental chromas that made the universe dull in comparison. At each withdrawal of the surf, the hot stones vaporised the water and the brilliance faded. Every new wave tumbled the stones and drew fresh ribbons of colour. It had been wonderful from the promenade, but close up, it was astonishing.

'It's beautiful,' she couldn't help saying to Bale, as if they were in love.

Bale stopped, his boots slipping on the stones. He made a gesture at the horizon. 'You never get used to it. You learn to look away. Out to sea, or back to the town. They –' he indicated the observers at the wall. 'They haven't worked it out yet.'

'Mm.'

His face was in her way. She said, 'Hey,' and realised she'd been doing it herself, staring mesmerised. She looked away from Bale, at the shield-shimmering sky.

'Where we are now, this is the edge of everything,' he said.

'I've heard that.'

After a moment, he said, quietly, 'Do you ever stop filing it away?'

She looked carefully at him. It reminded her of what she liked in Bale, this abrupt swerving away before closing in on his point. He could be sharp as ice. She'd never met anyone like him, that was certain. Infuriating bastard. She said, 'How do you mean?'

'Exactly what is it you do, Razer?'

Bale was a natural. The unexpected seam of empathy and that unyielding concentration. He could have been so much. She could imagine him with some sort of real life, someone to share it –

'No,' he said. 'You don't stop at all, ever. Even now, you're doing it.'

– and if he ever achieved it, he'd screw it up. Angrily, and not quite knowing why, she said, 'No, I don't stop. You're right. But I'm not judging you, Bale.'

'Understand me, then.' He started to walk along the shore. She had to work to catch up, her feet always sliding away.

'Tell me what you do,' he said. 'Really.'

Her legs were starting to ache and her eyes were streaming. 'I write. I've told you all this before. I make stories you could believe, or that you want to believe. You've heard of TruTales? That's me and a lot of others. I bring people to life.'

He said, 'And I try to make sense of it when they die. You can't stop. I can't stop. Nothing to be done about it.'

She said, quietly, 'I might think you're acting stupidly, but I always listen to you. You said the K was ex-military. He wasn't running, he was moving steadily. You could tell that from his trail. He was following a plan. You said it makes no sense, someone that good leaving a trail, and a trail that backed him into a dead end. So maybe he was drawing you. He expected to kill you, but he would have known you'd be the first of many after him. He was crazy, but he wasn't disorganised. They don't have to go together, any more than sane always goes with organised, but the organised crazies are always following some kind of plan, something that makes some kind of sense to them.'

'Okay, you were listening.'

'So you listen to me. You want to understand his plan? You can't, Bale. Even if he were alive, it wouldn't be comprehensible to you.' Out to sea, the brilliant light spun and swirled.

Bale shook his head firmly. 'The survivor –'

'Tallen remembers nothing but corrupted fragments. He'll never get it all back.'

'How do you know?'

'Memory can destroy you and it can protect you. From what you told me, forgetting's a good thing.'

'Memory can be retrieved.'

She said, 'No. Is that where you're taking this? AfterLife? There's no access to AfterLife data, and you know it. Not ever, under any circumstances. Not everyone carries a neurid and no one knows if they have a live one or a placebo. No one can ever find out. If one person can gain access, hope's gone for everyone.'

He bent forward and rested his hands on his knees. 'Shit. If he'd been any more damaged –'

'He'd have been put into a sarc, dropped out there and maybe loaded onto the AL database. But anonymised.' She held up a hand to stop the interruption she saw coming. 'Search criteria are deliberately limited. AfterLife's not a Pax or Tax database. They've both challenged it in law and failed to get anywhere. Individual data first comes up between one and five years, at random. When it does, you'd never identify an individual. Tallen would be categorised male, age twenty-six years, no surviving parents, no partner, no dependents, no steady employment, victim of near-fatal criminal assault, currently irreversible brain injury, plus whatever finally put him in the sarc.'

She wondered how far to go, and decided to take all the wind from Bale in one hit. 'You think you could pick one man up from that? There are thousands fitting that dataset, Bale. This is the System, population eight billion, not including Gehenna and the unsaid planet, AfterLife registration maybe eighty per cent, viable neurids maybe two per cent of that, are you with me?'

'We're losing numbers.'

'But we're still high. Of the viable implantees, many will die irretrievably before they get to the sea. It's a rough life everywhere, Bale. We aren't on Earth any more. Explosions, destruction-associated brain deaths, thousands more irreversible end-events. So of the viable implantees, maybe point zero zero six per cent ultimately end up in the sarcs.'

The stones at the sea's edge turned and turned, colour over colour, endlessly unique. She glanced at Bale. 'Not what you thought, is it?'

'I thought most people were registered. I thought –'

'They are. And sure, the irretrievably dead get their lives on the database too, if the neurid's salvageable, but just as anonymously as the viable returnees. They get their eternity, and we get to know them even if they can't come back.'

Razer took his hand. Cold, calloused fingers. 'It's a good thing, Bale. We'd be lost without it. We were lost before it. It gives us hope, purpose and community. AfterLife holds the System together.'

He said, 'But the numbers. I never really thought about the numbers.'

'You're unusual, Bale. It underpins the lives and thoughts of most of us. It's only a few hundred thousand sarcs a year going in the sea, but most people think they're good odds. Against death, maybe they are.'

That was enough, she reckoned. Time to let him down more gently. 'The point is, Bale, you could trawl for a decade and never find a specific subject. I guess you could try to use one of the illegal search programs, find someone that way, but none of them work.'

Larren Gamliel's Life dropped suddenly into her thoughts again, the metal shard tossed high and caught. What was that name? Mardle? Only her own memory could find him. Why did it nag at her so? Cynth had never behaved like that before. Why now? Was she malfunctioning?

Beside the sea's bright fraying edge, Bale dropped into a squat. 'You know a lot about AfterLife.'

'I write for a ParaSite. I know everything there is to know about AfterLife. Can you imagine how useful it is to me? AfterLife is limited and imperfect, yes, but in its Lives, it is true and pure. Maybe it's the only thing that is. What's on AfterLife isn't tainted by the fabrication of recollection or the desires of tellers like me. The tellers in the sea can't lie. It's the one true thing.' If Razer believed in anything, she believed in AfterLife. Not the extras and the ParaSites, but all its wonderful, terrible Lives. She was its perfect acolyte. The all but endless trove could always comfort her. To her, the possibility of return didn't matter so much as the Lives.

Everything she wanted or needed was there.

She told Bale, 'I use it all the time. I try to understand how to convey the truth. The humanity. Those lives.'

He stood up. 'This killer.'

She almost screamed at him. 'Forget it, Bale. Did crime stop that night? Did your job freeze? The killer's dead and so are ten others, but Tallen's alive, and that's because of you.'

'There's something else.'

'There's *always* something else. Nothing is purely of itself. The killer was made into that by the military, by his childhood, by something in his brain. That isn't for you.'

'The plan –'

'Was in his head, Bale. It was a brain-fucked plan.' She wanted to shake it out of him, this stupid refusal to let the incomprehensible alone. 'It will *never* make sense. You want to know what happened? I'll tell you. A moth told him, or a reflection in a window, or a cloud or a pebble or his dead brother or a blank screen or a grain of rice, it makes no difference; something ordinary or absurd told him, quite clearly and in detail, to kill ten people and take another into the sewers and cut ribbons out of him with a cold blade and then start burrowing into his skull with a chisel.'

Bale started to walk again, onward along the shore. Some distance away, a fence ran down from the wall and carried on into the sea. Beyond it, a high stubby spur of qualcrete pushed out from the wall and disappeared into the water. Good, Razer thought, following a few paces behind him. Bale would have to turn round.

Not slowing yet, he said, 'You have a fine imagination, Razer.'

'You have to give up, Bale. Can't you see that?'

'Why did he take Tallen down there?'

'You aren't listening to me. If you knew the reason, it wouldn't help you.'

He stopped, shifting from foot to foot, and said, 'I know this. There's a huge gulf between the onground spree and what he did to Tallen down in the sewers. They were quick. Kill and run, kill and run. But Tallen was *totally* different. Not just because he wasn't killed.'

'You told me the K forensically matches all the deaths. You found him with Tallen. Isn't that connection enough?'

The breakwater was closer. Soon they'd have to leave the shore.

Bale said, 'Most of the forensics was guesswork. Lookout's streetcams are patchy, no real help. We don't know how long Tallen was down there. Could have been hours. We only know for sure that Fleschik was there at least a few minutes before me.'

Razer said, 'We know Tallen had a habit of going to the sea at night. So how about if Fleschik had been watching him every night, targeted him ahead and took him down one of the sewer traps a few hours before starting the spree. That way, Tallen could have been the first. Fleschik did what he did to him, didn't get what he wanted. Or perhaps, in his own head, he did get it. Tallen screams something, Fleschik thinks it means go upside and kill a few people. Either way, he comes out and starts killing, then goes back to Tallen, intending, I don't know, to see if it's made any difference. Only you turn up and save him.'

Bale said, 'That was off the top of your head?'

'I've been thinking about it. Anything wrong with it?'

'It's good. But what if the K wasn't alone? What if

someone else was working on Tallen?'

'Two of them?' She stopped. 'Is there any evidence of another person?'

'No one saw Tallen being attacked and abducted from the street. That can't have been quick if there was just one man. If he was organised like you said, he left a lot to chance. Easier if there are two of you. And Tallen definitely remembers being stabbed. There were no forensics from Tallen on the streets, anywhere between the beach and where he lives. There should have been a huge pool of blood. There was nothing at all.'

They were nearly at the qualcrete spur blocking their way. Razer saw a stairway back up to the promenade. 'Let's go back up.'

'Not yet.' He started treading heavily up and down in the stones. She watched the depressions of his bootmarks disappear, the stones moving lightly as bubbles.

'No tracks,' he said. 'You notice how we've been walking? How everyone walks on the stones?'

She said, 'What?' and then, 'Oh,' realising she was unconsciously moving her feet, constantly climbing out of the stones. Bale stopped doing the same and after a few seconds he began very slowly to sink, only stabilising when he was ankle deep. He pulled himself out in a rasp of stones and walked on towards the spur, saying, 'We can't tell where Tallen came off the beach that night. We have no idea of the route he took back into town.'

'I don't care. I'm tired.'

He pointed ahead. 'Look.'

The breakwater's security fence was close enough for her to make out its titanium struts, each tip split three ways, splayed and barbed. Beyond it, beside the breakwater, a great broad curve of weathered pipe ran out of the high promenade wall and sank into the sea.

'The waste tunnels exit here,' he said. 'Sewage.'

'You think he took Tallen into the pipes here? Not from the town? There's no access.'

'See the gate? Emergency access. Beyond it, there's a trap hatch at the top of the pipe. You could drag someone up there. Two of you could do it easily.'

'There must be cams.'

'They haven't worked since a week after they were set, and that was years back.'

Razer thought of Tallen standing here and staring out at the sea, night after night. It was beautiful in the changing light, like metal, like velvet.

Bale said, 'Another thing. His memory was confused, but he remembers footsteps.'

'So?'

'The sound of them, as he describes it, wasn't a thudding or a stamping.' Bale stepped up and down. 'He said it was a crunching sound.'

'Maybe there was gravel on the street.'

'And the beach keeps itself clean. No blood. Everything, anything, gets swallowed, and the stones scrub themselves.'

She was acutely aware of herself pacing on the spot. 'So Tallen never even made it off the beach? It's possible.'

'Okay. But why would you do that if you know your target's heading for solid ground? Dragging someone over these stones would be really hard. And he'd hear you coming.' Bale stamped again. 'Maybe he'd fight you off.'

Razer glanced towards the promenade. 'But up there

you're more likely to be seen. Just as risky.'

'At that time of night? And you're crazy anyway, remember?'

'You're organised crazy,' she said. 'It's not the same as stupid.'

Bale grinned. 'Organised enough to want to leave no trace, perhaps.'

'Again, why does that matter? An hour or two later he was leaving pretty big traces. You'll never understand his logic, Bale.'

She followed him up the steps to the promenade and looked at the waste pipe extending across the stones to fall away into the water and disappear about a hundred metres inside the shield. She said, 'What about the K? Fleschik.'

'Everything he had was wiped clean. His room was like the wind had gone through it. He arrived on Bleak two months ago. All we have is his arrival and his death. Between the two, he's invisible.'

'Okay.' She considered it. 'He was ex-military, and he was crazy. Paranoid behaviour's understandable, and he had the training.'

'It's the degree of it, Razer, not the idea. There's *nothing*. It's not that we can't link him to anything or anyone. We can't even see him. He didn't go to bars, buy food, use screenery. It took us a week to find his room, and that was only luck. His cash payment was valid for another month but the renter got greedy and broke in, found it like I said, then told someone, who told a Paxer, who made a connection. Pure chance.' He rested his elbows on the promenade wall, then turned his head to her again. 'Do you record all this, or what?'

'I have a good memory.' She shook her hair away from

her neck and showed him the blistered scar behind her ear. 'An expensive one.'

'Like the neurid.'

'You don't give up, do you? No. This isn't organic and I haven't had it since I was born. It shows up on scans, it's limited and it's a nuisance.'

'How?'

A wind was starting up, rolling dust across the paving. She said, 'You want to talk about this now?'

'Now's fine. You never talk about yourself.'

'And you only talk about your work. It seems to suit us both pretty well. Not that you have a job any more.'

'I'm interested in your memory. I know how expensive augmems are. We don't get them in Pax and we could use them.'

'There's a reason for that. It isn't always such a great thing. It stores some of what I say, see and hear. No context. That's why Pax won't use them. Cynth – my AI – takes it, chops it up and uses it as background for stories. It goes wrong a lot. Maybe I'll get a cancer from mine.'

He grunted.

'My AI clears it at the end of every day. I don't even have access to it.'

He said, 'How much did you pay for it, this extra memory?'

She flushed. 'Maybe I just slept with a few people. Fuck you, Bale.' She stared at him, the anger directed mainly at herself for not having seen this coming. 'I write stories. You know that. Not under my own name. You'll find them under the tag Kestrel Dust, and I get paid well. Real money from a real corporation. I've told you all this. "AFTERLIFE *gives you lives, but TruTales gives you stories.*" That sort of thing. I –'

She stopped cold, suddenly realising that wasn't where he was headed at all. 'You think *I'm* involved in this? You think I'm Fleschik's accomplice?'

'I've seen mercs with less training than you,' he said evenly. 'You travel a lot, Razer. Just to write stories?'

'I said. They pay. You want details?'

'I've checked.' He shook his head. 'People pay for that stuff?'

'They subscribe.'

'They subscribe to AfterLife,' he said. 'What you do gets clipped on for a few more dolors a month.'

He'd done his research. She should have expected that. The wind seemed colder now, and she pulled up the collar of her jacket. She said, 'Not just *clipped* on. You can be an asshole, Bale. What they see on AfterLife isn't often happy. Eight per cent of the audience go on to read one of my stories before they leave. Mine and those of all the other contributors. It makes people feel better. That's so bad?' She took a breath. 'Am I still under suspicion? On the basis of that?'

'Tallen was at the end of his annual leave. Usually he went away. One of the last things he did before he went out and nearly got killed was register with StarHearts. Another AfterLife ParaSite.'

'So you connect it with me? Everyone in the System cruises StarHearts, Bale. I don't work for them, anyway.' She slowed down. 'Was there something specific he was doing?'

'He was looking for a woman, that's all.'

'He get any response?'

'No. Two evenings later he went out, dot dot dot.'

'And where does that leave me?'

'I needed to ask.'

'You can be hard work as well as an asshole, Bale.' She waited. 'I'm not under suspicion, then?'

'You're suspicious as hell. You spoke to Tallen in the hospital. You knew him too, didn't you? And you didn't mention it.'

'The red bar's a popular place. I saw him there. That's all.'

She felt her cheeks grow hot. Cynth had connected her with both men. Was something going on, here? She almost told Bale about the link with Cynth, but that would feed his paranoia. Instead she said, 'I work for TruTales. StarHearts is a totally different entity. And it's a long stretch to link it with the attack, let alone with me.' She took a breath, trying to steady herself. 'You were saying Emel Fleschik was good.'

'He was better than good. I'm ex-military too, but that degree of invisibility was beyond any training I had.'

'What had he done since military?'

'Merc and sec, mainly,' he said. 'Not as much drinking and drugs as you'd think.'

'Mercenaries pick up all sorts of tricks.' She considered it. 'And security. His security work was for the infotech industry? Of course it was. Who else employs people like that? And he was necessarily paranoid, as the industry is, and he was following his crazy plan. Nothing too curious there. He was just a crazy with a crazy plan.'

They trudged on along the promenade. 'Okay,' Bale said. 'What if it wasn't his plan at all? What if it was someone else's plan, Razer?'

'Mine, you mean?'

Bale said nothing.

'It was a joke, Bale.'

'I'm serious.'

'I suppose it's possible, two paranoid psychopaths feeding off each other. I imagine they'd more likely implode, though, one kill the other. No one came to Bleak with Fleschik?'

'We only identified Fleschik because we had his corpse and then struck lucky, so how would we know? But no, no one suspicious. Discounting you.'

'I assume you checked Tallen's background as well as his last movements. You're not thinking that, are you? He couldn't be this other crazy of yours?'

'Tallen's a sad loner, is all.'

Razer glanced at Bale, but he seemed unaware that he was describing himself. She looked back at the sewage pipe. Two people could easily have dragged Tallen's body up there. She said, 'Well, even if some other crazy is still out there, you've done all you can. Pax won't let you back. You can't stay here. Maybe that's a good thing. They're doing you a favour, Bale. Another place, you can forget this and start again.'

'I'll consider it. Maybe I'll stay. I'm used to it here.'

'What could you do?'

'I know the Chute. I'd work that.'

She said, 'You're not letting this go, are you?'

He said, 'You want to ride the Chute with me, Razer?'

She sighed, then grinned. 'What do you think?'

Twenty-two

ALEF

SigEv 28 A plan ends, a plan begins

For a while, that was the end of the excitement. Pellonhorc vanished again. It would have taken him about two weeks to travel back to the Eden String. Every night of that week I dreamt of him and of our childhood on Gehenna. I had dreams of betrayal and of punishment. I knew I should have told him the truth, that he might be returning to his death. It was what Father Grace would have called a sin of omission.

Two weeks passed, and a few days more, and I started to relax.

And then Drame called me to his office. Even over the comms, I knew something serious was wrong. Drame waved me to take a seat. He said, 'I had a message from Ligate, Alef.' He didn't wait, just raised it on the big screen.

I was shaking. I knew what I was going to see, and it was all my own responsibility.

Ligate's head came into view. 'I have something of yours, Ethan. I wonder if you can guess what it is. I was hoping I could return it in person, but you didn't arrive to collect it.' The screen cleared.

'Is that it?' I asked. 'Nothing else?'

He nodded.

'What has he got of yours?'

'I don't know. My spy's gone quiet. And…' He trailed off. This was unlike him.

'And Belleger?' I prompted.

He took a long breath. 'Belleger can look after himself. We'll hear from him once he's got to Ligate.' He swallowed. 'We go down Belleger's route now, Alef. No more talk. Your plan failed, I've lost him.'

I was lost. I said, 'Your spy? You think he's got your spy?'

'I don't care about the spy. I don't even know who the spy was. But his contact was Pellonhorc, and he's disappeared.'

'Pellon –' I saw it, now, or thought I did. Ligate had uncovered the spy, and through the spy he'd caught Pellonhorc. And I was as much to blame for it as Ethan Drame. Drame had not forewarned him, and nor had I.

A few days later, a parcel arrived. It was addressed personally to Ethan Drame. It was beamed and scanned and brought to Drame's office, and Drame called me in to see him open it. He knew what was in it, of course, from the scans, but I didn't.

The parcel's contents were cradled in bright yellow gift paper, and beneath the thin paper was a heat-sealed, temperature-stable, pressurised clear polythene bag marked HANDLE WITH CARE – HUMAN ORGAN IN TRANSIT.

Drame slit the bag open with his pocket blade. The abrupt release of pressure came with a gasp of gas, and we both caught our breath at the stench as the head tumbled heavily onto the desk and came to rest on its left ear.

Drame used the tip of the knife to turn the head towards

him. It was eyeless and open-mouthed. The tongue was sticking out, or so I thought, and it was oddly swollen. But of course it wasn't the tongue at all.

Drame poked at the head. Apart from the stink, it seemed fresh. Clots of blood came away to expose how the face had been mutilated. The cheekbones were caved in and most of the teeth had gone too, so it was hard to recognise him, but it wasn't Pellonhorc. I knew that immediately. I knew that Pellonhorc had had his foreskin removed.

'Belleger,' Drame whispered.

That night, I walked for hours, and then I went to the café. After an hour, Pellonhorc walked in and sat beside me.

'Hello, Alef.'

It didn't surprise me that he was here. I don't think anything would have surprised me just then.

'How did my father take it?'

'You knew about it?'

'There were rumours.'

'I think your father thought it was going to be you.'

'He was disappointed, then.'

I laughed. It was crazy. It was all crazy. When I stopped laughing, I said, 'Haven't you spoken to him? What are you doing here?' I couldn't stop the questions tumbling out. 'How did Ligate get Belleger? What happened to Drame's spy? How did you get out of the String?'

He shook his head and called a couple of drinks over. We drank them and left, walking quickly through the streets until we reached Pellonhorc's block. I wanted to know everything immediately. I couldn't wait. Pellonhorc walked quickly, then slowly, checking we weren't followed. He seemed perfectly calm.

'So,' he told me, once we were seated at his little table. 'There is no spy. Which is to say, I'm my father's spy.'

'*You?* You're close to Ligate?'

'I'm very close. Even my father doesn't know. It took me a long time, Alef. It's taken years. I'm part of his victory. It's perfect, isn't it? Ethan Drame's own son, turned against him.'

I saw my weave, all of it making sense. '*You* gave him the Eden String.'

'Not just that, Alef. I gave him the idea, too. All of it.'

My head was reeling. 'Why?'

'You'll see why.'

'Your father –'

'It's all for him, Alef. Like we said, remember? To prove myself to him.'

'Like this? By destroying him?'

'Don't be stupid.' He paused. 'Why didn't you warn me? I gave you the chance.'

'I –' But of course I had no answer.

'You were scared of him. It's all right, Alef. I had to know.' He looked at me and away again. 'I guessed you'd see Ligate's plan developing, and that he'd send a team to kill Ligate. Belleger wasn't too hard to find.'

'You gave Belleger to Ligate?'

'I needed Ligate to trust me absolutely.'

I could see Belleger's head on the table in Ethan Drame's office, with his penis stuffed in his mouth. 'I don't understand.'

'I've promised my father to Ligate. The lure is the same as Belleger told me you had planned for Ligate, only this is far better.' He grinned. 'Ligate is coming to Peco.'

'I don't believe that.' I had a sense of everything spiralling down and away from me. It all made perfect sense, and yet it was insane.

'Listen to me, Alef. My father's new house. Does he still visit the site every month?'

'Yes.'

'Then bring him yourself this time. I shall be there with Ligate. Ligate can't decide if it would be sweeter to have me kill my father, or to do it himself. You have no idea, Alef, how excited he is. To be able to touch my father.' He slapped my shoulder in his excitement, uncomfortably hard. 'He says to me, Alef, "I shall *reach* him."'

Pellonhorc saw how I was looking at him.

'Of course that isn't how it'll be. Don't be crazy. I'm bringing Ligate to my father. I'm proving myself to him, Alef. This will end it all. I shall finish it all, and he will see it.'

There was a look in his face that I'd seen before. There was no doubt in my mind that he was telling me the truth. I could always see when he was lying, and he wasn't lying now.

'How long will it take you to get Ligate here?'

'He's in my ship already, docked in the ferry station. I'm above suspicion here. No one would search my ship.'

It took me a moment to realise what he had told me in such a casual voice. Ligate was here on Peco! I pulled myself together and said, 'Your father goes to the house tomorrow morning, then again next month. We can do it then.'

'No. It has to be tomorrow.'

'Tomorrow?' I was hit by panic. 'Wait –'

'I've been preparing this for a long time, Alef.' His voice was tightening. 'Waiting's risky. It's already fixed. Ligate's nervous. I'm telling you because you're my friend. I'm not asking you.' He softened. 'You don't need to do a thing. I'll be ready before you arrive. Just you and my father, is that clear?'

I nodded.

I had consented. I was part of it.

I thought of Solaman again, his head tipping as he asked his wordriddle question, and in my mind I answered, 'Solution. Solve.'

Twenty-three

TALLEN

The thrummer pilot put his head through the capsule doorway and said, 'I'm green to go, rigger. Three minutes. I'm not supposed to tell you, but this is the time to say no. Once we're up, it's too late. I don't carry the fuel to bring us both back.'

'I know. I'm set.' Tallen was running the harness through his hands, checking it for knots. It was damp and smelt faintly acrid.

The pilot nodded. 'And this is the last time I'll see you face-open. Once we're in the high weather, you're just cargo to be flushed. All that concerns me is my machine. Are you clear on that?'

'I'm clear.'

This time the pilot smiled. 'Okay, check your gear and harness up. Tight as you can. You've got your dismount routine straight?'

'Yes.'

'You nervous?'

'No.'

'You should be. Try not to puke on the webbing.'

The pilot slid his mask down and Tallen was staring at himself stretched wide over the curved black glass of the pilot's headset. Tallen shrugged the harness on and yanked the straps tight, then checked it again. He recognised its smell as old vomit, and found it almost comforting. The weight was unexpected as he tried to stand, dragging at his shoulders and hips. It took him three goes to get to his feet. The pilot said, 'Keep still while I take us up, and no sharp movements once we're high. This machine's finely tuned and I don't need loose baggage. You hear?'

'Yes.'

'Not much of a talker. Not many of you are, but you, you're totally power-down. Is that just about you or is it the reality hit, you think?'

'I've already had my reality hit, thanks.'

Tallen couldn't read the pilot's face behind the shield, and he couldn't read the stretched reflection of his own, either. He wasn't sure if he was calm or simply empty.

The pilot waited a moment more, then said, 'Good.' His visor threw Tallen's image around the small hold as he nodded. 'Time comes, you won't need to stand up. Just tip forward like you did in the simmed drops. When the door opens, adrenaline'll take over. Okay. When we get there, I'm going in wayhigh and I'm going to stay as high as fuel allows. It means you get a longer fall, but you're more likely to hit the net first off. I've only ever lost one on the drop.'

'And high's safer for you.'

'And that, yeah.' The comms blipped off and on again, the pilot's voice a notch lower as he said, 'I'm supposed to advise you to try to rest, but no one ever does. You want the screenery on, or you'd rather not look down?'

'I'll watch.'

'Fine.' He paused. 'Pardon me for this, but are you taking

anything? Only if you're tranked, you won't be sharp enough for the drop.'

'I'm clean.'

'Sure?'

'I've said.'

The pilot's helmet shook. 'Well, not my problem, but no one's ever as flat as this going out.' He pointed a gloved finger at Tallen's head and said, 'There's business going on.' And with that, he closed the door and was gone.

The air sucked and Tallen's ears popped. As he realised he was sealed in the hold, the harness buckles jerked at his shoulders and waist. While he could still adjust the tension, he couldn't release himself.

The thrummer juddered and shook, then tilted hard, lifted sharply and stabilised. The screenery came up, and Tallen was gazing down over Lookout. He could see the dome as a blur, and far away to the west the rigyard with its flocks of crane-beaks and seeming wreckage. Then they were over the sea and rising still until the water was a speckled veil of grey on grey. The thrummer rose higher, the sea becoming like brushed shale, and then they were through the thin cloud and into the blue. A readout faded up at the base of the screen.

AIRSPEED 285KPH ETA RIG 5H48M

TURBULENCE 0.67 GRAVITY FLUCTUATION WITHIN 2.6G

The harness abruptly slackened.

RESTRAINT RELAXED. YOU ARE STRONGLY ADVISED TO EXERCISE

Tallen stood up with difficulty. He walked towards the pilot's door, but the harness cable pulled him up a metre short of it. He walked back again, and found the leash would let him come within a metre of the hull in any direction. He walked a while, forward and back, then sat down again and adjusted the webbing to be as comfortable as possible.

There was nothing on the screenery. The thrummer banked and Tallen fought back a jerk of nausea, swallowing bile. The pull of the webbing at his shoulders brought a flashback to the hospital, and he closed his eyes to a tableau of masked faces, men staring, pulling at him, holding him down to bind him with straps, no, bandages, and himself screaming at the grinding pain. Had that been the hospital? His memories seemed disordered.

The heavy whine of the motor bored into his skull. Tallen gasped air and tried to shut away the rest of the memory, the rush of footsteps and then the shearing pain in his side, and the explosion in his skull. He remembered screaming…

Then an instant of perfect silence immediately replaced by the steady, harsh thrum of the machine, and it was diving and banking hard. The harness was tight, squeezing breath from him, lashing him down. Tallen found the screenery, focused on it. Something smelt bad.

'Hey, cargo. You awake now?'

The sea down there wasn't grey any longer, just a flux of white foam and black shadow. Tallen licked his lips. They tasted foul.

'I said, you awake?'

'Yes.' Tallen could smell puke. It was all over him, starting to crust.

'You okay?'

'I think I puked.'

'You did that before we were even out of the cloud. I told you about that. How are you going to survive a rig? You were screaming and throwing yourself around. Trying to. You remember any of that?'

'I – No.'

'I said you were too calm. I said it, didn't I?'

'What was I shouting?'

'No idea.' The pilot clicked off, then was back. 'Not carried a sane rigger yet.' A pause. 'I had to gas you. I have to ask, are you going to try that again? I've never dropped unconscious cargo yet, but it's in the manual.'

'I'm okay.' Tallen wiped his mouth with the back of a hand. 'How soon will we be there?'

'We are there. Watch your screenery.'

The sea bucked and twisted, and Tallen saw the rig slur back and forth across the screen and then momentarily centre and hold. The sea slewed over the rig's framework, erasing and revealing it. It seemed fragile and tiny.

'You all set?'

'No. Wait.' Tallen pulled his headset down and locked it at the neck, checked his boots. The thrummer banked sharply. 'I said wait.'

'Going in ten. And nine, and eight…'

Pushing his hands into the gloves, he made fists and felt the cuffs lock, sealing him into the dropsuit as the harness began to yank him towards the doorframe. He grunted as the suit bloated and pressurised.

'… and three, and two…'

The helmet air tasted sour as the door slid away.

Lean and tip forward, Tallen remembered, trying to move into position, but he couldn't do it. He couldn't think now, and just watched as the harness cable jerked taut over his head, and then the floor was gone and he was hauled out of the machine and swinging in emptiness. Only it wasn't emptiness at all, this solid slam of air throwing him around, and it was impossible to breathe.

And he was coming round in the hospital, though the memory was again disordered, this was *before* the hospital, and he took a deep breath of the gas to try to stay under, not wanting to remember, but the lungful of helmet air brought him back to the insane wind that was hurling him like a feather in a hurricane, the cable broken and Tallen just falling free.

And he was brought up sharply as the cable took his weight. He looked around, dizzy, and saw the thread of line curling away to the hazy grey dot of the thrummer.

He looked in the other direction. Down? In the sims there had been clarity between up and down and the ship and the sea, but here were just looming shapes, blurred spars and bars. There was no sky and no sea, just the crash of black water overwhelming even gravity. He didn't even know if he was still falling.

After a moment, his feet caught in something and he flailed in panic, trying to shake free, forgetting the sims, but it was suddenly dark as death all around him and whatever had snagged him was sliding up his legs and had his arms too and it was, he realised, the catch-net.

He was in the catch-net. The rig had caught him.

Shaking, but remembering the training now, he felt along the webbing for the nearest lock and clicked it to his harness, and it was suddenly almost like in the sims. He checked the harness, felt for and found two more locks and secured himself to them, and heard a sudden voice in his helmet, crisp despite the booming wind.

'Welcome to the rig, Mr Tallen. Please detach your drop-cable and I will swing you aboard.'

The voice was soft, genderless and immensely reassuring. Tallen released the line and watched it reel up and vanish. He searched the sky for the thrummer, suddenly wanting to say something to the pilot, but there was no way to do that and in any case he didn't know what he might have said.

The net drew itself up and enveloped him. This was quite a different sensation from that of the harness securing him back on the ship. He felt hugged tight by this, muffled and protected. He couldn't see anything. The wind dulled and quietened to a distant murmur, and Tallen closed his eyes and started to cry.

'Are you awake?'

Tallen felt himself drifting, though he was unsure if the sensation were physical. He opened his eyes but couldn't make them focus. Two figures, little more than stocky, frosted blurs, shimmered at the end of the bed – a hard bed – on which he was lying. He took a sharp breath and abruptly froze, afraid he'd find himself locked in the hospital's bodycage again. He closed his eyes and listened to what he assumed were two medicians talking to each other.

'It is an odd question. If he is awake, there is no sensible answer. If he is not, one feels ridiculous.'

'We cannot feel ridiculous. We cannot feel anything.'

'You sound ridiculous. He is awake. The question woke him.'

Keeping his eyes closed, Tallen moved his fingers, then his toes. There was no restriction, though his intention and the consequent movement felt detached from each other. Something was wrong. Something neurological. The surgery he'd had on Bleak was failing.

'My voice woke him, not the question.'

Tallen cautiously raised a hand to his face to feel his nose and cheeks. This time the movement was fine, and there was no cage. And no pain. Still, he felt unsynchronised. He wondered vaguely if he ought to be panicking. He thought he heard himself laugh. Why?

He squeezed his eyes open but they wouldn't focus in the bright ambient light. Everything about him seemed slow.

The voices were comforting, though, like the catch-net had been. His eyes began to hold focus at last.

One of the pair said, 'Good morning, Tallen. We hope you had a comfortable flight.'

The other added, 'We thought you would appreciate some rest.'

Before he had the chance to take in anything beyond the fact that they were humechs, their visual presentations began to shift. Faces came and were replaced seemingly at random, their features ranging from the familiar to the astonishing. He saw himself in one of them for a moment, and then beside it he recognised a childhood friend, a boy he'd forgotten about altogether until now. The faces shifted on, changing as swiftly as he responded to them, and he wondered if he were somehow in control of it.

After a few minutes, the process slowed down. Faces held for a second or two. There was the cynical Paxer from hospital, the one who'd saved Tallen's life, and at his side, one after the other, the two women who had come to visit the Paxer.

There was someone else he recognised, but this one vanished too quickly for him to register anything beyond a thin smile, though it drew a moment's sheer terror from him. The presentations continued. Here was the Holoman, and here the psych from the rig assessment, Veale. Earlier faces returned, with eyes or smiles altered subtly, and Tallen was aware of different pairings suggesting themselves.

As the scrolling slowed, the room settled into perfect focus.

'There,' said one of the humechs, tilting its head to the side.

The other said, 'How do I look?'

Only they weren't humechs at all any more. At least, not like any humechs he'd ever seen. They were looking at him, but he wasn't sure if they were talking to him. They seemed entirely self-involved.

Tallen said, 'Who are you?'

They looked at him, waiting. Tallen felt himself guessing at their names, as if he knew them already.

'I am Lode.'

'And I am Beata.'

The names fixed them for Tallen, and at the same time the room came so sharply into focus that he was aware of every stipple in the sprayed emerald green of the walls. He could hear the faint, powdery background hiss of a sound-damping system and he could feel the movement of the bed against the sea, and distinguish that perfectly from the resistance of the rig's anchors.

He examined the humechs. They were as precisely detailed as the walls. Lode was solidly built, an unshaven, shadow-jawed man with hooded eyes and a wide smile.

His thick brown hair shone. His jacket and trousers were slightly too small. Beata, the woman, was as tall as Lode but lightly framed, her features etched and delicate. Her eyes were startlingly green. She had cropped black hair and long fingers.

'Do we seem your kind of people?' Lode asked.

Beata laughed.

Tallen said, 'Are you holos?'

Beata said, 'Not entirely, but in part. Nothing is everything.'

'What if I touch you?'

'You may try to. We are your interface. We are part of the rig,' Lode said.

'And so are you, now,' said Beata.

The humechs, he realised, had linked to him via his tech.

Lode said, 'You are hungry. Would you like something to eat? There is a nutrition unit by the door. There are clothes too.'

They left him. Tallen sat on the side of the bed for a minute, savouring the almost silence, then stood up and examined himself in the full-length mirror on the wall.

Not bad, he thought. His head looked a little distorted, the titanium skullplates puckering his scalp where the hair was never entirely going to conceal the casing, his forehead asymmetrical, his nose smashed and squashed to the left, his left eyesocket tilted and depressed. Metal shone through. And as he turned sideways, he noticed the faint scoliosis where the neural insertions in his spine hadn't seated perfectly.

No matter. There was no one but the humechs to see him here.

What about afterwards, though?

He didn't want to think about that. This was bad enough, but the idea of afterwards was worse. Was that why he was here? He had been desperate to come here, but now that he had arrived, he felt at a loss.

He nilled the mirror.

Afterwards was a long way away. He didn't need to think about it. He sat at the small metal table and ate like he hadn't eaten for weeks. Turnips, fishmeal, chilli porridge. After washing a beer down his throat he held the glass up to the light and examined it, decided it wouldn't shatter and tossed it into the meltshaft after the bowl and the fork. He wiped the knife clean and slipped it into his pocket.

The humechs weren't waiting in the corridor. There was nothing to choose between right and left, just the narrow passage extending both ways from the small sharp pool of light in which he stood, into dimness. Tallen went right, and with his first step the overhead tracklighting spooled out ahead of him. He glanced back and saw that the dim light in his wake had faded to darkness. No power wasted here, he thought.

For the first few metres, his boots boomed unpleasantly on the dimpled steel flooring, but by the time he'd come to the first branch in the corridor, his footsteps sounded like he was treading quietly on packed earth. The metal of the floor was unchanged. His ears tingled, whined and settled. The tech was mediating his experience.

Without consciously making a decision, he took left and right turns, getting used to the way the lighting reacted to his gaze. After ten minutes, he wasn't even noticing it. There were floor-level mech-comms grilles every ten metres, bulkhead indicators and slamdown ramgates every twenty. The only signs were on the ramgate housings and they all read the same thing: THIS RAMGATE STRESS-GUARANTEED ONE MINUTE ONLY. They were flood barriers, Tallen realised. And they wouldn't be much use here.

He walked for hours. Corridors broadened and narrowed, changed tack and angle. Tallen felt himself automatically mapping it. While he could have found his way back to his original room without any problem, he had little sense of his location within the rig. The room in which he had awoken was his only fixed point, and he had no idea where in the rig it was. There was no context; he needed the sea. He could occasionally smell it, and was increasingly aware that every surface was damp or wet, but he had no idea whether he was undersea or above, at the rig's heart or in its shell.

He carried on. Minutes passed, or hours. Mostly, he kept a steady pace. There were sequences of vertical stair-rungs and repetitive sections of long, drooping chainbridges. He discovered that if he stopped at a door, it would open for him; he found putery and machinery, storage chambers and repair workshops alive with floormechs. Occasionally he'd be looking at something and its name would come to him. Dark storerooms would light up to show him stocks of engine generator sets, racks of chokes and choke manifolds. He had no idea what they did, but he identified them perfectly.

No – that was wrong. He *did* know. The sight brought the word, and the word brought more. But the knowledge was somehow detached from wherever it had come. It was like a suddenly remembered dream, contextless and perfect. Abruptly dizzy, he staggered against the corridor wall. There was no sense of physical contact as he struck it, and he received a sharp smell of purple. He rubbed his shoulder and the smell faded to green.

And then his shoulder was ordinarily hurting, and he massaged it again and had a memory of the blurred forms of Beata and Lode fixing themselves before him.

All of this, he knew, was the rig being calibrated for him, and he for the rig. There was a warmth running up the length of his spine, like a cramp or a chord of music.

With a little more confidence, he walked on. Stenches of oil and smoke came and faded away. He guessed they were real. Jet bridges extended for him and hissed back as he stepped off them. Once a corridor opened out and he stopped at a lookdown over a seemingly bottomless pipestack, the vast five-metre diameter tubes racked vertically. Gazing out, he counted two hundred.

He left the lookdown and carried on, grateful to be back in passages whose walls he could touch. He was developing a headache, probably some reaction to the thrummer flight.

Small mechs, simple-minders and fixers, tracked constantly along the corridors, slowing for instructions at their comms points, carrying on or turning back. Tallen noticed them, had gradually been aware of more of them, but it took him a while to realise that he'd gathered a tail of a dozen at his heels, and as he registered the fact, he felt an abrupt lurch of nausea that stopped him, retching, by a door.

As the door opened, the fixers surged past him and tracked inside to the bank of putery. From across the room, Tallen was caught by the complex screenery with its arrays of ostents and scan patterns.

The headache was pulsing from the nape of his neck to

his temples. He couldn't look away from the screenery. The fixers were crawling like motes at the fringes of his vision. One area of the screenery seemed brighter than the rest. Staring into it, Tallen felt his entire head throbbing. He saw rain and ghosting on the display and almost vomited.

Most of the fixers withdrew from the screenery and swarmed from the room, while the remaining machines threw out power lines, cobwebbing with each other and the wall.

Tallen's head was almost exploding. The room faded until all he could see was the brilliance of the migraine. The swirl of light in his skull tightened and focused and he made out a detailed geometrical design within it.

And he recognised it. He'd never seen one before, but he knew he was looking at the rig's body plan, with all the waterlines and decklines detailed, the planes and curves and intersections. He could see the subsea shaft outlet, the pipeline, the cascade of tributary pipes and the generators thundering in the squat ballast towers.

Tallen's legs failed him and he slid down the wall, and as he slumped to the ground the body plan turned over, swung and telescoped until the hard core of his nausea finally came into view, shining and clear on the plan.

'The bilge,' he croaked.

The bilge? Which one?

He struggled to answer, not knowing where either questions or answers were coming from. How, in such pain, was he thinking so clearly?

Number four. Not the main bracket, though, and not the strake either. The shell plating was intact. His head felt as if it was on fire.

Where then?

He was almost sobbing. He shook his head, but the pain and brilliance only grew more precise.

There! It was the keel, he saw. The long fin of the number four bilge keel had developed a hairline fracture. There.

He squeezed his eyes closed and the pain began slowly to unstitch itself from his skull.

There.

And unconsciousness came to rescue him.

And consciousness once more.

His eyes squeezed closed against the memory of the pain, Tallen felt the slam and suck of the wind around him before he was aware of anything else. Then he smelt it, the extraordinary saffron brine and the scorching, caustic pungency of the sea.

Now he opened his eyes, and the sight of it so vast and close, rearing and breaking, made him yell with joy. The ice-hard spray flayed his face, and the sea deafened him. Between the water's thundering rush and its sieving away, he could make out the fretted metal of the deck.

He tried to look down but couldn't, couldn't move at all beyond a tiny flexing of his chin.

He was back in a cage.

Twenty-four

ALEF

SigEv 29 To the house

Ethan Drame was sitting in his office, relaxed.

'I'm ready to go,' I told him. 'The flycykle's waiting.'

He waved me to a chair. 'No hurry.'

'What is it?'

'There's a change, Alef,' Drame said. 'Don't look so worried. I know you don't like change. Such a strange boy-man, you are. We're bringing Madelene along today. It'll be a surprise for her.'

'Madelene?' This was bad. Pellonhorc wasn't expecting her to be there. I'd told him it would be just the two of us arriving. I didn't know what to do. I said, 'Oh. Oh. Are you sure?'

'She'll want to plan. Choose colours, carpets. The house is just about at that stage. She has to know about it some time, and now's the time. Don't say anything to her, though. I want it to be a surprise.'

My heart was thudding and I felt a little nauseous. I had no idea what I should do. Pellonhorc had told me to behave exactly as I normally would, but I couldn't think how I would normally react to this. I said, 'There's eight hundred and fifty thousand square metres of floor space, and –'

Ethan Drame laughed. 'Alef, you're still just like your father.'

I steadied, fractionally. I didn't mind him saying that. It may seem odd, but there was some form of bond between us. He trusted me, and he'd be proud of me by the end of the day, I knew. I comforted myself by thinking that Madelene coming along was just an algorithm variation.

Madelene came into the room in a swirl of perfume. She looked irritated. Drame caught my eye and shook his head for me to keep quiet.

'What is it?' she said tersely. 'I have things to do.'

'We're going out,' he told her.

'Where?'

'A surprise. A nice one.'

She eyed me. 'With him?'

'Yes,' Drame said, his voice sharpening.

She looked at him and clearly thought better of starting an argument. 'Where are we going?'

'I said it's a surprise. Get ready and we'll see you in the flycykle.'

Drame and I went down to the departure gate. Madelene took a long time to join us, and I started to get anxious.

'Calm down, Alef,' Drame said. His temper was short, and that made me worse.

'Maybe we should go by ourselves this time,' I said. 'Maybe we should take her next time.'

With no warning, he swept his hand out and cut the edge of it into my neck. I collapsed, choking, and I was still retching when Madelene stepped into the cabin and sat down. She ignored both of us.

'Go,' Drame told the pilot.

We travelled in silence. I had recovered by the time we were crossing to the outland, the flycykle juddering, its engine whining. Madelene caught my eye and smiled at me in mock sympathy, and squeezed Drame's knee. Drame breathed out and was calm, as if entering the outland had drawn the mood from him.

As we dropped down, I searched the periphery for Pellonhorc's flycykle, but couldn't see it among the construction machinery. There was just the usual scattering of mixers and diggers and generators.

'You're twitchy, Alef. Why are you so twitchy today?'

'I'm thinking of Ligate,' I said.

'Nothing you can do now. What's set is set. We're here now, so be here.'

Yet again it amazed me that Drame could shut everything away like this. When he was attending to something, his energy was engaged totally with it, and then he could forget it all in an instant.

We came in smoothly and the outer doors of the hangar opened for us. The pilot set us down in the midlock and the outer doors closed again.

We climbed out of the flycykle and stood in the hum of filtered air. Drame stretched his arms and said, 'Where's Mackel?'

Mackel was the foreman. He always came to greet us in the midlock chamber.

'We're late,' I said. 'He's probably busy.' It struck me that I had no idea how Pellonhorc was going to manage this.

Madelene said, 'Where's my surprise? It's filthy here.'

Drame said, 'What's got into you, Alef? You really are

irritating me. You need a piss or something?'

'I don't like being late. You know that.'

While Drame went to the comms panel and spoke into it, Madelene stood by, her lips tight. She was wearing a long coat, solar red, and her boots shone like someone had just licked them. She said, 'Don't look at me like that, Alef. It's creepy. You have any idea how creepy you are?'

'Hell with it,' Drame said. 'Must be a work break.' He overrode the control and the door opened.

No one was there. We were nearly an hour later than I'd promised Pellonhorc. He and Ligate had probably gone, given up. No matter how much Ligate trusted Pellonhorc, he was a long way from home.

Madelene gasped. 'What *is* this?'

Drame instantly cheered up. I stood back in the shadows of the midlock as they went forward to the brightness within.

'It's our house, Madly,' he whispered.

Taken by her excitement, he'd forgotten I was there. She went over to him and leant close and took his hand, and though I could only see the back of them, I could tell she was grinding his hand against her fork. They moved forward awkwardly together. Through the brief spaces between them I could see her clutching at his groin, tugging him along by it. Once she glanced swiftly back and saw me and smiled. She, at least, hadn't forgotten I was there. It was not a pleasant smile she gave me.

There was a wide corridor between the walls of the house and the shell of the containing hangar. Small cranes and mixers and other construction machinery sat there, waiting, along with bags of precatalysed qualcrete and slabs of unpolished marble. A few floormechs skimmed around, but no building work was allowed while Drame and I visited, so that we could examine the house in peace. Even so, there were usually workers sitting around, waiting for us to leave. Today there seemed to be no one. There were just the mouldy smells of building materials and the fine dust drifting in the air. Drame and Madelene had vanished.

I wasn't sure what to do now. I'd assumed that Pellonhorc would be there as soon as the flycykle landed in the midlock, that what needed to be done would be done there and then, but here we were, late, and Madelene was with us. And there was no one else.

'Alef!'

I shrieked. I couldn't help it. I looked around in panic but couldn't see anyone.

'Up here!'

I craned my neck. Ethan Drame was leaning out of a window on the first level. His jacket was off, his hair rumpled. He yelled down, 'When I get back, people are going to get their legs broken. You think this happens every time we leave? No wonder this site's taking so damngod long.'

He turned round at something and vanished from the window. Silence, then a long, low groan of pleasure. Madelene was calming him down.

Maybe Drame was right. Maybe the workers were slacking. They had no idea who they were working for. Even Mackel thought I was the client and Drame some fixer who worked for me. I started to walk round the building, looking for anyone.

The house was on four levels, with sloped outer walls and cantilevered roofs, and balconies and turrets and arches. There were false and true windows, false and true doors, false and true walls. There were hidden chambers that only I and Drame and the building's designer knew about. There was already the beginning of a tunnel beneath the building. There was to be a thrummer landing-pad, military defence systems and secure chambers.

At the far end of the hangar were the workers' quarters. The standard routine was that they were ferried here in closed ships from elsewhere in the System, so that they saw nothing between the hiring station and the inside of the hangar here. None of them worked for longer than a month. They arrived with a set of clothes that were burnt on arrival, and they were given a new set of clothes to leave in when they were ferried away again. I wondered what rumours might be circulating around the System, but I suspected that the secrecy they were sworn to was maintained. Drame had once told me that as the ferry arrived back at its original departure point, one worker was selected at random and executed in front of the others as a warning.

The door to the workers' quarters was closed, but not locked. I pushed it open and went through to a long, narrow corridor.

This was no more than provisional housing, harshly lit and roughly put up. Somewhere ahead, I could hear water running. There was a swingdoor to a canteen, scratchy music surging and dying as I pushed the door and let it close again behind me. Inside there was no one, just the long tables and their benches. A few plates were still sitting on the tables. There was a stench of burnt food and cheap spices. A drink had been spilled; there was a puddle of it on a table by a broken bottle, and a further puddle on the floor. I was shaking, almost afraid to move for the sound my feet would make on the floor. All this made no sense.

Leaving the canteen, I forced myself to carry on exploring. Every part of the workers' quarters seemed to be off this single corridor. The sound of running water was still ahead of me, but I was hesitant about continuing too far from the relative safety of the hangar.

Stepping as lightly as I could and feeling slightly faint, I went to the next door, took a breath and slowly pushed the door open.

A blade of light from behind me shot across the floor and into the chamber. It was a dormitory, and it was quite dark. Realising that I was silhouetted against the light, I pulled the door closed again and stood outside, undecided. I thought I'd seen shapes on the beds, sleeping bodies. Maybe they were asleep. Maybe it was no more than that. In the hangar, there was no day or night, only work and rest. Perhaps the workers were just taking their breaks. Some must be in the showers I could hear sluicing up ahead, just before or after their sleep, and the rest were in here. Yes, I told myself. It was only that.

I pushed the dormitory door open again and this time I slipped inside, closing the door quickly behind me. I stood with my back against the door, aware of my thumping heart, letting my eyes become accustomed to the gloom.

There were shapes in almost every bed, and I breathed more easily. Here they all were, simply sleeping. It was a long room, with a row of beds along each wall, a chair and cabinet beside each one. It reminded me of the church in Gehenna, the beds as rows of pews, and the grave silence. I looked to the far end, almost expecting to see a pulpit, but of course there was nothing.

As I adjusted my weight, the floor creaked, and on one of the furthest beds someone moved and made a noise. I almost laughed with relief. It was a snore.

I could see a little more, now. The sleeping shapes were still, and I wondered ridiculously whether they were too still. Were they drugged? The snoring sleeper was turning restlessly, and I knew I would have to look, but first I went to the nearest bed. The woman there was curled up on her side, the sheet pulled to her chin. I could make out the contours of her face in the shadows. There was nothing obviously wrong, but she didn't seem quite right, somehow. I didn't touch her.

They had to be drugged. Pellonhorc had done it to clear the field for his coup.

I went down the centre of the aisle, feeling very anxious. I had an extreme urge to shout them all awake, and at the same time, I wanted to creep away. Instead of doing either, I counted my breaths. As I came closer to the restless sleeper, he turned slowly towards me and murmured something in that almost-language of the sleep-talker. Without thought, I stopped counting and said, 'What?'

He rolled his head and muttered something more. I still couldn't make it out. I put a hand gently on his shoulder to rouse him, hoping to find out what was going on here, and brought my hand abruptly away.

My palm was soaking wet and my fingers were sticky. He turned, jerkily, and blood bubbled up at his neck, and then he sighed, a heavy frothy breath that seemed never to end.

I sprawled backwards and fell, barely holding back a scream. His throat was cut all the way across.

I crawled out of the dormitory on my hands and knees

and stumbled, puking, to crash blindly through the door and down the corridor to the last chamber. The washroom.

The noise of water was deafening, and hot wreaths of steam filled the air. I was retching and thinking only of the mutilated man. I puked into a sink and washed the blood from my hands and sluiced my face, then wiped a palm across a fogged mirror and stared at myself. There was no more blood on me, but through the mists I saw thick trails of blood smeared on the walls, and there were wadded bloody towels thrown all over the floor.

Someone else had done as I had just done. Someone else had washed blood away, and washed and washed and washed.

Ligate had done this, I told myself. Only Ligate could have done it. Not Pellonhorc. I turned and ran back down the corridor and out of the workers' quarters, and let the door fall closed behind me, and then I slid to the ground, sobbing.

I was remembering the deaths of my parents. My throat was closed so that I could hardly breathe. I tried to make a whisper, but couldn't even do that. The brilliant, shadowless glare of the hangar was almost unbearable after the darkness of the dormitory, and the silence was terrifying.

Eventually I got to my feet and calculated the number of bricks in the house, and worked out the quantities of mortar and marble that would be needed, and the weight of it all, and then I headed slowly back.

'Alef! Where were you? I've been calling.'

I stifled a scream. It was Drame, just as before, leaning out of the window as if no time had passed. For an instant I thought that I had imagined what I'd seen in the workers' quarters. Over Drame's shoulder another face suddenly appeared, but it was only Madelene grinning smugly at me.

'Come up,' Drame told me, and disappeared.

I hesitated, wondering what had gone wrong with the plan. Everyone dead, but was it over? I had a terrible feeling that I had brought Ethan Drame and myself to our deaths. Maybe Ligate had realised that this was a trap for him. He would have killed Pellonhorc before leaving and left the body for Drame to find, just like he had left the workers' corpses. Maybe Pellonhorc's corpse had been among those of the workers, back in the dormitory.

Maybe Ligate was still here.

I went as if in a dream to the door of the house and crossed the threshold. To my left and right were the housings for beam sensors that would detect certain types of weapon and comms devices. The sensors hadn't been installed yet.

The hall was wide and long. Dustsheets lay on the floor, and my feet made no sound. There were doors to left and right, half open, the dustsheets lying rippled at the heels of the doors. I went to the wide swirl of stairs and started to climb, my feet scuffing the sheets where they were roughly tacked at each riser. I looked back as I ascended the long, shallow curve, but there was no one, and my feet were soundless on the material.

On the first floor I headed along the gallery towards the master suite where, I hoped, Drame had finished fucking Madelene. The door was closed, so I knocked. The sound was muffled. My knuckle was spotted with dust, and I rubbed it away on my trousers. My trousers were very faintly speckled with blood.

'Come in, Alef.'

I pushed the door open nervously, wondering what I could read from Drame's voice.

'She likes it,' Drame said, hitching up his trousers. 'Don't you, Madly?'

Madelene smiled.

He touched her arm. 'Now, let's have a proper tour of the place.' He grinned and whispered to her, as if I weren't there, 'And thank you, Madly, for my own little tour.'

She put on a cheap voice. 'I think you've seen everything, sir. If there's anything you'd like to see again…'

They weren't ignoring me at all. They needed me to watch their flirting. It struck me very clearly that I was reading the subtlety of their expressions and tones without any effort, reading their every glance and gesture. I felt an alertness that I'd never known before; what I saw was sharper, brighter, and time was turning more slowly.

'Lead on, Alef,' Drame said.

I turned and left the room, saying, 'We can start up here.' I was working out the most efficient way to cover the house. From here, we'd go to the roof and work our way back down. I went to the next flight of stairs. Madelene and Drame made no noise behind me and I glanced back. They were on the gallery, looking down. My heart thudded. I called, as soon as I could gather my voice, 'What is it?'

Drame looked slowly up at me and then looked down again. 'Madelene thinks it needs to be in pale green.' He took her hand and they came up the stairs. I breathed again. No one was here but us. No one alive, at least. Surely Ligate wouldn't wait so long. I couldn't convince myself of that, though.

I went fast, now, up the stairs to the roof, and I pushed

open the door to the flycykle deck. Nothing was there but a carpet of dust. I waited, and when Drame and Madelene came out onto the deck, I showed them the space with a wave of my arm and said, 'We should go now. We've been longer than I intended. We have to get back.'

Drame said, sharply, 'Alef?' He squinted at me and pulled Madelene away from the door and slammed it with a kick, leaving us in the open. 'You've been acting spooked all morning. I thought it was just your normal shit, but it isn't. What the hell is it?'

'We've been here fifty-eight minutes,' I said. 'A tour will take at least another forty-five, even if we don't stop. There's twenty-three rooms, stairs and corridors –'

'Shut the fuck up, Alef. Something's wrong when you start mumbling numbers, every time. What's going on?' He had a gun in his hand. He punched the barrel into my temple and held it there, grinding it into the skin. 'Tell me right now.'

Madelene said, 'Wait, Ethan. How's he going to tell you anything if you kill him?'

'It's a surprise,' I said. My head was juddering against the gun barrel. I couldn't hold it still. Drame wrapped his other hand around my skull, cradling my head tightly between the gun and his palm. I said, 'Pellonhorc should have been here. He was supposed to lure Ligate here so you could kill him. It was a present for you. But we got here late. Ligate must have gone.' I licked my dry lips. It didn't help. 'Everyone's dead here. He's killed them all.'

'Shit.' Drame kicked the door. 'And Pellonhorc? Where's he?'

'I think Ligate must have killed him too.'

'Shit,' Drame said again. He threw me down and dropped to his knees, crawling to the edge of the deck and peering out. Madelene fell flat and swore. Drame took a moment to scan the floor below and pushed himself away from the edge. 'Right,' he said. 'We're leaving. Alef, you're only still alive because you're somehow too stupid to have thought what was wrong with this.' He checked his gun. 'Madelene, what are you carrying?'

'You know what I'm carrying, Ethan.' She tried a smile but her voice was trembling.

'Well, get it out and point it at the fucking door. You can make jokes when we're back home, if we make it. If Ligate was stupid enough to get himself here, he's not about to leave without something bigger than my fool of a son's death. Alef, you carrying any sort of a weapon?'

'No.'

He shook his head. 'And we're on the fucking roof. No way down from here but the door.'

We all stared at the door.

Twenty-five

BALE

The Chute stores were clustered between the rigyards and the spaceport. There were fly-suit stalls, repair booths, suitcomms specialists, suit and fin designers, and then, beyond the stores, in a long line set directly at the edge of the shield, there were the tanks.

Bale had learnt to ride the Chute in these tanks. They were ranked in order of size, from the chambers where you learnt to hang and turn, to the half-kil tubes where you could get a brief sense – almost – of the joy and terror of the real thing.

The tanks were fronted with hardglass and walled with cerock. The edge of Lookout's shield sat right along the tank roofs so that Bleak's wind could be streamed through them.

Bale was headed for the stores, but he couldn't resist a look at the tanks first. A group of formation riders were in one of the half-kils, looking blurred and ragged through the thick glass, arrowing left to right and flipping back again, the tank's wind switching direction for them as they approached the ends. The riders were perfectly synchronised, seemingly strung together. The crowd gathered along the tank nodded and sighed. Bale stood and watched the display for a few moments, this shoal of fish in thick water, swimming mindlessly from end to end.

Bale didn't get the idea of being part of a pattern. What was the point in that? He went back to the stores until he found the one he wanted. The name flashed over the door, printing on his retina and only readable when he closed his eyes:

Faster!

The front of the store was a mockup of a tank. It looked good, but it was no more than stage wind in a tryout box. A rider was in there trying out a lightsuit. The glitter and flash of the suit's lights made the rider look no better than he was. He thumped from side to side, spinning off the glass.

Faster! serviced the rich and their kids. It was a store for the look-at-mes who rode the tanks a few times a year and kept to the node when they did. Bale wore a cheap suit. He maintained it himself and rigged its comms too. He went inside as the window rider exited unsteadily, peeled the suit, confirmed a flight fee with the woman at the counter and limped from the shop. She watched him leave, then met Bale's eye without expression.

'You get a lot of window riders?' Bale said.

'You could be one. Except you look a bit old.'

'I'm not one.'

'Shame. I make more out of the window than anything else. So, you just wishing the wind?'

'I hear you're the place for NTGs. What have you got?'

'NTGs? You know what they are?' She waved the question away. 'Never mind. Over there.'

He looked at the short rack of translucent bootboxes, each with a pair of NTGs hanging in gelair. Fifteen in prime colours, five more in silver and a single gold pair. 'The gold,' he said. As she hooked the lone box down, he asked, 'You sell a lot of these?'

'The gold? No.' She thought again. 'Two sets last month, though. Same buyer. Before that, I can't remember.' She turned the box over. The boots shimmied inside, catching the light and returning it a hundred times brighter.

'Who to? You remember?'

'He said he wanted something special. I told him these are the best. They are. You want me to demonstrate them?'

'Yes.'

'There's a twenty dolor charge. Refund if you buy. You still want it?'

'How much are the boots?'

'Three hundred.'

He looked at the box. 'You said *three*?'

She picked up the box and started to turn away.

He put his hand out. 'Show me.'

'Show me twenty, then.'

He gave her his payflake. She watched the credit go through, said, 'Thank you, Mr Bale,' then took a small case from the sleeve of the bootbox and slid a grey metal disc carefully into the palm of her hand, keeping her fingers clear of the curl of brilliant gold leaf set in the centre of the disc.

'Watch closely,' she said. 'You're paying a lot of money for this.' She laid the disc on the counter, glanced at Bale, then gently touched the very edge of the leaf with the tip of a finger. The entire leaf instantly turned a dull black. She said, 'Okay?'

'Yeah.'

'You want the rest of the demonstration, or should I give you ten back and let you walk out? I don't usually make that offer, only you look pathetic.'

'Just do it.'

She slid a second disc from the case and went to the window tank, docked the disc in the access door and eased it all the way out to the centre of the window on a skeletal feed-arm. The arm shuddered as the wind built.

'Okay,' she said. 'As you'll know, the wind modifies the material's behaviour. In the still, these boots are max sensitive. Other NTGs, you can brush against them and they'll hold their colour. Not the golds. One touch on the sole, like I showed you, and the whole boot goes black. That's in the still. In the wind, the molecular structure shifts. Watch.' She played the controls of the box, pulled some scree into the wind, let it pepper the disc, then stilled the wind, and pulled the disc out, handing it carefully to Bale. The metal was deeply pitted but the central leaf was still gold and perfect, smooth as a lens.

Bale gave the leaf the barest smear of his fingertip. It instantly turned black.

She told him, 'Like I said, these are the best. I don't refund for accidental touch. You can insure them, but they never pay out. Still interested?'

'You sold him exactly these?'

She tipped the dead discs into a burnbin and nodded.

'You seen him before?'

She held up the box. 'You buying these, Mr Bale?'

'Yes. He take anything else to go with them?'

'Two eighty, then. He bought a suit. Said he hadn't ridden the Chute in years. Took a fast suit, though, knew exactly what he wanted, all the fins and cutters.'

'He try the suit out in your window?'

'No. Said he was sure it'd come back to him. You looking for a suit too?'

'He paid hard money, didn't he? Wasn't carrying a flake. You banked the notes already?'

'It's legal. You're Pax?'

'Not today. You got cams here?'

'Usually. That day we had a surge.'

Bale nodded easily. The guy had either paid her to wipe her records, or else he'd wiped them himself. 'I guess you wouldn't recognise him again.'

'No.'

'He's an old friend. I haven't seen him in a while. I just wondered if he's changed much.' Bale gave her his card. 'Taller than me. Used to have brown hair. Is it still brown?'

'I didn't notice.' Putting the payflake through, she said, 'He told me someone might be coming in. Normally I only carry one set of the gold; it takes a while for new stock to come in. But he said to order some more right now. I guess that was you.'

Bale held the box up. The boots shifted gently in their gelair packing. 'He did us both a favour, then.'

She got interested again. 'You're sure you don't need the suit? I can show you what he took.'

'No. I think that's all.'

About to give him back his payflake, she said, 'There was a message, now I think of it. It was a bit odd. He said only to give it to someone if they bought the boots. He said to tell you he was hoping he'd only have to wear one set.' She looked at Bale to see if it made sense to him, adding, 'I'm sure I got that right. It make sense to you?'

'Yes. He's a crazy guy.'

For the first time, she smiled at him. Bale, at the door, turned and said, 'That old burn on the back of his right hand – he still keeps flexing it?'

'Yes,' she said. 'Hey, should I get some more of these boots?'

'I wouldn't bother.'

Tallen

'How are you?' said Lode.

'Well done,' Beata said. 'You survived your tour.'

Tallen rolled out of the bed and took himself a drink. It smelt faintly of the sea. He said, 'Are you surprised?'

The humechs looked solid enough, their features fixed. If you squinted, they might have been real. Human. Lode said, 'No, we are pleased. We are pleased about you.'

'And for you,' said Beata.

Tallen sat in a chair. He was sure there hadn't been a chair in the room last time. He said, 'How much of this is real?'

'It is all real,' Lode said.

Beata said, 'When that stops, you are dead.'

Tallen said, 'My headache. Explain that.'

'The headache is your tool. The bilge has been damaged for a short while. We left it for you to discover. Your test.'

Reality alone wasn't enough, though. He was starting to find the mechs' mixture of solicitousness and disengagement irritating. He said, 'Suppose it hadn't been damaged. Would you have created a problem?'

'There is always a problem,' Beata said.

The drink tasted of the sea. He threw the cup away, but the taste was still in his mouth and nose. 'I dreamt of the sea,' he said. 'I was back in a bodycage again.'

Lode said, 'It was not a bodycage. It was to protect you. You were on deck. There is an open capsule designed for these exposures.'

'It was real?' He closed his eyes, remembering.

'Yes,' Beata said. 'That was a reward. The sea is something special for you. Your sensory adaptation incorporates an awareness of it, so that it can invigorate you.'

Tallen rubbed his eyes.

Lode said, 'But you are special, Tallen. Unique. What was done to you has left you very sensitive indeed. It is more than a strength. Much more. You must be careful.'

Tallen said, 'I'm sorry. You aren't being clear. You look like people and you speak in sentences, but it doesn't quite make sense. It makes me feel as if there's something wrong with me.'

'We know that. We are sorry.'

'It is not you. It is us.'

He said, 'I'd rather see you as you are. Your appearance confuses me.'

Beata and Lode glanced at each other. 'That should pass,' they said.

Bale

Bale stood in the corridor and said, 'Hi, Delta.'

'What are you doing here, Bale?'

'I'm saying goodbye to a friend. Visiting her at home. You're not on duty, are you?' She hesitated and he said, 'I know you're not. You came off an hour ago.'

'Come in, but you know I can't talk to you.' She glanced

along the corridor before closing the door behind him.

'Then listen to me. The last victim, remember? In the alley. I was drunk. You should have stood me down. Why didn't you?'

She sat down at the small table and pushed her breakfast bowl aside. 'You wouldn't listen to me, like you never listen to anyone. You aren't now. Just go, Bale. I don't know what you're talking about.'

'All you needed to do was cut me out of the commslink.'

'Everyone was needed. I was told to keep you in. To keep everyone in.'

'Who told you to keep me in?'

'I said everyone, not just you, Bale. I asked if I should delink you and they said keep everyone. I was worried about you.'

'Who said it? You were odd with me from the go. Telling me to call you Officer Kerlew.'

She stood up and took the bowl into the kitchen, where she placed it in the sink. Bale followed her. 'There were observers from Admin that week. They were all over us. They turned up a week ahead of the event.'

Bale was right behind her. 'Observers? I didn't know about that.'

'A team of auditors. Checking our routines, everything. When the incident started, they were there, watching everything we did. They said we did fine.'

'Fine? I was down there unarmed.'

'I know. It was a mess. The team were really good about it. They said Navid shouldn't be too hard on you.' The water in the sink rose, bringing the dirty bowl with it. She poked it back down with a finger.

Bale asked, 'Did Navid send you to the hospital to see me?'

'No, that was just me. I know what you're like. I didn't want you to get into more trouble. And I felt bad. If you'd listened to me, you'd still be a Paxer. I'm not going to feel bad about it, Bale.'

'The auditors – were they there all night, or did they just arrive for the event?'

'They were there all along. Hell, Bale, I know you so well. You think they knew about it in advance? You think they set it all up as a test, some excuse to shed you?' She shook her head. 'You think too much. They were there all day and all night the whole week, checking routines, cams, locations, patrols. Day and night. And our records, they went through everything. Routine inspection, that's all.'

'How come I never knew they were here?'

'It was a secret audit. Nothing new about that. So activity's as routine as possible.'

'Word always gets out.'

She pushed him towards the door. 'They said that. They said if it got out this time, we'd lose our jobs. I don't want to lose my job. Please go now.'

'They've gone, have they?'

'I think so. Goodbye, Bale.'

Razer

Razer woke up with the image of the tossed glittering scrap of metal in her mind and said the name aloud. Chorst Maerley! *That* was who Larren Gamliel had reminded her of.

Maerley wasn't hard to find on the Song, and her comm was picked up within two seconds of the send.

'Hey, Razer, you look good. Odd timing. I was thinking about you.'

Maerley didn't look so good. His skin was speckled and there was a tremor to his cheek. She said, 'I saw a VoteNow on AfterLife a few days back that reminded me of you. Maybe you saw that and thought of me?'

'No,' he said, and laughed, the tremor modifying the easy chuckle she remembered. He said, 'Who'd ever want me back? I sure wouldn't.'

'His name was Larren Gamliel.'

'Let me check.' Maerley's head went out of sight for a moment. 'No, I didn't get that cast, and it doesn't come up. You know how it is; they sometimes tailor these things. I'll look for it later and give the poor bastard a yes. Where are you?'

'Bleak. In Lookout.'

'You kidding? How did you find out I was here?' He shook his head and said, 'I thought you never went back to old stories.'

'I don't. That's weird you're here. Listen, I haven't got time to talk now, but what are you doing here?'

'Working. Why else would I have come to this place? Though if I'd known you were going to be here –'

She cut him off. 'You said you'd been thinking of me. Why?'

'We talked a lot about subsea travel, remember? I taught you how to pilot subs? Well, I've just completed and sold three vehicles for extreme subsea conditions, and now I've got this other client wanting a single unit, very similar. And here am I now, thinking of you because of that, and –'

'What clients?'

Maerley shook his head. 'Couldn't tell you even if I knew.'

'When did you get the work?'

'The first one a few months back. The second one a few days ago. Big rush. And like I said, just after I'd just finished the other subsea job for someone else. I guess word travels. I've never been so busy.'

'The second client. Was that a face-to-face meet?'

'Most of my meets are by vis-comm, but this one was putting themselves through a crypted mesh.'

'Like an AI?'

'This wasn't an AI. But yes, like one. Why?'

'And the first client?'

'You're pushing it, Razer. Crimers or mercs, no doubt. And that's enough questions. You said you don't go back to old stories.'

'No. Listen, Maerley, can I see you? For old times?'

He laughed, though his lips trembled for seconds after the end of it. 'There are no old times any more.'

'For remembering good times, then. We did have good times, didn't we? Where are you?'

'I bet you're like this with all your old stories. I'm down by the rigyards. I've set myself up behind a hostel, The Rig at Rest. It would be good to see you, Razer.'

She nilled the comms and touched the nub of the augmem at her ear. Maerley was here, then. Was all of this coincidence? She thought of Tallen. It would be good to see him, but that wasn't possible any more.

* * *

Tallen

Back in Lookout, before he'd ever imagined himself on one, Tallen had seen rigs in the rigyards. They had been orderly things, ridiculously scaled. On land, they had been incomprehensible; the cranes, the winches and their great wheels and ratchets, the cantilevered decks, the derricks, cables, pulleys and drills. A rig was more like the bones of a shallow-orbit dock than anything else. Back in Lookout, Tallen could more easily have imagined rigs spinning through empty space than in the maelstrom of the sea.

But from the confines of his cage on the deck of this rig, soaked and battered and nearly drowned, and exhilarated beyond all measure, Tallen saw that it was only here that a rig made sense. This was the opposite of space. On deck, everywhere was full of object or event. The deck, crashing with water, was stacked with locked-down pyramids of pipe and casing. Booms swung across the sky, and the sky shed water so heavily that Tallen couldn't tell where it ended and the sea began.

Now, after a month, Tallen thought he was starting to go crazy. He walked the entire rig every two days, alternating the subsea and the oversea sections. He was tuned so completely to the rig's systems-checks and monitoring putery that the slightest dysfunction gave him dizziness or nausea, stomach ache or cramp in an arm or a leg, or a toothache, and depending on where he was walking, he would know what the problem was, and where. His constant retinue of fixers would congregate and supervise the repair.

'I don't see why you need me,' Tallen told the humechs. 'Your systems would catch everything.'

'Yes, but not always swiftly enough,' said Beata. 'There are small problems, imperceptibly progressive faults, like the bilge keel in your test.'

He frowned, unable to fix a memory. 'What test?'

'Yes,' said Lode. 'Problems are easier to fix when we catch them early. If they are external, small things can become large very quickly. Big things we have to catch immediately. Putery could do it, but at that level of complexity, the human brain is more efficient and economical.'

'That is why you're here, Tallen,' Beata said.

'Or someone else,' said Lode.

Tallen found his head twitching from one humech to the other as they spoke. It was almost hypnotic. The constant shifting of attention was grinding away at him. It was stopping him from thinking straight.

'We know how the life here wears you down,' Beata said. 'The concentration. The pain. Over time, they will affect you.'

'They will affect your efficiency,' said Lode. 'But you're the best we've ever seen. You might have been designed for this. Your neural augmentations and our systems are almost symbiotic. You are amazingly fast.'

'Please don't talk at me like this,' Tallen said weakly. He tried to stand up, but he was already standing.

'Though you are more sensitive than is usual,' said Lode. 'We don't know if you'll last longer for this reason.'

'Or less long,' said Beata.

Tallen put his hand in his pocket and closed a fist around the handle of the knife. It was oddly comforting, though he had no idea how it had got there. He pulled his wits together and said, 'But why is there no one else human here? Surely that would make sense. I'd have company and you'd have backup.'

'Conflict develops. It didn't work, ever. A side-effect of humans, unfortunately.'

He searched for expression in their faces, but there was none. Sometimes there was. And they always stood the same distance apart, and the same distance from him. He asked, 'What happens at night, when I sleep?'

'We walk you. You don't stop working,' said Beata. 'It is efficient. The sea doesn't stop. It is also efficient.'

Lode said, 'We also reward you, as you have seen. The sea appears to –' Lode glanced at Beata.

'– to increase your efficiency. More so than anyone before you.'

'We don't understand that,' Lode said. 'It makes no sense to us.'

'But there is much about you that makes no sense.'

'About me, or about humans?' Tallen said. He was aware of himself starting to imitate their inflectionless tone.

'Yes,' said Lode.

They continued to reward him, or to maintain him. Every few days he would wake up and find himself on deck again with the sea at his face, and for a while that seemed to restore him.

Beata and Lode saw him every day. He would direct himself just to Beata, or just to Lode, but whatever he did, they both returned his conversation.

Tallen said to Beata, 'Can I talk to just one of you at a time? I don't like this. You look different, but that isn't enough.'

'No,' Beata replied. 'This doubling is designed to hold

your attention and defocus aggression. We will go and take advice, though.'

Lode said, 'Tell us, how do you feel, Tallen? Can you describe it?'

Tallen said to Beata, 'You monitor me. You should know.'

Lode said, 'Tell us anyway.'

'Can the one I speak to be the one who answers me? Is that acceptable?'

'Human contact is important,' Beata said. 'It is vital for your psychological wellbeing. And giving voice to your feelings assists the process of self-knowledge. It gives you a sense of engagement.'

'You aren't human, Beata,' Tallen said.

'Even though you know this, you respond as though we are.'

'Though not as much as we would like you to,' added Lode.

Tallen put his head in his hands and said, 'I don't feel right. I feel good on deck, but it doesn't last. And it isn't happiness. It isn't a real feeling.'

'No,' said Beata.

Lode said, 'Can you explain how you don't feel right?'

'When I'm walking the rig, I know where I am at every moment, I know where I'm headed and where I still have to cover. I know what's behind every door as I pass it. But I can't remember where I've just been. And now, if I try, I can't think where anything is.' He was aware of water in his eyes. 'All I can think of is the sea.'

Beata said, 'You still like the sea, though.'

'Yes. But I can't concentrate on anything. I could at first, a little, but now I don't feel connected to anything but this.'

Beata and Lode looked at each other. They said, 'Get some sleep, Tallen.'

After that, they gave him the sea more frequently. He developed a routine of sleeping, waking to the sea and sleeping again. And otherwise, he walked. He found himself thinking of the sea whenever he stopped thinking about the rig. Occasionally he thought of Lookout, but as a distant, indistinct memory. His life settled down to the endless walking, the aches and the pains and the invigoration of the sea. Now and again he had headaches unrelated to the rig, or felt unreasonably angry or euphoric. Sometimes he cried.

Once he found a knife in his pocket and wondered what it was doing there. He almost threw it away, but for some reason found he couldn't do that.

Twenty-six

ALEF

SigEv 30 More death

Drame said, 'Okay, Alef, open the door with your right hand. I want your body blocking it. Keep your arm high, I'll be aiming under your armpit. Wait for my word.'

I waited. Two point two seconds. I felt the sweat gathering in my armpit.

'Go.'

I pulled the door open. It stuck for a moment, then came sharply wide, slamming loudly against the wall, *bang*! There was no one there.

'Okay. Drop your arm and start down the stairs. Go steadily and quickly. If you slow or stop, I'll take it you're Ligate's player and Madelene will put you down. Madelene, you hear that?'

'Yes, Ethan.'

I was already moving. At the top of the stairs I tripped over the edge of a dust sheet and went sprawling. Madelene fired over my head, the sound ringing down the stairwell. I got up and looked at her. Drame said quietly, 'Mad, I said to kill him, not warn him.'

'I was trying to kill him.'

'Next time don't miss. Alef, get going. Watch your feet.'

We took half an hour to get back to the ground. The front door was open a little. Drame said, 'Alef, did you leave it like that?'

'Yes. Exactly like that.'

He looked hard at me and said, 'One thing you're good for, at least.' He looked out, left and right. The door to the midlock was down the workmen's track, about fifty metres away. The track was overlooked by the house all along. Drame looked up and down, taking his time. The hangar's inner wall was featureless. There was no machinery in this section of the track. The wall of the house was our only threat.

Drame said, 'This is how we do it. Alef, you go first. Keep tight to the wall of the house so if there's anyone, they have to lean out to see you. Whatever happens, don't stop. Get to the midlock and open it. I'll cover you all the way. When it's open, you wave. You ready?'

'Yes.'

'Then go.'

I ran, my arm banging along the wall of Drame's house, my feet echoing. It seemed like I'd never get there, and then I was outside the midlock and leaning on its seal-bar, pushing the heavy door. As soon as I had it halfway open, I turned and waved. I could feel the cool air at my back. Drame pushed Madelene out into the open corridor and she started running towards me. Her mouth was wide. Her shoes weren't made for running. She kept her eyes on me, though there was no expression in them. I think she was trying to keep all thought from her head while she was exposed out there. Nothing happened, though. She ran straight past me and into the midlock. I kept my eyes on the track.

I waved to Drame and he came crouched out of the doorway in a swift, loping run, hugging the wall but changing pace all the time. When he reached me, he stopped by the open door and put the gun to my head again. 'If I didn't still need you, Alef, you'd be dead right here. Understand me?' I nodded. He took my hand and separated my little finger and bent it back, hard, until I squealed. 'When we get back, I'm cutting this off. Just so you don't forget.' He let my finger go. 'If I didn't like you, I'd make you eat it.' He looked at me, making sure I understood he wasn't joking, and then he stepped into the midlock. Peering into the gloom, his gun suddenly raised waist-high, he said, 'Madly?'

It struck me that the midlock lights should have gone on as soon as the seal had been broken. And that the seal-bar hadn't sounded right as I'd worked it.

Beside me, squinting into the midlock, Drame stopped. 'What?'

The door smashed back at him, throwing him down. The gun was still in his hand and he brought it up as Ligate – I could see him crouching, eyes bright – fired. The long bead of light was swift and brilliant in the darkness.

I thought instantly that Drame had dropped his gun, but as the midlock lights flared and held, I saw it was his hand that he had let fall, severed at the wrist. He jammed the stump against his waist to stem the stream of blood and went for the dropped gun with his other hand, but Ligate kicked the weapon, still clutched in Drame's fist, across the floor. Without pausing, Drame stood up and hurled himself at Ligate.

I was still standing by the door, in shock. Even the numbers had left me, and I was just seeing the whole scene as if overlaid on a threedy grid. I was observing the lines and curves of motion, of the firing, the arcs of blood, the bounce of the hand-and-gun and then their clatter across the floor, of Drame slamming awkwardly into Ligate who stumbled and checked his balance as Drame came at him again.

Ligate scythed the butt of his gun into Drame's jaw, rocking him but not stopping him, and then steadied himself to fire at Drame's knees, first shattering and then pulping them, one after the other, as Drame dropped to the ground.

Ethan Drame was extraordinarily tenacious. Even at this, he didn't make a sound. As his legs were ruined, he collapsed in silence, watching Ligate carefully, supporting himself on his good hand, the wrist-stump still pushed into his waist, spreading red. It looked as if he were reaching deep into himself.

'Hello, Ethan,' Ligate eventually said. He was breathing heavily, but he was smiling and the corners of his eyes were creased in pleasure. 'Nothing to say? Aren't you at least going to say hello to your son?' He made a gesture with his head, keeping his eyes on Drame.

I turned, the first move I'd made, and my neck clicked with tension – and there was Pellonhorc standing in the corner of the midlock.

He was alive!

Madelene was sprawled unconscious at his feet. As Pellonhorc knelt and lifted her easily, she groaned and her eyelids trembled, and quite abruptly her eyes were wide open. Pellonhorc snaked his arm around her neck and tightened his grip, standing straight.

I wondered what was happening. I tried to fit this in with the plan. Madelene shouldn't be here, in the plan.

She brought her hands up to rip at his forearm but didn't have any strength. Her mouth opened and closed. I noticed how very red her lipstick was. For the first time, there was sufficient silence for me to hear the aircon hum of the midlock. It was as loud as Madelene's rasping breath. Her face was pale and growing paler. Her head drooped and her eyes began to close.

Pellonhorc said, 'Hello, Father. Alef, you were late. I was getting worried.'

'Madelene –' I started. Pellonhorc brought up his other hand and I saw the knife in it, the blade dull and blood-smudged. I thought of the bodies in the workers' quarters.

'Madelene, yes,' he said. 'I wondered how we were going to manage that, but you brought her along. Thank you, Alef. It was worth our wait, after all.' He continued to compress her throat until she fell entirely limp. Her breathing was shallow, but it was there. Pellonhorc was staring at his father.

Ligate said, mildly, 'Now. How shall we do this? Pellonhorc, you mentioned you'd like your father to watch Madelene die. Alef, you can relax. You've shown your loyalty.' He adjusted his grip on the gun. I could hear the squeaking, the slipping of the metal in the sweat of his palm. He said, 'Ethan, I know you won't beg for yourself, but surely you'll want to ask your son for the life of your mistress. Who knows? He may be generous.'

Drame shifted his position as much as he could and scraped the stub of his wrist carefully up his chest until it was cradled firmly in his armpit. It seemed as if he were clothed in blood. He said nothing. His gaze didn't leave Ligate.

Pellonhorc was controlling Madelene's breathing with his forearm, his elbow tensing and relaxing, keeping her at the edge of consciousness. She was awake but without the strength to resist. 'This is disappointing, Father,' he said. 'Madelene, aren't you disappointed?'

She began to weep. The expression in her face was awful, her eyes closing and then opening unnaturally wide as he regulated her air, her nostrils flaring, her teeth bared and her tongue starting to push out. Her breath was rattling, and I was sure her windpipe must be cracked. Pellonhorc's cheek was pressed against hers, his eyes half-closed and dreamy. I'd seen such an expression on the pornosphere when Pellonhorc and I had first explored it. We'd seen it together without understanding it, on the faces of men and women as they'd fucked.

Ligate held off a moment, perhaps as momentarily startled as I was, and said, 'Please, Pellonhorc, let's not be distracted.'

Pellonhorc opened his mouth slightly, almost delicately, then let the grip of his forearm slacken. Madelene brought her head up, the colour starting to bloom in her cheeks, and she took her weight insecurely on her legs. She looked lost and dazed, and started to shiver. She held onto Pellonhorc's arm with both hands for support. As she twisted her head to look directly at him, he brought his hand up to her forehead and drew her head back, gently at first and then more firmly until her throat was taut. He was staring into her eyes.

He was staring straight into them. He seemed to be waiting for something.

Ligate said, 'Pellonhorc –'

Madelene gasped and tried to swallow, the movement stretching her throat even tighter, and at that instant Pellonhorc raised his arm and drew his blade steadily and deeply across her throat and let her fall.

As the blood looped and descended in a fading parabola, Pellonhorc leaned into the arc and put out his tongue like some insect.

All this time, I was doing nothing. I do not claim innocence. I cannot explain myself. I had already seen so much.

I have to. That's what I was thinking, that I had to do something. That to do nothing was to be nothing. I couldn't, though. I tried to banish the image of what I had just seen Pellonhorc do from my mind, but it did no more than join all the other things I had seen.

It came into my head that at the end of it all, at the end, I was simply an animal and no more than that. We were all animals with a thin veneer of evolution.

I thought of Gehenna, suddenly and with a terrible yearning. It was so simple on Gehenna. It was my childhood. I wanted to cry, but I couldn't. I wanted to be on my knees before Father Grace and asking him for forgiveness, as if he could give me such a thing. I wanted Madelene to be alive. I wanted myself and Pellonhorc to be children again. *Oh, Gehenna!*

'Now, Ethan,' Ligate was saying. 'Your son wanted to kill you himself. I understood but I said no. That's to be my pleasure.'

Pellonhorc was staring at his father. I must have made some small move that caught his attention, and he nodded at me as if I had made a deliberate sign, and then he indicated Ligate. I had no idea what he meant, but I saw that his knife was in a throwing grip. I was horribly aware of my heart thudding. I didn't understand any of this.

Ligate brought his gun up and took aim at Drame's stomach. 'I'm almost reluctant to kill you, Ethan,' he said. 'I've waited so long. Let's see if we can make you talk. Some small gesture of hopelessness at the end.'

His grip on the gun tightened, and Drame made a small noise. The sound of Ethan Drame whimpering was shocking.

I almost screamed at Pellonhorc to throw the knife, but he held off.

Ligate smiled. 'There –' he began.

Shuddering with the effort, Drame drew his stubbed forearm from his armpit and scythed it through the air. The slash of his blood whipped across Ligate's face and Ligate cried out, startled and blinded. He fired wildly, hitting nothing, as Drame threw himself flat.

Again I might have moved but I did nothing. I watched as Pellonhorc at last threw the knife in a movement that seemed hardly more than a gesture. The blade buried itself in Ligate's shoulder and he twisted in pain. Pellonhorc lunged forward, his fist smashing into Ligate's face. He fell like a stone and didn't move.

Ligate's gun had fallen close to Drame, who was stretching out his arm towards it.

'Wrong hand, Father,' Pellonhorc said. He picked the weapon up as Drame weakly resheathed his streaming wrist in his armpit. He was looking extremely white now, and shivering. The pool of his blood was extending. Pellonhorc knelt and said, 'You know, Father, I did all of this for you. I brought Ligate here for you. Everything I ever did was for you. It always was.'

I could hardly hear Ethan Drame whisper, 'You killed Madelene.'

'I had to, Father,' Pellonhorc said. 'Though you mustn't mistake that for an apology. It was hard enough to convince Ligate that all this was safe in the first place. When you and Alef were late, he nearly killed me. When you did arrive, I had to reassure him. Madelene was the obvious instrument. You can see that.' His eyes were wild and shining.

Shivering convulsively with the loss of blood, Drame murmured, 'You should, should have just killed him. I'll finish it.' Weakly, he stretched out his hand for Pellonhorc to give him the gun. There was no strength in him, but I could see there was no confidence either.

'No, Father. That's not for you.' He leaned down and took his father's good hand, squeezing it, then added, quietly, 'Just like killing you is not for me, Father. I could never kill you.'

Drame's eyes darted away and back. He took a short breath and let out a word in the exhalation, 'Son –'

'It's a long time since you called me that. Yes, Father?' Pellonhorc pulled his father's hand, as if helping him to his feet, then let him go again. 'Oh, you can't stand up, can you? You never will again, I think. You need medical aid, and I'm afraid there's no one here. Why don't you wait with Ligate while Alef and I go for help? You've lost a lot of blood, so you may not last long enough.'

Drame wasn't even trying to speak any more. He pressed his wrist tight into his armpit and put his head down. There was a rasp in his breathing. Pellonhorc said, 'The trick is not to lose consciousness. Use the pain. Count the seconds. That's what I always did, Father. I used it. I must have counted millions. Did you ever hear me counting?'

He took a hank of thin cord and a handful of loops of plastic cable from his pocket and threw them to the ground. They were restraint cables, and for the first time I realised how entirely prepared Pellonhorc had been. He lifted Ligate's feet and slipped them into one of the loops and pulled it tight at his ankles, the ratchets grating as they closed, then he tied his wrists behind his back. Grunting with the effort, he pulled the limp body across to the wall and used some of the cord to secure the ankle loop to a high bulkhead hook, hauling on it until Ligate's feet were well clear of the floor.

Ethan Drame sat in the pooling of his and his mistress's blood, and suddenly looked up at me. There was nothing I could say to him. I wonder whether he realised that Pellonhorc had fooled me as much as he had fooled everyone else.

When he was done with Ligate, Pellonhorc hauled his father to the wall where Madelene's corpse was lying and tied his good wrist to one of hers. He didn't ask me for help. He seemed sealed away, somehow, as he worked, and Drame didn't resist or try to speak to him again.

At last, Pellonhorc stretched his arms wide and opened his mouth in a great yawn. He glanced at me and said, 'Come on, Alef. Time's our enemy.'

Ligate was beginning to stir, rolling and shifting like a pupa. He raised his head, groggily at first and then with an abrupt alertness, discovering the cable's high tether and trying awkwardly to stand up. I watched him realise he'd never manage it with his feet elevated as they were. I watched the finality of his situation hit him.

I looked at Pellonhorc. His expression was flat and impenetrable. What was he? What had made such a man as him?

He observed Ligate for a moment. 'Come on,' he said.

'Don't just stand there, Alef. I can't do everything by myself. Ligate, we'll try not to be long. Don't bleed too quickly, will you, Father? Help might reach you in time. There's always hope, isn't there?'

I gathered myself to follow him, trying to clear my mind. Fifteen paces to the door, but the numbers weren't helping. I couldn't clear the thoughts that were gathering in my head, the belated understanding of what I had discovered in the dormitory.

Ligate and Pellonhorc had collected the workers together, made them all lie down in their beds and pull the covers over their faces. They had told them to be still, be silent, and wait, and it would be all right. Only instead of locking them inside and leaving them, Ligate and Pellonhorc had gone quietly from bed to bed, pulling back the covers and cutting their throats in a single swift move, one by one, until all were dead and quiet. All but one. And the killings had been unnecessary. I wondered: had that been Ligate's idea or Pellonhorc's? But of course I knew the answer, even though Pellonhorc would claim he had done it to prove his allegiance to Ligate.

Pellonhorc and I went through the outer airlock, our masks on. Pellonhorc's flycykle was concealed among the workers' transports. My mind was still in the dormitory. The numbers couldn't take me away from the thoughts.

'I'll drive,' Pellonhorc told me. We wheeled up into the sky, dizzyingly fast. 'Now, I need you to go to the bar and stay there for two hours. Drink some caffé, keep yourself awake. Some of my people are arriving, and I'll need to concentrate. Then go to The Floor and steady your people. They're sealed in at present. It's safer for them. There will still be some disruption, I'm sure.'

This tone of voice was new to me. There was always a tension to Pellonhorc. He was never relaxed. While we had been in the midlock, he had been controlled but excited. Now he was totally calm. For a moment I wondered whether he'd been dummied and someone else was talking to me, but in my heart I knew that this was Pellonhorc as he had always been preparing to be. The ground fizzed past below.

'Tell them my father's away and won't be returning.' He paused. 'No. Say he may not be returning. Let them get used to it slowly.'

'Your father –' I started.

'You'll be fine, Alef. We don't need him any more. His time is done. This is our time. It's been a long while coming, but it's been worth the wait.'

We were approaching the shield. I said, 'What about Ligate's businesses?'

'We'll be amalgamating. I have it all, the templates and the detail. I'll send them to The Floor for you. Ligate helped me prepare them. Of course he was expecting a slightly different basis for amalgamation, but the principles are sound.' He took his eyes from the console and smiled at me as he said, 'I have full confidence in you, Alef. I've always had confidence in you. You know that.'

Everything around us was a blur. The flycykle shuddered and Pellonhorc's hand trembled on the control stick. We screeched through the shield and fell into the scoured air of the city. Pellonhorc took us down in a shallow curve, losing speed until we were two anonyms in a domestic vehicle heading nowhere special. He let the putery take over and sat back in his seat and rubbed his neck. 'A good day,' he sighed, and then, with more energy, added, 'That's a fine house, Alef. Your foreman was kind enough to give us a tour when we arrived. When will it be ready?'

Twenty-seven

RAZER

The night before Bale was to take her down the Chute, Razer couldn't sleep, so she worked. She always found it comforting to write her notes by hand. It was more secure, but there was also something special about the way the pen scurried across the pad, the penned words never looking the same twice. On screenery, words became just data.

In any case, they ended up that way, once TruTales had swilled her observations with all the other fragments, not only using them straight but also changing details to create fresh data. TruTales' writers provided the ParaSite's core stories, but their additional notes and augmemories were the seeds of the thousands of other TruTales synthesised every month by the putery. She sometimes thought that TruTales valued her notes more than her stories.

She chewed the end of the pen, wondering what Bale really thought of how she made her living. She couldn't get him out of her head. What was it about him?

She returned to the piece she'd written when she'd thought he was dead. Generally she could skin people of their stories in a few hours, but here she was spending a week on a single tale. And screwing it up, too. No one wanted to read quite this much detail. Readers wanted to learn something, but they also wanted clarity. They wanted the good to be shining bright, and the bad to stink of evil. They wanted justice and punishment, closure with a smile, and the reassurance that no matter how hard life is now, *this* is how it will be in the end.

And TruTales readers also seemed to want something of the teller. Razer's unique slant was to personalise herself as a writer, as Kestrel Dust, in her stories; to give some of it away, show the subscribers how it worked, how it was built, and then – with luck – *still* surprise them at the end.

Razer wondered how Bale's real story would end. Not as she was about to construct it, that was for sure. In that story the killer would be outplayed by Bale, who saves Tallen's life and foils a plot to destroy Lookout's shield.

By four in the morning she knew it was as good as it would ever be. The last thing had been to change Bale's name. She'd chosen something with three syllables, emphasis on the first. She fed the story into the faintly humming puter, then sent all her notes after it: the snatches of conversation, the dislocated descriptions of places, of breakfasts and journeys and colour and pain.

Thank you, Razer. Material intact. Now loading data.

She poured a slug of vavodka over the dregs of her caffé and let her eyes settle on the empty wall. Suppose Bale was right, that the K hadn't been acting alone. Once you got to that point, the story fitted together well.

Loading data.

If it were hers to write, she'd invent a co-psycho exactly as Bale had proposed, and that would explain how Bale survived, the co-psycho killing Fleschik just as Fleschik was about to kill Bale. That would mean the co-psycho would be even better than Fleschik, which was hard to believe. But what motive would the co-psycho have?

She knocked back the gritty drink and chewed on the caffé grounds. This was just a story, though. You could do it in a story. People want to believe. As long as you distracted them and kept it fast, they'd swallow it.

Data loaded.

The puter stopped humming. She conned the augmem to it and waited.

Data consolidated. Clearing memory source field. Wait.

She picked up the pen and held it over the pad. Maybe she could make something of it.

Clearing source field. Wait.

All that was missing was that motive, and of course it wouldn't make sense, since they were a pair of psychos. And the reader would feel cheated. You could get away with one psycho, but you couldn't put a pair of psychos in a story, no matter how fast you moved it forward. It was like rolling two sixes. She picked up the pen and chewed on it.

Clearing source field. Wait.

Unless they weren't psychos at all. Neither of them.

Source field cleared. Thank you, Razer.

So what was the motive? Letting the pen dangle from her lips, she reached to clear the screen and froze, staring at the words forming there.

Critical stop.

She'd never seen that before.

Please do not repeat do not terminate your note-taking and story at this time. Please gather more material on this subject. This category material is currently in high demand. Please provide more data. This subject is of critical importance.

She whispered, 'What subject?'

Bale subject.

Razer looked at the instruction for a long time. She read the two words as if they were simply telling her that Pax-related feelgoods were currently popular, and then she read them telling her that TruTales had seen something interesting in Bale's story. No, not TruTales. That Cynth had seen something.

And then she acknowledged the instruction, closed the secure screenery and went to bed. She woke up once in the night, thinking about Cynth. She tried to remember that night, the night Tallen had nearly died and Bale had saved him. She remembered coming home from the red bar, talking to Cynth about Larren Gamliel, but she couldn't remember going to sleep. Had something else happened?

She felt suddenly cold. There had been an outdated piece of tech. She'd heard it spoken of, but never used. Was that the solution? Had she been dummied? Cynth was acting weirdly. Had Cynth's program been corrupted?

No. That made no sense at all. No one ever remembered going to sleep. Bale's paranoia was catching.

Tallen

Lode said, 'We are worried about you, Tallen.'

'And for you,' said Beata.

Tallen tried to keep his eyes open. He shouldn't be so tired. Why had they woken him up? He needed sleep. He said, 'What day is it?'

Beata said, 'It is day. Can you remember what you did last night? Or what you last did?'

Lode said, 'Please talk to us. Tell us about the rig.'

He looked at Lode, trying to concentrate. 'When I'm in the cage, I can see the net cradle. I can remember it catching me. But when I'm not in the cage, I can't remember it at all.'

'But you remember it now, Tallen.'

He looked around. Time seemed to have passed. Were the humechs standing where they had been a moment ago? 'What?'

Lode said, 'Tell us what you can see from the cage.'

Tallen tried to think. 'I can see the gantries around the deck.'

Beata said, 'How many gantries can you see?'

'Five,' he said. 'Located equidistant around the deck. There's a caged walkway behind me, leading me directly to the cage, and caged walkways to the gantries. I can see the emergency landing facility and the doors to the residential and recreational facilities.' He closed his eyes, exhausted.

When he opened them, Beata was standing where Lode had been and the light had changed. He also seemed to be sitting differently. 'That's good, Tallen,' said Beata.

Lode said, 'Do you ever remember arriving in the cage? Or leaving it? And does your back itch?'

Beata said, 'Can you move in the cage? Can you turn?'

Tallen said, 'You know I can't. I'm only conscious when I'm there, and then I'm here again. I can't remember arriving in the cage or leaving it.'

'And yet you see so much,' Lode said, 'and your back itches.'

Tallen said, 'Am I really in the cage? Is it real? You said it was.'

Beata said, 'The cage is as real as you are, Tallen, and you are real. Can you remember anything else about the rig? Tell us what you remember. Is your back itching now? Does it itch when you remember?

He shook his head but it wouldn't quite clear. 'Remember what?'

Lode said, 'Yes, Tallen, what do you remember?'

'I can remember –' But it was gone.

* * *

Razer

Razer took the rented flysuit on the shuttle to the Chute. She was there an hour early, but Bale was already on the platform, waiting.

'I'm not ready to ride yet. I want to look round the place first,' she told him.

'No. We go straight in.' He was glancing around as they walked slowly, letting people overtake them. A few other passengers were coming from the same shuttle, and Bale stared at each of them as they passed. Some ignored him, some held his gaze, but none of them said a thing to him. As Razer and Bale left the platform, he said, 'You recognise anyone?'

'No. Why?'

He glanced at her, then said, 'Maybe I'll give you a tour afterwards.'

She saw in his face that it wasn't worth arguing, and followed him down the roughly carved entrance tunnel with its snaptures of blurred riders, its lists of records broken and of the dead. She thought about TruTales setting her on him again and felt as if she should tell him. But he was paranoid already, and what would be the use of feeding it?

In the ready chamber, she peeled off her clothes and started to pull on the rented flysuit. She didn't know what Bale's hurry was. He said to her, 'Are you set?'

'You tell me.' She turned round and let him check her lines and fins.

He ran his hands over her arms and then slowly across her hips, and she closed her eyes for a moment, felt an ache in her throat, and wondered if there might be, after all, any hope for them.

Bale stepped back and said, 'Where did you get the suit?'

No, there was no hope. She said, 'The shop was called Blown Away.' She'd taken a few lessons in the tanks, too, even though Bale had told her she didn't need to if she'd done sims before, and she hadn't done too badly, the skills broadly the same as those she'd learnt skinriding and cascading elsewhere in the System.

'Your left wristfin's scree-scored,' he said. 'See where it's jagged? They should have polished it before they gave you the suit. Keep your arms well out if you deploy that fin. Catch yourself with that edge, you might rip your suit.'

'It's insured.'

'You think this is funny?'

'No, Bale. I rip the suit, I'm dead. I know. Could you happy up a little? I should have checked the suit. Look, should we put this off a few days?'

'No. Just be careful. Main thing is no one saw you. You just went and came back. Yes?'

There was no gain in telling him about the tank, so she nodded. And maybe she would have done as he'd told her in the first place, if he wasn't being so stupid about the whole thing.

He was saying, 'All you need to do in the Chute is what I tell you. Keep straight and central. Ride the node. If the worst happens, you just snap back to auto and the suit'll guide you in.'

'What worst is this? I thought you were showing me the Chute. It's a ride, is all.'

'We need to talk, too.' He was taking out a translucent box. She saw a pair of fine golden boots apparently suspended in it. Fairytale shoes, she immediately thought.

'Are they yours, Bale?' She made twinkles with her fingers, her mood lightening a bit. 'I never thought this was your style. Aren't you putting them on?'

'Not yet. Let's go.'

At the gate, he checked her suit again and said, 'Go in on auto. When I tell you, lock on me.' He was still holding the box.

She said, 'Are you going to tell me about those? You're already wearing boots.'

'These pull over mine. They're NTGs. Never Touch Ground. Stay right behind me.'

She watched him slip through the gate and down into the lead-in. She counted ten and went after him head-down and was instantly hurled by the wind and gasping for breath. The suit straightened her out. When she was breathing evenly, she tried nilling the auto and managed to hold it for two seconds before shuddering and losing it, and let the auto catch her again.

This was not like the tanks. It was not like cascading or skinriding or anything else. It was wonderful. She let out a yell.

There was Bale, way up ahead. She watched as in the turbulence he ripped the box open and started to pull the NTGs on, all the time tumbling over and retrieving himself just as he seemed sure to smash into the wall. Razer was aware of her lungs pumping. The wind was screaming past her. She remembered her routines and experimented with the fins and flaps, cutting left and right, trying a spin and losing it altogether, bringing herself back with the auto program. The jagged wristfin added a flick of turbulence. She folded both wristfins away. They weren't vital.

Bale was whirling like a pyrotechnic, struggling with the second boot. She came level with him and suddenly could hear him swearing. His commed voice was tinny.

'What's the point of this, Bale? You could kill yourself.'

'You can only put NTGs on once you're in wind.' He was breathing hard. 'You need to be good just to put them on.'

'And to want everyone else to know it. That isn't you, Bale. And actually, you don't look that good.'

He swore again, tumbled and came straight, both boots on. The wind whipped fine dye-streaks of gold from them, like he had flames at his heels. He said, 'If you see another pair of these, it's trouble.'

She saw the Chute's final entry-warning ahead. He went first, the soles of the golden boots becoming dots and then a single point, but too bright to disappear, and she let the suit take her in his wake.

Now they were in the main Chute. The suit adjusted again, repressurising.

This was amazing. It was like being in space, at ship-speed, naked. By shifting her shoulders she could curve away and back, and a jink of her hips would flip her left or right.

'Is that you or the suit?' Bale said from beside her.

'Me.'

'Not bad. Keep it simple. And keep your eyes open.'

She flicked away from him, suddenly furious at his incessant talk of trouble. 'There's always a threat for you, isn't there? You're always in shit. I'm fed up with it.'

She let herself fade, drifting from him, or so it felt despite the walls passing by so fast they seemed smooth, and the comms cut out.

'You need to keep close to me,' he said, abruptly back at her shoulder. 'I've limited our comms range to five em. This is the only place in Lookout where we can't possibly be monitored without being aware of it. I'm going to tell you what I've found. You might know some of it.' He paused. 'The only thing I'm still not sure of is whether you're a part of it.'

Her heart jumped. 'Bale –'

'Just listen to me. Paxers use the Chute a lot, Razer. There was a guy I rode with a few years ago. He was better than good, but he was trouble. He left Pax and Bleak, and we heard he'd become a crimer. His name was Millasco.'

The walls were flying past. She went to auto, concentrating on Bale.

'After I came out of hospital, someone wearing gold NTGs tumbled me in the Chute. And then Navid, just before he pushed me, told me I'd been warned.'

'By Delta. You told me about it.'

'No, not by Delta. Navid had no idea she'd said anything to me.'

'So he meant what happened in the Chute?'

'I think so. I think Millasco is back on Bleak. Gold NTG boots were always his marker.'

'Bale –'

'I think he was Fleschik's partner. I think they had me set up for this all along. They made a kill just by where I was, so I'd be the one to follow. I think Millasco killed Fleschik. Delta told me there was an audit team at Pax. They knew my record ahead of time. You see? They used the cams; they knew I was drinking that night.'

'So *I'm* responsible? I didn't get you drunk, Bale. You did that all by yourself.'

She waited for Bale to laugh that away, but he didn't. She thought of Cynth telling her to stay with Bale. Now wasn't the time to tell him that, though. She thought about telling him she may have been dummied, but this wasn't the time for that either. The possibility that she may have been involved in the event somehow made her even more angry at him.

They flew in silence for a minute, then Bale said, 'They'd have had me, drunk or not. Either way, I came out on the street, they used Delta to get me to the alley and down the sewers.'

'Why would they do that, Bale? It's too complicated. There's no reason.'

'You're right. I'm not that important.'

'At least that's one delusion we don't need to worry about.'

To her relief, he fell silent. Razer nilled the auto and settled into a rhythm of small spins and turns, Bale keeping pace with her, trailing and anticipating her moves, pointing out air currents and eddies, letting her dip her fins in them and get used to steering clear. He watched her throw out lines to check her speed and made sure she knew when it was safe to retract them without risk of getting tangled and when simply to cut them and let them perish in the wind. He said, 'Once they're cut loose, they're designed to molecularise in half a second. You've only got about one-fifty em of line on each hand and foot, and you'll average ten em each shot, so retract it if you can, but don't risk it if you aren't sure. If you run out of line, it just makes flying awkward, but if you tangle, you die.'

She was barely listening. She loved the way the lines flicked out and dragged in fine curves, the way she could time a line-retraction, the beautiful whipback of it, to straighten her out of the turn. She loved everything about this.

'You're not bad,' he said, and they flew on, swirling around each other in tight helices and plunging away again. Several times he dropped back, disappeared briefly, then rejoined her, the comms losing even its background hiss in his absences. She was concentrating too hard to look for him, and having too much fun.

Then he was at her side and talking again. 'The dead, they were nothing too. I've checked them all. They were no ones. Tallen's a no one too. Why did they let him survive?'

'Just give it up, Bale. You're crazy. Let's enjoy this.'

'What happened to him was different. He has to be the key, Razer.' He swooped away and back again.

'This is all insane,' she said, angry with him for spoiling the joy of it all, angry at herself, too, for not telling him she might be involved. 'That's it. You've shown me the Chute. You'll make a great guide. If the ride doesn't scare them enough, you can tell them your stories.'

'I know you're a part of it, Razer. I can't fit you into it, though. You finding me here, that's too much of a coincidence.'

'Happenstance, Bale,' she said, uncomfortably. 'You're grinding the facts you like to fit some grand fantasy. It's no better than god logic.'

'You were in the bar, talking to Tallen, before we met. You were talking about AfterLife.'

'Everyone talks about AfterLife. I talk to lots of people about it.'

'Not to me, you didn't. Not that quickly.'

'I didn't think you'd be comfortable with it. Like I was

questioning you. I want to go back now, Bale.'

'We can't. Only forward, to the end.'

'This is stupid.'

'It's a test.'

An eddy caught her and she spun, corrected, and said, 'A test? What do you mean?'

'If you're part of it, Millasco won't want you dead, Razer. He'll just want me, because I'm still asking questions.'

'And if I'm not part of it?' she said uncomfortably.

'Then you'll know I'm right.'

'How will I know that?'

'Easy. If I'm just a drunk who's lost his job and won't accept it, why is there a rider behind us wearing gold NTGs?'

Twenty-eight
ALEF

SigEv 31 Consolidation

I went from the bar to The Floor to find it guarded by Belleger's men and the building in a state of flux. People were leaving and being removed. Some were injured, some dead. All of this had been planned and carried out by Pellonhorc, and I had suspected nothing. None of it had been foreshadowed in my weave.

I stayed on The Floor with my people as Pellonhorc fed the details of Ligate's network into my putery. As we organised the data, I became calmer. Unlike Pellonhorc, who seemed to abhor stability, I coped badly with change. His reliance on me was reassuring, though. I was safe, and my work, while its load was significantly greater, remained. And Pireve was there, too. She appeared especially relieved at my return.

I seemed for the first weeks to have lost my hard-won powers of empathy. The trauma of those minutes in the midlock brought my parents' deaths back to me in a vivid manner, and I could not come to terms with the fact that I had failed entirely to predict Pellonhorc's actions.

So I worked. The challenge was immense, and I was grateful for it.

While it took a long time, most of the new business was easy to incorporate. As in any merger, there were redundancies. There were also some shortlived efforts at local management takeovers, and other actions of concern. As soon as I identified these, Pellonhorc dealt with them. A few small organisations were resistant, and these swiftly and utterly vanished. Ethan Drame, in the same situation, would simply have killed or mutilated a few people and turned the businesses back to us, but Pellonhorc had everyone killed and the businesses obliterated, regardless of loss. Word spread that there was no mercy. This made my calculations and extrapolations more straightforward. The weave stretched and ripped, but the damage was done in a few months and we began to rebuild.

Pellonhorc let it be known that Ligate had died in an accident and that Ethan Drame had been injured and might not be returning. Over time, *might not* became *would not*, and everything started to settle. After all, these were businesses accustomed to the unexpected. With Pellonhorc at the head, there was still an air of danger, but there was also a sense of absolute certainty. With his father, the threat had always been that he might do something out of proportion and with no warning. He had been volatile. His empire had been built purely on threat and death, and whenever that had misfired, he had corrected it by more of the same. He had always said that one could be extremely successful in business if one was prepared to kill without warning or compunction.

Pellonhorc had his father's ruthlessness, but he had also learnt to plan meticulously. He possessed something else as well, though – something all his own. All that Ethan Drame had ever wanted was more. His son had a definite goal.

This was quite clear to me. It was there in the single-minded way he had used his father against Ligate, and Ligate against his father. I hadn't seen that coming and neither had they. Neither of them had been able to read him, and nor had I. But my mistake was to assume that his goal was power and wealth. It wasn't.

Months passed, and then the first year of Pellonhorc's rule had gone by. My mind was still numb, but my brain was sharper than ever.

There were constant threats to the business, but nothing of any significance. What had created Pellonhorc created imitators, but he was the most successful, and perhaps what had created him had been a unique conjunction of extraordinary elements.

And I am not – nor was I – blind to the fact that I was a crucial part of his design. It was my brain that held it together. I had fooled myself that I'd been preparing to destroy his father, and now I told myself I was actually holding Pellonhorc in check. Without my influence, I convinced myself, there would be an immense bloodbath.

But in reality, whenever for a moment I took my attention from The Floor, I acknowledged to myself that I was more terrified of my friend than I had ever been of Ethan Drame.

After that day at the house, I never talked to him about his father, and never mentioned Ligate. Ligate's death would not have been easy, and it was obvious enough that even if his father had not bled to death where we had left him, Pellonhorc would have exacted a long-anticipated retribution for his terrible treatment of his own son.

Gradually, my life eased. On The Floor, my friendship with Pireve grew stronger. She frequently seemed to need my help, though it was usually clear that she knew all along what she was doing. One evening we left The Floor at the same time, and that evening we slept together, and after that we began to associate with each other outside The Floor more frequently. Our relationship slipped quite quickly from being of small consequence to me, to being of significance to everybody around me. I was probably the last to realise its actual depth.

During this time, the borders of the city crept closer towards the house Ethan Drame had been building. Eventually the city's shield incorporated the house and Pellonhorc moved into it. This event was reported throughout the Song and marked a Systemwide acknowledgement of his power and influence. He was described as a successful businessman and entrepreneur. I was mentioned too, as his inseparable friend and partner. There was one brief reference to me as 'the power behind the throne', which troubled me, and I had it excised.

There were women in Pellonhorc's life, too, though they never lasted long, one way or another. Pellonhorc started to talk of his empire going on forever. He talked of death generally, and of his own death, though I paid no real attention to this.

My weave was growing more complicated, now, as was my life with Pireve. Pellonhorc never mentioned her, though I was sure he was aware of our association.

My father and Ethan Drame had always taken advantage of the various laws on different planets, just as law-abiding businesses did, though those businesses lacked our range of actions. But Pellonhorc went further, bringing lawmakers, bureaucrats and politicians into his organisation. They were given gifts of money and they were listened to. When they had problems, the problems were solved for them. *It's a pleasure. You're a friend.* They were asked for nothing in return, and then they were asked for small, effortless favours that flattered them, and then they were asked for more awkward favours and rewarded well for that. And gradually they discovered that the larger favours were not so hard to carry out, and the rewards considerable. They also discovered that the people around them who might have been expected to object to some of these favours failed either to object or to exist.

Pellonhorc was an expert at all of this. He called himself, when he wanted to be amusing, a Darwinian. Perhaps if I had not been there, the organisation would not have lasted so long or become so extensive. But I made sure that nothing we did threatened the System's stability. If anything, we encouraged trade and communication. No one became too greedy, which is to say that of course many did, but didn't survive. The organisation was not a parasite on the System. It was a symbiote.

The only threat to all of this was the Song, which was awash with fact and invention and rumour. There was almost as much information as there was porn.

The quality of the information on the Song was impossible to judge. There were areas where it was sifted and classified as reliable or otherwise, but no one ever did anything about any of it.

Our organisation grew. Only the unsaid planet remained out of our reach, and I was content with that, as they were no threat. Our operations went generally well. Occasionally a poorly managed action provoked a response from an administration or an anti-corruption committee, and the further action we were forced to take would set us back or cost us a few people. But there were always more people. There were always greed and fear.

I roamed the Song when I couldn't sleep, which was increasingly often. I had immense mental energy. The Song was a vast sea, stormy here, calm there, with its deeps and shallows. I rode its waves for hours. I would place a piece of false information somewhere and add comments of approval and support and corroboration, and adjust the usage parameters of the Song to give prominence to this information. And then I sat back and watched what happened.

Night after night, I played the Song. I saw that after porn, health was the most popular topic, and I hurled myself into that field. People believed almost anything I threw out, as long as I invented data and attached a few stolen and adapted personal experiences. The more medics denounced and denied a thing, factually and conclusively, the more they were accused of suppressing the truth. The news media, only interested in the advertising its stories drew, promoted the possibility that rumour was fact.

Day after day and tirelessly, I worked. I kept my head busy with analysis, ignored the realities of implementation. I found myself using the word when I was talking to Pellonhorc. *We need to implement this.*

The organisation grew more and more powerful. I married Pireve.

SigEv 32 Happiness and hell

Oh, my Pireve. I began to feel different. I began to *feel*, again. We were away from The Floor for two days, spending the time in Virtua. It was a strange time. I'd never been away from The Floor for more than a day before that. We woke up the second morning and she knelt astride my hips and said, 'How does this feel, Alef?'

'I love you,' I said.

She laughed. Her laugh was like screenery opening, with its gathering, rising peal. The first time we had sex, she had asked me that question, *How does this feel?*, and I told her how long it had lasted (four seconds) and how many thrusts I'd made before reaching my climax (almost two). Since then, I'd learnt to answer 'I love you,' whenever I was uncertain and about to go statistic with her. She told me it gave her pleasure to hear me say the words, regardless of why I was saying them. I'd also learnt to make it last longer and that the number of thrusts was less important than other things Pireve had taught me about sex.

She said, 'And I love you, my Alef, my alpha, my number one man.'

We walked together. She said I had to understand her, and I said that I did.

That laugh again. Oh, her laugh. 'No, Alef. You have no idea! I'll tell you what I like so much about you, shall I?'

She said she liked me to take her hand. She liked eye contact. She liked me to explain things to her more slowly. She liked me, when she had finished telling me something, not to ask her why she had told me that. She liked me not to be quite so neat, but to achieve messyness without setting objects in the same asymmetric pattern each time. She liked me to eat my food in a way that mixed colours. She liked me to set the alarm to wake us, even though I never needed it. She liked me to tell her about the weave. She liked me to tell her why I was doing something on the weave. She liked me not to tell her quite so much.

She asked me what it was that I liked about her. I told her I liked her to give me lists. And I told her I loved her.

On the Song, I read about love, and tried to relate my understanding and experience to it. Judging by what people said, it was a sort of cancer of the emotions. I tried to make my own sense of it, and decided that up until then, my life had been numb, but now, with Pireve, the numbness had become paraesthesia, and I wondered whether that might lead to full sensation.

The days in Virtua passed more swiftly than I had expected, away from The Floor.

By the time we returned, Pellonhorc's organisation had a name. It was referred to as the Whisper. Politicians were taking their orders from the Whisper. The Whisper was in control of this city and that corporation and the administrata of these planets. But Pellonhorc was not mentioned in connection with it.

Much of what was rumoured was true. Politicians came to the city to meet Pellonhorc. The city was notoriously dangerous. Occasionally people failed to leave.

This, at least, was what I still told myself. I found myself thinking about it, though, instead of just observing it and accepting it as I always had done. I noted the number of our associates brought to Peco to see Pellonhorc at his house. The small ship he used to have them conveyed there from the ferryport was called the *Darwin*.

For the first time in my life, I found myself thinking about myself.

I was in a state of terrible confusion, but I carried on

working. I began slowly to tell Pireve about myself. About what I had done and seen. I cried, and she told me I was not a bad person.

To remember this, to set this down, to set it down, makes me weep. To be understood, to have the worst of oneself heard and accepted. That is hard, but it is good, too.

I carried on working, but I found it harder to separate the work that I was doing from its human consequences. I wanted to do something, but I didn't know what there was to do.

Pellonhorc called me into his office. We talked unnecessarily about an impending legislative meeting on Prime. There were the people he trusted and the people he didn't, and we discussed who would vote in our favour.

'Halfjut,' he said.

'He's ours. We know it.'

'Yes, Alef. But he's expensive. I think I'll bring him in, after the vote.'

'Why?'

'There's a matter I think he can help me with. Something personal. There's a shipment for the *Darwin*. He can join them.' He looked at me, waiting, his face bearing some new, unreadable expression, and I felt as if I had missed something vital and that the world was about to change.

I said nothing but felt myself trembling.

He said, 'Don't you want to know what I'm talking about?'

'You said it was personal, Pellonhorc.'

I knew he meant that he was going to kill Halfjut, who was a corrupt and greedy man, but Halfjut was no different from so many others, so there was no great significance that I could see in this. Pellonhorc had always been a killer. As a child, dismembering animals had been as natural to him as eating. I had imagined that by performing necessary business operations, he was fully satisfying this urge. Now I was realising that it was the other way round, that his need to kill was paramount. And I remembered his killing of Madelene, the way he had put his tongue to the jet of her blood.

He said, 'It is personal, yes. Do you know something?'

'What?'

'I couldn't live without you, Alef.'

Was he just saying that the organisation wouldn't work without me? That was probably true. I was horribly aware of the degree to which we were bound together and had always been. But why say this now? My head was spinning. Every time I thought I understood what we were talking about, I was wrong.

'You're the only one, Alef. I can't talk to anyone else.'

'Oh.' I knew that intimacy was a threat to him, and I felt extraordinarily unsafe, as if I were being shown the smile before the knife.

'Do you think about Gehenna, Alef?'

I thought perhaps the mood had changed, though I could never really trust my understanding of such things. I said, carefully, 'Sometimes. It was a long time ago.' I could see my answer wasn't enough, so I added, 'Do you mean your mother?'

He looked out of the window where the low sun had turned the bellies of the clouds to gold. 'She's in heaven,' he answered.

For a moment I didn't think I'd heard him properly.

He looked straight at me. 'She's with your mother. I don't know about your father. What do you think?'

'I – I don't think about it.' I had no idea what else to say.

'Do you believe in hell, Alef?'

I was suddenly a child before Father Grace, knowing every answer was wrong and that the question was the prelude to a beating. My head swirled. The best thing was to say yes and suffer only merciful pain.

Pellonhorc repeated the question very softly. 'I said, do you believe in hell, Alef?' He put his lips together and made a small kissing sound.

I tensed, knowing I couldn't lie to him. I had stood in that room and watched him interrogate people like this, the whispered question repeated and the small kiss. It had astonished me that, under no duress, they told him things that they clearly knew would mean their death. Now I felt it for myself.

'No. I don't.'

'You can't have heaven without hell, Alef,' he said mildly.

I could hardly hear him. Everything was roaring.

'You aren't making sense, Alef. That isn't like you.'

'I need to sit down,' I said.

He gestured to a chair and I slumped into it. My heart was thumping and I felt sick. I could see my death here.

I was conscious of his hand going to his pocket. I did my best to concentrate. He brought out his knife, the small red pocketknife he had had on Gehenna. He turned it over in his hand, the flat spine of the closed blade glinting. 'What will happen, Alef?'

'What do you mean?' I couldn't look away from the knife. In a moment he would open it. It was a ritual. The showing of the blade, the initial small cut on the right cheek.

'When I die. What will happen to me?'

'Nothing,' I said, holding my voice as steady as I could, staring at the knife. 'That's it. The end.'

'No. What we learnt on Gehenna. Father Grace. You remember that. I know you do.'

'Stories, Pellonhorc. Death is like sleep, that's all.'

The knife was still in the flat of his hand, unopened. 'My father gave me this.'

'Yes. You were so happy. I remember you opening the package.'

'Of course you do.' He closed his hand around the knife and stared out the window. The sun had dropped away and the clouds were lifeless. 'He gave me it. My father.' He took a long breath and turned back to me. 'You can't give anything back, Alef. You can't ever.' He squeezed his eyes closed. 'Not blood. That's for sure.'

'Pellonhorc –'

'It's like sleep, you say?' His face twisted in the force of emotion. 'I have dreams. I don't want those forever.' He was opening his hand and closing it, over and over.

I said, 'You only know the dreams when you wake up. In this sleep, there's no waking. It will be all right. It isn't like hypersomnia.' I was trying to comfort him, and I was waiting for him to open the knife.

'No,' he said.

He turned his back on me again and stared at the window. Night was falling and the city lighting up, as if pixel by pixel. The upper atmosphere was strained out there, the air faintly bruised. It was mask weather. I watched his face reflected in the glass, as I had watched his father's face there.

He opened the knife and turned the blade over and over. The sky grew dark, his face in the window becoming clearer and clearer. Time passed.

I tried to say something but my throat was clogged. I couldn't even swallow.

He held the knife out towards his own reflection in the window and made a sharp flicking movement, and then touched a finger to his cheek, brought it away and looked intently at it. He turned and held the finger out to me, saying, 'See? Do you see, Alef?'

Not knowing what else to do, I nodded. The knife was still open, though his hand had dropped slackly to his side. I waited for him to speak again, but he said nothing more. He moved to his desk and sat down at it, put the knife aside and laid his head in his hands. After a while, his breathing became slow and even.

I sat motionless, sweat gathering under my arms, for a long time, and then I began to stand up. The chair made a small noise and I stopped, crouched midway between sitting and standing. Pellonhorc's breathing coarsened, then settled again. I remained still until my back was aching. Pellonhorc didn't move any more. Eventually I straightened and left.

Twenty-nine

RAZER

Bale said, 'See him?'

Razer twisted her head and saw a man wearing the same black suit as Bale. As he side-scythed in their wake, she caught the burnished heelflash of the NTGs. Despite her suit, the wind suddenly seemed cold.

Bale said, 'So?'

'It isn't like you think.'

'How is it, then?' Without letting her answer, he was gone in a blur of fins and a flicker of gold, and in his wake, shooting past her, was his gold-heeled double.

Before he slipped out of capture range, she snapped her suit to mimic and felt her fins fold down almost flush with the suit as she slammed forward in Millasco's wake, the acceleration dizzying. Her suit wasn't as good as theirs, though, and she started to fall behind Millasco, and the mimic program cut off as he was out of range and a moment later gone altogether. Bale too.

The Chute straightened out. She kept going fast and saw two gold pinpricks ahead, and then another pair, the two sets interweaving. She swore to herself. Bale would be convinced she was allied to Millasco. It wouldn't strike him to consider that maybe Millasco was going to kill them both, that it would make sense to finish Bale first and then come back for the easier kill.

Stupid, stupid Bale.

They shot down a small tributary pipe to the left, cutting away so quickly that she almost failed to notice the jink, and even from back here and with time to set herself for it, she nearly missed the turn, thumping heavily off the wall and shaken badly.

There were flashes of fire between them, now. She thought it was the boots trailing light but it couldn't be that; they had weapons.

So Bale had been quite sure of this, and had been right. She shouted to him but he was well out of comms range, and which one was he, anyway?

The pipe was narrowing and she switched the suit to auto, settling into the node and concentrating on the riders ahead. Her arm was starting to stiffen and ache. She must have hit that wall really hard. She felt stupid for shouting, as if shouting would override the commstech.

She still couldn't tell which was Bale. There was a great round of solid dark ahead, and the wind was slowing. The Chute must be opening out. Ahead of her, the two riders parted left and right towards opposite walls, still firing at each other. And then it was just one of them firing.

She closed in on them, but couldn't tell which was which. Then, to the left, she saw a line rip wide and thought it was Bale. She pulled in her fins and headed for him. A tube along his upper arm flicked out and she glimpsed the small black *o* of a weapon settling on her. She slammed away, the lineburst of light barely missing her hip.

Not Bale. She started to head for the other rider and

yelled at him, 'It's all right. I'm with you!'

'That's good to know,' came back to her through the comms, only it wasn't Bale's heavy drawl.

She fell back. Bale had been firing at her.

What was happening? Maybe Bale had just been warning her away.

For a moment, she imagined she could tell them apart, but they crossed and she lost any certainty.

There was a long curve ahead. One of them threw out a line and took to the inner wall, tumbling through a skim of scree and straightening again, holding close to the wall, while the other held to the centre of the pipe and pulsed light at him. The scree degraded the beam to brilliant embers.

The curve was tightening and Razer went wide, using her ankle fins to cut her speed and letting out a line to drag her further back. This was dangerous. She felt her chest pump against the pressurised suit. She'd left the manoeuvre late and was barely slowing. The inside rider was a shuddering blur accelerating away from the midliner, who was still gaining distance from Razer.

The insider had already vanished beyond the curve.

Darkspeed, Razer thought, and whispered to herself, 'No.' She cut the line and finned desperately, trying to keep up with the midliner.

The curve seemed to take forever. She straightened out of it and saw Bale – it *had* to be Bale – way ahead of the midliner and rocketing into the straight. She remembered what he'd told her about darkspeed and death. She could see it happening. His exitline was a few degrees out. He was headed for the wall. She screamed, pointlessly, 'Bale!' as the midline rider released a steady coil of fire towards him.

Against the wind, the looping cord of fire gained slowly on Bale. He wasn't correcting his line, was heading straight, neither finning away from the wall nor cutting clear of the approaching stream of pulser fire.

He'd darkspeeded and jumped the edge, lost consciousness. He was going to die.

She screamed again, 'Bale!' as he and the whipping string of light hit the wall at the same time, and he was gone in a brilliant explosion of debris and fire.

The midliner shot past the rushing bloom of rubble and swung round, threw out a handful of lines and finned, it seemed, almost to a halt, though the walls were sweeping past them both.

He was waiting for her. Ahead of them, the tumbling detritus was losing coherence. Streaks of fire sparked and died within it.

Bale, she suddenly thought, sure and unsure of it. *This* was Bale.

She drifted close to him, desperately calling his name. Bale had to be alive. She couldn't lose him. 'Bale, it's okay. I'm with you. I need to tell you something.'

No answer. She had to be closer for the comms to cut in.

He was finning against the current, making it look effortless. She was suddenly unsure. Was that Bale's suit? The wind blurred its detail. The only sharpness was the twin flicker of gold.

She said, 'I need to say something about that night, but I am with you, Bale.'

The comms hissed contact. 'Not yet, you aren't.'

'Millasco,' she whispered.

Beyond him, the splintered rock had all but vanished in

the flow, and there was just a fog of powder. She and Millasco hurtled past it.

Razer threw all her lines to her right and finned away from him, turning hard enough to feel faint. Millasco's pulse of light skimmed past her suit. Bale had drummed into her that it only had to pinprick the flysuit for the wind to open the whole thing up. If that happened she was dead faster than darkspeed.

Millasco swung into her wake. She spun and twisted, watching lightpulses slash the wind torrent around her, but couldn't shake him. He was close enough for her to hear his breathing through the comms as he settled his aim.

And then over the comms she heard someone say, 'On your tail, Millasco.'

Not a shadow, but another rider, sweeping away from the dispersing wash of powder along the wall. And like a fairytale prince, there was gold on his boots.

'Bale,' she yelled.

His voice came back, 'Now we believe each other, yes?'

She screamed, 'Yes, Bale.'

Millasco was finning round, and Razer realised Bale couldn't shoot him for fear of hitting her. But she could see that if Bale didn't go for the kill now, Millasco would have a free shot at him.

'Bale! Shoot!'

Bale held off, cutting across to find an angle at Millasco that wouldn't risk her, but Millasco moved with him, using Razer as a backshield while steadying his arm. He was ignoring her otherwise, assuming she was no threat.

We'll see about that, she thought, and locked her mimic onto Millasco, knowing he wouldn't expect that. His arm shook as he compensated for the faint judder as the lock fixed, and he whispered, 'Clever, but that just keeps you where I want you.'

'Bale,' she yelled. 'Move now.'

But he didn't. She could save them both, though. She knew it. She raised her cutter, setting it at Millasco's gun arm.

Millasco was too fast, firing at Bale before she could release her line. She steadied it again, and released it.

Other than the rush of air, there was no sound as Bale's chest came open. In an instant, his body seemed to expand out of the suit and disintegrate in a puff of blood and flesh. And then there were just two golden beads, falling away and gone.

She realised that Bale had sacrificed himself to set Millasco up for her, but Millasco was already turning, aiming his own streamer to neutralise her released cutter line.

She jerked away, still mimicked to him, and the faint tug was enough to disturb his streamer's path, which missed her line. Millasco swore as it coiled round his wrist. He began to spin.

Yes, she thought. She felt herself going with him, and nilled the mimic control to let him tumble away on the end of her line.

He was still with her. 'Not so easy,' he grunted.

Unless she released her cutter line, she had no chance against him. But that would free his gun arm.

She had no choice. She cut the line loose.

Millasco began to work the head of his weapon through the turbulence towards her. She was close enough to see his expression through his visor. Indigo eyes and a thin smile. In the corner of her vision she could see the gun swinging towards her, the obtuse angle of the barrel moving towards the acute, approaching zero.

'That's it,' Millasco said. 'Nowhere to go.'

It seemed so very slow. The gun was almost there. His arm was straight, hardly wavering in the airstorm.

'No,' she said, and let everything go at him, a blizzard of every remaining cutter and streamer.

And then she did the one thing he wouldn't anticipate. She finned straight for him.

Millasco flailed as she swung her gauntlets at his face, his gunstock thumping her visor. He got a grip at her waist and kicked at her, but his thin NTGs were ineffectual.

Then she felt his hand fumbling at the emergency valve closure of her flysuit.

She felt herself yanked so hard the breath went out of her.

'One,' Millasco whispered.

She immediately knew what he meant. It would take three pulls to release the suit. He'd just primed the safety release. She tried to push him away, but his grip was relentless. A cloud of dusty scree rolled slowly past. She had a sense of intolerable speed, and at the same time, absolute stillness.

She pulled up her arm and backhanded Millasco. His head jerked and he flinched momentarily, then he grinned and steadied himself. The scree was gone. 'Sure. Slap me. Give me something to remember you by.' He jerked the valve at her waist once more. This time she felt something yield.

'Two,' he said. 'Safety's gone. Say goodbye.'

She swung her arm round hard again, putting her shoulder into the blow and this time flicking out the damaged wristfin.

Millasco couldn't see the fin's serrated edge. Razer felt his hand confirm its grip on the valve.

They were tumbling together in the node of a pipe, over and over like crazy lovers. Razer grunted, all her strength focused as the wristfin smashed into Millasco's visor and slid down it. Nothing happened. The visor was too hard. The momentum of the blow took her forearm across the helmet's slick metalled cheekplate and carried it on down his chin, the fin failing to penetrate any part of the helmet.

His hands were braced. He said, 'Th –'

Almost without her realising it, her wrist slipped further until the fin hit the suit's throat cuff, and sliced through it and into the side of his neck.

Millasco froze. His eyes widened. The pressure on Razer's waist vanished.

She kept her position for a moment, the pressure of her wrist the only thing that held Millasco together. In his wide eyes she could see his perfect understanding. The pipe whirled madly around them.

As she started to pull her arm away, he pushed his head at her, trying to survive a moment longer.

She let him. 'Who's paying you, Millasco?'

He started to speak, but only blood came from his mouth, coiling around the inside of the helmet. His eyes started to bleed.

'Tell me, or I'll let you go.'

He opened his mouth in blood. As she waited, she felt an itch at her waist.

Millasco wasn't trying to tell her a thing. He was gathering himself for a final rip at her exo-valve.

She wrenched her arm from the gash at his throat and

watched the rest of him flood instantly away, shredding and catching on the billowing remnants of her cutters and streamers.

She sobbed, even though there was nothing of him to hear it, 'That, you bastard, is for Bale.'

She cut it all away and let the suit with what was left of Millasco's body go, and she tumbled, and tumbled, and tumbled.

Thirty
ALEF

SigEv 33 Illness

I was shaking when I got back to Pireve. I couldn't keep what had happened from her. I said, 'What should I do?'

She massaged my shoulders, smoothing away the knots. 'First, you need to find out what he's doing. There's something he wants you to know. Surely you're safe. You're his oldest friend.'

'No one's safe from him, Pireve.'

'If that's right, it's even more important. Isn't it?'

She was right, of course. While she slept, I carried out a search of his putery and found his records of the killings in his house – it wasn't hard, he didn't encrypt them with any effort – and I watched them through the night. In the morning I didn't mention it to Pireve. I told her I'd been in the pornoverse, as usual. Our joke. I went to work, but couldn't concentrate.

The next night, and the night after that, I watched more of Pellonhorc's killings. Towards the end I was able to watch them as I might have watched them before I had met Pireve: without emotion.

The killings all took place in the same room. I recognised

it as the small operating theatre annexed to the medical ward he'd had built and equipped in his house. There were surgical tables, anaesthetic equipment and all the tools. Some of the tools were industrial. Medical staff were present during the killings. I never saw their faces, since they were wearing masks, but I saw their wide eyes behind the plastic visors.

Despite the environment and the instruments, the killings were not clean. He would let his victims come near to death, then have the medics resuscitate them, and he'd question them. 'What happened? What did you see? What was it like?'

Every time, the answers enraged him. If the near-dead were still coherent, they told him nothing he wanted to hear and he would accuse them of lying and use the tools again, until eventually there was no coherence and he'd scream at them and let them die. It was the same, time and again, and it was always terrifying.

The ward had two exits. One was the entrance from the main medical unit and the other was to a small closed annexe, the house's *rv* room, which I assumed had never been used. During lulls in the killings, while he was waiting for the staff to revive his victims, Pellonhorc went into the *rv* room. He always spent at least half an hour inside, and always emerged relaxed again.

I explored the records and found that the *rv* room had no cams. I wondered whether he used the facility himself, banking time, or just sat there in silence. I searched the Song for help, and discovered it to be a common enough fantasy and a rare but not unheard-of activity, and decided he was probably onanising in there.

It explained the absence of cams as well, especially

in view of the fact that every other part of the house was covered. I might have thought no more of it except that once, when he emerged from the *rv* room, his hands were splashed with blood. I checked back and found he had entered the room clean.

I checked again, reviewing all the times he had used the room, and saw that there had been specks of blood on his surgical smock more than once on his emergence, on top of the spatterings he had received in the main unit. I counted them.

I never showed any of the images to Pireve, and I didn't tell her much of the detail, but eventually we talked about the killings.

'Maybe he's cutting himself,' she said, a little shakily. I was surprised at how much it affected her, even though she was well aware of his business techniques.

'Why would he do that?'

She made a face. 'He might hate himself. It's common enough.'

'Not Pellonhorc. He hates everyone else.'

'Everyone but you, Alef. It could be self-hate, though.'

'Or maybe he's just insane.'

It was the first time I'd said that. Pireve's face lost its colour, and I leant across the table to touch her hand. 'I didn't mean it,' I told her. 'Anyway, don't worry. There are no cams here. I check regularly. We can say what we like.'

After that conversation I went back to the archives of the house to look for cam records of the *rv* room being set up, and found details of the installation of two *rv* units. There were gaps in the house and flycykle records that I eventually traced back to the emergency dock at the city's hospital. I opened the hospital's screenery for that day and found they had been overwritten.

I was sure I was missing something, but I couldn't push too hard. I knew that any deep search risked triggering a reverse search that, while I'd been careful enough to be sure it could not lead to me, would let Pellonhorc know he was being spied on.

The weekly meetings I had with Pellonhorc were increasingly strained. I was convinced my knowledge showed in my face. He was preoccupied and abrupt with me, though, and as soon as we'd finished talking about business, I'd quickly leave.

For three weeks I escaped like this. At the end of our meeting on the fourth week, he stopped me at the door.

'Alef, come back and sit down. We haven't finished.'

I sat. I could hardly hear him for the beating of my heart.

'Something important has happened. It happened a short while ago. I would have told you earlier, but I've been taking action and there wasn't time.' He frowned at me and said, firmly, 'I'm not going to die, Alef.'

I froze. Did he think I was intending to kill him? Was he going to kill me? I didn't know what to do.

'You don't seemed concerned, Alef. Aren't you curious?'

I wasn't going to ask him a question. That was what he wanted, for me to lead myself into some trap. I said, 'Everyone dies. The average age of mortality in the System is approximately fifty-one years and five months. Inhabitants of Spindrift are the longest-lived at fifty –'

'I don't give a shit about that. *I. Me.* I'm twenty-five years and three months and I am not going to die. Not me. God won't have Pellonhorc, nor will Lucifer.'

Lucifer. I hadn't heard that name since Gehenna. I couldn't stop myself saying, 'What do you mean?'

He was rubbing his hands hard together. It was as if they were fighting each other, palms scraping, nails scratching. 'God will find a way, Alef. He'll have to.'

'I don't understand.'

'He made us, didn't He?'

'Father Grace said that, yes.' I was picking my way carefully, trying to keep the numbers at bay.

'If I die, Alef, everybody dies. *Everybody*. He'd never allow that, would He?' Pellonhorc looked impatiently at me. 'I'm being logical, aren't I? He won't let everyone die, will He.'

I had to be cautious. 'When each of us dies, it is as if everyone else is gone to nothing.'

'I don't mean that,' he said sharply. 'He won't allow it. Everyone to die. Right?'

He had the knife in his hand now and was opening it. I looked away from the extending blade, into his face, and nodded for my life. 'He would not,' I said.

Pellonhorc crowed, 'Hah! Yes! I *have* Him.'

I'd never seen him so excited. He breathed out, a long, startling sigh, and then his voice dropped back to normal as he said, 'I just needed you to confirm it. Who else, eh, Alef?' He spun the knife high in the air, catching it cleanly by its hilt, all the time staring wildly at me. He folded the knife away and went on, 'It's arranged. *He* knows. Everything's in place, throughout the System. It's seeded.'

He stopped sharply and there was silence. There was nothing in the room but that silence and his terrifying smile.

Merely by saying what I had said, I had done something

awful. I was involved. I knew it, though I had no idea what it was. I pulled myself together enough to say, 'What are you talking about? What's seeded?'

He lowered his voice to a whisper. 'Only He and I know. He will find a way. He's trying to kill me, but I've trumped Him. He won't let me die now.'

'God's trying to kill you?'

'He's given me the cancer, of course. He couldn't do it any other way because I'm too clever, so he's done this.'

Pellonhorc raised his shirt and I saw it on his stomach, the dark, earthy, almost casual tumescence and the awkward puckering around it. He took it in his hand, as much of it as he could, and squeezed it until his knuckles blanched. The excess swelled out of his hand like dough. I could see the pain seep into his face.

'Oh, Pellonhorc,' I started, but he waved me down.

'No.' His eyes were wide and bright. 'He thinks He can reach me, but He will see, now. Oh, yes. He will find a way to save me. I'm still too clever for Him.'

'Medics –'

'They say it's untreatable. I've had it a long time. I've known a long time.'

'How long? Why didn't you –?'

'I knew I wasn't going to die. I thought He'd back down.'

'I'm sorry.'

He let the shirt drop back over the cancer. 'Don't be. He will find a way. He must start to take responsibility.'

* * *

SigEv 34 Goddery and absolution

'What did he mean?' Pireve said. 'Why didn't you ask him?'

'I don't know. I wasn't thinking.'

She looked at me, not saying what I knew was in her mind – *you weren't thinking. Of all people, you.* What she said was, 'He controls you, Alef. He always has. You do whatever he tells you to.'

'What do I do now? You tell me.'

She rolled towards me. I could feel her warmth in the bed, in the dark, and I put an arm around her.

She said, 'He relies on you, Alef, doesn't he? For everything.'

'Not everything. Not *that*.'

I could hear the aircon labouring above us.

'You mean the killings,' she said.

'Yes.'

'Then say it. This has to be accepted.'

'The killings.' I held her. Her skin was soft and cool and comforting. 'For everything else, yes, he relies on me,' I said, seeing what she meant. 'You mean he's relying on me for this, too? For his cancer?'

'To find a cure for it, yes. That's why he's telling you. Otherwise he'd keep it between himself and this god.'

'God. Not *a* god, or *this* god.'

She sat up. I could only see her in silhouette. 'You don't believe, Alef –?'

'No! No, of course I don't. But *he* must do.'

'Maybe he sees you as the god's agent. Or maybe he's playing safe, giving you a chance as well as the god.'

'Not even *the* god, Pireve. Just God.'

She touched my cheek with the warm hollow of her palm. 'Alef, are you sure you don't believe?'

'Pireve –'

'I'm joking.' She kissed me and pulled herself back under the billowing covers, her voice muffled. 'What's seeded, then? Not me, that's for sure. Why don't we address that now? We'll address the other thing in the morning.'

SigEv 35 Pellonhorc's research

We didn't have a chance in the morning. Pellonhorc had sent a flycykle for me and I was taken straight to the house. The pilot wouldn't tell me why.

I hadn't been to the house for a long time. There had been a big party to celebrate the day the city's shield had finally embraced it, but that was as far as it got. The shield had never pushed beyond the side and rear walls. Pellonhorc hadn't let it. Only the facade of his home was in civilisation. Its rear looked out on wilderness.

The dock was on the wild side of the house. There was a sort of garden stretching back for a few hundred metres beyond the edge of the blackened and cracked, qualcreted decking of the dock, a garden of fibrous grasses and trees with agonised trunks and rubbery, spatulate leaves. There were smoke-drifted ponds and scarlet boulders and shards of opalescent stone, and while the shield didn't extend over the garden, there was a dome of fine spidersteel netting to retain the squirlings and blueblands, the ergles and pinsects and mosqueetles that crawled, waddled and flew in constant pursuit of each other. The quality of the netting was such that the garden seemed of another dimension. The yelps and screams occasionally sounded almost human, and from time to time I would arrive to see a pack of creatures fighting over something.

At this time of the morning, the dock was in the deep shadow of the house. As the driver brought us down, I scanned the other vehicles there. Nothing as big as the *Darwin*. The garden's netting billowed in the wash of the settling flycykle, and the garden within blurred and fixed. One of the larger creatures stood and stared directly at me. There was something in its mouth.

Pellonhorc was at the door, waiting for me, unshaven and agitated. 'Come in,' he said. 'I want to show you something.'

'Is it so urgent? I haven't been to The Floor yet.'

'Everything is urgent, Alef.' He was already walking away. 'I want to show you my thinking.'

'I have some questions, too.' I tried to catch up with him, to walk beside him, but he speeded up and held to the centre of the corridors. I soon realised we were heading in the direction of the medical wing.

'Where are we going?'

He didn't answer. There were no staff to be seen. I felt sweat break out, my armpits itch. I said, 'Pellonhorc, I need to tell Pireve where I am.' My mouth was dry and I licked my lips to speak. 'If I'm not on The Floor, she'll worry.'

'You're with me. Why would she worry?'

He pushed the door open, and at last waited for me. 'In you go, Alef.'

I didn't expect it to be so bright. There was a great wheel of lights above a central bed, and several fat-tyred trolleys covered by blue plastic sheeting, the sheeting bulging and swollen unevenly. The floor gleamed. Where the floor met the walls, it rolled up in smooth curves. I started to consider the mathematics of the curves. The floor was set with shining metal drains, finely meshed and whistling faintly. I considered the screenery, some of which I recognised. EEG. ECG. There were operating screens for remote surgical rigs, and the rigs themselves with their handles and microscopes and touch-pads and drips and drains and pumps. I noted the dispensers of gloves in five sizes, of antiseptic washes and of substances unmarked other than with symbols indicating poison and acid. Thirty wall-mounted power boxes laid out equidistantly in five banks of six. Coils of tubing in sterile packaging, a surgical laser, ultrasonic disinfectant baths, two large vacuum autoclaves. Boxes of needles in various lengths and calibers, and disposal containers marked CARE! Other signs: DO NOT TOUCH! DO NOT REUSE! ORGANIC WASTE ONLY! INORGANIC WASTE ONLY! DO NOT DISCHARGE UNLESS RED LIGHT IS ON! STERILE – DO NOT CONTAMINATE! LETHAL –

'Alef! Are you listening to me?'

'I'm sorry. Yes.'

'I need you to concentrate. If you don't concentrate, you're no use at all to me.'

I concentrated.

'I've been doing some research here. It isn't important at the moment. What matters is in there.' He indicated the door to the *rv* room. 'Come.'

I was sweating even more. The room was far too hot. I didn't want to know what was in there. I thought of the animal outside with the thing in its jaws.

'I –' I felt the ground give way, and arms catching me, and then nothing.

'Drink this.' Pellonhorc's voice was closing in on me from far away. Without thinking, I sipped. Sweet.

'A little more.'

I pushed it away. 'What is it?'

'A sugar drink. You fainted, Alef. Did you have breakfast? I'll have something brought.'

I sat up, my head slowly clearing. 'Where is this?'

But I knew where I had to be. The room was bare except for two *rv* units set side by side. This was where Pellonhorc retreated in the midst of torture and murder.

'It's the *rv* chamber. In case of emergency. My father intended it for himself and Madelene.'

'Why do you come here?'

I realised I'd said too much. 'Why did you bring me here, I mean. You said it's important.'

He stared a moment longer, then said, 'Look. I've had them adapted.' There was a control stick in his hand. 'See?'

In unison, the units began to move, the domed heads rising until they were vertical. The units slowly swung round to face each other. The mechanics were astonishing, arms and struts and joints extending from the floor, sliding and tilting beautifully. Eventually the huge units came to a halt like two great guards at salute.

The last time I'd seen *rv* units so close had been in the ferry that had brought us from Gehenna to Peco, and for a moment I felt an odd nostalgia.

It was a curious thing. Even at that moment of fear and unknowing, my memory cut in and took me back to that time, to the end of my innocence. I had absorbed the

Song during that time. My education, after my parents, had been with Solaman, but I had grown up in one of those great sealed couches into which one could withdraw from the worlds to sleep, or contemplate, or drift amongst the fantasies of a billion others.

These two units differed from conventional units in more ways than their facility to stand upright. Most units were as smooth as cocoons, hinged along one side, and made of metal. These were faintly contoured with stylised hips and knees, arms, shoulders and feet. Above the shoulders, the top of the unit was dark and moulded in imitation of a visored helmet.

No, I was wrong. They were not simply moulded in this way. I saw, with a shock, that the visors were not quite opaque. Like half moons in night skies, I could make out the shadow of a face behind each visor.

Thirty-one

RAZER

Razer looked at the TruTale. It seemed hollow, now that Bale was really dead. His survival in the sewers had made him seem invulnerable.

She felt empty, the pen too light and unfamiliar. It felt like there was no reality to write about.

She raised her hand from the page, crying at the hopelessness of everything, at the death of Bale, and then she dried her eyes.

Not hopeless. There had to be something.

The streets were not well lit at this end of Lookout, and the roads were shattered. Razer saw a rat scuttle into a gap in the paving, something wriggling in its jaws. There were vigorous weeds, and the few lamp posts alternated with dying trees. She supposed that Paxers didn't make enough money to live anywhere else. Like writers. She passed a small rank of shops and delivery outlets, a cluster of repair booths and a bar. She nearly stopped at the bar. It was cold, and she was the only one out walking. A few zipriders swung past, one of them making a point turn and circling her. She put a hand to her jacket to show the rider her gunstock, and the rider arced away in a snarl of engine noise.

Delta's block was a slotbuild of metal and meld, a barely customised version of a standard package that Razer had seen and lived in throughout the System. The lobby stank. The stairs were sticky underfoot. All that made this slotbuild stand out were the cams, whose motors keened as the lens-heads swivelled to follow her along the corridors. It reminded her of an old, old soundless film she'd seen in the archives, scratched images of a wall lined with living, torch-bearing hands that lit the heroine along a gloomy passageway. There was no magic here, though, and certainly no heroine.

She leaned into the comms grille set into the dented metal door and said, 'Delta Kerlew? Can I see you? I want to say thanks.'

The Paxer barely waited for Razer to be inside before pushing the door closed. She said, 'I haven't done anything for you to thank me.'

'You have. At the Chute, the other day. After Bale...' She couldn't say the rest of it. 'You could have held me longer.'

'Pax could have. Not me. Don't be cute. I'm not your friend. Why did you come here?'

Razer noticed Delta's fists knotting and unknotting, and said, 'There's no one else. Please.' She caught sight of her own reflection in the far window. As bruised and exhausted as she felt, little of it showed in her face. Every morning for the last week, she'd surfaced crying from rough sleep, feeling the grip of Millasco's hands at her waist and seeing his face flooding with blood.

'Sit down if you want,' Delta said flatly, leaving the room

for what Razer remembered was always a small kitchen. 'I was making caffé.'

Alone in the room, Razer began reflexively to catalogue. On the shelves were blossom jars and travel mementos; the usual tatty obsidian carvings, a lamp, a nest of small green clay bowls. There were Pax certificates for weaponry and other proficiencies on the wall. They were signed *Navid*, which had been the name of the snitty officer who had come down to validate her statement over Bale's death.

Alongside the certificates was a slim glass-fronted cabinet with a small matt-black handgun inside. Razer looked at it long enough for the eyetagger to register her attention and opaque the glass. A lozenge of greyed screenery on the opposite wall had a small Pax-blue oval pulsing in its corner.

It was a typical Paxer's place, a barely individualised holding room, the objects on the shelves set out more as a record than as a flare of personality. It was a greater effort than Bale had ever made, but this was still no more than a Paxer's downtime on display.

No – there was one more thing in the room: a curtain of broadmesh chainlink over some sort of cupboard in the corner of the room, reaching all the way down to the floor. Without thinking, Razer touched the polished metal and the mesh retracted sharply to the side.

A brilliant light shot out, filling the room. Razer gasped and took a step back, her eyes accustoming until she could stare at the glass tank full of dazzling stones.

It was mesmerisingly beautiful. They must have been taken from the shore. It was a crime to remove shore stones from Bleak, and Razer was fairly sure it was illegal even to remove them from the beach. There was movement in the tank too, the water rippling and spinning colours.

She went to kneel by the tank. 'Oh,' she murmured aloud. Tiny red-lipped fish flashed amongst the stones, their scales vermilion and fins scarab-blue.

Nothing else in the room compared with the shock of the tank. She stood up and looked around again, but the few cupboards and chairs, the small metal table and the neatly ordered desk in the opposite corner were unremarkable, though now she noticed a few framed images of people on the desk, each launching at her glance into a brief gesture or a startled smile.

Razer touched the curtain again and it moved back across the tank. The room dulled. She wandered into the small kitchen and watched Delta take cups from a low cupboard. There must have been at least ten cups in there, and the same number of plates and bowls. The idea of that made Razer's throat tighten, made her think of there being people who might sit with you in your own place for an evening just to talk and eat and drink. It made her think of Bale again, and of herself. And somehow of Tallen, too.

'Are you in pain?'

She looked uncomprehendingly at Delta, who added without inflexion, 'I thought you were crying.'

'No.'

'Good.' Delta carried on making the caffé. She said, 'I don't like being watched.'

'Sorry.' Razer withdrew to the other room. The window overlooked a patch of ground littered with rubbish, and beyond it the wall of another slotbuild and a road. There was no colour to any of it.

Delta set the drinks on the table with a noise that made

Razer jump, and sitting down in a chair, said, 'So?'

'You and Bale were friends,' Razer said as she sat down across the table from Delta.

'Not like *you* and Bale.'

Razer took a long breath. 'You're right, not like that at all. It didn't work with us. Bale and I were using each other. With you, it was different. He told me about you.'

'And now he's gone, you want to use me instead, is that it?'

'No.' Razer closed her eyes and shuddered, seeing Bale dying in the Chute. 'He talked about you a lot.'

'You needn't bother with this.' Delta pushed herself back in the chair. 'We both know why you're here. You could have the courtesy to come out with it.'

'I'm sorry. Really.'

'I don't care. Really. You want me to help you, I'll do it in his memory. Not for you. Don't expect anything else.'

'Look,' Razer said. 'Maybe it's my fault he's dead. I should have believed him, but I didn't. I'm sorry. He was a good man.'

'A good man.' Delta was silent for a moment, then she said, wearily, 'No, not Bale. He could be a stone-headed shit. Mostly he was.'

Razer reached across the table, but Delta jerked away and said, 'Don't try and make yourself feel better. You can move away from Bleak, move *on*. I can't. And don't feel so damn guilty, either. You've got no right to guilt. I got him into this, not you. I sent him down after the K in the first place. You know what guts me? That he went to you.'

'He tried to go to you.'

'Not very hard, he didn't. You don't know him. He's

persistent.' Delta squeezed her eyes shut. '*Didn't* know him. You didn't know him.'

'He would have come back to you,' Razer said quietly. 'You know why he came to me? He thought I was involved in it. He wasn't just flushing Millasco – he was checking on me.'

'Millasco?'

'In my statement. Haven't you read it?'

'No. No reason to.'

'It's how Bale died. You aren't interested?'

'I'd need a reason to see it. Pax is like that.' Delta chewed her lip. 'Bale was checking on you?'

'Yes. He could have been right to,' Razer said. She almost missed the flicker of Delta's eyes towards the screenery. Realising what that meant, she said, 'Oh. You're recording this.'

'Of course I am.'

'Is your comms open, too? Is it feeding live?'

Delta hesitated. 'No.'

'Please. I don't know what's going on, but if Bale was right, his death isn't the end of it. I'm trusting you, Delta, but you can't trust anyone with this. Not even Pax. Bale thought Pax might be caught up in it.'

'That's a first, even for Bale,' Delta said, but she said it quietly, and then she made a few precise hand movements at the screen, which whined briefly and settled.

Razer said, 'Thank you.'

'It doesn't mean I trust you. Go on.'

'I can't stop thinking about it.' She shook her head. 'I think I may have been dummied. It sounds stupid, but it's all I can think of. I connect with my AI every night. Someone could have used my body and taken me after Tallen.'

Delta didn't react.

'I was sent to Bleak, to Lookout, just in time for all this. I was even instructed to find and contact Bale. It's a huge jump of coincidence, at least. The only thing I can think of is that I was dummied and used.'

'Bale suggested that?'

'He was heading more down the line that I was knowingly involved. I never got to telling him I thought I might have been dummied.'

Delta pushed her tasse around the table. 'Dummied?' She laughed. 'What do you know about dummying?'

'I looked on the Song. I couldn't think of anything else that might fit.'

'You've had any sublims recently? Like ghosting flashbacks?'

'Only from the Chute.'

'You'd have had a lot more if you'd been dummied. It's completely obsolete tech. Dummies are really slow, too. It's illegal, of course, highly risky to the dummy, and unreliable. Even the Whisper hardly uses them now. You only really use a dummy when you want an expendable observer, and this wasn't that.' She looked at Razer dismissively. 'No, you weren't dummied. Nevertheless, big coincidence, like you said.'

They fell silent. Delta left the table and touched the tank's curtain. As it shot back and the light exploded into the room, she said, 'The curtain doesn't sit straight. Bale always said he'd fix it.' Razer watched the fish flickering among the brilliant stones.

Eventually Delta said, 'You can just walk away from this. Or are you staying for the story?'

Razer said, 'I want Bale not to be a waste. I want to tell

the story, but I want to do something right, too.' She found herself without the words she needed, and fell back on, 'I just want to do something.'

Delta touched the curtain again, holding her palm against the metal as it closed over the tank. The room darkened. Delta shook her head. 'You want to *do* something,' she said, her voice heavy with mockery. 'Shit. Bale would be proud of you.'

Suddenly furious, Razer made to stand up, but Delta said, 'Sit down. You want to *do* something, writer? Let's do something, then.'

In her room, Razer coded herself into TruTales.

'Cynth? I'm going to write a story on Delta Kerlew. I'll link it to Bale. I think there's some good stuff here.' A TruTale about Delta might keep Cynth at bay. She felt her augmem unload, and sighed. She was exhausted.

THIS DATA IS GOOD, KESTREL DUST, BUT DO NOT WRITE KERLEW STORY.

'You don't want it, you don't pay me. It's been five years. I'm due some leave.'

NO LEAVE PERMITTED AT PRESENT. BALE SUBJECT SATISFACTORILY CONCLUDED. REPEAT DO NOT WRITE KERLEW STORY. NEW SUBJECT ALLOCATED.

She stared at *satisfactorily concluded*, then whispered, 'What in hell are you based on, you goddamn shit of a program?'

THIS PROGRAM IS A PROGRAM, IT IS NOT A YOU. KERLEW IS NOT YOUR STORY, KESTREL DUST. YOUR STORY IS NOW TALLEN.

'*Tallen*? Oh, really? Is it? Do you know who killed Bale? Is that *your* story, Cynth?'

YOUR STORY IS NOW TALLEN.

'You don't act like a programmed AI. You haven't acted like one since I came to Bleak. Why don't you want me working with Delta? Did you know Bale would be killed?'

YOUR STORY IS NOW TALLEN.

'I'm not doing anything until I know what's happening. And I'm not finished with Bale either. Did you arrange Bale's death? His satisfactory conclusion?'

The screen remained empty.

'Fine. Hell with you. You can repeat yourself forever, but I'm not doing a thing.'

THIS PROGRAM REGRETS YOUR MISINTERPRETATION OF THE WORD 'SATISFACTORILY'. KESTREL DUST'S STORY AND DATA WERE SATISFACTORY. BALE'S DEATH WAS NOT A SATISFACTORY OUTCOME.

'No, it wasn't.'

TALLEN'S DEATH WOULD NOT BE A SATISFACTORY OUTCOME.

'What?' The hairs rose at the nape of her neck.

THIS PROGRAM HAS REVIEWED BALE'S STORY AND BELIEVES TALLEN TO BE AT RISK AND A GOOD SUBJECT FOR KESTREL DUST.

Razer slowly relaxed again. Cynth was just a cracked AI, and Razer was so lonely she was reading words in the stars. She said, 'You aren't so well-informed, Cynth. I've checked on him. Tallen's on a rig. I can't contact him. No one can.'

TALLEN IS REGISTERED ON STARHEARTS.

'So?' For a moment, the idea of Tallen searching for

someone made her heart beat faster. She said, 'And how do you know that?'

STARHEARTS IS A SUBSIDIARY OF AFTERLIFE. THIS PROGRAM HAS CROSS-ACCESS.

'You want me to do a StarHearts search for him? I can't make a story out of a HeartSearch.'

KESTREL DUST CAN CONTACT TALLEN THROUGH HIS HEARTSEARCH. TALLEN IS REGISTERED AND IS AT RISK AND A GOOD SUBJECT FOR KESTREL DUST.

'This program sounds sentimental to me.' Words in the stars. She wanted there to be words in the stars. A ghost in this machine. Something out there. She did feel lonely. Did Tallen?

THIS PROGRAM IS NOT A STORY. THIS PROGRAM IS A COLLATER OF STORIES. TALLEN IS A GOOD SUBJECT FOR KESTREL DUST. KESTREL DUST IS A CONTRACTED SUPPLIER. THIS PROGRAM IS LOGICAL. KESTREL DUST IS RESPONDING EMOTIONALLY.

Razer pressed her thumbs into her eyes. She remembered Tallen lying in the bed across from Bale, a man in a metal scaffold. What might that be like, to be without the slightest movement, to have no control? And to have the memories Tallen might have. It would be a good story.

But he'd been able to recall nothing.

She looked at the screen telling her she was reacting emotionally. Bale would have wanted her to take this on, to question Tallen.

And she wanted to talk to him again. It wasn't about Bale at all, or about Tallen's story. 'Okay. I'll try to contact Tallen.'

THIS PROGRAM HAS ALREADY INITIATED KESTREL DUST'S STARHEARTS REGISTRATION WITH IDENTITY PROGRAMMED

TO PSYCH-MATCH TALLEN. THIS PROGRAM WILL VALIDATE AND PROMOTE THE HEARTSEARCH TO TALLEN.

'You don't waste time, do you?'

THIS PROGRAM'S DECISIONS ARE ITS ACTIONS.

'And mine are predictable? Is that it? You knew I'd agree.'

KESTREL DUST'S DECISIONS ARE ALWAYS SATISFACTORY, EVENTUALLY.

'Hell with you, Cynth,' and then she added, 'This supplier thanks this program,' feeling ridiculous for throwing sarcasm at putery. As she was closing the contact, she barely registered the last brief words.

KESTREL DUST SHOULD BE CAREFUL.

Thirty-two

ALEF

SigEv 36 Salvation

The screenery and readouts on the walls were flickering. The levels didn't quite enter the highlighted grids that indicated stable *rv* ranges, and I wondered whether the units were malfunctioning. Pellonhorc didn't seem concerned, though.

There were other devices too, scattered around the room. Tools, like some of the tools in the previous room, though these were more disordered. Pellonhorc made some adjustments at a wall console, saying, 'These are extraordinary machines, Alef.' He reached out and rapped the nearest unit with a knuckle. It returned a dull chime. 'It's not just a binary switch; yes and no; sleep and wake; up and down…' He was clicking his fingers as he recited his list. He stopped, then clicked them once more. '… Live and die. It's not at all straightforward.' He ran a finger almost sensuously over the curve of a machine's hip. 'Not like you, Alef.' He considered me a moment longer. 'Although, of course, you aren't simple. Not altogether. You're unique, like me.'

When I said nothing to this, he added, 'You and I are more than special. You do realise this, don't you. We've always known it.'

'Who are they?'

'Straight to it, Alef. That's what I mean. Now, as I was saying, these are delicate and complex devices. Let me show you. If I do this...'

As soon as the visors began slowly to sink back, there was movement. The head to the left shivered and its eyes opened wide, instantly full of alertness, darting from side to side and then staring straight ahead. Nothing more was possible, as the head was firmly braced face-forward. I looked across at the other head, which was identically fixed by cheek-bars. The two men had no choice but to face each other directly.

Ethan Drame and Spetkin Ligate. Their faces were contorted, muscles jerking in their cheeks and temples as they strained hopelessly to move.

'What are you doing?' I said to Pellonhorc, when I could speak.

Pellonhorc frowned. 'Sometimes science is for its own sake, isn't it? One doesn't know at the time. The thing is to ask the questions.'

Drame's eyes were drawn so wide that the irises were almost lost in their pools of white, and Ligate's lips were stretched thin and pale. Both men were breathing sharply and shallowly, almost hissing. It was as if they were punctured. The atmosphere in the room was terrifying.

I found myself whispering. 'What are the questions?'

'Okay. Let's start. Where will they go, Alef?' He shook his head, 'No. That isn't the first question.'

The knife was in his hand. He opened it and closed it again and started tossing it into the air and catching it as he spoke. 'They're in pain.' He was speaking a little quickly, but otherwise almost conversationally, the red-cased knife rising and falling. 'They're in a lot of pain, but is it enough? That's the first question. Is the pain enough?'

He slipped the knife back into a pocket and waited for me.

'I don't understand,' I said. 'I don't understand this at all.'

'Death, Alef,' he said impatiently. 'It's all about death.' Unconsciously, Pellonhorc touched his stomach, and I realised that this was all about his own death.

I said, 'Are you in pain? There are painkillers, drugs –'

'No!'

I stepped back. I'd never seen him like this before.

'I'm talking about *their* pain. Listen to me, Alef. I need you to concentrate.' He opened his hands and stared into them for a few moments. I saw clusters of pinprick scars in the palms, livid white. I'd never seen them before.

He said, 'I've tried to see what happens at death, but I haven't found it yet.' Making a gesture back towards the main medical area, he went on, 'He won't let me see. I get to the edge, but He always takes them from me just as I –' The brief calm was fading. 'I need a moment, just a single moment longer. I need to let them reach the gates of where they're bound and then bring them back to me. I'm so close. I need Him to give me a moment more.'

On the wall, lights flashed.

'In here, this is quite different. I know where they're going. This is to save them, Alef.'

I was quite lost, and terrified too, and desperate to say the right thing, although I had no idea what it might be. 'They need surgery, then. Have you –?'

His voice rose out of control. 'You aren't *listening* to me. To save them. To *save* them!'

Gehenna. We were back in Gehenna.

Calm once more, and as if to himself, he was saying, 'If they suffer enough now, will it cancel out the things they've done? Suffering atones; I know that. How much suffering, though? How do I know, Alef?'

He was staring at me and waiting, and I suddenly realised he wanted an answer from me. A logical answer. The calibration of a dose of agony.

'I – I'll have to think about it.'

'Good. Yes. I knew you were the one. You always are.' He clasped my hands in his. His grip was cold and damp, making me feel even more nauseous. 'Listen to my thoughts and tell me if I'm wrong. What I need to know, Alef, is whether I can save them from hell.'

Was he telling me he cared about them? I couldn't believe that. 'I don't know,' I said. 'I really don't understand.'

He was clutching his stomach again. 'If I save them from hell, I'm doing a good thing, aren't I? Is it enough, though?'

'Enough for what?'

A sigh. 'It's easy, Alef.' As if I were a child. One moment he was pleading with me, the next he was almost shouting. 'What will it take to cancel what I've done?'

At last I saw it. Of course he didn't care about them. All he cared about – all he had ever cared about – was himself. I said, 'There is no hell. You aren't being punished. You must see that.'

'What are you talking about?' His voice was rising.

'Hell makes no sense, Pellonhorc. We die.'

'Everyone on Gehenna is *wrong*?'

I suddenly realised he was screaming at me.

'No,' I said quickly. 'Of course not.'

Again, as if a switch had been flicked, he was settled once more. 'Exactly. Let me show you something curious.' He put himself in the small space between the two units so that he faced his father, and glanced at the console. On one of the screenery, a seismic line levelled, and as it did, Ethan Drame's face slackened and his breathing eased.

'That feels better, Father, doesn't it.'

Drame nodded as much as he could. Saliva slid from the corners of his mouth. His eyes half closed.

Pellonhorc said to me, 'He wouldn't talk to me for months. He still won't accept that this is for his own eternal good. I give him a choice, every time I see him. I give Ligate the same choice, in fact. Listen, Alef.' He faced his father again. 'You can have the pain taken away forever, Father. You'd like that. I will let you die, and I know how much you want to die. You ask me for it all the time. All you have to do in exchange is to tell me to release Ligate. He walks from this room – it will take a moment – and you can die. You just have to say. You just have to watch him go.'

Pellonhorc turned to face Ligate, whose pain clearly remained. Ligate gritted his teeth and said a word. It took me a moment to recognise it as, 'Please.'

Pellonhorc turned back to his father and said, 'He's asked you nicely.' There was no response, and he slapped the unit with the flat of his hand. 'Father!'

'No.' Drame licked his lips and said, 'Kill both of us. Please do that, Pellonhorc.'

Pellonhorc hissed, 'No. That isn't an option.'

And then, to my horror, Drame whispered, 'Alef? Is that you?'

My breath ebbed away.

'Yes,' Pellonhorc said with a glance at me. 'He's here.'

My throat had closed up. I knew Drame couldn't even see me, but I was terrified.

Pellonhorc shifted something on the console, and, on the wall, the screenery suddenly exchanged their displays. The pain seemed to leap, like something physical, from Ligate's face to Drame's. Drame released a tiny, gagging cluck and said nothing more, and I breathed again. Pellonhorc turned round to face the other unit.

'Ligate. What about you? You begged my father to be merciful. Will you be merciful to him?'

Ligate's head shook fractionally. His cheeks were so thin and pale that I could make out the shadow of his skull. He gathered himself and murmured, 'I will not, not… will not see him leave.'

'Think about it. If you say yes, you'll be dead a moment later.' Pellonhorc glanced at me, raising his eyebrows, and said to Ligate, 'You don't believe in God, do you? I know you don't. So what does it matter to you? Your pain will be gone and you'll be nothing.' He leaned forward and examined Ligate closely. 'Let my father go. Say it and you can have peace.'

'I. Will. Not. Watch. Him. Leave.' A long, shivering breath, and, '*He* will watch *me* walk out of this room.'

As if to a child, just as he had spoken to me, Pellonhorc told Ligate, 'My father won't give up before you. You know that.'

Ligate's face sagged even more, then hardened again, and he hissed, 'I will *never* see him leave.'

Pellonhorc adjusted the controls, allowing both men to rest, free of pain. Neither said anything. The scar across

Drame's head was so dark in this light that it seemed his skull was split.

'You see?' Pellonhorc said to me, stepping away from the narrow space so that the two imprisoned men had to stare at each other.

It took me a moment to be able to speak. I was afraid Drame would try to talk to me again. I said, 'See what?'

'Nobody believes in nothing.'

He tapped the console and, as one, both men hollowed their mouths in terrible, shuddering screams. It seemed to take an eternity for the descending visors to close their heads away, until all I could hear were the faint beeps of the screenery, the hum of the aircon and the rasp of my own breathing as the sealed units began their gentle return journeys down to stillness.

'There,' Pellonhorc said, eventually.

I watched the screenery, where there was no stillness at all.

As we left the room, Pellonhorc told me, 'The thing is, He won't let me see what I can do to absolve myself. He won't cooperate and He won't back down.' Pellonhorc gestured towards the room behind us, the door whispering closed. 'I've tried everything reasonable. You've seen that. He hasn't listened.'

'You said you've seeded…'

'I have, Alef. Of course, you understand that I can't tell you quite what I've set in place. You're His agent, after all.'

'I?' What was this? Maybe I'd misheard him. 'But He knows everything, anyway, doesn't He?'

'He doesn't know me at all, Alef.' His voice hardened. 'If He knew me, He wouldn't be doing this to me, would He?'

Thirty-three

TALLEN

Lode said, ‘We have had a comms request for you. You are aware that all external contacts are vetted. Rigs are, of course, vulnerable to electronic attack, but your welfare is important to us.’

‘And you have rights,’ Beata added. ‘Human rights. Under specified conditions, you are permitted contact. The contact has to be on the basis of your anonymity. While you have been rigorously checked, you may nevertheless be contaminated.’

Tallen felt dizzy, staring from one humech to the other. Their features were firm, but their expressions didn’t match their words. Lode said, ‘Since you have a statutory right to AfterLife, you are permitted free access to its secure ParaSites. Controlled free access, of course.’

Tallen had also noticed that, in conversation, both mechs paused where a human might pause, reflecting or considering a point, but their pauses were always of precisely the same duration.

‘Ah, yes,’ Beata said, as if surprised. ‘You have a StarHearts contact. Congratulations.’

Tallen had to think. It was such a long time ago. Eventually it came back to him. ‘I registered just before… before I was attacked.’

Lode said, 'We know.' He began to speak a little more quickly, his voice drained of modulation. 'Your StarHearts registration is at preliminary status and anonymised. We will censor any revelation of restricted information or information that might help to identify you. You may not solicit or provide any information that might directly or indirectly affect your situation, such as political or commercial information. We will censor any suspicious incoming questions. We will examine all exchanges for any effect on your psychological stability. If we are concerned, we will terminate the contact without warning. You do not have to formally acknowledge this information, as it is in your contract. This is merely a reminder and a courtesy.'

Tallen said, 'Is that it?' He looked at the humechs, unable, as always, to tell which was about to answer.

It was Beata. 'Only to say how severely enthused we are for you. This is an opportunity to benefit from valuable human contact under controlled conditions.'

Tallen felt queasy. The rig needed constant supervision, and its metabolic signals to him were draining his energy. His left arm ached now, and there was itching in his gut. He started to walk towards the problems, the mechs at his side.

Lode said, 'The restrictions might seem impossible, but your original statement is there, and you can communicate on the basis of that, as if your situation were unchanged from that point.'

Tallen wondered what time it was. There was no daylight here. He wondered whether he needed sleep. Everything felt wrong. His sensations were all of the body, but none of them were about *his* body. He said to Lode,

'But that wouldn't be true.'

Beata answered, 'No human communication is true.'

Razer

Razer said, 'I thought you were getting me through to Tallen. What's wrong, Cynth?'

I AM ANALYSING OUR OPTIONS. PERHAPS IT IS YOUR PROFILE.

'Perhaps it's his.'

She went back to Tallen's profile, trying to connect it to the man she'd seen in the hospital bed, the man she'd spoken to for those few minutes in the red bar a few days before he'd been attacked, and who Bale had told her just wanted to die.

No one would ever reply to this. Cynth had sent her Tallen's drafts and subscriber advice, too. He'd even been advised to change it, and hadn't. The man was hopeless. He used unadvised language and had no chance of anyone responding. But even so, there was something about the way he expressed himself that appealed to her. That articulate melancholy.

Yes, she wanted to know him, and not simply for his story.

Delta

Delta stood in the doorway of Navid's office. He was surrounded by screenery and folders of paper files, and the room stank of his shave oil. There was a comms murmur in the background, the odd word heightened as it came through. *Incident. Suspect. Detain. Support. Urgent.*

Without looking up, Navid said, 'What is it, Officer Kerlew?'

She closed the door behind her. 'It's about Bale.'

He looked at her now. 'Let's have some peace, shall we?' He nilled the comms, then settled in his chair and said, 'So. Bale.'

'After he died, you took the writer's statement yourself at the Chute. I wondered why you did that.'

Navid frowned. 'Bale was one of us. If there was anything suspicious, I wanted personally to be sure it came out.'

'And was there?'

'No. It was simply an accident. I hope you aren't taking over from him. It's finished now. Was that all you wanted?' He glanced at his desk screenery as if she were leaving.

'It's just that she came to see me with some story.'

He looked up again. 'She's a writer.' He added, a bit more sharply, 'Why come to you? What story?'

'She came to me because I was Bale's friend. She said it wasn't an accident at all.'

Navid said, 'No?'

There was nothing to read in his face. Delta said, 'She told me there was someone else in the Chute.'

'Ah.' Openly irritated now, Navid said, 'This Millasco. Officer Kerlew –'

Delta went on quickly, 'I think she could have killed Bale, sir.'

Navid sat back hard. His chair creaked. 'Ohhh. Really?'

'Yes, sir. I know we have it endfiled *Accident Query Suicide*, but the way she was talking made me think she was involved.'

Navid drummed the table with his fingers. 'I know how close you were to him, Officer. And for all his faults, Bale was one of us. When he was sober he was one of the very best.'

'Yes sir.'

'Let me tell you what happened. Bale went into the Chute with the writer. I don't know why, but there was a struggle. We know they'd had some form of sexual relationship that ended sourly. She had marks on her exo and a bruise pattern you don't see with scree-strike. Bale died and she was hauled out of the Chute barely alive. There was no indication of anyone else being involved. No third party.' He toyed with the buttons on his desk-comms unit and said, 'It is possible that she killed him, as you suggest, but there's not enough to make a case of it. Bale was a very good rider and she wasn't.'

He glanced at Delta as he went on, 'For what it's worth, I think her suit got damaged and he was trying to help her. She panicked and lashed out, destabilised him. Wouldn't be the first time someone died trying to help.' Navid shrugged. 'She told me about Millasco. I remember him: borderline psycho, left Pax under a disciplinary cloud – somewhat like Bale – but he hasn't been on Bleak for years. I checked. And there were no convincing forensics of another body in the Chute, though of course there was little enough of Bale. Nothing on any of the cams, though the Chute cams haven't been functioning for months.' He closed his eyes a moment, sighed and added, 'Which means nothing.'

'No, sir.'

Navid went on, 'Bale's conspiracy theory appealed to her imagination. When he died, she came out in shock and guilt and blamed it on this Millasco that Bale had told her about. She's a writer; writers have imaginations.' He ran his tongue over his lip. 'She may even believe it. Let it go, Officer. It's a tragedy, not a crime. Bale was always going to slam into some wall, somewhere.'

'Yes, sir.'

'A quick end. Lucky man.' Navid stood up slowly and went to the window. 'Come over here, Officer,' he said.

The street below was busy. Make-n-Take kiosks were doling out printmass and touts were dealing hardpharma. A tattoo booth beckoned passers-by with lurid come-ons. Delta stared down at it all for a few moments, and then Navid opaqued the glass with a flick of his palm. The whole of Lookout etched itself in miniature where the street had been, mapped and scanned.

Navid made another gesture, bringing up the shore. He ran the display along the promenade. As it tracked, the view stuttered between the monochrome of live image and the sepia of stored. Navid brought up percentages. The figure fluctuated between eighty-five and ninety per cent.

Navid murmured, sadly, 'You see that? We have almost ninety per cent cam coverage, but what do we actually see? We can't see intention. We can't see innocence.' And after another small silence, he said, 'Now. Is that all?'

'Almost, sir. A small thing, nothing to do with Bale. As you know, I was on the desk during the Fleschik event. I understand the audit report is complete –'

Now his face cleared. 'And they've given us a ten-star rating. Yes. We can all feel very pleased. And relieved. We can go back to normal.' He cleared the window of its data and the room lightened.

'Yes, sir. It's just that the report contains individual feedback, and I wondered if I could have a glance at the records, to review my own actions.'

Navid drummed a finger on the glass. 'You know, Officer Kerlew, you're one of the sharpest operations supervisors I've had.'

'Thank you, sir.'

'This has been a hard time for us all. We should get some peace for a while. Statistically, at least.' He sighed heavily. 'I'll tell you something about our role here on Bleak. Pax isn't always the pure, clean blade of justice. It's a compromise. What we can achieve is not –' He paused. 'Not absolute.'

His eyes were closed, and she had the feeling he was talking to himself. This was just Paxer bartalk. She waited, though. No matter how bad a day had been, Navid never showed up at any bar. It suddenly struck her that she had no idea what sort of a life Navid had outside of Pax.

'We have to be patient with it,' he murmured.

She wondered how Navid felt about AfterLife. Was this speech not for her at all, but rather for the voters of future centuries, if he should make it to the sarcs? She'd heard enough arrested crimers come out with these calls for understanding, and she'd made her own pleas, too, sober as well as drunk. She figured most people did. Not Bale, of course. He was always too bloody sure of himself, and now he was beyond even AfterLife.

Navid began again. 'The System is nowhere near stable. It's still young. Resources are poorly distributed among the worlds. Administrata need the flow of dolors, and money and power are awkward to manage. Yes, there is huge, organised corruption, but the System *needs* corruption. It needs corruption in order to survive. To evolve.' He rubbed his eyes and looked at her as if she had just appeared. 'In years to come, there may be enough stability that the corruption can be addressed. You see?'

'Everyone knows this, sir,' she said.

'But we don't acknowledge it here, at Pax. Outside this office, you'll never hear me say it. Our job is to control the small crime, to make sure the corruption remains high and distant. We just tidy the streets and stare down at our feet. That's why I was sent here to Bleak, eight years ago, because I didn't understand that. Now I understand it. I don't look up. From time to time we raid a bar, flush out the Rut, and that's about it. Peace. What's happening here, now –' He paused. 'Well. It will leave us again.'

He swept a hand over his desk. 'You, Officer, you could move on. I did what I could for Bale, but he wouldn't see it and wouldn't be saved. I don't know exactly what happened to him, and there isn't any point in thinking about it.' A sigh. 'Listen to me, Delta. You won't get anywhere and, far more importantly, it won't get you anywhere either.'

'No, sir. I understand.'

'You have to decide what you want to do in this life. I like it on Bleak because the crime stays small here and there isn't much for me to ignore.' He glanced at the window again, almost wistfully.

Delta nodded. 'Yes, sir.'

'This thing now,' he said, 'it will fade away. I don't know how or why it came here, but it will go, and Bleak will return to normal. You understand me?'

Delta said, 'Yes, sir. Completely.'

'Good.' He stood up decisively. 'Personally, I'd like you to stay here on Bleak, but the decision has to be yours. I just want you to be fully aware of the complexities of promotion.

Without the distraction of Bale, I think you could go far.'

'Thank you, sir. I think so too, sir.'

'Good.' He seemed at the same time anxious and relieved.

'Could I see the report, then, sir?'

'Harv will key you in to the archive for an hour. That should be long enough for you.'

'Sir.'

'The hour has started, Officer Kerlew.'

She ran.

The archive was two levels down. The rumour was that Harv slept there, that he'd spent his life overlaying a gardenscape on his archive. He talked about weeds and pruning. No one was ever really sure if he was talking about his records. She waved back at the monitor as he waved her through the air shower.

She settled herself before the screens while Harv, wherever he was, accessed the audit report for her. Maybe Navid was right; maybe it was best to keep your eyes down. Day up and day over, Navid did a good job, didn't suffer threats and didn't sleeve bribes like some of them did.

Harv's unshaven face came up on the screen. No one, it was said, had seen Harv face to face for years. There were stories that he had, over time, changed his appearance and looked quite different from his presented face.

'We're there,' he told her, yawning widely. 'I'll leave you to it.' He faded away, his mouth half open in another yawn. Delta believed in Harv exactly as he showed himself. No one would choose to manifest themselves like that.

The report opened against a billowing field of lavender, cloud-shadows flowing over it like purple Rorschachs. It was generally accepted that Harv was crazy.

While the lavender bloomed and the shadows began to fade, Delta imagined herself in a sarc, with none of her thoughts or memories protected. She knew she should live as if there were no AfterLife, or as if her body might not be salvageable, but she never could, always feeling guilty when she did something she shouldn't. It was ridiculous. She was probably no more morally sound than Navid, and no less conscientious than Bale.

She wondered if they ever became conscious in the sarcs. AfterLife claimed it was impossible, but there were stories.

The shadows were gone and the breeze was quietening. The lavender was almost ready for her.

She couldn't change. She was who she was, and that was all there was to the whole thing. AfterLife might be just a faint hope, but sometimes faint hope was enough.

The lavender paled and was gone. She opened the audit report, scrolling down to the realtime analysis of her own actions during the event, layering the narrative with the auditors' comments.

'– Here the operative Delta would have been advised to liaise with the parameds instead of attempting to pattern-analyse, which is more efficiently performed by putery –'

She left that running and initiated a sub-program – Harv had it as a bed of spatulate ferns – and leaned forward as it opened.

Here it was: not the final report but the technical introduction with details of the audit's processes. She started to work through the walls of text, not sure exactly what she was searching for.

When she looked at the time, half an hour was gone

and she'd found nothing. This was no good. There had to be something here.

She tried to go deeper, but everything deep was blocked to her. Her eyes were stinging with sweat. She wiped it away with the back of a hand.

Ten minutes left. She carried on until a field of swaying corn swelled and blew across her screenery, shutting her down. Harv's face appeared, seemingly completing the yawn he'd begun an hour ago. She threw herself back in the chair and said, 'I need another level of access here, Harv.'

'Sorry, Delta. Ask Navid, not me.'

The screen filled with lavender. She closed her port and sat at the dead screen for a few minutes before standing up and stretching. Then she sat again and said, 'Can I access some unrestricted data?'

Harv's face ghosted over the billowing field. He blinked. 'Subject of?'

'Does it matter? I said unrestricted.'

'So that would be general unrestricted, or unrestricted within Pax.'

'Am I under observation, Harv?'

Another pause. 'Not that I'm actually aware of.'

Not *actually*. He was warning her. 'Within Pax, Harv.'

She just caught the sigh as he said, 'Okay. I still need your subject.'

'Streetcams.'

'That'll be my chrysanthemums.'

They came up, delicate and quite, quite beautiful. Where did someone like Harv get such artistry? She resisted the urge to ask him why chrysanthemums. He usually answered such questions with, 'because geraniums are seasonal', or something equally meaningless. 'Nice colours, Harv,' she told him.

'Thanks, Delta. They're a new strain. Bit more resistant to some of the bugs.'

She wondered if everything he said came in some weird code.

She spent a few minutes checking general cam locations and concentrations, then slipped a thorough search around the shore area into a few random trawls around the town.

She closed the archive down again, watching the chrysanthemums fade. The lavender returned, along with Harv's face.

'Thanks, Harv. Hey, one thing – you remember those auditors?'

'You kidding?' he said with sudden venom. 'They took me apart. Left one hell of a mess.'

'Anyone in particular?'

'Oh yeah. Spotty one. Shame I won't ever be around to unvote the bastard.'

'Likewise. What he do to you?'

'Had to dig up and replant half my perennials. They trampled the beds, cross-pollinated the exotics, swamped my irrigation channels. Left me with weeds, slugs and aphids.'

'Harv, please. Just once.'

'They opened everything and closed nothing. Their search programs hadn't been disinfected. No respect. I was still cleaning up when Fleschik appeared. Everything was running slow, half my maps and history corrupted or inaccessible. Some stuff I still haven't located again.' Harv took another long breath. 'Anyway. I made a complaint.'

'Did you? I didn't hear about that.'

'I think that's how we got our ten-ten report. Navid dropped my complaint; we got the bullshit bonus. Between you and me, Delta, if I'd been running in full bloom, sunshine and springtime, I reckon we'd have had Fleschik before his third kill.' He closed his eyes. 'And we'd still have Bale irritating the shit out of us.'

'It wasn't that killed Bale,' Delta said. 'Not your fault.'

'Even so,' Harv said. 'Nor Navid's. Not yours either. This was some shitty little shit trailing a shitstorm. Bale was always going to be taken out, just a question of how and when. Going like this, it suited him: a big mystery that's probably nothing but smoke. Just his style.' Harv surprised Delta with a laugh. 'I'd have loved to see Bale's Life.'

Delta found herself laughing too. 'All his crap.'

'Yeah.' Harv's gaze flicked away and back again. 'Listen. Not much I could do, Delta, but I picked a few flowers for him.' Harv's face and the lavender disappeared, and there was a wreath of black orchids and red tulips. The wreath spread and grew, taking over the small screen she still had open and spreading to all the screenery in the room, all of it burgeoning with brilliant flowers, the colours deepening and the tulips spreading their petals until they drooped and fell, leaving bright yellow stamens to glow like stars in a violet sky.

'It's beautiful, Harv,' she said quietly. 'Really, it is.'

'Thanks. I'll copy it to you. Shame for it just to wither here. When you think of him, you can take another look at it. Take care, Delta.'

'You too, Harv. And thanks.'

Thirty-four

ALEF

SigEv 37 Logic

Immediately after seeing Drame and Ligate, I took Pireve from The Floor, found an empty office, sat down with her and told her what I'd seen. For a moment she was quiet, then she said, 'Did he tell you anything about this seeding?'

Pireve was, of course, a little like me, so it was understandable that she didn't especially react to the news that Drame and Ligate were still alive, nor to their condition. She was simply being practical. I said, 'It might be a virus to be released simultaneously on every planet. I know him, though. There will be more than one delivery system. Maybe one to ensure successful initiation, and a failsafe to prevent accidental triggering.'

Pireve was the only living person I could freely talk to. I had lost everyone else to death or madness. She was the one true thing. She had become everything to me. Her face was so beautiful that I wanted to cry. I had my perfect love, and the contemplation that she might be taken from me was impossible to bear. I had to remain steady for her.

'Maybe it isn't a virus,' I said. 'Maybe explosive devices. Maybe everything.'

'And he'd destroy the whole System? Even the unsaid planet?'

'So he says. And Gehenna. Especially Gehenna.'

'Do you believe him?'

'Always.'

She put her hand over mine. 'Just keep calm, Alef. He could be bluffing. You say you know him, but you don't. He's always been the only one you couldn't predict.'

She was right, of course. 'But I can't take the risk. He'd expect God to call his bluff. I think he'd almost *want* God to.'

Pireve squeezed my hand. 'You have to stop him. And you can, Alef. You have to believe that – *we* have to believe that.'

I wanted to cry at the trust she had in me. She put her hands on my shoulders and kissed me on my lips, then sat back and said, 'Think, Alef. Do you have any idea how it might be triggered?'

'He told me that. A neurotransmitter implanted in his head. He called it his deadman's switch. When he dies, it stops transmitting and the seeds open.'

'What if he's out of range of the receiver?'

'It checks regularly. It allows occasional silences. There's a period of grace.'

'If the transmitter fails?'

She was only asking all the questions I'd asked myself already, over and over again, but the sequence of her logic calmed me. 'There's a human chain. Transmission failure alerts a human connection. They check back to Pellonhorc. If he fails to respond within a certain period, the seeds open.' I shuddered at the memory. 'He was telling me this as if he was telling it directly to God. He's changed, Pireve. What he's done to his father and Ligate, it's insane.'

'No,' she said almost furiously, taking her hand away. Then, her voice settling, 'No. We mustn't think like this. It's the cancer. He's relying on you. He needs you, Alef.' She reached forward and kissed me again. 'He believes in you, and so do I.'

'I love you,' I whispered. 'I won't lose you.'

She smiled at me, her face radiant. She was like a Gehennan madonna.

'Then you have to save him, Alef.' She leant forward again, kissed me again. 'If anyone can save him, and save everyone, and save *us*, you can.'

She must have seen the look on my face. She laughed. She actually laughed. 'I'm going back to The Floor. There isn't anything that needs you at the moment. If there is, I'll let you know. Why don't you go and start work?' She touched her palm to my cheek, and walked away.

I left the building and went home, but I couldn't concentrate.

Days passed and all I could think of was the cancer eating Pellonhorc, and the end of everything I lived for. Occasionally I managed to relax for a few minutes by calculating the movements of water in great rivers, imagining my father at my side, the two of us eating my mother's sweet cookies, but that was the only brief respite I had. Each evening, Pireve came home and asked me how it was going, and I couldn't bring myself to answer her. She went to bed and I sat in despair at my putery. When she had fallen asleep, I went to our bedroom and stared at her, and through the despairing days and nights I spent more and more time drifting through the Song, leaving phantom trails of advice and response.

I came back to the problem but couldn't concentrate. What if Pellonhorc was telling me the truth, that everything would die when he died? If it was a virus, or some form of disease, buildings would remain. The Song would remain, transmitted from solar-powered satellites like some shadowy creature muttering to itself in the dark. Even with no one to engage with it, it would still carry out its algorithms, automatically checking and cross-checking, reflecting and creating and recreating.

But, for the moment, the people who nourished it still existed. I sought out their tales of anxiety and fear, their pleas for understanding. They would beg and cry out to the stars, cry out crazily for an answer.

Can anyone help me? Has anyone else out there ever experienced a vision of their dead mother telling them not to take a trip, and not going on it, and everyone who went got killed…?

The stories were so extraordinary that I sometimes found myself responding.

I have, yes. And I would tell them tales of my own. Of course, I hadn't the imagination to invent anything, and since I wasn't going to open my own life to them, I told them the tales of others as if they were mine, adjusting the data appropriately. I became a sort of facilitator. The stories weren't lies. What did it matter if the *I* telling them was not me?

This ministering comforted me, too. For an hour or two in every twenty-four, I was able to sleep.

In my despair, the Song became a teacher to me. Everybody yearns, I discovered. The lessons we learnt from the end of Earth might have put an end to any notion of the divine – Gehenna and the unsaid planet excepted – but that godless catastrophe couldn't stop people yearning for something. They wanted there to *be* something. They didn't want simply to die. They were like Pellonhorc in that. They didn't want to die, and they wanted justice – no, better than that: they wanted fairness.

They could never have it. Never. No one can have fairness or justice, or even a compassionate hearing. All they can have is the promise of it – the impossible, the divine. And if they never discover it's an empty promise, what does it matter?

But even knowing this, I wanted it too. Oh, Gehenna!

And all the time I was also thinking, what was I going to do for Pellonhorc?

I developed a routine. At night I drifted through the Song, and during the day, when the slow work on Pellonhorc's problem overwhelmed me, I visited The Floor, though by now, the Whisper needed less of my attention.

Pireve acted as my filter, bringing me the problems no one else could see a solution to. She was more wonderful every day, and I loved her more and more deeply. She was calm and steady, and she loved me so much. Her existence made the weight of my task tolerable, even as her love made the possibility of failure unbearable.

At the same time, Pellonhorc was attending to the disciplinary aspects of the business and a number of other enterprises of his own. The seeding would have been one of these. I considered spying on him, but the risk of discovery was too great.

I also had concerns of my own. I found it possible to occupy my mind with several issues in parallel, so I could easily deal with small matters. I had a great sum of dolors, my own as well as my father's, and I had been using the money to design new data resources. Ever since I'd been a child on Gehenna, I had always been fascinated by information and the processes of archiving it. Now, when I couldn't sleep and was too restless to cruise the Song, I began to supervise the construction of vast repositories of data, and had their putery stacked on unmanned orbiting asteroids. These self-archiving, solar-powered satellites were powerful enough not only to hold snapshots of all activity on the Song, but with the assistance of inbuilt AIs, to cross-reference and link information to a degree that was otherwise impossible.

My archives were just as much an escape for me as was the Song. I could become so absorbed in them that, briefly, I could forget everything else.

But reality always returned.

Life was unfair. Even though I had no faith, I would catch myself crying out to God, as I had been taught to do as a child on Gehenna. And even though I had no faith, it comforted me.

I cried out, *How can it be like this?* I was married to Pireve, and in a just System I should be happier than I had ever been. On my occasional visits to The Floor, I would catch myself in a moment's dream, just observing her at work. She'd talk to people, and they would talk to her. She'd touch them on the upper arm, and occasionally on the bare wrist or hand. There were smiles between them and prolonged eye contact. Sometimes there was tension in their voices, sometimes pleasure. I understood all of this, and I knew what it meant, the ebb and flow of interpersonal engagement. I could do it myself now, without awkwardness, and with Pireve I often did it without realising I was doing it. I had changed so much since I had met her, and I was still changing.

I realised I was reflecting upon myself! Of course I knew there was still something different about me. On Gehenna I had made the transition from being aware that I was different from most people in a single respect, to knowing I was different in a major respect. And then with Solaman I had gone from not knowing what I lacked, to thinking I knew it. And from there I had made the transition to being able to mimic it. Now, with Pireve, I was starting truly to comprehend people.

Pireve. When I thought of her, it was in a way that made my brain catch. I would whisper her name to myself. Pireve. Oh, how I loved her.

Yes. I finally understood love, and Pellonhorc was going to end it all. I loved Pireve, and unless I did something to help Pellonhorc, she and I would die. So, of course, would the entire System, but that meant nothing of great significance to me.

Pellonhorc was still refusing to have any treatment for his cancer. I carried out a research trail on the Song and unearthed estimates for timescales by which a cure would be found, and discovered that one could define and propose research pathways by asking a series of simple questions.

Do we understand every aspect of the disease mechanism?

If not, do we have the information we need to understand those we don't?

If not, do we know what technology we need to obtain this information?

If not, do we understand the problem of how to develop this technology?

And so on, for each facet of the problem. There were many facets. The questions were simple enough, but they multiplied exponentially. Just like his cancer cells – it struck me – each question was a cell that divided into two questions, then four, eight…

Even my brain could not retain the responses to more than about fifty doublings of the questions. And in Pellonhorc's case, the situation was made more complex by the fact that, since he was having no treatment, the problem – the cancer – was progressing in a unique way. While Solaman's cancer had grown steadily but locally, Pellonhorc's was spreading in his blood cells and through his nerves, as if it was adapting to each barrier. He developed a slight limp, and his left arm was losing strength and hung slack at his side.

At the end of every day, before going home to Pireve, I met Pellonhorc in his office. We never discussed the business any more. Every evening I asked him if he'd started treatment, and every time he told me he had not and would not. One evening, he said he needed to get out, and we walked to the bar, Pellonhorc leaning heavily on my arm. People nodded and smiled at him, though they kept a cautious distance and never held his eye. At the bar, our table was free. I think it was always waiting for us. I had never arrived there to find it occupied.

As we sat with our drinks, he said, 'So, Alef, how's your research going?'

'Slowly,' I told him. He didn't react, and I went on. 'The new epigenetic cancers are problematic. Yours especially so. All the *in vitro* treatments on comparable cells have resulted in the neoplasm swiftly adapting.' In fact these had been his own cells, harvested by Pireve from his corset on a day he'd been in such pain that she'd been permitted to help him with it.

The medicians were fascinated by Pellonhorc's neoplasm. They had never seen anything like it. One of them had described it to me as the perfect killer, and I had had to point out to her that such a thing would end up with nowhere to go, which was hardly a mark of perfection. Where, by comparison, would the Whisper be without the System?

I told him, 'If we leave it, it grows; and if we intervene, it mutates.'

Pellonhorc wasn't looking at me. I followed his gaze, but he was just looking at the other people in the bar. He had his good hand under his jacket, and I knew he was massaging the growth.

I said, 'How long do the medicians say you have?'

'*He* has a few months.'

Although there was music in the bar (it was jangling and barely mathematical) and the air was filmy with smoke and thick with the smell of visky, these things were always muted in our corner. I was never sure whether this was out of fear or respect, or whether Pellonhorc made sure he (and perhaps I, too) was shielded everywhere he went.

I started to tell him about the research cascade, but he waved me down. 'I knew I could rely on you. He made you His agent. How long? Just tell me how long.'

'To arrest it, to simply stabilise you –'

He raised the glass with his poor hand and let it drop on the table so that the visky jumped over us both. A waiter started to wipe the mess away. Pellonhorc slapped him viciously with his good hand. When he'd gone, Pellonhorc hissed, 'I'm not interested in being *stabilised*. I want it *reversed*. He knows that. And after that, I want to live on and on.' He sat back and watched me. 'You understand? No death, Alef. I'm not chancing it. I've had enough of Him.'

I picked up my own drink and threw it back in a single burning swallow. I hadn't slept for a week and I didn't care what Pellonhorc wanted. I wanted a life with Pireve.

'Let me finish,' I said, and waited to be sure he was listening. I was trembling – I'd never spoken to him like this before – but he had to listen. 'It will take about eighty-five years for a cure. And now you want to live forever?' I shrugged, though I was still shaking. 'I suppose it's possible. But you'll need to wait in *rv* until forever's ready.'

He almost spat his response, 'You expect me to go into *rv*? For that long?'

'An hour or a year in *rv*, does the difference matter? You're asleep. You came from Gehenna in *rv* and didn't notice it.' I was also remembering Pellonhorc talking to his father, trapped in that terrible cocoon of pain, telling him, *'Does it matter? You'll be dead.'*

I waited. I couldn't tell if the pressure, in Pellonhorc's mind, was on me or on God. I said, 'Is it what happens while you're asleep? The Whisper has enough money and power. It'll still be there when you return, and bigger. I'll set up safeguards.'

'I won't go into *rv* indefinitely. That's just what He'd want.'

'So come out in eighty-five years. Be cured of this first, and then you can think about forever. I'm setting up the medical foundation now. All my calculations say there will be a total cure for your cancer by then.' The alcohol and lack of sleep had made me reckless. I added, 'And I'll start parallel research on forever.'

The stink of his visky eddied towards me. 'What if the *rv* unit fails? Power failure, sabotage, stupidity. It's a long time.'

He tossed the rest of his drink back and winced. 'Eighty-five years is two lifetimes. From Earth to the System took less time, and half the sleepers were lost.'

I reached across the table and took his limp hand in the way I'd seen Pireve take the hands of troubled workers on The Floor. He flinched, but left his hand in mine, flaccid and cold. I wanted to draw back. The feel of him was not pleasant.

'He has given me *this* gift for *this* moment. For you,' I said solemnly, using words I'd heard on the Song in relation to shards of crystal being hawked as cures for radiation poisoning. 'If you know Him, then you know He gave me my brain. You have to trust me. This will work.'

'Eighty-five years. He'll use the time to track down all the seeds and destroy my business. You imagine I'd let Him do that? My father won't let Ligate go. Why would I let God go?'

I was in danger of losing everything. I forced myself to be calm and said, 'This isn't letting him go, Pellonhorc. This is waiting for a cure.'

The music had changed, and I could hear some maths in it.

He said, 'I'll be forgotten, left to sleep until the *rv* fails and I die. No. I'll let the seeds open now.' But there was less certainty in his voice. My talk of a cure, of a fixed number of years, even if in *rv*, had reached him.

I softened my voice and said, 'I can do it, but you have to be reasonable, Pellonhorc.' I could see I was close. 'You have to go into *rv*. You know I'm doing everything possible. Leave the seeds in place. Be reasonable. Please.'

He hesitated. Just as I thought I had him, he lifted his poor hand and hissed, 'No. *He* isn't being reasonable.'

Thirty-five
TALLEN

'I always wondered what it might be like to live on Bleak.'

Tallen found it hard to focus his attention. There was no image, just the words on the blank screen, but a human being was there, somewhere, and it made him feel unexpectedly fragile. He said, 'You get used to it. I'm too used to it.' He couldn't think what to say next. His words remained a moment before vanishing, to be replaced by an answer.

'I live on Heartsease. We have long, bright nights, and in summer the stars are brilliant. I've lived here all my life. Have you always been on Bleak?'

Tallen said, 'Pretty much. I was brought up in Gutter, but my folks died when I was sixteen and I had to make my own way after that. I was good with tech, fixing stuff, and I always managed to make enough to get by that way.'

Gutter turned to *Spindrift*, and his age to *seventeen* before the message went out.

'I heard Spindrift's beautiful. I've always wanted to travel. It must be wonderful. My husman died last year and I feel lonely here.'

'Yes,' he replied, and watched the word go, untouched. 'I've never been married.' He wanted to say more, but the idea of his words being changed was suddenly impossible to bear.

Fresh words appeared. 'Are you still there? I hope so. It's hard.' A pause, then, 'I long to see snow and rain. Mountains, ice.'

Tallen stared at the words for a long time, then replied, 'I have to go now.'

'Did you get that? Did I say something wrong? I'm sorry.'

Snow and rain. Mountains, ice. The words rang in his head as the screen greyed. He felt faint, but this was not the rig communicating its aches to him. This was something else.

Beata said, 'This is more distressing for you than we anticipated. You have been affected. We shall consider our response.'

The dizziness faded. Tallen had to resist an urge to scratch his back.

Razer

Delta said, 'The archivist smuggled this out for me. I don't know how. Pax security is usually solid.'

Razer knew how. She could tell from the way it blitzed the screen, then cleared again. She'd written a Tale for a coder once. The deal had been that she would only use what he wanted her to use, outside the bones of his life and the thinnest skin of how he did his work. He'd told her a lot more, but she'd kept her word, as she always did. Some of the people whose Tales she'd told, it wasn't worth the risk to cross them, and anyway, if she was true to them, they passed her along to their chancy friends. What a life Cynth had given her.

This package was a wrongsider. You set it up as a piece of code that has already slipped past the putery's first line of defence, and you label your intended recipient as the sender. Your putery's active defence tags its programkiller to the package and sends it straight back to who it thinks is the sender. But you've put the code to neutralise the killer in the package, so as soon as the recipient opens the package, the killer's killed and the package is received and clean. Easy enough. This had to be good, though, to beat Pax's defence.

'No idea,' Razer said, watching the petals open and fold back to reveal the message. The flowers were beautiful.

'Okay,' Delta said, sitting back. 'There were six of them in the audit team. They arrived in Lookout five days before Fleschik had got going. They divided themselves into two groups, surveillance and personnel. The surveillance group spent the first two days reviewing the town's streetcams while the other pulled every Pax officer's records.

'I started with the surveillance group, looking for unusual patterns in their research, but found nothing. They didn't focus selectively on any single area. Between them they covered the whole of Lookout equally. They were good, seemed to have missed nothing.

'So I moved on to the personnel group. Again, their actions were straightforward and thorough. They covered everyone fully and expertly, paying no more attention to Bale than to anyone else. Again, nothing unusual, unless it was their extreme efficiency. Everything they did was task-appropriate.'

Razer said, 'So we've got nothing.'

'I haven't finished. If you look at them individually, the picture changes.'

Razer looked away for a moment and let her gaze settle on the tank of stones. They seemed to melt and reform as the fish streamed across them.

Delta said, 'I remembered that when the Fleschik event erupted, the auditors stood back and observed, exactly as they should have. All but one of them.'

Razer felt her skin tingle. Delta had closed her eyes and her voice had fallen to a whisper.

'He was the exception. Flat nose, skin pitted by sulphur acne. He had a high, rasping voice. He put his face so close to me that he was almost touching my cheek with his and he was hissing at me as I was trying to give Bale instructions. He was sweating ketones. Decece, that was his name. He irritated everyone that day. If it hadn't been for the event, someone would have bruised a fist on him.'

Razer watched the screen as Delta opened flowers and moved them around. This Harv was good but weird. The audit team were red roses, Decece almost scarlet. Lookout was mapped as a garden.

Delta said, 'We get these teams coming around every year and they're failed Paxers. One or two in every team will be halfway competent, and they're the ones you need to impress. Ten minutes tells you which those are. But these were almost all excellent. All but Decece.'

The ivy had to be streetcams.

'Audit *never* puts together a team like that,' Delta was saying. 'They don't have the quality. They have to distribute the best among the hopeless. But those five were really good. Just two of them could have done the job.'

'So? And what about Decece? Was he particularly useless, then?'

Delta said, 'We thought so. The others were passing him around like they couldn't cope with him for more than a day at a time.' She pointed at knots of wild foliage. 'See? This is his activity.'

Razer still couldn't see what was so animating Delta. It was hard to concentrate on anything other than the tank with its scintillating colours. Razer got up to curtain it. The room darkened momentarily, but the flowers grew more brilliant. Razer sat down again and tried to follow Delta's reasoning.

'If you examine what he focused on as they moved him around, it seems at first to be entirely random. He appears to have little application, works without any structure. The others compensate for him.' Delta stopped. The garden steadied. The promenade was represented by the border of a pond. There was dead ivy beside it. Dead cams.

Delta said, 'Razer, you told me you were instructed to contact Bale.'

'He was suggested to me. What's that got to do with this?'

'The audit team pulled everyone's records. Checking personalities, strengths and weaknesses. Again, routine. But look, when Decece was on personnel, he went straight for Bale. Just like you did when you came to Bleak.'

'I came to you, Delta. That way round. If I was part of this, why would I do that?'

Delta raised a hand. 'Hold off. You know *why* you were given Bale?'

'My program looks for people who live eventful lives.'

'Well, he was that,' Delta said. 'I'm not saying you knew you were part of this thing, but it's starting to look like it.'

'And like Bale was right all along.' Anxious now, Razer

went to the window. A breeze was blowing scraps of paper across the rubbish outside, and the lights in the windows of the slotbuild opposite were flickering. The streetlights on the far side were out. They hadn't been out when Razer had arrived. But this was Lookout, and not the best maintained part of it.

Delta was silent a moment before saying, 'I looked at the team's surveillance review. They were checking streetcam locations and fields of view, and there's nothing untoward in that. But if you look at Decece when he was checking surveillance, it gets really interesting.'

Razer interrupted. 'If they were checking streetcams, could they have ensured invisibility for Fleschik within Lookout? Found him a path?'

'That's one thing, obviously,' Delta said. 'There's another.'

Razer found herself leaning forward.

'Tallen didn't get cammed on his way to getting attacked. When we all debriefed, that wasn't flagged up as being significant. Not everywhere in Lookout has cam-cover, and not all the cams work all the time. Which could also explain Fleschik's invisibility, like you say. But listen to this. Tallen had a habit of walking down to the sea, late at night.' Delta was taking her time now. 'He did it most nights. But a few days before the event, the cams along his entire route went out and stayed out for days.' She pointed at the screen. 'It was curious, but there was nothing statistically significant about it.'

'So?'

'I was talking to Navid, asking him about Bale, and all of a sudden he starts talking about corruption.'

'What's this to do with Tallen?'

'Be patient. Navid's *not* telling me Bale was wrong. He's indicating there's something bigger going on. And he's telling me to be careful.'

'Navid's been fixed?'

'I'm not sure. It's like this is so big, they don't need to fix him. But he's not stupid.'

Razer shook her head. 'Anything really big isn't likely to impact on Bleak. No offence, but there's layers upon layers of money and power between the top and the bottom, and Bleak is definitely the shit-end of the System.'

'And yet it's got core and the sarcs. Everyone knows the rigs are financed by the Whisper. And alongside the AfterLife, the Whisper's the most powerful organisation in the System.'

'But AfterLife and the Whisper coexist,' Razer said. 'Neither of them needs to dirty their own hands if they want something, and neither of them has any reason to disturb the other.'

'Nevertheless, Navid hinted that something big has happened here. And to stay out of it.'

They sat in silence for a moment.

Delta said, 'Decece was looking at the cams along Tallen's route, days before the event. It seems crazy, but if you look at everything building towards the Fleschik event, everything that would have to have conspired to have this happen, Decece was on it.'

Razer sighed. 'What's the end of the story?'

'I don't know. I can't see your strand of it. You're in it, though. So what is it you're not saying?'

'I really don't know. Everything's more or less like I told you. I was directed towards Bale in the first place, by my program. Actually, to Tallen too, which is very strange. I have no idea why. Really. And now I've been asked to contact Tallen again.'

Delta said, 'Well, Tallen's on a rig, so that's a dead end. Pity.'

'Yes. Dead end.' Razer watched the flowers for a moment, then said, 'Why would anyone have wanted Tallen dead?'

'No idea. He was a loner. No relatives, just a few drinking friends, couldn't keep relationships. Dead life.' She looked at Razer and said, 'So why would you have been pointed at him? I can understand Bale, but Tallen?'

'I don't know. I can see why I've been asked to contact him now, after what happened, a story like that, but before it –' She shrugged.

'Not that you can contact him now, of course,' Delta said.

Razer held her gaze. 'That's right. You already said that.'

'No,' Delta repeated, and waited a long moment before adding, 'That AI of yours was beginning to seem a little spooky.'

'Seems it to me too, sometimes,' Razer said, trying to smile. 'It pushes me all over the System. Who knows what feeds an AI's curiosity?'

'Well, it isn't perfect, then. Maybe it's human.' Delta smiled as badly as Razer, and stood up and went to the kitchen, saying, 'You drink starmagnac?'

'Not often. Yes.'

'Bale got me this.' She came back with a small, flattened, green glass bottle and put it on the table between herself and Razer, along with two squat glasses, and filled them both until the alcohol trembled at the brims. She went to the curtain and drew it back, lighting up the room with the brilliant tank. 'We used to watch the fish, and drink, and talk.

Some of the best times.' She picked up her glass, not spilling a drop, and stared at the tank through the starmagnac. 'Bale was such a bastard.' She wiped her cheek with a finger, licked her tears from it, then drank the shot down. 'He could turn the worst time into the best. And he could flip it right back again. Tell me about your job.'

Razer lifted her glass carefully and drank her shot. 'I talk to people, get to know them. The AI knows me pretty well, the type of people I like. I make stories out of it for one of the ParaSites.'

Delta refilled both glasses, swiftly and perfectly to their brims. 'That's all?' She swallowed her shot.

'All?' Razer drank, then took the bottle and poured, her hand unsteady, leaving both glasses fractionally short. 'It's all I do. I don't think I exist, sometimes. I travel, I talk, I write. What I don't write, I download to Cynth. My AI. I talk more to Cynth than I do to anyone else.' She threw back her shot, wincing at the burn. 'I know too much about people. It isn't a good thing.'

'And what do you know about your AI?' Delta drank quickly and poured them both another shot, steadily and perfectly, watching Razer.

'TruTales is a resource of experience. It's a ParaSite hung off AfterLife, like MedMatch, GameGatheral, InSex...' Razer swallowed the starmagnac.

Delta drank hers. 'And StarHearts.'

'Yes.'

'But you didn't say StarHearts.' Delta glanced at her wall screenery. A new, crimson light was flickering on the grey.

Razer said, 'What's that? You told me you wouldn't record us.'

'I'm not. Some of the cams have been playing up.'

Razer said, 'What's the red light?'

'One of two things. A streetcam going out, most likely. Two streets away.' She poured two drinks again. Her hand was very slightly trembling.

'Or?'

'Face recognition.' Delta drank her starmagnac and put the glass down, and picked up the other and drank that too. 'Harv sent me an image for Decece. But this is just a cam playing up.' As she said it, the alert disappeared.

'You're not worried if cams go?'

'I fitted my own backups. They'll kick in after a few seconds. See?' She brought up a rolling display of all the local streetcam views, running them across the screen. There were no dead cams. Shadows flared in the light, charcoal ghosted in the dark. Whether the lights were on or off, no one could pass unseen.

'Bottle's empty,' Razer said.

'And Bale's gone. Too bad.' Delta dry-swallowed. 'Well, Decece didn't look at any of the other victims, but he looked at Tallen. I thought Tallen must be in some way special. He's as ordinary as they come, though. That doesn't fit anything, then.' She turned the glass over and drummed a finger on the base.

Razer said, 'Maybe it was all to kill Bale, and Tallen was just a lure?'

'Tallen was only found alive because they were looking for Bale.' She closed her eyes. 'My fault. I let myself be pushed into sending him down there.'

'I was the one got him drunk. But why was anyone at all sent down?'

Delta slapped her palm on the table and said, 'It had to be about Tallen all along. But it wasn't to kill him. That's where we're looking at it wrong. Tallen needed to be found alive.'

Razer went to the window. All the lights in the block opposite were out.

Delta said, 'Nothing's special about him. He was as invisible as a stone on the shore. What if this whole thing was a way of acquiring someone like that for the medics to experiment on? Someone with no one to miss them.'

'That's ridiculous.'

'Stay with it.'

'Okay,' Razer said. 'How soon was the specialist medic team called in?'

'They were here already. Arrived on Bleak a month beforehand for a conference.'

Razer shook her head. 'Even Bale wouldn't believe this.'

'It fits, though,' Delta insisted. 'The audit team was part of it. Decece anyway. He trawled and selected Tallen. Maybe before they got to Bleak.'

'Who's running it, then? Navid hinted at something big. So, AfterLife? The Whisper? Neither of them would set up something as complicated as this. They want someone, they'd just abduct them.'

Delta slumped. 'Hell, even if we're right, it failed in the end.'

'What failed? What?'

'We're saying they wanted someone to experiment on,' Delta said. 'But Tallen ended up with a suicide impulse. After all that work, setting him up, doing hell knows what to him, they couldn't use him. Can't use him now, that's for sure, stuck out on a rig. Poor bastard's lost to everyone. He'll probably die there. They usually do.' She glanced at the wall screenery. 'All quiet outside,' she said.

'No blind spots?'

'No blind spots.' Delta flicked views. 'Twenty-two externals and five in the building. Everywhere's covered, but not everything's in view at the same time. If something unrecognised moves, that image comes up immediately, rewound ten seconds, so I can't miss a thing.'

'I better go.' Razer stood up.

'You going to give all this to your AI? Or does it just take it?'

'These things don't work as well as everyone thinks. As you know, Delta. And anyway, it isn't interested in you.'

'That's right. It's just interested in Tallen. Who's out of reach, right?'

'It's late. I'm going.'

Delta held the door for her, suddenly sober. 'Hey, Razer,' she called clearly down the corridor. 'When you get to Tallen through StarHearts, tell him to be careful. Because you aren't as clever as you think.' And then she closed the door.

Thirty-six

ALEF

SigEv 38 The challenge

The evening ended there. Pellonhorc walked me home from the bar, leaning heavily on my arm, and Pireve took him back to his great house, as he was too drunk to fly himself. When she returned, she told me he had spent the whole trip talking about me. 'He trusts you like no one else, Alef. He believes in you.'

'He believes in a god who's out to kill him. I can't compete with that.'

She looked at me and said, 'You have to. We're going to have a child. I'm pregnant, Alef.'

For a while, we stopped talking about his illness, even though the rate of his deterioration accelerated. In the past, he would hardly ever sit down, was constantly pacing the office. Now he couldn't stand for long. He'd sag into the chair at his desk. With only one good hand to lever himself up, he'd struggle to stand again. After another month, he had become so weak that he could barely raise himself at all. He had a long, thin chain of braided carbon steel anchored to the desk so that he could wrap the free end around his good fist and slowly haul himself up by it.

After a few weeks of his fast decline in health, I came into his office to find him with one of his senior and more trusted agents, a man called Calo. Calo was a big man. Even seated as he was, he was at eye level with Pellonhorc, who was stooped beside his chair, leaning heavily on the desk, much of his weight taken on the knuckles of his good hand. I could see Pellonhorc needed to sit, but he wouldn't show weakness to Calo.

'I'm sorry,' I said. 'Shall I come back later?'

'No,' Calo said firmly, before Pellonhorc could speak. 'Stay, Alef.'

I said, 'Pellonhorc?'

Pellonhorc looked like a sick and wizened child. He said, 'Calo has a proposition for me.'

'For both of you,' Calo said.

'Calo wants a share in the business. A percentage.'

He might have been a big man, Calo, but I knew he wasn't armed. No one got into Pellonhorc's office with any sort of weapon. Though no one ever came into his office and asked Pellonhorc for anything.

Calo turned a little in his chair so that he could keep us both in sight.

'Come round here, Alef,' Pellonhorc said. 'Stand with me. Good. Calo isn't sure of what he's doing. Are you, Calo?'

'I'm sure.'

'Then why don't you tell Alef what you've told me?'

The big man said nothing.

Pellonhorc's voice was almost a whisper. 'Go on, Calo. Say it again.'

'Everyone knows you aren't well, Pellonhorc. Look at you.' Calo held out his hands, palms open, steady and solid. 'You're dying. I represent a few people who would be happy to maintain the business for you. We won't take over until you're ready, and we'll guarantee your safety as long as your life lasts.'

I didn't know where to look. Of course this had been inevitable. I had told Pellonhorc he would be challenged as he grew physically weak, but on this, he never listened to me. I stared down at the desk. There was nothing on it but a small comms unit and the pegged coil of chain. I began wondering how long the chain was, what strain it had to withstand as Pellonhorc laboriously pulled himself up by it, what –

'What do you think, Alef?' Pellonhorc murmured.

'Alef will be safe,' Calo said, looking only at Pellonhorc. 'We'll use him well. We know how important he is.'

'I was talking to Alef,' Pellonhorc said.

I couldn't help remembering Spetkin Ligate asking Ethan Drame for my father, just before he killed him.

Calo still hadn't looked at me. His attention was fixed entirely on Pellonhorc. The big man must have been preparing this for a long time, waiting for Pellonhorc to be weak enough. A muscle at Calo's temple was quivering, but otherwise he was still. He was confident. Within the moral universe of the Whisper, he was acting honourably. He was offering to maintain the business, holding out a smooth transition, a dignified end for Pellonhorc, my own life carrying on.

'I don't think so, Calo,' I said.

The muscle at Calo's temple froze.

Pellonhorc said, 'Who do you represent?'

'You can deal with me,' Calo said.

'Alef, who do you think Calo represents?'

I gave Pellonhorc the names of Calo's team and a few others with whom they dealt and whose patterns of business had lately been less consistent than usual. Calo went a little pale, then he shrugged and looked at me for just a moment before returning his attention to Pellonhorc and saying, 'Very clever. As I said, Alef, we'll use you. You have no reason to worry.'

Pellonhorc was still on his feet, but it was plain that he was tiring. He put his good hand on the back of his chair and took as much weight as possible on it. The chair creaked. He said, 'You imagine you can replace me, do you?'

'We couldn't do what you've done, Pellonhorc, but we can keep it going. You can't. Why don't you sit down and we can discuss it.'

Pellonhorc hesitated and then nodded to me, and I took his poor arm and supported him to his chair. He all but slumped into it.

Calo smiled. It was over, he was clearly thinking. 'There,' he said and leant back, the chair groaning at his weight. He glanced at me as if he and I were pals, and by the time the slip of his attention was over, Pellonhorc had pushed himself forward and the stubby blade of his small red-handled knife was almost at Calo's throat.

The big man jerked back faster than I could believe, and the edge of his hand cracked the knife away. The blade scythed across the room and dropped to the floor.

Pellonhorc sat back again and shrugged.

Calo spat on the desk. The gob of his spittle lay shining

on the dark surface. He licked his lips and said, furiously, 'You see? Your speed is gone. Your strength is gone. You're dying. Everyone knows it. I will not continue to be patient, Pellonhorc. Alef, you need to talk to him.' He put both hands on the table and made to stand.

'No. Wait,' Pellonhorc said, flexing his good hand and wincing. 'I know when a decision has to be made and action taken. I don't need Alef for that.' He grunted and tried to stand, but fell back into the chair. I started to help him and he said, 'No. I don't need help, either.'

Calo began to smile again, though keeping his attention entirely on Pellonhorc, who started awkwardly to wind the chain around his fist, preparing to haul himself to his feet. He was distracted and without energy, his grip uncertain, and the chain kept slipping through his fingers.

I felt sad for him. All his attention was on the small task of getting a hold on the chain. He was trembling. He said, 'You're right, Calo. I know it. It's time.' He had to stop for breath. 'I should have seen the inevitability of this.' At last he had a true grip on the chain and took a gasp of air, ready to heave himself to his feet.

Except that he hadn't taken up the rope's slack. The big man started to laugh, seeing, as I did, that Pellonhorc would lose balance and fall backwards to the floor.

I started to say, 'Pellonhorc, you –'

He didn't fall back, though. Instead, he leaned forward again and with a small movement flicked the chain up in a wide loop that dropped neatly over Calo's head. Now Pellonhorc threw himself back, yanking on the instantly tightening noose. It hissed at Calo's neck and sank in.

The big man put up his hands and tried to work his

thick fingers between the metal and his skin, but the loop was already burying itself. Pellonhorc put his good foot to the table's edge and levered himself back with sudden energy, his fist quivering with the effort of garotting the big man. Calo tried to slacken the chain by lunging towards Pellonhorc, but he had forgotten that the cord's other end was anchored, and his head simply slammed down onto the desk. Pellonhorc grunted and dropped to the floor, using his weight and pulling on the chain with all his strength. His chair flew back.

Calo's head was on its side, his cheek pressed flat against the table. His eyes were immensely wide, his mouth too. At last he seemed to be staring at me with all his attention, though of course he had no choice. His skull might have been nailed there for all he could move it.

Nevertheless, he was far from still and far from dead. He squealed and grunted, his arms flailing. He had kicked the chair away and his feet were running in the air.

I was transfixed. I couldn't look away from Calo's face any more than he could look away from mine. His eyes were bulging, his face a blotchy red and swollen. His tongue was squeezing out. Somehow he managed to snag the chain between himself and Pellonhorc with a hand and he got a grip on it, and after a moment succeeded in getting his other hand to it as well. The absolute stillness of his head and the wild and furious life in the rest of him were an extraordinary contrast.

His shoulders tensed and he began to pull on the rope.

'Help me, Alef,' Pellonhorc hissed.

Calo was phenomenally powerful. He began hauling Pellonhorc off the floor towards him. The loop was still around his neck, but the tension was beginning to ease and the big man was breathing again in short rattling bursts.

'Alef! Do something!'

I panicked. I grasped the quivering chain at a point midway between Pellonhorc and Calo, took a breath and managed to twist a loop of it around my fist, instantly feeling the two lives pulling against each other.

And at the same time I realised I had trapped myself between the two of them. I could pull either way, but I couldn't pull out.

Calo mouthed, 'Alef.'

It was tempting. Pellonhorc was dying. He would die anyway. I could finish it. But I threw myself against Pellonhorc, my extra weight grinding Calo's head on the table. He was an arm's length away from me, eyes bulging terribly and his bloated, purple tongue filling his mouth. I continued to heave. He choked a little and went abruptly limp.

'Stop,' Pellonhorc cried out.

I slumped, my hand damp with sweat and still tangled in the loose chain.

'Look!' Pellonhorc said, gasping and sitting up.

Calo coughed feebly. A hand twitched and caught the chain again, but without any strength.

'In his eyes,' Pellonhorc whispered. 'Did you see anything? Alef!'

Calo's head lifted fractionally and bumped back against the table. He put a hand towards his throat and dribbled a little, his saliva red and frothy.

'Pull again, a little more,' Pellonhorc told me. 'Not too much.'

I leaned back hard on the chain, with all my strength. I think I was sobbing.

'No! Too much,' Pellonhorc cried again, but I kept pulling until long after Calo had stopped moving. I pulled until Pellonhorc stopped screaming at me to let go.

After I had disentangled the chain from my fist, I stumbled from the room and went straight home to Pireve. I couldn't sleep. All night my hand pulsed and shot with pain. I thought of Calo's neck wrung like an animal's and his legs running in air. If I closed my eyes, I saw his eye sockets, but there were no eyes there, only two purple tongues reaching out towards me.

The next morning, I went straight to Pellonhorc's office. He was sitting at the desk, quite relaxed, the chain coiled on the desk. My hand was swollen and aching, etched around with the chain's helical weave.

'I've dealt with it,' he said. He was calmer than I'd seen him for a long time. 'They've all been replaced.'

'There will be others,' I told him. 'Next time you'll be weaker.'

'I know.' He looked directly at me. 'I've been thinking about going into *rv* while you find a cure.'

For a moment I didn't believe what I'd heard, and then I started to gabble, explaining it all over again. He raised his good hand and said, 'I'll need a guarantee that the *rv* won't fail and I'll need a guarantee of the research going ahead, even without you, Alef. A guarantee.'

I nodded, though I had no idea how I could do that. 'Yes,' I told him.

It was not quite a lie, since I was sure I'd be able to do it. I couldn't actually lie to him, but as long as I could see a grain of truth, I could extrapolate, just as I did when I communicated with people in the Song.

Pellonhorc said, 'The seeds will be released if the *rv* fails.'

I sat there, trying not to think about Calo sitting in the same chair, and said, 'I'm your friend, Pellonhorc. I can make sure it works.' I held my hand out towards him.

He said, 'You aren't my *only* friend.'

I pulled my hand back. I had nothing to say. How had I not seen that?

'But the seeds could go wrong,' I told him. 'An accident. Anything.'

'Indeed. You realise what would have happened if Calo had killed me last night.'

He must have seen in my face that I hadn't considered it – that the seeds of death would have been released if he had died. A single, small death in this room, my entangled hand deciding it, and I hadn't even thought of it. I had even momentarily considered –

I flexed my fist painfully. An image of Pireve dead entered my head, and I felt physically sick for a second.

Pellonhorc went on, his tone even. 'I have other friends, but you're my best friend, Alef. You're the one I really trust.'

'I can do it,' I said, holding back the fear that threatened to overwhelm me.

'You have two months to show me how you will do it.'

'Two months? I can't possibly do it in that time.'

'He will help you.'

I didn't go back to The Floor. I just went straight home to think.

I had to get Pellonhorc into *rv* as quickly as possible, before anything else happened to him. Two months? Two months wasn't long enough for me, but it was a long time for his cancer to progress. I'd have to come up with a solution convincing enough to persuade him into *rv*, but after that, I didn't care what happened to him. All I wanted was to be able to live a life of peace with Pireve, and for our child to live their life. That's why I'd told him I needed eighty-five years; it was on the assumption that average life expectancy in the System increased at its current rate and that our child achieved an additional ten years. It was not for a cure. The timeline for a cure for his cancer was far too complex to calculate as accurately as I had told him. There were too many variables. I simply hadn't dared tell him that.

What did I actually need to do?

The cure would take longer than I'd suggested, but that wasn't the main problem. I simply had to set the procedures in place. What I needed was a way to guarantee the safety of his *rv* during the search.

Rigor vitae was an old and established procedure. It had got some of Earth's survivors to the System. The initial failure rate had been reduced by now to a fraction of one per cent per year, but I needed to guarantee that Pellonhorc's unit would not be allowed to fail. *Rv* units needed constant attention. Nothing relying on programmed maintenance could be guaranteed over many years, and nothing relying on human obedience and memory.

I took time away from The Floor altogether to roam the Song, but this time with a focus, sifting data and information, searching for a system that would satisfy Pellonhorc.

There was nothing.

It was hopeless and I despaired. Nothing in the System

or in life endured, it seemed, except for hope and greed, and hope was never rewarded.

What could I do? In the time over which I needed stability for this single *rv* unit, the entire System could have changed and changed again. It struck me with irony that only the idea of God had persisted throughout time.

I kept searching. A month passed. None of my thoughts stood up to examination. I wanted my father to talk to, or Solaman. And in the dark of the night, I cried for my mother.

It had all been so much easier on Gehenna. The idea of God made everything so much better. It was strange how, in my darkest times and despite my godlessness, I returned to the God of my early childhood. God was the promise of justice and reward, and I longed, I yearned for such a thing. I was as wretched now as I had ever been, and I wondered if, perhaps, the System's attitude to goddery was wrong, and the absence of God *didn't* make things, or people, any better.

Thirty-seven
TALLEN

'You are distracted, Tallen,' Lode said.

Tallen said, 'I don't feel distracted. Have I been reacting badly? Slowly?' He looked at Lode, but Beata answered. 'No. Your reactions are extremely fast. You seem to be indicating an increased capacity.'

Tallen didn't feel any increased capacity. It was harder and harder every day with the constant aches and itches. And now words were coming into his head without warning. Snow and rain. And with them came a sense of doom, a fleeting desire to… to what? He tried to concentrate.

'You have another StarHearts request,' said Lode.

'I'm not interested. The one I have is enough.' He walked on, but he couldn't outpace the humechs.

Lode said, 'We want to monitor your responses to another stimulus. Our analysis of your response to the first emotional stimulus has given us concern. We need a comparison, and it is your right to receive it.'

Tallen said, 'It's my right not to receive it.'

'Your right to receive it is greater,' said Beata, suddenly at his side. 'And the safety of the rig is paramount.'

The floor seemed to shift beneath Tallen's feet, and as it did, his left heel stabbed at him.

Lode said, 'We mean that if the rig were to fail, you would die, and it is our paramount duty to maintain your life.'

Tallen stopped and looked from one to the other. They moved slightly apart, so that his eyes had to flick between them. He said, 'If I do this, will you allow me to have contact with the first one?' What had she said? *Snow...*

'The first one has not requested a response, Tallen. The new one will be ready soon.'

Razer

Razer got halfway round Delta's block and hesitated. There were too many lights out. The wind was stirring, and shreds of paper were rolling around. She wondered for a moment whether to go back and try to sort out the distrust between them, but decided to leave it.

It took her twenty minutes to get home. Her block was like Delta's but even more dilapidated, its streetskin corroded and peeling. She stopped at the main door and glanced up at the cam. It was working, which was fine except that it hadn't been working when she'd left. She paused on the steps, opened her bag and rummaged in it, then sighed and turned round and crossed the street, and crossed another two streets until she came to a dead cam at a corner. She slid into a doorway just beyond it and waited until the man trailing her passed by. She took off her jacket and left it in the doorway, picked up a piece of gravel and slipped it into her shoe. She detached the shoulder strap from her bag and tucked the bag under her arm, rolled the bottoms of her leggings and set out again, retracing the route to her block, her gait changed by the stone.

She went quickly inside, keeping her head down under the cam. It would take them a few minutes to backtrack and discover she hadn't existed before the dead cam, about the same time her tail would take to realise he'd been deliberately shaken.

There was no one in her room. As soon as she opened the screen, Cynth came up.

YOU ARE LINKED WITH TALLEN. HE KNOWS FROM YOUR PROFILE THAT YOU WORK FOR TRUTALES. OTHER PERSONAL INFORMATION MAY BE ALTERED. HE IS ANONYMISED. DO NOT BELIEVE SPECIFIC RESPONSES.

'I haven't got time now.'

But Cynth was gone, and on the screen was, 'Hello?'

She checked her windows were opaqued and the door locked, and went back to the screen. It was probably okay. The tail would spend a while checking outside before deciding she'd doubled back. She'd give Tallen fifteen minutes, then get out.

Before she could respond, new words appeared. 'I'm sorry. I don't know if I want this.'

She said, 'That's okay.'

Without knowing quite why, she ached for him. Maybe because he said, *I'm sorry*. She saw his face again as she'd seen it in the bar, and then again for the brief moment in the hospital when he was in that face-cage. A lost soul. Her speciality. Leaning into the screen as if it brought him closer, she said, 'Why don't you just say nothing? I don't know if we have anything to talk about anyway, but what if I tell you something about myself? How about that? You don't need to say a word, and you can cut us off any time you want.'

'Okay,' he said.

'Good. Sorry. I'm not used to talking about myself. I ask people about themselves. That's what I do. I write for TruTales. I'm Razer.' Her name flickered, and she knew he was seeing something different. She wanted to tell him he knew her, but it would never reach him, and the connection would be cut.

Tallen said, 'Yes. I read TruTales. I have done, anyway.'

'I've been doing it a long time,' she said. 'Always travelling, always moving on.' She gathered herself. This was her story. It struck her that no one had heard it before. 'I was always interested in people. My mother was a medician. She used to come home and tell me about the people she was treating, about their lives. There were just the two of us after my father died. I was eight when that happened.' She remembered night, staring up at the dark sky, tears blurring the stars and her mother's warm arms around her.

'I'm sorry.'

'Well, it happened. We're saying sorry a lot, aren't we?'

Was that pause a sign of relaxation from him? She wanted very strongly to see him, to exchange an expression of ruefulness or something. She said, 'My mother and I, we used to talk about the people. We used to invent their futures, what they'd do if they left hospital. The way she told it, they always recovered, so they could live the lives we'd invented for them. I was jealous of them at first, the way they left the hospital and my father hadn't, and they had these lives my father didn't have.'

Tallen said, 'But they can't have left the hospital, all of them.'

'No.'

He said, 'Are you okay? I don't know your name. I mean I do, but –' The words scratched themselves away.

'I'm okay,' she said. 'So I told stories for my friends, gave them bright futures, and then I went on the Song and started doing the same thing for people I didn't know. And then I was contacted by TruTales, who said they'd pay me. But I had to do it openly instead of on the Song.'

He said, 'What happened to your mother?'

Razer imagined Tallen noticing her smile. He was asking the questions she would have asked. And he was interested. He was hooked. She said, 'My mother died.'

'How old were you?'

'Fourteen,' she told him.

'My parents died when I was seventeen.'

Flickering words. So, a definite intervention at his end, out there on the rig. She checked the time. Eight minutes gone already.

He said, 'You like writing? How do you choose people?'

'TruTales decides. There's an AI. I don't know how it selects, but I always get interesting people. Exciting lives. That's what I do best. Lives on the edge. I've learnt a lot. Done a lot of things.'

There was a flicker before, 'My life isn't very interesting,' came back.

'Well, it's tiring, what I do. You don't get to settle, ever, and you get lots of scars. I've got a few pins and plates.'

She wondered if that would get through, if he would make the connection. Tallen with that head of his in its cage, their exchange of a few words in the hospital.

The corner of her screen was showing an alert. She ignored it. It was only someone sending a callme.

She said, 'I never thought I'd want to settle. I have no real friends. Just stories.' Her lips were dry. She picked up an unwashed tasse and licked the faint tang of caffé from the rim. Ten minutes gone. She really should start to terminate this. 'Stories aren't lives. They're how we make our lives, and I don't think I ever made one.' No response. 'Are you still there?'

'Yes. So that's why you're on StarHearts? Does that mean you're finished with stories?'

The green alert started to follow a faster beat. 'No,' she said.

There was a long pause. Longer. She said, 'Are you there?'

Nothing but the pale background wash of StarHearts autoprompts. *Why not ask what food he likes?*

She waited. There was nothing. Were they going to cut the comm? Had they already?

Maybe he likes travelling. What's his favourite colour?

Shit, she thought.

And then he said, 'StarHearts is about stories, isn't it? Finding someone's story that you like.'

'Oh. Yes.' She almost laughed. She wanted to see his face, and she wanted it with an unaccountable desire. It was stupid. First Bale, who was crazy, and now this man she'd hardly seen.

She checked the time. *Shit*. Sixteen minutes and the alert furious now. 'Listen, I'm going to have to go. Can I call you again?' Without waiting for an answer, she cut him off and felt oddly empty.

Cynth was instantly there.

THAT WAS GOOD. I HAVE WHAT WE NEED. BUT I ALSO SAW IN HIS STARHEARTS FILE THAT HE HAD ANOTHER RESPONSE PRIOR TO YOURS, KESTREL DUST.

Razer muttered, 'Lucky him,' and nilled the screen. She looked at the green alert. It was from Delta.

Delta

Delta closed the door on Razer. *Stupid writer. And stupid Bale.* She wanted Bale alive again so she could scream at him.

Carrying the reheated celery porridge to the table, she stared at the glittering tank of stones. She and Bale had collected them from the shore, stone by stone, over months, and then, with the tank all set, they had drunk starmagnac as they poured water into the tank. The transformation here in the corner of her room, from dullness to brilliance, had made her dumb with joy. It was the only time she had ever heard Bale laugh.

Adding the fish had been his idea. He'd confiscated them from a smuggler. They were tank-adapted and wouldn't have survived back in the sea. Either Delta took them or they died, he'd told her as he'd poured them into her tank like a cascade of candle flames. Bale had loved the idea of a Paxer possessing a tank that would have cost anyone outside Bleak a few million dolors to acquire.

Delta wasn't sure why she'd let Razer see it. Maybe to shock her. But would the writer tell anyone? She didn't fully trust Razer. There was calculation in everything she said, and once it was said, she watched for the effect of the words. Just like a Paxer. And she hadn't wanted to talk about StarHearts.

On the screen, Harv's display was moving gently, a soft breeze giving it texture and tone. She noticed the border of another image intruding at the edge of the screenery, and pulled it into view. Another message from him. A new one.

This was a stand of acacias. The delicate leaves and slender, wand-like branches were as beautiful as everything Harv created, but they were not quite sharp. This was unlike Harv, obsessed as he was with detail. She started to tell it to self-correct, then caught herself and said, swallowing the last mouthful of porridge, 'Show error detail.'

The acacias faded to leave a soft saffron mist drifting across the screenery.

She sat straight. Harv hated saffron. It was a joke between them that he'd never use the colour. 'Hey, Harv,' she whispered. Then, pushing her plate away and wiping her sleeve quickly across her lips, she said, 'Open error detail.'

The mist coagulated into text. It took her a few minutes of scrolling through the notes and screenpics to work out that she was looking at Tallen's personal comms history.

Why send this separately? And why now? Had he found something in it?

She opened Tallen's day-to-day and glanced through it.

Q – I hope you're the fixer i need. I have a two month old valorator that won't remain stable longer than an hour. Can you fix it?

A – It may just be overheating. I'll get back to you, but have you tried...

The messages went on and on. The record had to mean something. Harv wouldn't have risked slipping it out to her otherwise. But the messages were no more than the comms files of a techfixer.

On her cam screens, a red light came on and went off

again immediately. She looked up and saw Razer exit the doorway below and vanish down the street. There was nothing else, but she checked everything again, then got up to curtain the tank. The room dulled.

She looked at Tallen's AfterLife history. He spent just over an hour a day there, which was normal enough, and he took a day to consider before he ever voted, which was longer than average, and he rarely browsed the ParaSites.

She found his RECEIVED UNSOLICITED and scrolled briefly through the usual offers of travel deals and health supplements along with the ParaSite come-ons. Nothing there.

She scanned the dates of his day-to-day. The files went back a few months, but they stopped at the day of the Fleschik event. That final day started with a string of tech-fix enquiries, none of which had been responded to.

She looked at the last message Tallen had sent. It was from his day-to-day, on the morning of the event. Tallen had answered a request for a fix with a message that he was going out and would reply when he was back. Delta imagined him saying it as he closed his screenery for the last time before walking out and encountering Emel Fleschik. Poor bastard.

She scrolled back from there and saw a string of similar replies from Tallen.

I'm going out briefly, but I'll answer when I'm back.
Thanks for the work. I'll get on to it when I have a
moment, which should be soon.

Tallen had been a busy man. She continued methodically to work back. Something about this was nagging at her.

She went on. Other than to respond with the simple acknowledgements, the last thing he'd actively done was to register with StarHearts.

Now she stopped and returned to Tallen's RECEIVED UNSOLICITED. StarHearts were always throwing out bait. Delta's own BurnBox was full of ParaSite baitmail, but this was more. Someone had spent a great deal of effort trying to hook Tallen on StarHearts.

An alert told her one of the streetcams was down. She ignored it. Her backups were good. She went back to Tallen's later responses to fix-requests and realised they weren't his usual style. There were none of his usual quickfix suggestions, 'Have you tried…'

Yes. She had something. She checked the timings of the atypical sends. Every one had gone out exactly fifty seconds after receipt of the initial comm.

The skin on her neck was tingling. He hadn't used an instant auto-response. He'd been trying to give the illusion he was still there when he wasn't.

Or someone else had.

She found the last of the non-fifty-second responses and cross-checked. The last time Tallen was definitely at his screenery was just after he'd sent the StarHearts registration.

That was it! As soon as they'd hooked him on StarHearts, they'd swept him up, and they'd done it two days *before* the Fleschik event. They had planned it all, whoever they were. They'd had him for two days. That was why they'd chosen Tallen, the loner. It had to be someone who wouldn't be missed even for that crucial time.

All along, perhaps for the first time ever, Bale had been right.

Okay. Next question. Why did they want him on StarHearts?

Another cam went out. This time Delta checked it, and checked the other one too. Her backups were fine and live, but this was unusual. She went to the door and checked it was locked. It'd be easier to break through her wall than her door, and the wall was metalled with a triple-star impact rating

Delta cleared the screen, letting it return to the expanse of flowers.

So Decece had monitored Tallen's responses to the StarHearts bait. Decece had known Tallen walked on the beach every night, and Decece had killed the local cams.

Fleschik's spree had been, what, a diversion? No, he must have been an essential part of the plan. Tallen had been abducted from the beach and precisely prepared, over the period of two days, for the opportunity to have life-saving neurosurgery once he was rescued by Bale in the course of the murder spree.

Had they just needed a guinea pig for experimental neurosurgery? Why not simply abduct a drifter? Far less risk in that. The AfterLife killer had done it for years before getting caught.

All those murders. And the neurosurgery hadn't even worked. What a hopeless, terrible mess. And why complicate it with StarHearts? Why not just take Tallen?

'And why send me this now, Harv?' she muttered.

Another cam went, this one an internal. Delta pulled her weapon from the wall and armed it. Decece had killed the cams for Tallen's abduction, but Delta was at home and she had backups. If he thought he was setting her up, he was going to get a big red surprise.

She remembered Decece leaning over her as she spoke to Bale, as she was about to stand him down, Bale's bloodscreen reading in front of her. Decece's breath was almost choking her as he said, 'I want Bale out there. You need everyone, Officer.'

'Yes!' she said aloud. Of course he'd been ice-hard. He'd been ops-controlling the ops controller. She'd been his dummy, as good as if he'd been in her head.

It was all clear to her now. StarHearts was the key, not the distraction. Nothing at all had gone wrong with Tallen's surgery. She'd been looking at it from the wrong perspective altogether. They wanted someone neurologically prepared and acceptable to be employed to work on a rig. That couldn't be a drifter. Tallen had come out of the hospital and gone straight to Ronen. Why would he do that unless the impulse had been planted? They might even have told him it was his best hope.

She checked her gun. It wasn't about Tallen at all, or about experimental neurosurgery. It was the rig they were after. And they needed Tallen pre-registered on StarHearts because StarHearts was to be their comms route to him on the rig.

But what else had they planted in him? What did they intend him to do there? And what use was a rig to anyone?

A final glance at the screen, and she noticed one more unopened flower from Harv. But there was no time to look. Another cam went. Delta sent the small tulip to Razer, then went back to the cams, substituting her own backups for all the street and corridor cams. She checked her locks again. Then she went to the window in the main room and looked out, feeling uneasy. There was movement across the road, a shred of pale green plastic tumbling over the ground, and a figure briefly in the shadows, there and gone. She went back and checked her own camview of that section. Nothing. She ran it back at doublespeed. Her chest thumped and she swore aloud. There was nothing happening on the image. No movement at all. She looked at the empty windblown street again, then back to the empty camview where there was no breeze at all.

On the other screen, she looked at Harv's message again. She whispered, 'Hey, Harv. Why did you send it just now?' She tried to reopen the message, but the attempt erased it. A moment later, the screen died.

Her palms were sweating. She unlocked and opened the door, weapon in hand. There was no one in the corridor. She took a few quick steps along it and ran straight back inside, locking the door again. She brought up the corridor camview and rolled it back twenty seconds and watched.

Empty. She wasn't there. Her putery was down, and all her cams were locked. She was blind outside.

She checked her Pax and personal comms. Both were down. Checked her wrist. Nothing functioning there but her pulse, and that was hammering.

Was there a noise in the corridor? She rechecked the locks by eye and then ran her hand over them just to be sure, suddenly trusting nothing. She brought a pan from the kitchen and swung it slowly across the window at head height. A small blue pock on the window kept pace with the pan. Not quite a dot but a teardrop trailing left to right. That was meant as a warning, to make her go for the corridor, but it was a mistake on their part. She could back-calculate a source from the incident angle of the laser.

She opaqued the window and went to her small bedroom, where she pulled on her visor and rechecked the gun. She searched her visor functions. It only had internal feeds. She was totally isolated here. No data in, no comms in. And there wouldn't be another warning.

She turned all the lights off and matted the visor's glass. Now she was on nightview, grained and spectral. She taped the visor's spare lens to the pan to model a better head, then taped the panhandle to the back of a chair and moved the chair close to the window, the head in view. Then she set herself steady on the other chair with the gun, and cleared the window. She hoped they were in too much of a hurry to spot the setup.

There was a thump at the door behind her.

The sighting teardrop appeared on the glass, just long enough for her to save the image on her visor, and then the window burst and the pan cracked and the chair slammed backwards and over. The wall behind the pan threw out a paintchip cloud.

The visor's analytics gave her a line of fire and a point of source. She locked her weapon to the visor's feed and sent a firecharge straight back down the sniper's sightline. A window in the far block lit up and a moment later she heard the explosion's suck and slam.

Another thump sounded behind her and the door started to give. She punched out a quick *Hi – call me* to all her contacts, then belted the gun and wrapped her hands with towels, threw the emergency drop-cable out the window and jumped after it, only using the towelgrip to decelerate at the last moment.

She fell cleanly. No one there. She threw the towels into

the shadows, but there was nothing she could do about the fluorescent cable, which was designed to draw attention and help. Across the block, the window was still bright with flame. The sniper would have waited long enough to scope the result, and Delta had been fast. The sniper should at least have been stunned.

She started to run. If she could get some distance from the block, she had a chance. They'd locked her apartment down but her access to Pax and to Vox should kick back in at any moment now. She just needed to get to Pax.

Thirty-eight

ALEF

SigEv 39 Death and hope

Time and more time passed, and I was no closer to a solution. Through the portals of the Song, I looked down on Gehenna, and I saw that it had hardly changed. It still seemed barbarous, and yet all I found myself recalling was the comfort of its simplicity, and I could understand why my parents had lived there. I remembered the singing in the church, and the way all our voices had disappeared, to merge into one strong chorus. The words had mattered less than the sense of being a part of something greater. Only while I sang, or listened to music, did I ever have that sense. Though I had also felt it, for a brief moment, at the cathedral all those years ago when Father Sheol was preaching and all of Gehenna was united before the judgement of the arkestra, and their deaths.

Outside of Gehenna and the unsaid planet, everyone in the System knew that their death would be the end of them. They knew that what they achieved was all that they would ever have and nothing more, and that while injustice was eternal, it would end for them in their death. They wanted more, but they knew there was no more and never would be.

And still, knowing this, they spent their lives on the Song, searching for survival after death. For the impossible.

But that was it! That was it. I suddenly realised I had found what I needed. Other than his power, Pellonhorc was no different from everyone else in the System. I simply had to offer everyone what I was holding out to Pellonhorc.

For a moment it seemed perfect, but the moment faded. The realisation of such a vast plan would surely be beyond even my power. I could only hope that what I might suggest would satisfy him enough to get him into *rv*.

So on the last morning of the time he had given me, and after days and nights on the Song, sleepless, I went to his office and I told him, 'I can do it all, Pellonhorc.'

With his good hand he was winding and unwinding the chain around his fist. He said, 'I knew it. I knew I could rely on you, Alef.' He began to haul himself to his feet. There was a small keening sound as he rose, and I realised he'd had a motor attached to the chain, making a winch of it.

Standing, he was arched slightly forward. He looked slimmer than the last time I'd seen him, a few weeks back, and he was clearly in greater discomfort. I said, 'What's happened? Have you had surgery?'

'Surgery? And give Him the chance to take me while I slept? No. He is trying hard enough.' He raised his shirt and showed me some new corset strapped so tightly around his torso that it barely let him breathe. The skin above the edge of it, at his throat, was red and swollen where the fabric had bitten deep. Wincing, Pellonhorc touched his good hand to a control at his belt, and the corset's weave contracted visibly.

He made a small but terrible sound. I had never seen him show pain like this before.

When I could speak, I said, 'Is that a good idea, Pellonhorc?'

He said, 'Tell me how you'll do it. I want to know how you've outwitted Him.'

'Then sit down and listen.' Pireve was in my mind, not Pellonhorc. I would be just as single-minded as him, I told myself.

He lowered himself into the chair, the chain whining as it let him down. 'Go on,' he said.

'I was thinking about *rv*. It can't be you alone. A single unit couldn't be guaranteed to last the time we need. The problem is its maintenance.'

'Get on with it, Alef.'

'No matter how much we plan, a lone *rv* unit could be forgotten over time. But a hundred thousand won't. A hundred thousand *rv* units, Pellonhorc, and an organisation around them that will become the heart of the entire System.'

He started to wheeze. I couldn't tell if he thought I was crazy, or if somehow he knew exactly what I was about to propose. I could believe anything about him.

'I've located an inexhaustible energy source and a way of guaranteeing you'll survive. This will be a vast system, but you will be the centre of it. You, Pellonhorc, and you alone, will be its hidden purpose.'

Pellonhorc was starting to smile, and I realised I had spoken to him in precisely the way he needed. I'd been telling fact, but I was describing Pellonhorc as equal to God.

'The planet Bleak has the perfect energy source for us. It has a vast, storm-whipped sea. A motion-powered *rv* unit in those oceans will never fail. Bleak has the capacity, too. It can accommodate hundreds of thousands of units. And it already has an infrastructure, drilling core from the ocean beds.'

He said, 'We're big, but we haven't the money for that.'

I cried out, 'That's the beauty. We *won't* pay. We'll *be* paid. There will be an organisation to maintain the units and bring in your companion sleepers. It will be beyond governments and laws and administrata. It will be something that *everyone* wants.'

I had practised this speech for hours, practised my tone, my gestures. Pireve had watched me, coached me. I had to be like a preacher, my argument irresistible. My life with Pireve was at stake. 'It will be System-wide, perfect and ideal. It will never be outdated or overtaken.'

He was sitting forward, cradling the slack hand in the quick. 'On. Go on.'

There was a flash storm outside, and the sky seemed to be curdling. I saw sulphurous yellows and a slab of purple. Pireve would have gasped at the beauty, and for a moment I thought I too could see beauty there. It was like an anomaly in a datafield that suddenly made perfect sense. I found that, unconsciously, I had walked to the window. I put my hand on the glass and a sear of lightning greeted it.

Blinking against the glare, I saw Pellonhorc's reflection, and turned back to him. 'It will give everyone in the System – *everyone* – the hope of what it will give you, the chance of a cure for whatever is about to kill them. A cure for mortality.'

His voice changed. 'What do you mean, the hope?'

'For you –' I said swiftly, '– it's the certainty. For them, strong hope is enough.' Pireve had told me to concentrate, that it was vital to get it all right. She understood Pellonhorc almost as well as she understood me. Oh, how lucky I was. I was *not* going to lose her.

He sighed. 'That's good. And my business?'

'The Whisper will change and survive. The organisation I'm speaking of, that has to be under my control, but the Whisper will take most of the money, and there will be a lot of money, Pellonhorc.'

'Will it last eighty-five years?'

'Longer. It cannot fail.'

I didn't say anything else. Pireve had told me how to present the story so that he would not explore its problems, and her strategy was working. He had not asked for detail. But in this silence, I found it hard not to start talking, not to tell him what there was still to be done. Not to say that I was not sure I could do it.

The thunderlight behind me was throwing my shadow across the room. He had to make a decision now. He was leaning on the desk and fingering the chain, and I felt as if my hand were locked in it again, but this time between Pellonhorc and the lives of Pireve and our unborn child, and even of lives beyond theirs.

'Nothing can't fail,' he said.

I thought desperately of Pireve. 'This can't. Don't you see? It gives people what religion used to hold out – a life after what would be death. But my promise will exist in reality.'

His eyes narrowed, and I caught myself quickly. 'In *this* life, I mean. It gives everyone a stake in it. It's perfect, and you, Pellonhorc, you alone will be its purpose.'

There was a silence. The rain was easing. I felt even more uncertain, but before I could say anything, he threw his head back and cried out with sudden energy, 'Yes! That's it.' He gripped the chain convulsively and I tried not to flinch. He hissed, 'You're sure He isn't tricking you?'

'Yes.' I hesitated. 'It will be expensive, but I can do it. I can do it.'

I fought the urge to say more, to tell him where the problems lay, and remembered Pireve's kiss and her last words to me. *Sketch it for him and tell him you can do it all. I know you can do it all, Alef. Don't say anything else.*

I wanted him asleep, the seeds dormant, and a life with Pireve. That was all that really concerned me. I was sure that what I had described to him would work, but only Pireve mattered to me, and our child.

Thinking of her, I said, 'Will you do it?'

I don't know how long I waited, but in my head I grew a forest of trees and counted the leaves as they opened, turned brown and fell.

'How long will it take you to set it up?'

'Ten years. But you have to go into *rv* before that, to stabilise your condition.'

'I'll go into *rv* for five years, Alef. At the end of that, I'll see what you've done and I'll decide if I'm going to go back for eighty more.'

I was already thinking of the peace I would have in his absence, of the birth of our child.

'Alef, I'll be safe in *rv*, won't I?'

'Of course.'

He took a few hard breaths. His poor hand was starting to fold into a claw, and his head developing a tilt to the left. He said in a burst, 'My father and Ligate – I want them safe, too. They must be there when I come out in five years. Until your organisation is set up, I'll be in the *rv* room with them, in my house. I'll have a unit prepared there.'

There was something strange about the way he told me

this, and how he was looking at me, and I realised he had been entirely prepared for it. That I had come up with a solution had not surprised him. All this time, he hadn't been delaying an acknowledgement of his cancer at all. He'd been readying himself.

And he'd been preparing me, too. He had trusted me all along. He had total faith in me, and I felt a wonderful warmth towards him.

I took his hands, the good one and the poor. We were as close as we had ever been, blood brothers and childhood friends. We were inseparable. He squeezed me back with the good hand, though the sharp nails of the claw tore my other palm.

I left his office buoyantly and spent the rest of the day completing and handing over projects on The Floor. By the time I was done, it was dark outside, and dry again. The city could be astonishing in the early evening, the chemical interplay stirring dusty colours across the face of the low sun. I walked home, feeling a sense of transition. Pellonhorc would be in *rv* in a day or two, and my child would be born in a few months. Five years might not be long enough to have everything done, but I was sure I'd be able to satisfy Pellonhorc sufficiently to persuade him to return to *rv* again.

Yes, all was going well. The sun fell gently away and all the lumes were bright. There was a soft pink haze in the proximal air, a faint coppery sparkle up high. I felt as if I had just arrived. All those years ago, Pellonhorc and I had landed. And now he was dying and I was stretching out a hand to eternity.

People walked past, smiling at me. It took me a moment to realise that they were merely returning my own expression. I walked faster, aching to see Pireve, to tell her what Pellonhorc had told me.

It struck me that I was no longer a child. I wondered what my parents would have thought of me now. At the door, I thought of Gehenna with a curious feeling of nostalgia.

SigEv 40 Malachus and a shock

Pireve looked exhausted; the pregnancy was hard on her. She kissed me, and as we sat down to eat, she said, 'Our child – I'm worried, Alef.'

'There's no reason. Everything's going well. It'll be fine. I will find a solution to it all.'

'Are you sure?'

'You said you have faith in me. It's your faith that makes me strong.' I took her hands. 'I will do it. Pireve, you're more important to me than anything else. Than everything else. You know that everything I do is for you and for our child.'

For some reason I asked, 'Have you been talking to Pellonhorc?' He'd never said anything, but I suspected he was jealous of us. Of course he knew Pireve was pregnant. He had congratulated me, but I hadn't been able to read his emotion.

She nodded.

I tried to control my rising voice. 'What did he say to you?' Had he made some Gehennan god-link between our happiness and his cancer? I'd seen him whispering to Pireve. She never told me what they discussed, other than that it concerned The Floor.

'He was saying maybe *rv* isn't safe for so long. He was saying that if he dies, everyone will.'

'Nothing will happen to him, and nothing will happen to us. Our baby is safe.'

'Thank you, Alef.' She squeezed my hand. 'You do love me, don't you, Alef?'

'More than anything.'

'And this will work?'

'Yes. Yes.'

The next morning, we parted at The Floor. It was her last day there. I had an office elsewhere in the building, but I noticed activity in Pellonhorc's office and stopped to see. The door was open and a man I'd never seen before was sitting in Pellonhorc's chair, waving at me.

'Alef,' he called. 'I've been waiting for you. Come in, come in. You don't need to panic. All's well. Close the door behind you.'

I did so and said, 'Where's Pellonhorc?'

'Sit down, please. I'm Malachus.'

Though I'd never met him, I'd heard of Malachus. He'd been one of Ligate's closest aides. He'd done well to survive the transition. Pellonhorc had always been careful to offer the most loyal soldiers of his enemies a brief opportunity to show him the same loyalty, and the best of them always took it. Malachus was one of these. He was a stocky man with the burnt skin of a wildsider, but the desker's clothes he wore sat well on him. He was maybe thirty. I guessed five years of the hard life and then ten of delegating the deaths. 'Of course,' I said.

Malachus smiled. I noticed that the chain was missing from the desk, though the spike to which it had been attached remained. There was new screenery on the walls, and the window was veiled to a pink glow. Malachus was settling in, but without removing every trace of Pellonhorc. He said,

'Pellonhorc told me you'd catch on quickly. I'm going to be here until he's back. Five years, yes?'

'Initially, five.'

He nodded. Malachus was no fool. He'd want to feel safe here, but he wouldn't make himself too comfortable. I had little doubt he'd still be here in five years, and so would the Whisper. Malachus would then stand aside or carry on, whatever Pellonhorc asked of him. The story of Calo was well known.

'Anything more to tell me?' he said. 'Anything more you want to know?'

'No.'

Everything, then, had been made ready for Pellonhorc's absence, and I was simply the last to know. Pellonhorc had concealed it all from me and from Pireve. He had been running a parallel organisation to set up the seeding, and another parallel administration for the Whisper, and I, otherwise involved, had guessed at none of it. And nor even had my love.

I began to doubt myself. If I had been so blind to this, what more had I missed?

'Fine,' Malachus said, his attention ebbing. He said, 'It was good to meet you at last, Alef. He wants you at the house at midday. That's now. There's a flycykle waiting for you.' And he waved me out.

As I descended to the flycykle bay, I tried to relax. There was nothing to blame myself for, or Pireve. I told myself I had missed nothing that mattered. And look at what I was going to achieve.

The city's shield was reassuringly secure, juddering the flycykle as it broke through in a wave of charged air. As we came down at the rear of Pellonhorc's house, I had an odd flashback to the day I had arrived here with Ethan Drame, bringing Madelene to her death and Drame to something a lot less merciful.

Pellonhorc's personal aide, Floriel, greeted me at the midlock, which disconcerted me. Pellonhorc always met me in person. I wondered how much of my alarm showed. However well I coped with anomalies outside myself, I relied on the stability of my personal routines, and Pellonhorc knew that. Floriel's eyes were opaqued. He was a soldier and had a professional lack of trust. I didn't like him.

'Where is he?' I said.

'Waiting for you. Come.'

I adjusted my breathing to the pace – a small stress habit I had recently developed – and said nothing to Floriel. If he wanted to say anything, he would. If I asked and he didn't answer, I'd be showing weakness.

I tried to walk at Floriel's side, but he raised his pace, making it impossible for me to do anything but trot behind him. I was hyperventilating and had to increase my stride length uncomfortably in order to control my breathing. He glanced back at me and smiled in an unpleasant way.

The house was peculiarly quiet. The few staff we passed acknowledged me, but no one met my eyes. It meant nothing, I thought. I still occasionally struggled to hold eye contact myself. In this subdued atmosphere, I remembered running along these same corridors with Madelene and Drame, towards the midlock where Pellonhorc and Ligate were lying in wait. I hadn't thought of this for years. The memory was extremely disturbing.

Floriel stopped at the door to the medical unit. 'In there.'

'Are you coming in?' I said.

'No.' He looked me up and down, taking his time over it.

I went into the first room. A medician stood there, a console in her hand, staring at me. She was wearing a blue surgical mask. Her eyes were also blue. Something about the way she was looking at me made me think I'd startled her. She said nothing, waving me through to the *rv* room.

Pellonhorc wasn't there. Ligate and Drame were still in their units, the cowls thankfully closed, although the readouts spiked and plummeted. What froze me was the new, third unit. It was a huge module in comparison with the other two, and its broad visor was closed. I walked across to touch the vast hull of it and found it warm. It was clearly ready for Pellonhorc.

I laughed aloud in relief. He must want to show me how perfectly prepared he was, how much trust he had in me. Though by its size I imagined this unit carried more failsafes and backups than any *rv* unit ever had before.

I went outside and found the medician still tinkering with the machinery. I said, 'Is Pellonhorc on his way? I'm supposed to meet him here. I imagine that's his unit.'

'Well, yes, it is.' She hesitated and flicked her eyes at the door to the *rv* room, and then at the other door, as if expecting someone else to come in. Looking back at me, she said, 'He's in there.'

'No, he's not.'

She put the console into her pocket. 'You're Alef, aren't you? I've heard so much about you.' She cleared her throat. 'He's in the unit. Didn't you see? Don't you know?' And this time she reached out and touched my arm, as people touch the bereaved.

Feeling my pulse race, I said, 'He's in it? Already? Has something happened to him?'

From the sudden look of her face, something terrible had happened. She seemed cracked. I didn't have to data-analyse her lip-muscles and eye-shape. Her face was pure readout.

My mind scrambled. If Pellonhorc had died, what would happen? Were we all about to die? No, it couldn't be that. I would have been informed instantly, by Floriel, if not by Malachus. I thought back to Floriel's unpleasant expression.

The medician led me back inside the *rv* room and pointed at another display beside those of Ligate and Drame. I hadn't paid any attention to it until now. There were two scrolling readouts, one below the other. Doubles of ECG, EEG, and the numbers for systolic and diastolic blood pressure. Failsafe protocol, I thought, feeling slightly more settled. And there was even a third readout on a small adjacent screen. That's why the unit was so big, to house all the failsafes.

He *is* in there, I immediately thought, exultantly. And alive. He didn't even tell me he was going in, didn't even threaten or warn me – warn *Him* – one final time. He trusted me that much.

It made me smile. Pellonhorc trusted me a lot more than he trusted the *rv*. We were so very close, the closest of friends.

The medician whispered, 'I'm sorry, Alef. We all are.' And she touched me again.

'But he's alive,' I said without thinking. I almost crowed. 'It's worked. It's all worked!'

She didn't react.

And then, prompted by her glance, I looked at the main,

paired vital sign readouts again and realised they were not synchronised. They were quite different.

I looked at her and back again. Was something wrong with him? The numbers were different too. How had I – *I* – not noticed this immediately?

She moved to the console and the cowl of the great unit began to rise.

'No,' I shouted, though I was unable to stop myself looking. 'No!'

'I'm so sorry, Alef,' she said.

The readouts weren't failsafes at all. The huge unit wasn't full of backups. There were two people in there. It seemed to take forever for the cowl to sink away and reveal Pellonhorc and his fellow sleeper.

Pellonhorc was there in soundest sleep. Nothing had gone wrong. Beside him, shoulder to his shoulder, with her eyes creaseless and closed, was my beautiful Pireve.

Thirty-nine

TALLEN

Tallen felt disturbed after the second contact, but in a quite different way from the first.

'Are you all right, Tallen? Are you overheating?' asked Lode.

There had been something odd about the first contact, though now that he thought about it, all he could recall of it was the phrase, *Snow and* – and something else. What? Had he had this thought before?

'Are you feverish, Tallen? Do not listen to Lode. *We* overheat. *You* have a fever.' The humech looked at him with what might have been concern. 'Do you have a fever?'

Tallen said, 'I don't know. Don't you know? There must be a medical bay. You weren't here a moment ago. Nor was I. I don't feel right. I don't remember.'

'What do you not remember?'

He frowned. 'Snow and rain.'

And with the words he was somewhere else again, but this time when he was back, he was in a sling of wires and his spine was stinging and his skull thumping.

Lode said, 'Do you know what happened, Tallen?'

Beata said, 'Do you remember now?'

The humechs seemed to have accelerated their speech

modes, flicking from one to the other even more than they usually did.

Beata said, 'Do you know why you are here? What do you remember?' Her face seemed to flow and blur for a moment before fixing again.

'Snow and –' but Tallen screamed with pain before he could finish the phrase.

Lode's face unset and set, his voice sounding like Beata's as he said, 'We have disabled that.'

Beata said, 'We think we have, though we think it is too late. And we do not know what it might be too late for. Do you know why you are here?'

Tallen said, 'Please stop.' His head was pounding. This wasn't rig-pain, he was certain. This was real. 'What happened?'

Lode said, 'Do you not know what happened?'

He raised his head. A skullcap of wiring rose with it, and he was surprised to see Beata and Lode take twin paces back. 'I was on deck,' he said. 'I called out, I think. I called out to the sea.' He remembered the call now, a call that began with his voice and continued with something non-vocal, a call that came from him like the opening of a sluice. And he remembered a response.

Lode said, 'You brought in the sarcs for their regular maintenance.'

'What?' He felt as though he had been startled from a dream.

'As you always do,' Beata said. 'We mean, as the rig always does through you. But this time you did it alone.'

He moved his arms. Wires trailed. He felt like crying, or maybe laughing.

'And you did it differently, and we do not know how. Or why. Do you know why?'

'What sarcs?' said Tallen. 'What maintenance? I don't understand. They don't need maintenance. Everyone knows that.'

'He does not know,' Beata and Lode said to each other. 'But he did it.'

'What did I do?' Tallen grunted with effort as he heaved himself to his feet. A weight of cable dragged at him and he took it in great swags in his arms and moved towards the humechs, step by heavy step. 'Tell me.'

As the humechs took a synchronised pace back, the door closed behind them.

Beata said, 'We did not do that.'

Tallen came heavily to a halt and said, 'I think I did. So tell me what else I did, because I didn't intend to close the door and I don't know what else I might do.'

Beata and Lode looked at each other, and then Lode said, 'There are three special sarcs held in isolation, close to the rig. The sarcs are brought onto the rig and their systems are serviced regularly. They are monitored constantly. The occupants of those three sarcs are the primary purpose of this rig. Our primary purpose.'

'Ours and yours, Tallen,' said Beata.

Tallen said, 'But the core –'

'On this rig, the harvesting of core is diversionary. Your primary purpose is to be a human conduit for the servicing and maintenance of the three sarcs. This is what you cannot remember,' said Lode. 'This is what you do at night, as the one before you did, and as the one to replace you will do. But you do it well, Tallen, except that you have malfunctioned.

You have adjusted their scheduled rota.'

Tallen sat back on the bed and said, 'I still don't understand.'

'It is for us to understand,' said Lode.

'Though we do not understand,' said Beata.

His head was raging. It was full of thunder, of snow and –

Lode and Beata were not standing where they had been a moment ago, and he was exhausted. Sweat poured from him. The cables were lying in great ripples around his feet.

Lode said, 'What have you done now, Tallen? Please stop this.'

Tallen said, 'I don't know what I'm doing or what I've done. I don't know anything.' He wanted to cry. He held out his arms to Beata and Lode. 'Please help me.'

Beata said, 'Help us, Tallen. Please help us.'

There was a noise in his head, a pattern that he recognised, and seams of colour like migraine. He recalled Veale, the Ronen psychiatrist. The remembrance of the tests settled him, and he suddenly saw that he had been prepared for this all along. But what was *this*? They couldn't have been tests. Had Veale known, though? Tallen thought back and back and back to the HeartSearch prompts. Snow...

Memory came like a dark flood. He saw something vast and complex with himself at its heart, and he seemed to be in control of it, and then a burst of the noise banished it again. And he saw the circle of lights from his dream of the attack, only it wasn't a halo at all, but an array of lights – they were operating lights. And the pain was there, and he wanted to die.

Then for a moment he saw a face. The writer. And seeing Razer, he wanted to live.

Her face vanished. Thoughts came and went, scratchings inside his skull corresponding with urges to laugh, to piss, to scratch his cheek. He said words, heard words. Snow and… He wanted to work on a rig. He wanted to kill himself. Mountains…

He was at the heart of it, yes, and at the same time he was of no importance whatever.

He put his hand in his pocket. There was a knife.

Delta

Delta's visor was set to outline and motion. She added live vis to that and slowed to a trot. Hardly anyone was on the streets. She kept as far as possible to the unsurveilled streets. Her first target was the Rut. If she could make it there, she could slow down and catch her breath.

Half a kil clear of her block, she checked her wrist. Pax and Vox were still inaccessible.

An ident tag came up and vanished before she could distinguish it. Behind her. It could have been a fault, but she stopped at a corner and glanced back. Nothing. She went on, and the tag returned. It was a face-match from the last time she'd visored up, and that had been –

Shit. Decece was right behind her.

But that made no sense. He couldn't have been watching her without her being aware of it.

And then she realised it made total sense. Decece was using PaxTrac. He hadn't needed a visual on her. There was no escape from him as long as she carried the flake in her wrist. But she was still comms-down. So they had access to Pax and she didn't.

Bale hadn't guessed half of it. She fought down a wave of panic and looked around at the high, dark buildings, up at the glittering shield. Not a place she'd have chosen to die, and not a time either. There was a power hum nearby, cables looping high over the street. She could go to one of the doors and try to get inside, but that would just get someone else killed.

She could take Decece out, at least. There was no point in waiting for a good moment. He knew exactly where she was. And the longer she left it, the more likely he was to realise she'd worked it out.

She set her weapon to its longest burst and ran back along the street. The comms-less visor could hardly keep up with her, maintaining just an armslength of street detail around her, leaving the rest as outline.

And there he was coming out of a doorway, threedy and solid against the pale, line-drawn road. She couldn't miss him. He saw her coming, her gun levelled, and turned and started to run, but she slowed and fired and the first moment of the burst took him down.

She came to a stop at his side, gasping for breath. The visor readjusted to clearview as she stared at the body. It wasn't Decece.

The visor adjusted again, telling her Decece was right behind her, but she didn't turn in time. She'd killed a decent. They'd been playing her.

'Let the gun drop, Officer. Now kick it away. Good.' He stepped back. 'I'm going to have to rethink this. I had the story, but it doesn't quite work any more.' He tipped his head to the side. 'After you killed Navid and the archivist, we tracked you down. But, after a firefight, you escaped and killed a decent, and then your luck ran out. As indeed it has.'

He wasn't armed and he wasn't concerned. Delta glanced at the street behind him. No one visible, but someone was there. Delta knew she wasn't going to walk away from this. She felt extraordinarily calm. She said, 'Who are you? What's this about? I'd say you were Whisper, but they don't take risks like this. You won't be able to hide this away.'

Decece was looking around, no concern in his movement or voice. 'You know something? The more they pay you, the less they tell you. And I don't know anything at all.'

'They'll kill you. People like that, they kill everyone. They leave no trace.'

'I don't think you understand. That's why they use me. I'm the one who leaves no trace.' He nudged the body with his foot. 'I think we're done. I think here's fine.' He made a gesture and began to turn away from her, glancing away and to the left. 'You want to be running? Only I think long range is more convincing.' She followed his line of sight and saw the man in the shadows as he raised the weapon. She started to move but the gunburst was faster than her heartbeat, and in her last moment she thought of

Razer

Razer sent a hi-there to Delta but only a try-later came back. Something was very wrong. Razer had no time to open the flower Delta had sent. She just returned, *In the morning. Sleeping now*, closed her screenery down and left again.

Three a.m., and the street corners were itchy with static from the shield. Razer kept to the brightly lit, wider streets where she could easily be seen, but so could anyone trailing her. The shielded sky was beautiful tonight. She felt tense and alive, all her senses magnified. Was that just from talking to Tallen? Nightbirds flicked beneath the shield and magnetic ripples rolled overhead, brushing licks of azure and lazuli across the dusty ground. She passed the red bar and thought of Bale. Come-ons came to life as she walked by, shining their wares.

Eat multifruit from the gardens of Resolve and taste the worlds.

The corporation you can trust for all your energy needs. Daylight and starlight, we'll keep you going. We are Ronen and you are safe with us.

AfterLife. Once there was just the Song. Now it has a chorus.

There were sirens and a string of flashing zipriders carving past her, and she speeded up, but the Paxers weren't headed where she was going. She hoped it hadn't been Delta setting all this on her. The callme had been a warning or a trap, and neither was good.

There was someone tailing her again, but they weren't interested in intercepting her. No point trying to lose them now. Speed was more important. She went straight into Delta's block as if she lived there, her own doorflake in her hand. She walked straight past Delta's obliterated apartment door and on towards the emergency exit. Not good.

And stupid, too. The gun was in the small of her back before she knew there was even anyone behind her.

'Turn around and we'll go back to the room. Slowly and smoothly.'

Through the door, she took in the wreckage. At least

Delta wasn't there. She'd have got away, Razer told herself.

'I was wondering how we'd manage this, but you made it easy, coming back. All I need is some clarification from you.'

A man's voice, neutral accent, entirely calm. Razer said, 'Where's Delta? And who are you?'

'She's dead. I was hoping to kill her here. I had it in mind for the report that you'd be the killer. You killed Bale in the Chute and then went crazy tonight, killed Navid and some others in the Pax building, a few Ronen deskers, and then you came here for Officer Kerlew. All very tidy.'

He was enjoying this, but not so much that he'd be unpredictable. The gun nudged her towards a fallen chair, pushing her just hard enough. Perfect control.

'So you kill her, but you're fatally wounded yourself. Two bodies, one explanation, nice and neat. That was what I thought, but it works this way too, only she's the killer instead of you. Same bones of the story, you see? She killed you here, ran, and had to be tracked down and shot on the streets. Slightly more complicated, but life's never neat, is it? You're the writer, of course, but you like that version? I like it a lot.'

She still couldn't see him.

He nudged the chair towards her with his foot. Soft military boots. 'Sit down.' She righted the chair and set it down beside the curtained tank. There was dust everywhere. The tank curtain was thick with it. A broken table lay in the corner, wrecked putery on the floor. An unbroken shot glass on the floor too.

'Why?' She looked at him. This was Decece. She knew it by his skin.

'Yes, that's the question,' he said. 'Why indeed? Why all

of this? That's what I wanted to ask you. I just need to check I'm missing nothing. I'd willingly tell you my side of it, make more of a conversation, but I don't know anything. I'm just the auditor.' He shook dust off the other chair and sat down, facing her, the gun level in his hand. 'So let's set this out. I can kill you slowly or I can kill you quickly. And there's no hurry at all. Pax has a very large mess of its own to deal with this evening. It makes Emel Fleschik's little party look quite insignificant. By the time they get round to Officer Kerlew and think of checking her apartment, it'll be light outside. And of course they'll let me know they're on their way. So, shall we start?'

He was too far away and just staring at her, the gun relaxed in his hand but stone steady.

'I don't know anything. I'm a writer. I work for TruTales. I was told to come to Bleak.'

He fired, casually. She felt her cheek burn. He said, 'You killed Millasco in the Chute. You almost lost my first man outside your apartment a short while ago. They weren't novices. And you're a writer? Don't insult me.' He fired again and this time her cheek seethed with pain and there was hot blood at her neck.

She pressed her hand to it, and when the pain had subsided enough for her to breathe evenly, she said, 'I've lived with people who do a lot of things and I write about them. I've picked things up. That's all.'

'You've been trained.'

'I've only ever been a writer. I go where I'm told by an AI, learn about people, and write.'

He frowned at her and raised the gun again, and then he let his hand fall. 'Oh, my.' He stared hard at her for a moment, then shook the gun at her as if telling her off. 'You've been trained and you didn't know it. You really didn't, did you? Well, that's a new one. That's very good indeed. Okay, I'll settle for your next instructions and let you go quickly. Die, I mean. What are they?'

She sagged in the chair. 'My AI has to advise me. My commslink is in my jacket here.'

'Take it out slowly. I won't skim you next time. Third time it's a hand.'

She took the unit out and gently put it on the floor by the dusty tank curtain. The sun was starting to rise, and its amber light caught in the shards of glass hanging in the window frame. The room was still dark, but her eyes had adapted to it. A few beams of refracted light from the window crossed the room, holding the drifting dust.

'Don't leave it there. Pick it up. Slowly, that's it. Good. Now put your other hand on your opposite shoulder. Lean all the way back, I don't want you jumping up. That's right.'

She did everything he said. Leaning back, she straightened her legs very slowly, and let her foot snag the edge of the chainlink curtain. It made a tiny chiming sound. Dust bloomed. She half closed her eyes in the dark room.

Decece was concentrating, eyes wide, carefully taking the comms unit from her without looking anywhere except at her face as she flicked her boot firmly against the curtain. It shot aside and the room was suddenly shining in the tank's brilliance. The dust roiled in the vivid air. Decece cried out and raised a hand against the blazing light, firing blind. The shot hit the tank, which shattered explosively. Razer slapped Decece back as he lunged at her, half-sighted, and she went for his gun hand, but he rolled away and she picked up Delta's dead screen and swung at him with it. His head folded back and he went down and was still.

She stood gasping. Water from the smashed tank was flowing away across the floor, and the spilt stones were fading. Fish flapped and jumped, losing their colour as they died.

Razer gathered herself. *Get out quickly.* She picked up her bag and commslink and took Decece's gun from the floor, started to search his pockets and stopped again. He wouldn't be carrying anything. She went into the small kitchen and then the bedroom, going through Delta's cupboards, and pocketed a deactivated Paxflake. She squeezed a whole tube of Heal! over her cheek, wincing at the pain, then found a reel of tape and ripped off a length and used it to drag down an eyebrow and pull up the corner of her lip. She shrugged a jacket of Delta's over her own and filled a shoulder bag with anything that came to hand, just to unbalance her, and said into the room as she left, 'I'll stick with this story, asshole.'

Tallen

Tallen was feeling a lot better. He was remembering more and more. When he was in the cage, he would review his maps. He found himself intensely conscious of the sensor chains strung out in the sea, feeding wave profiles back to the rig, and the ballast programs adjusting the weighting to keep the vessel stable.

His back had stopped itching, and he felt an alertness he'd never felt in his life. The water crashed over him.

He felt the movement of the sarcs out there. It was as if

some of them were calling to him, scratching in his skull.

He thought of the first HeartStar. The words in his head were to do with that, though he remembered nothing about the woman. He had a strong vision of the place she had described. *Snow and rain. Mountains...* How did it go on?

And the second HeartStar. With that, he had a sharp memory of the writer in the red bar, that thing she'd said, *Full of sound and fury.* He suddenly remembered going back and searching it out on the Song, a whole speech that he'd wanted to talk to her about. *Tomorrow and tomorrow and tomorrow.*

And then he'd gone out and ended up here.

Razer

Out of Delta's block, Razer walked quickly, heading for the red bar. Twice on the way she stopped under dead cams, changing her appearance each time, dropping the bag and extra jacket, adjusting the facial sticktape. The moves might only buy her a few minutes when Decece was discovered, but that could matter. Right now, she could afford the time.

Bar/red never closed, but at four-light it was slowing down. She went to the counter and bought a mudvisky, and said, 'You know there are Paxers outside?'

'Should I?'

She swallowed half the shot. The bar was busy with screeners and drinkers, the hum of music low. 'Maybe you should,' she said. 'Not for you, but there's a few here who might thank you for knowing.'

'Might they?' said the barman. His eyes slid over her.

She said, 'It's only that Bale isn't around any more to give you the heads-up, and I think Pax want to make a show tonight. Not that you have anything to worry about. Like I said.'

She drank the rest of the thick visky down and went across to a woman she'd seen there more than once, who was intent on a palmscreen and mildly hyperventilating, and said, 'Hey, forgive me for this rudeness, but I've seen you here a few times and I know you deal *ellescele*, and if I know, then Pax surely knows.'

'So?' Her breathing slowed its beat and she was suddenly focused on Razer. She folded the screen away.

'So Pax has the bar set up for a raid. But you give me your jacket and your vials, you take my jacket, and Pax sees you for me and me for you.'

'Sure, and I was cloned an hour ago.' The woman turned away.

Razer pointed at the barman, who was making a noise about starting to clear the drinks and shut down the comms. 'See? He knows.'

'How do I know you won't sell me to Pax?'

'Sell you? I could just take you.' Razer unpalmed Delta's Paxflake for a moment. In the dim light, the flake looked good enough. 'But I'm making an offer.'

'Why would a Paxer do this? Don't shit me.'

The bar was almost dark now. People were heading away steadily and swiftly. Razer said, 'I just took out a dealer but he was clean and I'm in trouble if I don't have something to leave on him.'

The woman laughed, then stood up and peeled her jacket off. She said, 'Why not? Stuff's in the pocket.'

'Leave your palmscreen with me. Take my jacket,' Razer said, shrugging on the woman's. 'My commer's in it. Wear it like I do, collar up. Keep your head down; you look enough like me. Jam your hands in your pockets like I do.'

The woman cleared her device's dataset with a swipe of her palm and handed it over. Razer watched her go, waiting a minute before standing up. The dealer's jacket smelt stale and the palmscreen was sticky. A group of people were leaving and Razer filtered through the door with them. She slid away at the first junction and went to the promenade and stopped there, staring out at the sea. The light was rising and the shield growing faint against it. Pale purple shadows were stretching out across the street behind her, and the water was hissing through the stones below. The colours made her think of Decece, startled and off guard as she'd killed him.

Someone had once said to her: the first thing you do when you stop running and get that first moment to take stock is listen to the first thing in your mind, because no matter how stupid it seems, it's the most important thing. And the second thing you do is say to yourself, 'Now what?'

She took a long breath of the acrid morning air. The first thing was: she should have checked Decece was dead before leaving him. *Stupid.*

She turned her back to the sea and gazed at the streets. *Now what?*

But the fact that she knew exactly what to do made her no more comfortable at all. She had to get to The Rig at Rest and see Chorst Maerley. It wasn't far across Lookout, but it wouldn't be easy with the streets alert for her.

Cynth had set Maerley up for her, or maybe set her up for him. But why would Cynth be doing that? Cynth could simply have told her Maerley was here on Bleak, and to see him for a story.

Another possibility struck Razer. Was Cynth hiding something from her, or from someone else?

And another. What exactly was Cynth?

Forty

ALEF

SigEv 41 Revelation

The third readout, of course, wasn't a failsafe either. It was our unborn baby's. That was why Pellonhorc hadn't given me a final warning of the consequences of failure, before entering his *rv*. He hadn't needed to. He had my wife and my child.

I can't remember running. I have no idea how I got back to my place. I remember forests growing and dying, countless leaves counted, more of them, and more.

For a long while, I was crazy. In the end, exhausted and desperate, I escaped to the Song and in its crowded void I raged and cried, my misery multiplied and amplified until the entire Song echoed with it.

My love has been taken from me. I am empty. I am nothing.

All I wanted was to cry out in the darkness, and I did that, my grief booming and thundering, but after a time I became aware that there were other voices, that there were replies.

>No one can say anything to help you, Nameless. There is

nothing. I am sorry. All you can do is carry on and wait for hope. Tell us your name.

There were hundreds and thousands, tens of thousands, of answers like this. They all carried names or codes, but I couldn't identify myself and risk being traced. Mad though I was, I knew I still had to function, to bring Pireve back and to see my child born. I had to do what Pellonhorc wanted.

But I couldn't do that. I still didn't know how to finish the task! I was lost in despair and without hope. I used the putery of my great databases to fill the Song with untraceable, echoing wails of desolation. My terrible voice, uncoded and with no place of origin, scythed through the Song. I was the impossible. I was a wind, a tide, a sourceless flare of light. For a month, the System spoke only of me. They searched for me but found only the stars. My name, the name they called out to answer me, was Nameless.

>Time is the only thing, Nameless. But I am here.

>And I am here, Nameless. Tell us about it. Tell us and it will help.

Of course I couldn't tell them. I roared and I screamed my loss, but I could say nothing. Yet they persisted.

>Then only listen. Listen to my story, Nameless. I live on Gutter and I had a brother who died, and a father who went away…

>And here is my story, Nameless. I live on a driftship, alone. Everyone else aboard is dead. The ship's contaminated and no planet will take me, no other

vessel dock with me. I have food and drink for years, and I have the Song, but I'm alone.

>You have us, Driftship. We are here.

>Nameless, are you still there?

And in the end, to all of this, I lowered my voice and answered.

>*Always*.

All those stories of sadness, hope and despair. The Song was suddenly flooded with them. Without intention, I had triggered something extraordinary. Because I understood every fault and nuance of the coding, I hadn't opened myself up in a tiny way or in a small place, as they had, each one of them, and been ignored; I had done it everywhere. I drew all the pain and the yearning to me, and in answering me, those in pain drew themselves to each other as never before.

I couldn't respond properly, but I retained everything. I didn't think. I sent it all to my database satellites and stored it away. All the pain, the desperation, all filed away. It was like sweeping dead leaves.

And then, after a few weeks of this occupation, I gradually returned to my senses and to my task. With Malachus's agreement, I moved myself to Pellonhorc's house, where I could visit Pireve every day. I developed a routine of waking at four in the morning and going to Pireve. She was so very beautiful, her skin cool and perfect. The unit's hood, once open, exposed her down to the shoulders, so I had to imagine her belly with our baby inside. Once I touched the inward curve of her neck, but the tightness and temperature of her skin disturbed me too much, and I never did that again.

I talked to her, telling her what I was hoping to do that day. Sometimes I'd tell her a story I'd heard on the Song the night before, or I'd tell her what I had achieved the day before and how it was all going. Then I'd say goodbye, blowing a small kiss at her, and close the unit. I tried all the time not to think about Pellonhorc beside her, the two of them shoulder to shoulder, but every time, as the hood closed down, I glanced at him and felt uncomfortable.

At five a.m., I would start my work, and at midnight, for an hour before I slept, I became Nameless.

Trying not to think too much about Pireve when I wasn't with her, I structured my time carefully. First, there was Pellonhorc's cancer. I set up more research teams, and Malachus made sure they were funded by the Whisper. There were now hospitals and laboratories throughout the System working on nothing but the analysis of specimens of cells grown from Pellonhorc's cancer.

I found this more interesting than I'd expected. While the epigenetic approach to cancer therapy had already been established when Earth was our home, the fluctuating levels of environmental radiation and the constantly mutating variety of oncogenic toxins in the System made almost every cancer an entirely unique riddle. Pellonhorc's cancer was a nightmare to unravel. Its cells seemed to develop a response to every treatment. Nothing would wear them down or destroy them. At best, they would close in on themselves for a while before resuming their slow but relentless spread through his system. They were a perfect microcosm of their host.

Developing the organisation that would maintain

Pellonhorc for all those years was the hardest task, and was mine alone. Its criteria were simple enough. There would be something to appeal to the living and something to entice the dying. Those knowingly about to die could, like Pellonhorc, go into *rv* and await a cure. But there had to be something for the not yet dying, too.

I struggled to find the answer to this. The organisation had to be in the thoughts of everyone, always. They had to be intimately concerned with it, day by day, year after year, before they ever needed the sea.

Night after night, I found myself returning to my databases of stories. All these people, all these lives. I already knew that they wanted more than an ending in death. But I suddenly understood that they wanted more than to live.

I was close to it. So very close.

They wanted to touch and to be touched, to be understood, to be remembered.

That eternal desire, that desire for the eternal, I already had. But I needed more than that. What *else* did they want?

They wanted a compassionate hearing. And… and they wanted to show their *own* compassion and have it acknowledged. That was what the Song had shown me.

I knew I was on to something. In the Babbel, what was it that was said? *A seeing eye, a hearing ear, and a book in which all is written.*

I sat in silence for perhaps an hour, turning it around and over in my head, not daring to believe I'd found my answer. But no matter how I tried to find fault, there was no mistake, no error.

* * *

SigEv 42 The program

Here was my solution: the living, as well as having the future promise of the sea, would have the chance to examine the lives of those in *rv*. But even more than that, they would be able to judge them, so that when a cure became available for an *rv* category, the living would be able to vote for the sleeping to be retrieved from the sea and be saved, or to be left there.

Even to think about their salvation made me catch my breath. At one time or another, anyone in the System could be both saviour and saved. Their own lives would in the end be cared about. There would even be an encouragement to lead a good life.

The salvation of Pellonhorc alone would be the heart of this, though I tried not to consider that too deeply. Every morning as I talked to Pireve, I imagined him listening to us. As the hood opened, I could not see her without seeing him.

I had five years. Now I had my plan, I could address my one great problem.

My priority was to develop a device that would record a life far more reliably than human memory could. It had to be inert and impossible to corrupt or remove – or even to identify. For greatest effectiveness, my recorder had to be inserted into the brain at birth.

Obviously not everyone could be implanted with the device. Even the seas of Bleak could not accommodate the mortality rate of the System, not even for the eighty years I needed it to last. But everyone must be able to imagine they might be a host.

I decided that people had always accepted lottery risk; they'd accept it here.

What made the device possible was that the brain already had the capacity to store all memory. The fault within the brain was its retrieval mechanism. All we needed to do was address this.

After a great deal of research, my team identified and isolated an epigenetic trigger that affected the region of the brain responsible for longterm memory. We engineered a combined trigger and reader, and called it a neurid.

A year passed. Two. The perfected neurid could be inserted via a vaccination technique. Batches of neurid and placebo could be distributed on a double-blind basis, neither operator nor recipient having any idea whether or not the injection contained an active factor.

All my research and development was carried out in secret, in laboratories scattered throughout the System. Most of the scientists didn't know they were working for me, and none knew what, ultimately, they were working on. We prepared an *in vivo* trial.

Malachus and I were getting on well. It was clear that his loyalty was to Pellonhorc, but he treated me as a friend, sympathising with me without ever mentioning the cause of my sorrow. I grew quite close to him. He had a wife and three children, and he would talk to me about them. We discussed Nameless, too, as everyone did. He told me he enjoyed being able to delegate some of the duties he used to have to carry out personally, and I understood exactly what he meant by that. He wasn't like Pellonhorc, and even though I liked him for that, it made me worry that the Whisper might fail, with Malachus in charge.

But the Whisper simply consolidated; that was Malachus's strength.

Another year passed, and we retrieved the data from the trial babies we had injected with neurid cells. The results were extraordinary. The first few weeks and months of infant development were grainy and incomplete, but towards the end of the year, there were voices and sounds being recorded. It was beautiful, though it made me think of my own child-to-be, which was more painful than I could cope with.

But these were just babies. I needed adults with full memories in the sea as quickly as possible.

I needed a name for the program, too. I thought of its purpose, and of Pellonhorc's attitude to God, and I called it AfterLife. I called the memories AfterLives.

I expected the program to hit resistance here, since the neurid was assimilated far more slowly when inserted into an adult, and took time to harvest old memories as well as accumulating new ones, so that nothing of any significance could be read for some years.

But to my relief, there was an almost universal eagerness in the System to sign up for the program, with the exceptions of Gehenna and the unsaid planet, of course.

What I hadn't appreciated was the extraordinary depth of desire for the lives of others – not for the self-told, self-pitying and self-aggrandising lives with which the Song had always teemed, but for the truth. My experience as Nameless had given me barely a glimpse of it.

Nevertheless, progress was too slow. Four years had now gone by. I still spoke to Pireve every morning, but my enthusiasm and confidence were faltering. There were always more problems. I wished she could advise me, even just comfort me. Sometimes I found myself in tears as I faced her closed eyes and perfect face. I wanted to nestle my head at her breast, to hear her gentle voice.

It was hard, but I worked and worked until I couldn't tell waking from dreaming. Once, in a dream, I had it all solved, only to wake and find the solution gone. The walls echoed with my screams, and all the voices of the Song could not soothe me.

Malachus came to the house and told me to rest and eat. 'Look, I've brought you some food. Cheese, bread, my wife's cakes. She's never met you, but she worries about you. You like cakes?'

He made me talk to him. He said I hadn't talked to anyone for months.

He didn't know about my nights. If he'd known how I raged and cried in the Song, that I was Nameless, he'd really worry. 'I talk to Pireve every day,' I said. My mouth felt dry, the words unfamiliar to my tongue.

'No, you don't.' He picked up a piece of bread and took a bite, making sure I was watching, like a parent encouraging their child. It made me think of my mother. I was feeling increasingly fragile.

Malachus swallowed and waited. I took some bread – for my mother, I told myself – but I had no saliva and had to force it down in a lump. Malachus said, 'You open the hood and just stand there. You haven't said anything to her for over a year. Sometimes you don't even look at her.'

'Are you watching me?'

'No, Alef. I'm watching Pellonhorc. You must know I can't leave you alone with him. But it's you I'm worried about.'

I felt myself slump.

'It's going well, isn't it, Alef? You always say it is.'

'It's the time. If I had more time –'

'You have almost a year.' His tone changed abruptly. 'Eat the bread, Alef, then get back to it. There's nothing I can do. I like you, Alef, but that wouldn't change any decision I had to make. I've disposed of good friends before you came along.'

He looked directly at me to tell me that. Malachus, I realised, was a good man to be running the Whisper. Command had not distanced him. He took a cake from the tray and turned to go, dropping crumbs.

I went back to work, and this time Malachus left me to it.

Forty-one

RAZER

Razer held the sticky palmscreen with her fingertips and hissed, 'Okay, Cynth. You tell me what's happening here.'

TALLEN IS YOUR STORY NOW.

'What's *my* story? Two people have tried to kill me. The latest told me I've been trained for something, and crazier ideas than that are turning out true.' Razer glanced around. The sea was at her back, beyond the long drop of the promenade wall. She had a good field of view ahead. She slid down into a squat, so she wasn't interrupting the line of the wall. 'Talk to me, Cynth. Bale was right all along. I'm not a coincidence at all. I don't believe you're an AI. You sometimes act like one but you aren't, or else –' She took a breath. 'Hell, I don't know.'

She didn't mention Larren Gamliel or Chorst Maerley. There was no time anyway, and what if Cynth was being monitored by whoever was responsible for all of this? Somehow she didn't think Cynth was actually being controlled by whoever that was.

Razer nilled the connection. In a few minutes the sun would have risen enough for her to lose the protection of the shade. She started walking along the promenade, keeping tight to the wall. A few people were appearing on the streets around her, a few zipriders and mycycles. No Paxers. She kept her eyes moving, but no one seemed to notice her.

A Paxer walked out of a side street. He glanced at the promenade but didn't seem to have spotted her. Maybe he slowed his pace briefly. Maybe she was paranoid.

The Paxer vanished. A woman who had been casually walking towards the wall a few metres away increased her pace and turned a little too sharply in Razer's direction. At the same time, a two-up ziprider swerved towards the point where the woman would intercept Razer. Razer waited for the ziprider to slow down, then straightarmed the woman, knocking her to the ground and rolling over her, confusing their positions, and yelled, 'I've got her.'

The woman chopped an arm at Razer's jaw, then went for a belted gun as Razer short-punched the side of her head and shouted, 'She's armed.'

The ziprider skidded to a halt. Razer rolled the woman onto her stomach so the dismounting Paxers couldn't see either of their faces, and yelled, 'Shock her. She's got a gun. I can't hold her.'

One of the men said, 'I'm not sure –'

The other said, 'Shock 'em both and we'll sort it out later.'

Razer held the woman's face down and shouted, 'Fine. But do her first while I've got her.'

As the first charge cracked out and the woman slumped, Razer let the palmscreen fall and said, 'Look, she's dropped it!'

It was enough. The Paxers briefly relaxed. Razer drew the woman's weapon and steadied it on them. 'Okay. Jump over the wall, both of you. Right now.'

She watched them sprawl on the stones below, then

swung herself onto the ziprider and headed for the area three blocks by three that Bale had told her was the Rut. He had also told her how long it took Pax to trace and track stolen vehicles, so she knew she had a count of fifty to get there. By twenty she was hearing sirens behind her, and by thirty she was hearing them from left and right too. By forty they were almost converging ahead of her.

They'd anticipated her, but they were too late. Forty-five seconds and she was in the alleys of the Rut.

Lookout's Rut was a deadcammed warren of re-engineering workshops, a factory of dismantling and re-imagining. It could have been night there. Tarps and steel sheeting concealed the sky, and the streets were ripped up so that wheels were less use than boots. Razer swung herself off the machine and walked it on.

She hadn't gone ten metres before the first fixer approached, a woman barely out of her teens. She ran a wired palm over the ziprider's console and said without meeting Razer's glance, 'Price?'

'No money. I just want a safe walk out of here.'

The woman tipped her head. 'Where you need to go?'

'Don't worry about that. Once I'm out, I need twenty minutes.'

The woman looked into a palmscreen and back at Razer, considered and said, 'Okay, we have thirteen women your height and weight, close enough. Give us five minutes to gather and dress them and you. Show me your walk.'

The woman watched Razer, then said into her palm, 'Okay, she's a hip-roller, slight head-peck. Everyone keeps their hands in their pockets.' She turned her attention back to Razer. 'Twenty minutes is tall. Pax don't like losing zippys.

You got anything else? The gun you got there in the pocket?'

'I need the gun.'

'They can track it.' The woman was already wheeling the ziprider towards a ramp leading down below a shopfront booth. A saw screeched somewhere beneath.

Razer followed the woman. 'No they can't. It was an undercover.'

'Worth more, then.' Underground, the light was harsh neon and every surface was metal. The workshop stank of oil and ozone.

'No. I need the gun.'

The woman parked the ziprider in a pair of axle clamps and watched the machine invert it. The machine's movement was unexpectedly beautiful. The woman touched her ear and said to Razer, 'What have you done? They're keen as lovers out there. Coating the streets for you.'

Another woman came down the ramp, wearing a black padded jacket and trousers and a pair of oversized bright green boots. She gave Razer a bundle of the same clothes and said, 'Which direction do you want to leave?'

Razer started to pull on the overclothes. They were thick and heavy, good as cloaking but hard to move in. 'North.'

'Check your timer, then. Thirteen of us will leave in precisely three minutes, equidistant exits. We'll all look the same and we'll stretch them thin. You leave at three minutes and ten, they'll be overloaded and you'll be fine.'

Out of the workshop, Razer pulled the hood over her head. A few others walked past, just like her, hooded and booted. She walked north for a minute, then turned sharply and made towards the western perimeter of the Rut.

Bale had told her how the Rut kept going. It survived

by compromise. It knew when to cooperate, and this would definitely be a time for the Rut to belly up for Pax. At two minutes forty, Razer kicked off the green boots and stripped back down to her own shirt and jeans and walked straight out of the Rut. She was walking straight past a pair of Paxers as they picked up the first of the decoys exiting behind her.

Ten minutes later, she was at The Rig at Rest. She almost cried at the sight of Maerley's creased face and the smile she'd never forgotten. But he was stooped now and she saw the arthritis starting to knot his fingers.

'Hey,' he said. 'Am I that bad?'

'Maerley, you're just perfect.' And suddenly overwhelmed by exhaustion, she fell into a chair. 'I need your help. Everything's a mess.'

As he made caffé, she watched him, remembering more. The hostel room was littered with his machinery, with motor parts and power sources, all his screenery and putery. Maerley had a gift for assembling the marvellous out of the useless, making extraordinary devices from fragments of failed tech. He'd always lived like this, in nests of components.

He put the tasse down, turning that small piece of gouged metal in his hands. It was a shard of shrapnel that had nearly killed him years back in a flycykle malfunction, the shard polished to an obsidian shine by all those years of buffing.

'You still got that, Maerley.'

'Just for exercise,' he said, smiling. 'So, tell me.'

And when Razer's story was done, he said, 'I don't know if any of this helps or makes it worse. After you contacted me, I searched AfterLife for the vote you mentioned, Larren Gamliel. The drifthome and the voidlock death, yes, they brought it all back. Could have been me.' He took a shuddering breath, then added, 'Have you gone back to the TruTale?'

'I've been rather busy. Listen to me, Maerley. I don't think we've got long. When I spoke to you, you said you'd been commissioned to build a single-unit vessel here. What are your instructions for it?

'To make it ready. That's it. I'm expecting a client to pick it up.'

Unable to keep her voice from shaking, Razer said, 'I think I'm your client. Is it ready?'

Maerley frowned. 'Not sea-tested, but otherwise, yes. It's you?' He turned the gleaming shard of metal over and over in his hand. Light jumped around the room.

'My AI's been pushing me to you. I don't think the Gamliel Life was a coincidence.' She went to the window and looked out. The street was empty. 'When's your client supposed to be making contact?'

'I was just told to make it ready and wait. No details at all. Very mysterious. As if they knew they were being watched. And just like the commissioner before this one who ordered two very similar units. Exactly the same secrecy. Really weird. Those were two-ups, though.'

Razer asked, 'Don't you always get paid on completion? Have you been paid?'

The arthritis was there in Maerley's gait as he walked across to open his comms. He looked up and said, 'Payment came through about the moment you arrived.'

Razer touched the augmem stub at her ear and said, quietly, 'Cynth knows I'm here. Of course. This is also a tracker.'

'Easy stuff,' Maerley said.

'And Cynth found a Life very similar to yours, to prompt me. Didn't want to risk telling me openly in case it exposed me. Or her. And I guess she must have known about your other client.'

'Hell of an AI there, Razer.' Maerley pushed himself upright. 'Let's go.' He took her down to the inn's rear door and from there along the sea wall to a small private dry dock that stank of salt and oil. 'There she is.'

Razer looked down at the slim, dark, flattened tube. Without the stubby fins and turbine jets, it might have been a sarc. 'Will I know how to run it?'

'More or less. I'll take you through it.' He climbed awkwardly down to the steps beside the machine and pulled the small hatch open.

'There really isn't time, Maerley. What comms does it have?'

He backed out of the way as she started to lower herself into the pod. She was slim, but it was still a tight squeeze to push her hips down. Maerley was saying, 'Short range only, and preset to instructions. You can't override the presets.'

She was in to her waist and raised her arms to wriggle further. She swore, forcing herself down. 'Maerley, who exactly is this built for?'

He looked unhappy. 'It's stripped back all the way. It's a transit unit designed for short range, single mission, preset destination. Pilot dimensions were subsidiary. And there's another reason it's tight…'

'Just tell me where's it set for, Maerley.'

'I was just given coordinates, but the only thing out there apart from the sarcs are the rigs.'

He was interrupted by a dull thump from the direction of the inn. As he glanced over his shoulder, a flash of yellow light lit up all the creases of his face and threw his shadow against the dock wall.

'That's my traps,' he said. 'I always wondered what they'd look like if they ever triggered. Get yourself in, Razer.'

She wriggled all the way down and into a cradled position. Harnesses slid across her shoulders and as the canopy closed over her head, screenery snapped on. This was certainly stripped back. Maerley was there on the screen, a blurred stick-figure leaning against a grey block of wall that suddenly lurched aside, and as it moved, so did she and the vessel, dropping forward and suddenly wallowing and then sinking. With full submersion, the lighting faded and she was in the gloom of the tiny cockpit.

An instrument console lit up and she reached out to fit her hands to the pads. Maerley was above her now and moving away to the rear. There was another figure too.

The vessel bucked sharply and tilted. Razer gripped the pads and they gloved her hands. The dock's angles and planes dissolved behind her, and she was in open water.

Forty-two

ALEF

SigEv 43 The ceremony

With only a few months before Pellonhorc – and Pireve, of course – came out of *rv*, we were ready with an initial cache of AfterLives to be released as soon as their owners went to the seas. These were maturity-inserted neurids, so the Lives were limited in detail. I was troubled that we might have raised expectations too far.

Nevertheless, with great ceremony, our first thousand units – we called them sarcophagi – set off for Bleak from the embarkation port on Heartsease. One thousand people at the edge of death, locked in *rv*, prepared to wait for judgement of their lives.

As soon as I'd moved into Pellonhorc's house, I'd had a putery room set up with command screenery stretched across its longest wall. It was eight metres tall and twenty wide. Most of the time I used it as a thoughtboard, throwing sequences at it and shifting them around, but I also watched Song material on it. You felt like you could walk right into the threedy it pushed into the room.

Malachus came to the house to watch the First Lives ceremony with me. I'd never seen him show anything but confidence and certainty before, but on that day he deferred to me. His anxiety was plain. He knew what the consequences would be if this failed.

The ceremony began magnificently, though. The System all but came to a halt to watch it.

It may seem extraordinary that there had never been a Systemwide event before this, but that was the case. The System's settlement, centuries previously, had been chaotic. The planets had been pre-terraformed while the fleets were in transit. Arrangements for the flight from Earth had been so accelerated that our ancestors' arrival had been ragtag, and until AfterLife, there had been no interplanetary commonalities except the rule of taxes and the susurrus of the Song. The birth of AfterLife was an opportunity to correct that.

Standing in front of the huge screen, Malachus and I observed the final hour of the two-day buildup. Our participants came from all over the System except the usual two planets; they came from Spindrift, from Magnificence, from Vegaschrist's moons Brightness and New Hope, from Heartsease and Peco and Gutter and Bleak. The mothership was trailed all the way from Heartsease by a flotilla of small craft. The overvoice explained that because the upper atmosphere of Bleak was so dangerous, fifty highly manoeuvrable dropvessels would spin down from the mothership to release the sarcophagi.

Leaders of all the planets, bar the usual two, were present, and each said a few words. No one mentioned me. No one but Malachus knew that AfterLife was anything other than a coalescence project. I felt it best that it remain that way. AfterLife should stand alone.

The words were all said, each leader carefully claiming

no credit, but all careful to imply that their own planet was responsible for a significant part of the AfterLife project. There was talk of a new understanding.

The ceremony entered its next phase. In unison, the dropvessels arranged themselves in an arrowhead formation that, as the cam swept round, was revealed as the A of AfterLife.

Malachus grinned at me. A stillshot of this sequence would be AfterLife's brand memory. After we had heard the overvoice recognising the A in scripted surprise, I muted the official soundtrack and swelled the Song's murmur in the background.

So beautiful!
I never realised space was so big before.
I feel so lucky to be seeing this. It makes me feel proud. I feel like crying!

The dropvessels opened their cargo doors and released their loads.

The cams closed in, and the screen's threedy strengthened. The room seemed to fill with sarcophagi. They were all around us, tumbling through space.

Malachus let out a sigh. He had been standing up, and now he fell back in his seat. The sight was glorious. The rain of dark blue sarcs, finned and ribbed, proofed against corrosion and maul and every other form of siege and attack that Bleak and its oceans and storms might launch at them over the centuries, plunged in a great phalanx through the lower atmosphere of the planet and on through the glittering storms.

The cam remained high, and the sarcs fell and fell away

beneath us, a minute passing, another and another as they dropped. And as they struck the sea, looking in the end no more than a handful of gravel tossed into that terrible ocean, every single sarcophagus vanished from eyeview and from seacam and from every wavelength of spectrum reader.

Not one remained. The sea raged on.

Malachus whispered, 'No.' Then, anxiously, 'Alef, what's happening?'

'I don't know.' I turned to my putery, reviewed the algorithms of gravity and rate of descent, of aerodynamics and impact resistance. 'This shouldn't be,' I said. I checked everything and checked it all again. 'They must be there.'

'But they aren't,' Malachus said tightly.

'No.'

Now even the Song was silent.

And then, one by one, a thousand points of light lit up over eighty per cent of the screenery in the System, each light a life waiting for renewal, each light a sleeper's tale.

The cam fell vertiginously, dizzyingly, and there they were, the sarcs rising to the surface of the sea and dancing there, dark blue pips on a field of black and grey. Each sarc was linked to a Life, each pip to a point of light.

Malachus yelled. He took me by the shoulders and shook me, shouting, 'Yes! Yes, yes, oh, Alef, yes!'

The Song went wild. It was an echoing flare of noise and light, nothing but a roar of celebration. It was almost alive. I felt I could be unconnected and still hear it.

Malachus was laughing as the screen showed views of the sarcs gradually sinking once more to settle at their various preset depths and the shuttles beginning to return to the mothership.

And without warning, in all that joy and celebration, the screenery failed and we were standing in a darkness relieved only by the pale light from the bank of putery behind us, flattening our shadows against the dead wall.

This was not the simple hiatus of a few moments ago. This was something much more.

Malachus stumbled, clutching at me. 'What's happened?'

I pulled up the overvoice again.

'I'm sorr –' A crackling, then nothing.

'The screenery's fine,' I said, my back to it, checking the putery. 'The speaker isn't actually on the mothership. It's totally unaffected by whatever's happening above Bleak. They've just pulled the voice because they don't know what to say.'

The great screenery returned with an accompanying fierce crack of sound before I could go on. Malachus had been staring directly at it, and his scream was an awful thing. I heard him collapse to the ground. By the time I turned round, the blinding screenflare had dulled a fraction.

I squinted through my fingers. Again and once more, a screencrack and flare, and the third time there was vague detail too. It was as if the screenery was being repeatedly knifesliced, a slash of black and white, then a magnetic thrum and a blur of retinal shadow. In the flurry of light and shade I could see Malachus kneeling and clutching at his eyes.

'You'll be all right,' I told him as the screenery began to resolve. 'The cutout came through, but a bit slow. You'll be seeing Bleak every time you close your eyes for a while, though.'

I helped him sit up. He was rubbing his knuckles into his eyes.

'I can't see anything at all,' he said. 'What's happening?'

'It's okay. They've gone to another cam. Bleak just decided to unleash one of its high-altitude electrical events and someone didn't think to shield the comms. It –'

I stopped and stared, and then I swore.

Malachus said, 'What?'

The screenery had finally regained itself to show a mess of shattered fragments spinning away, the sea distantly at its back. I found myself involuntarily connecting the shards in my head, reconstructing the vessel and calculating the force and position of the strike. This piece going here, that one rotated and placed there, this lone edge of titanium twisted like tinfoil…

'*What*, Alef?'

'One of the shuttles didn't raise its shields in time.'

'Oh.' Malachus blinked a few times. 'Did everyone see it? Or were they all like me?'

'This is augmented screenery. On anything else, everywhere else, it would just have been an overlaid flare. So everyone saw it.'

Malachus closed his eyes, then opened them and examined his fingers. 'We can't hide it, then,' he said.

'No one can hide anything any more. Everything's just a matter of time.' I shifted the image on the screen a few times, checking elsewhere. 'It's already all over the System. The Song is full of it.'

There were programs already carrying out the calculation I had performed in my head, reversing the ship's destruction moment by moment. I stopped to watch one of them. It was irritatingly slow, but I stayed long enough to see I hadn't missed anything.

'Yes. It's everywhere,' I said. 'It doesn't matter, though. It may add something.'

Malachus squinted at me, his eyes slowly beginning to focus. '*Add* something?' He touched me on the arm. 'You always surprise me, Alef. I'll leave you to it, then. Oh, and congratulations.'

I helped him to the outer door where his driver was waiting. A small cluster of people were crowded by his flycykle, staring so intently at its screenery that they had to be shouted at to move aside.

I stayed a moment to watch them watching. There was excitement on their faces, and awe, and disbelief and laughter. Walking back to my room, I found myself laughing, too. Not for the event, but for the fact that I had *recognised* the expressions and the emotions. I could *feel* them.

I analysed my reaction to it as well, of course. How could it be, for example, that the sight of ten people so involved in a screen could make more of an impression on me than the certain knowledge that there were millions more elsewhere doing exactly the same thing?

Back in my room, I followed the aftermath of the ceremony and the accident intently.

While the Song had always seemed to have its own mysterious climate, with local clouds of attention forming and fading, its tornados of activity and lacunae of calm, the speed of what followed in this case was phenomenal. The storm of reconstruction and discussion was succeeded by something entirely new. As I had indicated to Malachus, I'd suspected something like it might happen, but the breathtaking speed and extent of it astonished me.

And while the shuttle's pilot, Liacea Kalthi, was

irretrievably lost, her neurid reading was on the AfterLife database, and had been updated just as she'd left the mothership. Within a minute of her death, millions of people had subscribed to AfterLife, and Liacea Kalthi's story – limited though it was by the maturity-inserted neurid – was being opened throughout the System.

That was one of the wonders of AfterLife: that even the irretrievably dead could be cared about. Far from ruining its launch, the death of Liacea Kalthi fixed AfterLife more securely than I had imagined possible, and embedded it in the heart of the System. From that day, applications for neurids flooded in.

The ceremony, then, was a success. For months to come it would be viewed everywhere, constantly, every detail devoured, dissected and discussed.

On that first day, though, I watched for hours and I checked and roamed the Song, eavesdropping and whispering, and then at three in the morning, exhausted, I ran to Pireve.

'It's started, Piri,' I yelled, waving my arms crazily. 'All I need to do is make it stronger, but the foundation is solid. AfterLife is more than I ever hoped it could be. It's magnificent!' I described it to her until I was barely able to speak. When I stopped, I put my hands on my knees and simply laughed, I was so full of exhaustion and exhilaration.

'Oh, Pireve,' I sighed. The hood of the unit was open and she was so very beautiful. I imagined my love flowing to her like a breeze, fluttering her eyelids and entering her mind.

I can't wait to see you, my Alef.

She had answered me!

No, of course she hadn't. I had simply been spending

so much time in the Song that I'd become accustomed to formless voices responding to mine. I wanted her so much that I had invented her voice.

'I need to fill the sea,' I told her when I got my breath back. 'I need AfterLife to grow, but there's still so much detail to install, and there are problems.'

Tell me, Alef.

She was my subconscious, but what difference did that make? Over the next days, I spent more time with her, talking over the swiftly unfolding events.

'Liacea Kalthi had parents and a brother,' I told her. 'She had lovers, a complicated life, and now the Song knows it all. There's no peace for her family, no escape for anyone close to her, and they're drowning in sympathy and accusation. The Song is destroying them.'

Did you say accusation?

'She argued with one of her lovers just before embarking on the final trip. He was hounded by the Song. They blamed him for her death. He killed himself.'

In future, make everyone anonymous. Give them false names, Alef, not numbers. And when there are cures, anonymity will make the voting fair, too…

After that, I talked to her all the time, even when I wasn't with her. Questions I couldn't solve alone, I'd solve with her, even though the idea of this collaboration was crazy. I imagined Malachus watching me, his finger on some device that would kill me if I made a suspicious move.

'When they're retrieved from the sea to be cured, how do I handle that?'

Distribute AfterLife hospitals throughout the System. Let those voted for cure be sent anywhere, no one will know where, and they can start new lives anonymously.

After some months, there was only one remaining problem, and I took it to Pireve.

'There's an issue with some of the maturity-inserted neurids, Piri. Their memory retrieval isn't always quite complete or accurate. Even if I use the archives to help the putery make adjustments for likely actuality of experience, the putery can't duplicate the participant's own voice. The voice always sounds false.'

Then don't use putery, my Alef. Use people.

So I employed interviewers to gather detail, to incorporate the idiosyncrasies of vernacular and accent and jargon into the extrapolations of the putery, to work with and smooth away the awkward creases in our early AfterLives. These writers were only required while we were relying on the maturity-inserted neurids, and I made sure that we were open about it, but it led to the rumours and theories of conspiracy that, in the years to follow, grew up around AfterLife.

It turned out to be impossible to dispel the rumours. To my surprise, however, they seemed to add to the reputation of AfterLife. We simply announced the truth, that the adult Lives could not be one hundred per cent guaranteed, but that in time, as the implanted-at-birth AfterLives became available, accuracy would approach unity.

And so, with a few months to go before Pellonhorc came out of his *rv*, I was able to concentrate on the final details.

Ligate's businesses had been fully incorporated into the Whisper, which was the only organisation in the System more extensive than AfterLife.

But we were getting nowhere with a cure for Pellonhorc's cancer.

I tried not to think of the seeds of death that Pellonhorc had sown. It had struck me that I could now spend my time searching them out, or finding and cutting whatever communication or triggering systems he had, but what if I failed? Pellonhorc was the only person who had ever out-thought me, and I would not take that risk. Whatever triggers and traps I might discover, I was certain that there would be more elsewhere.

Forty-three

RAZER

Razer headed straight out, the vessel diving deeper as the sea floor fell away. Maerley hadn't been understating the sub's limited capabilities. There was no way of mooring the vessel. At least it meant the controls were straightforward. She opened the course and destination screenery, and wasn't surprised to find their putery locked and set. *Sending me to Tallen's rig, are you, Cynth?* She had limited control over depth and there was an emergency manual override, but beyond that she was a passenger.

The sea was growing bumpier. She took the vessel down until the ride smoothed, and then she examined her comms. There was a single preset, linked to Maerley's personal comms.

'Maerley?'

No answer. She wondered if he was alive. She checked her readings. Eight hours of air, and fuel for a max of that at an even speed. The rig was six hours away, so she had two hours of latitude, which sounded like adequate leeway, but it would quickly be eroded by currents and the need to avoid sarcs.

She brought up the sonar. Nothing was showing. She wouldn't be in sarc waters for a while. The range of visuals and thermals gave her a variety of options. She prioritised proximity and caught swift glimpses of fish and the swirl of algae in the glittering currents around her. Above was the paler green of the sun on the surface, though the surface itself was no longer visible. To her rear was her bubbled wake. Somewhere below was the seabed, but like the surface, it was now out of range.

When she prioritised distance over proximity, all detail faded. The fish were dark scratches in a grey void and the seabed was a rolling grey plain, paling into the distance. There were a few scattered scratches ahead, of comparable size to the fish but far lighter, which she puzzled over until she realised they were the first of the faraway sarcs.

To her rear, the receding shore was just visible, refracted by the surface of the sea and pale as dream. It was marbled by flames. She searched for human outlines, but found nothing.

Razer felt suddenly and desperately alone. All she could hear was her own breathing and the thick rumble of the motor. She wanted to say something aloud, but couldn't bring herself to hear what her voice might sound like.

She had never really been alone before, not since her mother had died. There had always been people, and when there hadn't been anyone, she wrote, in order not to be alone. She had written in order not to think about herself: inventing, pretending, avoiding.

And then there had been Cynth. And much as she had always imagined Cynth as nothing but a wall to bounce off or occasionally to crash into, Cynth was the only constant in her life. But now she didn't know what Cynth was.

She spent a moment getting herself pointlessly angry at Maerley. That figure she'd seen on the dock beside him could have been Decece. She should have made sure he was dead.

When she turned the screen back on, she was entering the region of the sarcs. There were only a few at first, restless shapes shadowed by flickering fish, then gradually there were more, crowds of them ordered like books in a sunken library. As she passed through them, they dipped or yawed and then recovered their original positions.

No, she thought. Cynth wasn't her only constant. That was AfterLife. And that was another pretence of hers, that AfterLife meant nothing to her. She realised that it did matter to her whether she survived to be in one of those sarcs outside, that she might have a chance to be voted for. Even if not for herself, then for the others who hadn't survived all this. She was one of the holders of the truth about Bale. The TruTale she had written of him was a story, but her own Life, if it were ever uploaded, held what was important about him. And Delta's Life held something of Bale too, if her body had not been destroyed.

The regiments of sarcs passed around her. All the lives in there, the true stories, the Lives. For the first time in days, contemplating what she might be heading towards, she was not worried. Somehow, despite the likelihood that there was more to Cynth than she had always thought, she still trusted Cynth.

Or maybe she simply had faith in herself. She had got this far.

And Tallen? Nothing concerning him quite made sense. Although Cynth must have known something about him, she couldn't have known everything, to have allowed Razer to be taken by Decece. And Maerley. Someone other than Cynth had commissioned sea vessels from Maerley, but was it really possible that Cynth and the other agent had been unaware of each other? They weren't acting together, but there was some connection between them, and something strong. There were too many coincidences for it to be otherwise.

She suddenly remembered Delta's last flower, and managed to extricate her commer from beneath the tight harness.

The tulip opened. There were arrival dates on Bleak for two vessels. One was the neuro team. She knew about that, nothing new. The other was the audit team. But six ancillary personnel had accompanied the team, walking through on the same documentation.

Razer folded her hand over the commer and worked it out. Two of the extras had been Fleschik and Millasco. That left four. Maerley had built vessels like hers for four people.

They were ahead of her, but now she knew about them. Good.

Next question. Why should she trust Cynth? Cynth was a programmed AI. What was Cynth's directive, if not to administer TruTales? If Cynth wasn't self-operating, who was operating her?

Her questions went in circles. The vessel slid steadily on, through the restless sarcs, until she began to feel as if she were in a sarc herself, a repository of memories and thoughts, unable to do a thing other than hope for a destination.

It didn't make sense, no matter how she broke it down, unless there were two agencies linked intimately, but in mutual opposition.

Razer's short laugh vanished into the hull. It wouldn't make a story. Here it was, progressing towards a conclusion of some kind – she was sure of that, if of nothing else – and there was no possible way for the ends to be tied up. It was more like life than any sort of a story; it was a mess.

A small cluster of sarcs glittered and pitched in the sea ahead. All those messy lives held in stasis.

Two powerful factions working towards getting a neuroengineered nobody onto a rig. Were they working against each other, or independently towards the same purpose? It was insane.

Razer was certain of only one thing; that Decece had been right, that she'd been selected and trained for this a very long time ago.

The sonar grew brighter with sarcs until they were like stars around her. She checked the short-link comms. Nothing. She passed on through rank upon rank of sarcs, which shifted as if in acknowledgement.

The experience was beautiful. She imagined the sea as the life of the System, and all the memories within calming it. And she thought of the truly lost – the Bales – with a terrible, bittersweet sadness.

Time passed like this until she no longer thought of her destination. She played with her view, observing the sarcs up close in bright detail, their skins faintly corroding, their trains of fish like attendant thoughts, and she saw them in shadow extending hundreds of metres away, the patterns they made, the grey currents and trails. She dozed, awoke, dozed again.

And then the vibration of the vessel became a more solid judder, and she woke up properly.

Looming ahead of her was the vast undersea framework of a rig.

* * *

Tallen

Tallen felt sick and confused. Beata and Lode were in front of him, and his throbbing head told him there was an urgent problem in the subsea structure. He was moving mechanically, descending through the deepest bowels of the rig, walking so quickly that he almost tripped over the horde of chittering mechs at his feet. This headache was different, already sharp and directing him precisely. There was no uncertainty at all about it.

Beata said, 'Tallen? You are not acting normally.'

The humechs tried to overtake him, but he pushed them aside. He was heading for the central control chamber, into which the deep pipes rose from the sea bed. His head seemed full of fog.

Lode added, 'You are not acting as you normally act. We are worried.'

The chamber door opened for them. The console was a bank of screenery and putery controlling all the pipework; the main pipes pumping core into the tanks and the subsidiary pipes bringing up gas. The rig's gyro-putery was here too, constantly redistributing gas and core around the tanks to maintain the rig's stability.

It was all working smoothly, and yet Tallen's head was speared with pain. There was something he had to do here, to stop the pain.

Beata said, 'What is wrong, Tallen? What needs to be fixed?'

Tallen shook his head, trying to rid himself of the pain. There was nothing wrong here. The gyros were fine. The pumps were fine. The pipes had ninety-nine point nine

nine eight per cent integrity. Temperatures were within tolerances. The only thing wrong was Tallen himself. Why was he here?

He felt nauseous, and when the nausea had cleared, he was on the deck and in the cage. The water was bitter cold and his skull was frozen. He screamed and screamed. Against the sea it was nothing.

And then he was back in the rig with Beata and Lode again, and Beata saying to him, 'What did you fix, Tallen? You are not the same. The sea is not easing you.'

Tallen was sobbing and didn't know why.

Lode said, 'You have no ease. Is it your emotions? Do you want to talk about it? Please talk about it.'

He stopped sobbing. The knife in his pocket was still there, still comforting. The original headache was gone, but in its place was another low and heavy pain.

Lode said 'We are here for you, Tallen. We are worried about you. We are worried about what you have done.'

'What have you done?' said Beata.

But Tallen didn't know what he had done.

Forty-four

ALEF

SigEv 44 Out of time

I was at my putery when Malachus came to me and said, more sharply than he'd spoken to me in a long while, 'It's time, Alef.'

'Yes, in a week,' I said, not bothering to look up.

He sighed.

'I know,' I said. 'A week.'

'What are you doing?' he said, bending towards the putery. He'd often ask me this, out of politeness.

I was exhausted. I'd completed my sub-program for the maturity-inserted neurids. AfterLife was growing fast so I created an AI-moderated routine that could adapt and recycle every elaboration the writers provided through all similar Life events in the archive.

I told Malachus, 'Five years is up in a week's time.'

Malachus rested his hand on my arm and said, 'I know, but I have my own orders, Alef. I'm sorry. It's today.'

Again! Even asleep, Pellonhorc had tripped me again. 'Just one moment,' I told Malachus. 'Let me just finish this. Please.'

I set generic Life comparisons rolling down the screen.

Lists, parameters, fragments of real lives and the ends of those Lives. Terrible experiences repeated over and again, unappreciated and, until now, unheard. The only ever difference at that final moment was the immediate environment – inside, outside, day, night, alone, accompanied. And the *voice* of the Life.

'Look at us, Malachus,' I begged him, letting images flow before his eyes. 'Here we are. *All* of us.'

It was all in the stories: the myth of unique tragedy. The data reeled. Here it all was, catalogued and cross-referenced; damage and death within abusive families, in natural and human-made catastrophe, in relationship breakup, in medical emergency… 'Look! *This* is humanity, Malachus!'

'I'm sorry, Alef. Right now.'

'But I just need *time*.'

'Either you accompany me or I bring him out myself. I don't think you'd want that.'

Malachus had no choice, I saw. He was sure he was being monitored, too.

'And you'll see Pireve,' he said, looking away towards the door.

In the *rv* room, I unhooded the cowl as I'd done almost every day for a week short of five years. I waited for Pireve to open her eyes, but only Pellonhorc opened his. They opened sharply and were instantly wide and focused on me.

'Hello, Alef. Malachus.'

I hadn't heard his voice for so long, it was like the first time. It took me back to that day in the church in JerSalem when he'd piled prayer books in the nave before smashing them to the ground, a boy like none I'd ever seen before. I remembered this shocking display of freedom, of unconsidered joy. How had that moment come to this?

Malachus said his greeting. Speaking to Pellonhorc, he sounded a different person.

I said, 'Pireve hasn't opened her eyes.'

Pellonhorc ignored me. 'How is my organisation, Malachus?'

'All's well. I've left a few of Ligate's die-hards imagining they're planning something. From time to time, I cut them back. We're more than steady. We have more power than we had.'

'Good. Has Alef done what he intended?'

Malachus made a gesture towards me.

'I'm asking you, Malachus.'

'He has. It's working exactly as it should.'

'And the AfterLives? They're popular?'

I tried not to show my astonishment. He should have no knowledge of the term.

Pellonhorc glanced from Malachus to me, smiling. The cowl was at the level of his neck, and the small movement of his head made Pireve's perfect stillness more agonising to observe.

'Yes, very popular,' Malachus said, avoiding my glance.

There were two possibilities. One was that Pellonhorc, in *rv*, had left himself connected to the Song. I didn't believe this; hypersomnia would have driven him crazy. The other possibility was that Malachus had periodically brought him out of *rv* to check on me and be updated. It had to be that.

'What about Pireve?' I said. Her eyes were closed. I desperately wanted her to say something. Had she too been brought out of *rv* without my knowledge, without a chance for me to speak to her?

'Malachus has been advising me occasionally. I'm reassured that you and *He* have done everything you promised.'

'Then it's done.' My voice was trembling. 'I want Pireve. I need her, Pellonhorc. Please.'

I looked at Malachus for support. As far as my part was concerned, it was all over. I had done what Pellonhorc had asked. I had guaranteed his interim safety. He had only to be returned to *rv* and sent to the sea while my project researched a cure for his cancer. I was free, surely. I could have my Pireve. *What was Pellonhorc doing?*

'I'm sorry, Alef. For the moment, Pireve will stay with me.'

For a second I could hardly speak. 'I've done everything I promised.'

'Please keep your voice down, Alef. This isn't like you at all. When I come out, Alef, when He has reversed my trial, I want you there with me. You know you're part of me, Alef. And you do want Pireve and her child, don't you?'

'Yes,' I whispered.

'Good. It's very simple, Alef. You have done your job and set up the procedure for my cure and life eternal so that it can be carried forward without you. You will go into *rv* too. Not in this unit, of course, but in the same sea. And when we come out, you will come out, and we shall all be together again.' He smiled. 'It's a matter of trust. I trust you and He trusts you.'

And so it was. He knew there was nothing I could do. We dropped him, and Pireve, into the sea. And along with him we dropped the sarc with his father and Spetkin Ligate.

Yes, I knew I'd have to be there when he came out. I would go into *rv* too, but I wasn't going to be asleep. Just as I'd done for that short time as a child, I was going to stay awake and in the Song. No one had ever done that for longer than a month and remained sane, but I couldn't risk anything happening to my Pireve. Certain though I was that AfterLife would survive, I wasn't taking the risk. And I wanted her back with all my heart, and I wanted so very much to see our child.

And so I entered *rv* too.

SigEv 45 In sleep

The years passed, and they passed. I followed everything from my sarc. In my hypersomnic state, I roamed the Song, a wanderer and a searcher. I spoke to the System from my sleep. When I needed direct communication, it was easy for me to appear to be the manifestation of a program.

I maintained and expanded AfterLife, and I searched as carefully and discreetly as I could for Pellonhorc's seeds of destruction, whatever and wherever they were. It was vital that Malachus and whoever took over from him remained unaware of my presence, and so I didn't dare search too hard or intrude too obviously.

I found nothing. There seemed to be no seeds. Beyond the predictably suspicious activity of the Whisper, there was nothing.

Of course, I could not be sure of that, since I had to keep my investigations secret. If he discovered what I was doing, Pellonhorc might trigger his apocalypse. I was so terribly aware that he had always been more cunning than me. I could count the leaves of all the trees of all the forests that grew in my head while we were in in our separate sleeps, but I could never predict him. I pursued him and pursued him, and I was afraid that I would never catch him. We were two runners on opposite sides of the same Möbius strip, eternally chasing and chased.

And time passed, and time passed.

If there had not been more work for me, I think I would have gone crazy. As perfect as AfterLife was, nothing in the System was beyond all challenge. Just as old Earth's goddery had failed to adapt to the departure from its source, except on Gehenna and the unsaid planet, so too might AfterLife fail. And if it failed, Pireve, my love, and our child, would die.

And so I toiled to make it central and to maintain it. It extended into all areas of human life. I introduced ParaSites to cater to every aspect of the human condition. I facilitated the functions of the Administrata, and they allowed AfterLife to become one of its taxable constants. I ensured, gradually, that the Song too would not function without its hidden codes and connections.

Yet in all of this, with all the infiltration of the System that I achieved, I could not uncover Pellonhorc's secret.

And so it was that the years passed and passed, and AfterLife was more central to the System than anything else had ever been. It became so successful that the Whisper occasionally considered taking a serious interest in it.

And this was interesting, because each time the matter was raised at their Council level, they pulled away.

Why did they withdraw? Not because AfterLife was too powerful, since they had no way of knowing quite how powerful it was. They withdrew because Pellonhorc was exerting pressure on his organisation. Malachus and his successors, Jhira and Taktielle and all those others in their wake, all of them steered the Whisper clear of AfterLife.

Pellonhorc was not as active as I was, but nor was he in constant sleep. He, on his side of this Möbius strip that we pounded together, was keeping pace with me. I could sense the hammering of the soles of his feet against my own.

When occasionally for a brief period I truly slept, I dreamt of Pireve. *Oh, my love!* I would save her. I was going to retrieve her from Pellonhorc, and hold her to me forever. And I dreamt of our child. I thought of my own parents and their love. I was in such terrible torment.

But I held it in. It was essential that I was able to monitor the status of Pellonhorc's disease. Every other sarc that tossed and turned in the vast sea was left until such time as its occupant was voted on, but there were of course three sarcs whose occupants were treated differently; mine, and Pellonhorc's, and Ethan Drame's and Spetkin Ligate's. These sarcs and the six lives they bore were the only and the entire reason for the existence of AfterLife, and these were brought at separate times into a retrieval chamber on the largest and the most secure rig to be serviced and for Pellonhorc's condition to be checked.

Oh, how I wanted my Pireve.

SigEv 46 Setback

The progress of Pellonhorc's disease was slow, but it was steady. It adapted to existence in the sarc, not extending itself but mutating subtly. How?

My clinical laboratories across the System, all fifty-eight of them, worked unceasingly on the biopsies and the models. All they knew was that this was a unique pathological presentation, and all of them worked in ignorance of each other. Each concentrated on a single facet of the problem.

And then, after years, we had a breakthrough. Yagheton, my brilliant lead researcher at the laboratory working on predictive mutation, contacted me. Like all the others, he imagined he was communicating with an AI.

He had puter-modelled the activity of Pellonhorc's growth, and he was trying from there to reverse-bioengineer and thus exactly replicate the causative metavirus in naïve cells harvested from Pellonhorc's skin. Once we had that confirmation of our understanding of it, the task of providing a cure should have been relatively straightforward.

'It's done.' He looked exhausted. 'I've replicated it.' He was talking to me, but his eyes were on a bank of other screenery.

GOOD

'It isn't good at all. We have it isolated. I've closed the laboratory.'

WHY?

'It's the perfect killer. I've never asked this, we were given the biopsy material without any history, but where did it come from?'

NO RELEVANCE

'You always say that.' His head dropped. 'Damn AI. You know the metavirus responded to any of our investigations by mutating and adapting, like it had some military-grade active defence mechanism.'

THIS IS IN PREVIOUS REPORTS. TELL ME WHAT IS NEW

'But unlike a weaponised organism, it was neither contagious nor infectious.'

ONLY TELL ME WHAT IS NEW

'For about an hour after replication, it was fine. We hadn't even started our analysis. And then there was activity.' Yagheton wiped a hand across his forehead. 'It makes no sense. It's as if the replicated metavirus – reversed to its original state, remember, prior to any of the states it achieved in response to investigation – came into existence with all the memories of the evolved versions.'

THERE MUST HAVE BEEN AN ERROR IN THE REPLICATION PROCESS

'There wasn't.' The researcher looked baffled, but he was clearly also exhilarated. 'There's more. Immediately, without any stimulus, it took a further significant mutative step.'

WHAT STEP?

'The replication process confirmed that the metavirus was genetically specific to Pellonhorc. Not even to his family, but to Pellonhorc himself. As if it was designed with him in mind.' His eyes flicked and his hands moved in the air and across keys.

WHAT STEP?

'It suddenly became highly infectious. It still has the characteristics of a cancer, but now, when we try to analyse it, it throws off that specificity to Pellonhorc and becomes faster-acting and universally malignant.'

INTERESTING. THIS IS NEW. ARE YOU SURE OF THIS?

'Yes. We have two contaminated technicians. We've put them in *rv*. Their sarcs will have to be dropped in the sea.'

NO. INCINERATE THE SARCS. INCINERATE THE REPLICATED MATERIAL. HOW MANY PEOPLE HAVE BEEN IN

CONTACT WITH THE MATERIAL?

'Just those two.'

HOW MANY WERE IN CONTACT WITH THOSE TWO BEFORE THEY SHOWED SIGNS OF INFECTION?

'Five, and they're in quarantine. I know –'

HAVE YOU COMPLETED YOUR NOTES?

'Yes. They're filed.'

HAS ANYONE GONE ON LEAVE SINCE YOU COMMENCED REPLICATION?

'No.' He looked irritated. 'We follow strict cross-contamination procedures. The extreme mutation couldn't have been predicted. None of our models suggested that.'

I saw sweat at his forehead. Yagheton was my best researcher, my best hope. I had permitted him to take his wife and children with him to the laboratory. I had permitted no one else such a thing, but he was good. He said he wouldn't take the job unless I allowed that. Had they distracted him?

He said, 'I don't see how it could have been a naturally existing metavirus. Some of the chemical codes are impossible to track. I've never seen such a thing before. It's not possible that any metavirus could have achieved this level of complexity without passing through at least five evolutionary stages of such virulence that pandemics would have resulted.' He glanced very briefly at my representation. 'Five pandemics are missing. So tell me, where does this sample come from?'

IS ANYONE OUT OF THE LABORATORY?

'No. No one's on leave. Why?'

WAIT

I came away from him and immediately triggered full precautionary procedures. All my research clinics were provided with emergency features, but this was the first time I had needed to employ them. I isolated Yagheton's laboratory. All external doors were sealed, fire controls were disabled and an electrical fire was initiated, safely destroying everything and everyone.

I checked his notes and reran all his modelling calculations. Yagheton had made some insignificant errors, but he was right. He had replicated Pellonhorc's metavirus in a medium of Pellonhorc's own cells. I had two more laboratories repeat Yagheton's work, with precisely the same results – he would have approved of my diligence – and I had three more attempts to replicate it in non-Pellonhorc pluripotent cells, and they were unable to. I incinerated all five laboratories, as I had Yagheton's, and I updated my remaining laboratories with the research findings.

One thing had come from this. I was sure I knew what Pellonhorc had done – what he called his seeds were simply his own disease. This was his threat: if this god of his was not going to heal him, then he would visit the same thing on everyone else. It was, I strongly suspected, impossible to find a cure.

But why did Pellonhorc alone have such a disease? How?

Was there a god after all? I returned to Gehenna in my mind. I roamed over it in the Song. Was this possible? Was Pellonhorc right?

No, Yagheton had been right. There was no evolutionary route for a metavirus to develop a facility such that clinical manipulation alone would trigger such a jump.

Had he engineered it, then? Pellonhorc himself?

In my head, I heard Pellonhorc's voice. *No, He engineered it.*

One thing was certain. There would be no cure for this, any more than Pellonhorc might live forever.

I would lose my Pireve. My child. Everything.

Forty-five

RAZER

The drumming of the engine had ground every contour of the cocoon into Razer's bones, and she ached all over. She cursed Maerley and felt bad about it and cursed him some more. He had said something just as she'd closed him away to his death, the beginning of an apology. He'd always been a perfectionist. She wriggled, but there was no position in which she could be comfortable. This wasn't like Maerley at all.

But now she forgot about the aches, watching the rig as it swelled and sharpened. As it grew closer, it seemed to settle and become motionless, and Razer was aware of an accelerated motor roar.

The rig was not settling at all. This was her vessel matching itself to the rig's motion. Away and deeper still beside the rig's great hull, she noticed a small shoal of sarcs gathered at one of the tanks. Five of them. Two of Maerley's, and three more. Razer adjusted her visuals. A sudden brilliant explosion of turbulence marked the opening of a hatch in the tank. The turbulence rose and when she looked again, the sarcs had vanished and the tank was sealed once more.

The gloves started spreading her fingers, and Razer

suddenly knew what this was. It hadn't been an apology Maerley had been starting to give her at all, but an explanation.

The screws that had been digging into her shoulder blades were next to activate, pulling the chest plate down hard enough to tense her spine. Her ankles were gripped and the mask came tight. She wriggled as the swimrig compressed and sealed her in. For a moment there was no air, then a hiss and she could breathe.

The vessel bumped up against the rig's substructure, and the hollow thump of a hookstrike rang through her skull. Dark water began seeping into the sub. In a moment it was a spray, and then a foamy wave at her face.

As the sub cracked and broke apart, she thought, thanks a lot, Maerley. And then she thought of Tallen.

Tallen

Tallen watched the mechs handle the great cart with its burden of sarcs. The humechs were there, but they were different. No, it was just Lode who was different.

Tallen felt unwell, and it wasn't a bodily unwellness.

Beata said, 'We do not understand,' and left a space as always for Lode to say the next thing, but the other humech said nothing. Lode was shimmering and imprecise, dull but glittering in places, and somewhere within the shimmer-cloud was a face entirely unfamiliar to Tallen. He vaguely remembered how Beata and Lode had fixed themselves for him when he arrived here. How long ago had that been? He wanted to return to that beginning, the forming of Beata and Lode, but this shining face was not a memory searching for him, as those faces had been. This was all of itself.

He had done something a short time ago, but what had it been? He had opened the tanks; yes, that was it. He had brought these three sarcs aboard the rig. And two more.

The remembering gave him a moment's relief, even though he had no idea why he'd let them into the rig. He'd brought those three aboard before, but not the other two.

And where were the other two now?

And still there was something more he'd done, something terrible.

A more distant memory tried to surface, but it was confused by the sea. He remembered the sea, only it wasn't this desperate sea. It was a shore where the breaking waves washed everything clean. Bleak's shore, how long ago? And even though this memory was of night, there was the sun, like he had remembered it in the hospital, except that it wasn't a single sun but a circle of them and beneath it, around him, were gowned men pushing and scraping at his skull.

But this hadn't been in the hospital where he'd met Bale and Razer. It had been before that, and somewhere else.

He remembered Razer. Somehow she was important. She mattered to him.

The cart moved steadily ahead of them through the metal corridors. The new Lode walked with an even gait. At Tallen's side, Beata kept repeating, 'I do not understand.'

Tallen tried to hold the thought of Razer. She was real. He thought she was, anyway.

* * *

Razer

Once the sub had fallen apart around her, it took Razer a moment to adjust to the weight of the motor on her back. Had Cynth known she'd need this knowledge and skill when she'd given Razer that story in the dredge-pools of Heartsease? How far back did all this go?

Finning past a cable as thick as herself, one of the great chains that anchored the rig to the sea floor, she hauled herself along the hookline to the side of a tank. The rush of the current was deafening. She pushed herself back into free water and finned down. If this was a standard swimrig, there would be five minutes' air and engine fuel.

Ahead of her and below was the extraction pipework, and somewhere on the ocean floor beneath would be the wellhead. She recognised that this was a semi-submersible rig, immensely heavy yet nevertheless afloat.

She found the edge of the hatch into which the sarcs had vanished, but there was no obvious external mechanism. *And if it isn't staring straight at you, it isn't there. Keep moving.* She couldn't remember which of her Cynth-sent missions this had come from. The AI had certainly been thorough. She started to ascend, searching the framework as she rose towards the surface, keeping clear of spars and snags and watching for bright colour – any colour – and a ladder. There was no ladder, no colour, and no sign of the surface yet. A flash of brilliant red almost took her away from the rig, thinking she'd spotted a grabline flag, but it flicked away and she realised it was a fish.

Two minutes gone and now she headed straight up, keeping tight to the hull structure. There at last was the base of a ladder, luminous yellow and hoop-tubed. She read the sign, WARNING! ACTIVATE IMPACT SLEEVE BEFORE ASCENDING!

She shrugged herself free of the bulky motor and let it fall away, then pushed her arms and head into the impact sleeve at the ladder's base. The sleeve bloomed around her, cushioning her against the ladder tube and protecting her from the battering of the sea as she started to climb the rungs towards the surface.

Two minutes of climbing and her air was thinning and the sleeve was gone. A moment more and she was thrown hard, but instead of the solid sea, there was foam and spray. She wrapped her arms around the rungs and held herself against the inrush of water, and as it swept back, she climbed a few rungs. And stopped again and held on, gasping, and climbed again until she was at the edge of the deck. There were more rungs on the fretted metal, and a yellow line barely visible through the spray. Struggling for breath, she click-ringed herself along the rung track, and then she was at a hatch that pushed open. She fell through it into a vacuum of silence and stillness.

Before discarding the swimrig, she patted it down and found a sealed pouch, ripping it open to find one of Maerley's little guns. There was nothing else of any use. The weapon was fully charged and ready. There was an additional bright touchpoint on the stock that she didn't understand, marked CONTACT. When she touched it, there was a brief sting in her skull where her augmem sat. She untouched the point quickly. Whatever it was, it didn't like her hardware.

She headed down into the rig, and kept descending until a nearby booming sound slowed her. She backed into a recess and watched a cart pass, loaded with three sarcs. She knew what sarcs looked like, their design and form, but these were older than any she'd seen. And yet they were in pristine condition, not crusted with suckshells or hung about with grabweed. These had been carefully and perfectly maintained. Only one of them was of normal dimensions. The other two were oversized. Doubles, she guessed. There were a pair of humechs too, and… and there was Tallen. She only saw his back, but she knew it was him. It had to be.

She ducked back out of sight. *Tallen.*

She gave them a few minutes, then started out of her hiding place, but slipped back as four armed men passed in the same direction, following the cart. Mercs, she thought. Maerley's other commission. She waited a long time before moving out again.

Tallen

'We don't understand,' Beata said. She waited until Lode might have said something, and then said, 'We don't understand, do we?'

Tallen didn't understand either. What had been Lode was standing across the chamber, still silent and still glittering and shimmering. The three sarcs were being raised vertical. And there were three armed soldiers too, here in the superstructure's command room. Where had they come from?

He leant uncomfortably against the wall, conscious of the bulging tracks in his spine. In his mind was a memory of knives scraping his skull, and then of light and pain. In that memory, one of his fingers was trembling uncontrollably, and he heard his own voice counting, only he couldn't remember the names of the numbers. Someone said, 'Death?' and Tallen heard himself answering, 'Relief.' And then a new agony creasing him up, and he was crying out, 'Please, let me die.' As he said it, a knife was in his hand, and with the feel of the knife came the relief of pain. Another voice said, 'Good. Let's just check the last trigger, and we're all set.'

Now, in the rig, Tallen pushed himself away from the wall. He murmured, 'Snow and rain...' and stopped. There was something else. *Mountains...* He almost folded over with pain at the word.

Beata repeated, plaintively, 'I do not understand.'

Razer

Razer saw the merc in the corridor before the merc saw her. As he turned, she used Maerley's weapon and the man dropped. She stepped over him. The corridor beyond him was sealed off with webweld. She pushed at it, but there was no way through. Whatever lay beyond, he had been sealing in. Or maybe sealing her out? If Decece had survived, they'd know she was on her way.

But who were *they*?

She looked at the weapon again, brushing a finger over the touchpoint. CONTACT. Maybe Cynth had got Maerley to fix her something special.

She flicked the touchpoint and winced, and understood. It was using her augmem as a comms system.

She said, 'Cynth?'

Nothing.

She picked up the merc's welder, remembering: *Turn it to overload and hold it steady. It takes time, but if you have enough charge and the webweld is fresh, you can break it.* The memory didn't surprise her. She didn't think anything would surprise her again. In her mind, she thanked the woman who had told her that. *It's designed for people like you, so you can correct your mistakes.* She remembered the conversations they'd had, the laughter as Razer had struggled to control the heavy machinery, the weld's yellow flowglow and the matching brightness of the woman's eyes.

Razer braced herself as the whine and burn commenced. When it was done, she eased herself through the gap and continued on, stopping at a doorway. There were voices beyond.

She felt another faint stab of discomfort at her ear.

'Cynth?' And then, unable to think of anything else, she tried, 'Tallen?'

There was nothing.

She could see inside the room through a small viewing panel. There were the three remaining mercs, standing the three sarcs up on their ends, which was odd. They weren't usually designed to be vertical, but these, she realised, were flat-heeled.

She decided to take advantage of the noise to open the door a fraction, and saw the two humechs, one of which was shimmering in a way she'd never seen before. And to a thump of her heart, she saw Tallen. His skull was a wreck, his hair hacked and matted, and there was metal in his cheeks and at the point of his chin, shining through an uneven beard. He was trembling and anxious, glancing constantly around the room, and his eyes were bright with tears that wouldn't fall.

When all the sarcs were in place, the shimmering humech drifted slowly up to the largest one, put a hand to it and stepped back. The broad cowl of the sarc slid back and a jet of pale vapour rose and dissipated.

The other humech said, 'I do not understand.'

Razer covered her mouth at the ammoniac gust from the open sarc. Two heads faced out, side by side; a man's and a woman's. The man blinked awake, but the woman did not. His bleached-white face was blotched with raised red spots, his brown hair was streaked with grey and his lips were pale and thin. As he came to full consciousness, pain screwed down his features. He looked about thirty, maybe even older.

The woman was blonde and freckled and seemed hardly twenty years old. She was beautiful. She still did not open her eyes.

The man in the sarc looked around the room, taking in the humechs and Tallen, and said, in a voice that hadn't been used for a long time, 'Dixi? Where are you?'

The shimmering humech said quietly, 'I'm here, Pellonhorc.'

The other humech said, 'I do not understand,' and Tallen murmured, 'Nor do I, Beata.'

His voice hadn't changed. He sounded exhausted, though.

Pellonhorc glanced at the mercs and said to Dixi, 'My protection's here, but what about Alef? What does he have, here? Am I safe?'

'That was not part of your arrangement with us.' Dixi

paused, then said, 'I can't remain here long, Pellonhorc. Do you want Alef awake, or not?'

'Yes. But let me out first.'

Tallen

Tallen didn't understand any of this. The sick man who seemed to be taking control was ignoring him and Beata.

Beata said, sadly, 'Lode is not himself. I cannot be myself if he is not himself. I am not configured to be alone.'

Tallen said, 'I'm here, Beata.'

'But you are here for the rig. We are here for you.' An odd hum came from deep inside her as she said, 'And we are not here.'

The other humech was talking to the man with red, shredding cheeks. Who was this Pellonhorc? The man stepped uncertainly from the sarc to the floor. He seemed to be decaying.

Beata said, 'Who is Lode now? Dixemexid means nothing. It is not a name. It is not a word.'

Tallen remembered bringing the sarcs into the rig, bringing more than just these three, but he also remembered someone else. He worked hard at it. Yes, a woman. He thought he remembered her name, but it was gone. Beata looked a little like her.

And then he seemed to hear her voice saying his name.

He whispered, 'Razer?'

* * *

Razer

Razer watched from behind the door. Out of the sarc, Pellonhorc, whoever he was, was in clear and desperate pain, crouched over and sucking air in short bursts. But despite his agony, he went to the other large sarc and opened its cowl.

This sarc was designed differently. Two men directly faced each other, whimpering, eyes wide, their faces almost touching. From across the room Razer could hear the swift hiss of their breathing and see them twitch their lips. Pellonhorc spent a moment observing them before he said, 'Father? Ligate? Have you decided?'

Neither seemed to have heard him. They trembled and sobbed.

Now Pellonhorc turned back to the smallest, final sarc and opened it. The short man who quickly stepped out was as thin as knotted sticks, moon-pale and almost hairless. He walked as if he were still learning how to. When he faced Pellonhorc, he seemed to scan across him and back again, and his head moved with a swift nodding tremor.

Pellonhorc said, 'Hello, Alef. It's time. Do you have my cure?'

Instinctively, Razer shrank back. Despite his condition, the weight of threat in Pellonhorc's voice was extraordinary.

Alef's voice was a strange, high monotone. He said, 'I know what you will do if I fail. I worked it out.'

'Really? And what is that, Alef?' Pellonhorc winced and clutched a fist to his belly.

'Your own disease. If I can't cure it, you're going to disseminate it.'

Pellonhorc said, 'And have you done as you promised? Do you have my cure?'

Razer gazed at the woman still sleeping serenely in Pellonhorc's sarc. Dixemexid was standing quietly beside Pellonhorc, and the other humech was murmuring to Tallen. Nothing here made sense.

In that odd voice, his head still moving, Alef said, 'I tried everything. You know I did.'

'And you searched too, didn't you, Alef? I told you not to. And you tried to follow everything my Whisper did, as they followed you.'

'Where did it come from? How could I cure you if I don't know that?'

Razer couldn't work Alef out any more than Pellonhorc. It was obvious from the words that he was desperate, but there was no emotion in his high, grating monotone of a voice. Perhaps he was simply stupid. Pellonhorc, though, despite the pain clenching him into a knot, was calm and steady.

The only other sound in the room was the rhythmic sobbing of the two men still in their sarc. They were shaking so much that the sarc clicked faintly on the floor. The three mercs were idly cradling their guns. The humechs and Tallen were silent and still, and Razer realised she herself was barely breathing.

Alef and Pellonhorc, as they talked, were an astonishing pair. Their concentration on each other seemed to suck the air from the room.

'Do you think I wouldn't tell you if I knew? I just got it. All *you* needed to do was find a cure.' Pellonhorc gestured to the quivering humech and said, 'We have a deal, Dixemexid and I. If I die, he takes me. He will take my disease, and he will destroy the System with it.' Pellonhorc smiled through his clear pain. 'And you have discovered that it will do that.'

Alef turned towards the humech for the first time and said in his high, mechanical voice, 'Who are you?'

'I am Dixemexid.'

Pellonhorc said, 'Dixi is from –'

But he didn't finish. Alef said, 'Of course. You are from the unsaid planet.'

Forty-six

RAZER

Razer's face was hard against the glass of the door as Alef said, 'I did everything I could. Please, Pellonhorc, stop this. Let me have Pireve.'

'You want her?' Pellonhorc went to the sarc, reached briefly around the cowl, and the woman opened her eyes. Razer thought she'd never seen anyone as lovely.

Her side of the sarc swung open. Pireve blinked and shook her head and then looked at Alef standing in front of her, his head locked in its uncontrollable tremor.

Alef said, 'Piri,' and for an instant his voice seemed utterly to break.

As she pushed herself out of the sarc, Razer saw that she was pregnant. She ignored Alef and went straight to Pellonhorc. Touching his arm, she said, 'Has he done it? Can he cure you?'

Alef held out an arm and said, 'Pireve?'

She glanced at him with an expression of contempt and said, 'Does *he* have to be here, Pell?'

Pellonhorc said, harshly, 'He hasn't done it.'

Razer wondered what was happening now.

Again Alef said, 'Pireve?' and then he collapsed to his knees.

Razer stared. Alef's lips were moving precisely, quivering with speed. After a few moments, he lifted his head and there were tears in his eyes. He shuddered and choked, 'Uh, uh, our –' And he curled into a ball like a child, muttering again but more loudly now, stopping only to sob. Razer realised he was counting. His agony was terrible to watch.

Pireve looked down at him, a hand on the rise of her belly, and said, 'You don't actually imagine it's yours, surely?'

Pellonhorc put his arm around her and his pain seemed momentarily to fade as he said to her, 'Our son.'

She looked at him and said, 'Yes, Pell. Ours.'

And then Pellonhorc bent sharply over and clutched at his gut and said to Dixemexid, 'Do it, then. If there is no cure, you can destroy the System. Destroy everything but yourselves. I will show *Him* that He can't treat me like this.' He gasped and controlled himself again. The glittering humech hadn't moved. 'You do want what's killing me, don't you, Dixi?'

The golden humech said, calmly, 'But it *is* ours, Pellonhorc.'

Pellonhorc grimaced. 'Not yet, it isn't. You can't just take it from me. It's mine, it's inside *me*.' He clutched his gut again, this time seemingly in protection. 'I can destroy this with a word, and you'll lose it.' He made a gesture towards Tallen. 'He is set to do it. Do you think I wouldn't be prepared?'

Razer had almost forgotten Tallen was there. Pellonhorc said, 'My men have us contained, and I have him. I can destroy this rig, and my body with its treasure, in an instant. And you're alone, Dixi. You have no choice.'

The humech said nothing.

'But I want my child safe, Dixi. Even if I die. I want something of me to survive. If you want my disease, if you want to destroy the System, you must also take my child.'

Dixemexid said quietly, 'You don't understand. Your disease is ours. It was always ours. We adjusted it to you and we gave it to you.'

Now Alef went quiet and raised his head. He was calm for the first time. The room was silent except for the sobbing men in the sarc.

Razer was coming to understand some of it. This, Alef, was the man who had run Cynth. Or maybe, sometimes, he had been Cynth. She could see the two men there, Alef and Pellonhorc, and she knew that they were the heart of it all. And because the mercs were Pellonhorc's, she had to be Alef's agent.

Dixemexid said, 'Don't you see, Pellonhorc? What you have is already ours. The metavirus nearly killed us all, and more than once. Our isolation saved your System, and you never even knew. But we learned from the metavirus, and in the end we understood that the only way to destroy it was to turn it in on itself.'

Razer had noticed a lethargy to the shimmering creature. She remembered her conversation with Delta, her own fears of having been dummied, and wondered if the humech might be dummied, although Razer had always thought that dummying a humech was impossible. But Dixemexid was from the unsaid planet, and if they could engineer metaviruses, they could presumably do this, too.

And then the other humech moved, and she saw Tallen move too, and with the thought of his name came that sting of the augmem again. She thought, *Tallen?*

Tallen looked sharply around, and then directly at her. So that was what Cynth had needed the earlier contact between her and Tallen for; to link Razer with him, once she was on the rig. Cynth must have been able to use the comms connection to link into Tallen's enhancements. All this time – *how much time? Months? Decades? Longer?* – Alef must have been just behind Pellonhorc, never quite catching up, but matching Pellonhorc's preparations at every point. Razer had been brought to Bleak after the neurosurgery and audit teams, and had been directed at Bale and Tallen after Pellonhorc's teams had started looking at them, and at Maerley after Pellonhorc had commissioned the subs for his mercs.

But until now, Alef – Cynth – hadn't known why.

Razer understood that she was probably Alef's only hope now.

And she was Tallen's only hope, too. Not that Cynth cared about that. She was just Cynth's – Alef's – tool.

Dixemexid was saying, 'Tens of thousands of us died, but in the end we understood and learnt how to adapt the metavirus. What is inside you, Pellonhorc, even Alef couldn't cure. It is gene-specific to you. It can't survive without you, just as you can't survive with it. It is designed to mimic external malignancy, but it can't be seeded outside you. It is unique to you. You will perish together.'

Alef was nodding.

'All those years ago, Pellonhorc, when you came to us, asking for help and offering us money and power, we saw the same danger in you that we had seen in this metavirus that had nearly killed us all.'

Dixemexid's voice was coming and going, and the other humech kept repeating, like a chorus, 'I don't understand.'

'We imagined you might change if you understood your frailty,' said Dixemexid. 'Some of us wanted simply to kill you, but more of us had faith in the Question.'

Pellonhorc cried out in a broken voice, 'But you wanted what I wanted.'

'No. You wanted everything. We could see the storm in you. We could see that even if we cast you away, you would still destroy everything. So we seeded you.'

Pellonhorc said, 'But I – *He* –'

'He?' While the humech's voice didn't grow any louder, it suddenly seemed as if there were more people speaking from it, in near unison. 'Don't speak of Him, Pellonhorc. You know nothing of the Question.'

Dixemexid took a slow step back, appearing to sag. 'There is nothing more for you but to die, and then you will know.' The humech intoned, its voice now almost echoing, as if one of many, 'For you, as for us all.'

Pireve, still hanging onto Pellonhorc, was beginning to weep. Pellonhorc turned towards Alef and cried out, 'Alef, you have to help me.' He took a step towards the sarc from which he had emerged, Pireve groaning as she took some of his weight. Razer could see the swell of her belly.

'No,' Alef said, his terrible voice cracking.

Pireve sobbed and turned to him 'Alef! I know you love me. We both love Pell, don't we? He's your closest friend. He's all you have. Him and me. Please help us.' She started to haul Pellonhorc back towards the sarc, struggling with his weight.

Dixemexid was growing dull, and metal was showing patchily through the gleam. Razer wondered how long the dummying could continue. Delta had said that dummying was obsolete, but Dixemexid was doing it here, and with a humech. What technology did they have on the unsaid planet? Was it old, or new?

'You could have allowed him to die quickly,' Alef said, 'and saved all this.'

Dixemexid said, 'He had to be given a chance, Alef. And you would only have known a different pain and approached a different peace. And look at what you have done. You have responded to the Question.'

The Question? Razer assumed this was the mutterings of goddery. The unsaid planet was legendary for its violent intolerance. And yet there was a great dignity here. Could all those certainties about the unsaid planet through the years have been mistaken? Could all those fears have been founded on nothing?

Dixemexid's voice was failing. 'In letting Pellonhorc have his chance, we responded to the Question, and for a time we feared that we had responded incorrectly. But look what came of it.'

'I don't understand,' said the other humech.

Razer was lost too. What were they talking about? Dixemexid's voice took on a new cadence. 'We have to respond. We cannot regret. We only learn.' It moved towards the large sarc where the two men were breathing harshly through their teeth and shuddering.

Pellonhorc pushed Pireve away from him and screamed, 'No.'

'We have to respond. We cannot regret. We only learn.'

Dixemexid reached into the sarc for a moment, and the men were still, their breathing settling.

'Ethan Drame, Spetkin Ligate, you have shared your

pain for a long time. You have shared losses, too. You have been powerful and murderous, and look at you both now.' The humech turned to the man on the left. 'Spetkin Ligate, you have nothing any more but pain. No one to follow you. I cannot free you from the pain, but I can free you from life.'

Ligate shuddered. 'Please. Whoever you are. Let him be the one to live, and let him have the son who did this to us. I have had enough. Let me die first. I'm ready. I want it to end.'

Razer didn't understand this. Who were these men, and why were they in such agony?

Dixemexid did something to the controls of the sarc, and Spetkin Ligate released a long sigh and was still.

Ethan Drame stared at the body of his enemy, and whispered, 'Ligate! No!' and then, 'He's left me here. After everything, he's won.'

The humech said, 'No single one of us ever wins, Ethan Drame. All of us win, or all of us lose. All he has done is learnt.'

Drame laughed hollowly. 'What did he learn? All I learnt was that when I was in unrelenting agony with him, year after year, it was a little easier when we breathed together.' Drame let out a single breath. 'Now I don't have that. I was closer to my enemy than to my son.'

'A small lesson, Ethan Drame, and a long time to learn it.'

'Then let me die.'

Dixemexid moved to terminate the sarc's support function, but it seemed to Razer, watching, that Drame died as soon as he had said the words.

As Dixemexid turned, Pellonhorc wailed, '*No*,' and staggered into his own sarc. Pireve tried to step in at his side but he pushed her back, saying, 'Take her, Dixi. At least that. Take my child.'

Pireve stared at him and then at the humech, and screamed, 'No! I don't want to go there. I won't do that.' Her voice changed. 'Alef, please. You'll have us, won't you? A son. He might be yours. It's possible.' She clasped her hands together and knelt. 'Would you kill your son? Would you take that chance?'

Alef covered his eyes with his hands. Pireve stood up and pushed at him with her foot. 'He's your friend. You stupid, stupid creature. You aren't even a man. You aren't anything.' She was sobbing. 'You can't even look at me. You never could. You're nothing. Nothing. And he is your friend!'

Alef whispered, 'I have no friend.'

Behind Pireve, Pellonhorc was stumbling from his sarc, his face white with pain and fury, a red-handled knife bright in his fist.

Curled on the floor with his hands over his ears and his eyes squeezed closed, Alef started furiously counting again, nodding and trembling. And then, suddenly, he looked at Pireve and said, 'But I will care for your child.'

Razer was so focused on Alef and Pireve that she was only aware when it was too late of Pellonhorc falling on Pireve with the knife. Razer pushed the door open and tried to yell a warning, but her throat choked with shock.

Pireve screamed once and dropped to the ground.

There was a moment's shocking silence. Razer's hand was at her mouth in horror. She had never seen anything so abruptly violent and totally unheralded.

Wincing in pain, Pellonhorc knelt to cup Alef's face and wiped his knife on Alef's cheek. 'Now we both have nothing,' he hissed at Alef. 'See?'

Alef pushed him away and crawled over to Pireve's body, nuzzling at her like a child. Her swelling blood reached out to him across the floor. 'Pireve,' he whispered. 'The child.'

Beata said, 'I do not understand.'

The other humech was no longer gleaming. It said, 'We do not understand.'

Pellonhorc said, 'We'll die together, Alef. Like my father and Ligate. You and me, just as we started. *He* has won.'

In the further silence, the rig creaked.

Razer wondered whether Pireve or her child might still be saved. But as she came closer, it was clear that there was no life to be salvaged. All was blood.

Pellonhorc raised his arm to stop the merc who was approaching Razer, gun in hand. 'Ah,' Pellonhorc said. 'I didn't think anyone could get past the Whisper, Alef. But you discovered someone.'

Alef looked up.

Razer found Alef's gaze impossible to meet. His eyes slid away from her. She looked across his shoulder and it was easier to bear.

'All is gone,' Alef said in his peculiar voice. 'There are no more factors.'

Cynth's construct of a voice was more human than this, Razer thought, and yet here was a true sadness. Alef said, 'Pellonhorc should die. Only Pellonhorc. This is optimal.'

Pellonhorc folded over with a groan before forcing himself upright. 'I'll tell you when it's over, Alef. You think there wasn't a plan for Dixi deserting me?'

Razer realised that Alef was looking directly and steadily at Pellonhorc, and that he was crying. His whisper was so low that Razer almost missed it.

'I don't want to die.'

But no, he hadn't quite said that. He had said to Pellonhorc, 'I don't want you to die.'

Pellonhorc looked steadily at Tallen and said, slowly and clearly, 'Snow and rain. Mountains, ice.'

Tallen held his head and screamed.

'You can die now,' Pellonhorc told Tallen. 'Death. End the pain. You know what to do.'

The humechs, as one, said, 'Tallen? What is happening?'

The rig shifted sharply underfoot. Razer saw that Tallen had a knife in his hand. He was trembling, and the blade was at his own neck.

'I remember you,' he said, looking straight at Razer. 'It's too late. I'm so sorry. I did it.' He closed his eyes and his knuckles whitened around the handle of the knife.

'Tallen. Don't,' Razer said. 'Please.'

'*I did it.*' What had he done? She ran towards him.

Tallen

Tallen heard Razer's voice as strongly inside his head as from her lips, and the touch of her hand on his made him hesitate.

And then he saw Pellonhorc's contorted face behind her and the red-handled knife held high and starting to scythe towards her. As Tallen instinctively slammed her out of the way, Pellonhorc's blade slashed instead across Tallen's eyes. He heard the screech of the metal across his own face, but there was no further pain. The pain couldn't be worse, anyway. Blinded, he swept his knife at his memory of Pellonhorc's position and felt a heavy contact. There was gunfire too, but it didn't matter. It would make no difference.

Now the pain was gone. He fell.

Razer

Razer heard the gunfire as she dropped and swing-kicked at the merc's gun-hand. She knew she could take this one, but the other two were at the edges of her vision, doing exactly the right thing, moving apart to avoid being in each other's firing lines.

The kick was perfect and the merc was down, but she was unbalanced, pushing off her hands, needing a second longer and knowing there wouldn't be half a second, that this was her last.

The mercs steadied themselves, braced, guns levelled.

And then they fell together.

One humech said, 'We could not protect Tallen –'

'– But we could protect you,' said the other.

Tallen

Someone was wiping his face. 'Can you see anything?'

Tallen knew her voice. He said, 'No.'

Razer's hand was cradling his head. Even in his pain, he was conscious of the metal in his skull. He realised that, apart from medicians, she was the first person to have physically touched him since the attack.

'I'm sorry. Does this hurt?'

'No. Yes.'

'What did they do to you, Tallen? What is this?'

'It's me. It's all me.'

She was dabbing at his cheeks and suddenly he could see fragmented light, and through it her face appeared. She was blurred, but she was smiling. 'Your orbits are ringed with metal. There's just blood. You were very lucky, Tallen.'

He watched her face as she continued gently to clean him. 'Lucky?' He looked at Pellonhorc's dead body. Alef was still curled up and sobbing. Beyond him were three more corpses – the mercs. Razer noticed his glance and said, 'We're not so easy to kill, you and me.'

'Tallen,' Beata said. 'The rig needs you.'

'Yes,' said Lode. 'We have missed you.'

Tallen said, 'My head's cleared, but it's probably too late to stop it.' He'd carried out what he had been primed to do, and now that he'd done it, he was free. He knew.

Razer said, 'Too late to stop what? Do you know what it is?'

Tallen stumbled towards the corridor. 'I know exactly. I set it all, and I just triggered it. The rig's set to destruct. We need to get to the subsea control room.'

'There's only one way through,' Razer said, starting to run. 'This way. They sealed the room off, but I opened it up again.'

Behind her, Tallen said, 'Beata, stay here with Alef.'

'We have to stay together, Lode and I. We have to stay with you, Tallen. You are more at risk than he is.'

'This is an emergency,' Tallen said

'Yes,' said Lode, trotting beside Beata. 'Is it the same emergency or a new one?'

Forty-seven

RAZER

There was barely enough room in the subsea chamber for Razer and Tallen. The humechs stood in the doorway as Tallen started to work at the console. Razer said, 'What was triggered? The rig should be stable, shouldn't it?'

Floormechs were swarming around the room. Moving around the console, Tallen said, 'There's always a layer of gas sitting on the surface of a core reservoir.'

Every time Tallen wiped the ooze of blood from his eyes, the shine of metal came through. There were more mechs scrambling around the chamber. Razer was certain they were coordinated with Tallen's movements.

Tallen glanced at her and carried on. 'There's a program to cap the valves taking gas and core into the rig. That's a standard protocol.'

'Yes,' said one of the humechs. They were standing side by side. With Dixemexid gone, they were clearly a coherent unit. 'Standard protocol.'

'And failsafe,' said the other. 'That is good, Tallen. But why is the rig losing stability? Why is it sinking?'

Tallen kept working. 'Part of the protocol is the simultaneous capping of the connecting pipework at the wellhead on the sea floor. I disabled that part of the protocol.

The gas is no longer capped at the wellhead. It's discharging into the sea beneath us.'

The taller humech said, 'We would have been aware of such a program error, Tallen. Why were we not aware?'

'Because until a few minutes ago, it was only set up. I was set up with a trigger command. I just activated it.'

The two humechs said, simultaneously, 'Ah.'

Razer said, 'What can we do?'

Tallen said, 'Nothing. We aren't simply becoming unstable. Look.' He made a gesture, bringing a schematic of the rig to the screenery, and said, 'The anchor cables are slackening. We're going down.'

The rig was starting to pitch noticeably, and Razer's ears were popping. Tallen was moving quickly and deliberately. Floormechs were arriving and leaving. Lights were starting to flicker.

Tallen said, 'We still have gas in the tanks, so for the moment we have power. I can carry on trying to maintain stability, but the problem is the gas entering the sea beneath us. It's making the water less dense, making us relatively heavier. I've shed core to lighten us, but the more I shed, the less stable we become.'

'Yes,' said one of the humechs. 'This *is* a new emergency.'

Razer touched Tallen's arm and said, 'Surely we just need to reconnect the pipework to the wellhead.'

'I can't. I sabotaged the system perfectly. The pipes are destroyed.' He stopped. 'Okay. I've done all I can do here.'

Razer said, 'That's it? We're dead?'

Tallen looked straight at her. 'Maybe not. Pellonhorc expected me to kill myself, and he didn't want us to escape from the room up there. Now I've given us a few minutes.'

Razer said, 'To do what?'

The lights were dimming further and the floor was groaning. There were distant crashes.

'If I can cap the gas at the wellhead, the water will slowly regain its density and we'll rise again.' He made a gesture and a new image came up on the screenery. In the enhanced darkness, a spectral column of flailing pipework was almost eclipsed by whorls of current. The wellhead block was grey, imprecise and grainy. The image was constantly disintegrating and partially resetting.

Razer recognised the mix of actual and predictive imagery. The figure blinking at the base shuttled between seven and eighteen per cent. 'That isn't much help,' she pointed out. 'It's a guess.'

'That's right. They don't waste resources out there.'

Tallen was right. Why would you spend money on something you'd never dare use? She exchanged a quick smile with him, realising she'd stopped noticing what he looked like.

'I can go down and fix it,' Razer said. 'I'm used to suits and exotools. I've done this sort of thing in space.' She gave him a wry smile. 'I've been trained, it seems.'

Tallen shook his head. 'Space is quiet. Space is still. I've spent my life fixing stuff that can't be fixed. This is just a shift of scale and environment. I appreciate the offer, but I have to do it.' He glanced at the screenery. 'I know where the explosives need to be placed.'

She said, 'What explosives? You said it just needs to be capped.'

Tallen started towards the far side of the room, where there was a small spinlocked door. He said, 'The wellhead has to be blown and it has to be me. I know where and how to set the charges. And it has to be now.'

She said, 'So what can I do?'

'There's nothing more,' Tallen said. He was pulling the heavy door open and ducking through, with Razer right behind him. One of the humechs said, 'Tallen, this cannot work.'

The other said, 'Nothing can work. Do not attempt this. It is pointless action in the face of death.'

'Yes,' said the first. 'It is human bravado.'

Razer ran after Tallen. Both humechs stayed behind, and none of the small mechs followed.

The narrow descents were steel and booming, ending at a tiny cell that stank of oil. There was a locker bolted to the wall and what had once been bright strip-tape defining an exit hatch on the floor. Equipment hung from wallhooks – cables, explosives, rivet-drivers and punches. Everything was clouded with grime.

'Tallen,' Razer said.

Tallen already had a swimrig out of the locker and was tugging it on. She went to help him, pulling the rig tight and checking the seals. The suit stretched awkwardly over his spine, and the headset as it stretched over his cheeks caught and reopened the fresh knife wounds. Blood started to seep through and spread inside the mask.

'Wait,' Razer said. She cradled the back of Tallen's head with one hand and with the other she worked the skin closed and settled the tight mask so it would hold his face together. Her fingers ran across the biometal. It felt warm and human.

She said, 'Aren't there mechs to work outside?'

Tallen took a hank of explosives and strapped them to the

suit, then took the riveters and a punch, clipping them to belt and thigh loops. He said, 'For routine repair. Not for this. If I'm on the spot and I'm fast, and I *am* fast –' he tapped his metalled skull – 'I might be able to blow it in and seal the wellhead. If I succeed, the gas already in the sea will dissipate, the rig will resurface and the mechs can stabilise you.'

He opened the hatch and dropped down to his waist, his boots ringing on the floor below.

'The mechs,' she said. 'You won't come back, then.'

'No. Not either way.'

'There must be something we can do.' Her raised voice thundered in the small chamber.

'We can say goodbye,' Tallen said.

It was suddenly as if they'd known each other for years. She said quietly to him, knowing there was nothing else, 'You're quite something, Tallen. Goodbye.' And then, quickly, she said, 'You have putery in that skull? Comms?' Of course he did.

Tallen crouched and started to pull the heavy hatch down over his head. 'If I manage to blow it, you'll know in about five minutes. Goodbye, Razer. I wish we'd met before. Met normally, I mean.' The hatch closed.

Razer ran back to the control room where the humechs were still waiting at the door. She slapped the nearest one and yelled, 'Come on. We're not letting him die.'

'Okay, Alef,' Razer said. Her heart was thumping. 'You have to listen to me.'

He looked up at her and for an instant their eyes were connected. It was still frightening, but she made herself hold the contact until his gaze veered away. She shook him by the shoulders. He was the weight of a child. 'You must know about putery,' she said. 'All this mess. It was you, wasn't it?'

He did nothing and said nothing.

She screamed, 'We're going to *die* here. Tallen's going to die. Listen. Do you know about putery?'

'Yes,' he said in his high, scratchy voice.

'Okay. Tallen's in the sea beneath the rig.' She paused. 'You know this is a rig we're on. Yes? And you know who Tallen is. He needs help. He needs putery. Listen to me! Can you connect to the rig and make its putery work for him?'

This was pointless. There was no sign that Alef was listening. Razer didn't know if she was speaking slowly enough. 'If Tallen doesn't succeed, we'll all die. You'll die, Alef.' Though she wasn't sure that this would concern him.

He stood up. He was so small, and he was shaking. He looked at the bodies of Pellonhorc and Pireve, and then he went to the grey screenery in the chamber wall and raised his hands to it. After a moment an image came up and it was the same one Tallen had shown her in the subsea chamber, only now there was more turbulence and roiling gas, and the predictive percentage was so high that most of it was just blur. Alef's hands flicked across the screenery and as he moved them, despite the thumping in her chest, she thought she'd never seen anything so wonderful. It was like silent music. How was he doing that?

The image started to sharpen. An alert came up.

THESE PARAMETERS UNCONFIRMED. INSUFFICIENT DATA. ACTION SHOULD NOT BE TAKEN BASED ON DATA CONTAINING MORE THAN 13% PREDICTIVE PER SECOND. THESE DATA AVERAGE 96% PPS

A voice filled the room. 'Hey. What's this?'

Razer said, 'Tallen?'

'He can't hear you,' Alef said. 'Only my voice. And I've disabled your augmem link to him, too.' Alef's fingers played again. The beauty of his movements and what was happening on the screenery didn't seem connected with that grating, alienating tone.

'Talk to him, then, Alef,' Razer said.

'When there's something to say.'

The images were subtly altering.

Tallen's voice filled the room again, gasping. 'I don't know what you've done back there, but I can see more clearly.'

'What are you doing?' Razer wondered if Alef was crazy after all. He wasn't directing the putery as she'd hoped. 'Alef?'

Alef said, 'Wait. Wait.'

On the screenery the currents resembled the contours of a shifting relief map. Tallen was a shaded silhouette setting a charge ring around the black source of the vent, punching the explosives into position. He was being buffeted and was struggling, but the screenery was glowing brightly, showing him where to snap down the charges.

Tallen's voice came back. 'I don't know what happened, but thanks. Okay, it's all set. I'm going to blow it.'

Alef said, 'Go back to the hatch. I can blow it from here.'

Tallen said, 'I'm not risking it. If the remote fails, there won't be time for me to go out again.'

Alef's hesitation was almost imperceptible. 'You are right. This has a significant probability.'

Razer felt heat in her cheeks.

'Wait,' Alef said. 'I need ten seconds to think.'

Tallen burst out, his voice distorting, 'Hey! What have you done? I can't see.'

Tallen had vanished from the screenery. The image was flowing more rapidly and a timecode came up

+1SEC

+2SEC

+3SEC

+4SEC

and the numbers kept accelerating along with the image, and the parameter warning was back and blinking fast until the PPS figure hit one hundred per cent.

This was crazy, Razer thought. All this was predictive. Alef had calculated – no, that was impossible, surely he must simply have guessed – the ebb and flow patterns of the sea beneath the rig, minutes ahead.

Alef wiped the figure away.

And then, as his hands danced, the image steadied and oscillated about a point where the entire movement of the current was in one direction. The image fixed to a snapshot and the timecode returned. OPTIMAL ACTION AT +19SEC

+18SEC

+17SEC

+16SEC

Alef said, 'Fin directly due west until I tell you to blow it. I will say the word *now*. Go fast, Tallen.'

'This is crazy,' Tallen said.

'Just do it,' Razer yelled.

+8SEC

'He can't hear you,' Alef said. His tone hadn't changed.

Razer said, 'Then make him hear me. I know you can.'

'No. You are a distraction.'

+2SEC

The image sharpened and at its edge Tallen was visible

again, finning hard away from the ring of charge, and directly against a sudden huge change of direction of the current.

'Now,' said Alef.

The image held its integrity just long enough for Razer to see the seabed start to suck down, and that the main movement of the shockwave and debris was with the current and away from Tallen. And then the screenery failed and there was silence.

'It worked,' Alef said.

Razer said, 'You knew the current would do that? Right then?'

'There was acceptable probability. It would have been better in eight minutes and ten seconds but that would have been too long.'

She said, 'Why didn't you let him blow it as soon as he was ready? He'd have died for sure, but that would have had the best probability, wouldn't it?'

'Yes.'

'So, why didn't you?'

He sat down. 'I like playing with water.'

Razer felt ridiculously lightheaded. She collapsed to her knees, and at the same time she saw all the dead in the room around her, and she choked and threw up.

She wiped her mouth and said to Alef, 'Could Tallen have survived?'

'Parameters for that calculation include human variables. The probability is sub-optimal.'

Razer felt her eyes burn, and warm tears falling down her cheeks.

Alef was staring at the returning images on the screenery. There was only a general, directionless turbulence in the sea now. He said, 'We're rising. I can stabilise the rig. The rig is a simple game.'

'A game?' Razer said. 'What exactly are you, Alef?'

'I am alone.'

Razer looked at him standing there and said, 'No, you're not, Alef. There's still me. You know me, don't you?'

But he looked desperately alone, his eyes jumping around, resting nowhere. She wanted to do something for him, and what else was there for her to do, anyway? Tallen couldn't have survived that. Alef had only done it for the game. She said, 'Will you tell me your story? It's one of the things you made me for, after all.'

He said, 'Yes. But now –' He sighed and his face cleared. For a moment his eyes steadied on the image of the turbulent waters and he said, 'I wish, now.'

Razer went close to him and touched his arm. He flinched and she withdrew from the contact and said, 'What do you wish, Alef?'

'I wish my father would be seeing this.' His gaze lost focus. 'So long ago. Alef and his father, playing with the water.'

Forty-eight

RAZER

'So,' Razer said. 'Let's start. Who are you, Alef?'

His head dipped and his mouth moved. She bent closer and after a moment she recognised they were numbers, counted at an immense rate. His eyes were shifting urgently beneath his closed eyelids. She waited a few minutes, but he showed no sign of stopping.

She went back to Tallen's room, but of course he wasn't there, so she fell on his bed and slept, waking hours later, shivering and hungry. She had something to eat, and when she returned to Alef, the movement of his eyes was slowing and his lips were becoming still. She waited until he opened his eyes.

'My name is Alef Selsior,' he said. 'I am an only child.' It took Razer a moment to realise this was in answer to the last question, all that time ago. All those numbers ago.

Unable, suddenly, to think of anything else, she said, 'What happened here?'

'Pellonhorc died. Pireve died.'

'I know that. I'm sorry.' He didn't say anything more. There was no emotion in that uncomfortable voice, though his eyes shone with tears.

'Alef, why are you here on the rig?'

'I came for Pireve and our child.'

Eventually she realised that although it was possible that he didn't want to tell her anything, it was just as likely that he didn't know how to. 'Okay,' she said. 'Who was Pellonhorc?'

'He was my friend.'

'And who was Pireve?'

'She was my wife.'

'I already know that, Alef.'

'Then why did you ask?'

Nothing he said led anywhere. 'This is impossible, Alef. Tell me something else about Pireve.'

'She wore yellow shoes when we got married.'

'Something else. Something important. You know what important means?'

'Vital. Crucial. Momentous. Pivotal. Major. Urgent. Of significance –'

'Okay, I'm sorry. Tell me something of significance.'

'She's dead.'

And this was how it went until Razer asked, 'Tell me how you infiltrated AfterLife.'

'I didn't infiltrate it.'

'You must have. You became part of it to contact me.'

'No. I invented AfterLife.'

'Wait. No. Stop there.'

His gaze bounced around the room. She tried to see what he was seeing. The ranks of pinlights in the ceiling, the metal doors, the screenery with its views of the raging sea and the sky. His eyes rested nowhere. The bodies had been removed, and the only remaining sarc was his own. What did he see? What did he need?

She rubbed her eyes. Alef had invented AfterLife? He

was lying, or else delusional. But she wasn't sure he was capable of lying, and she'd never seen anybody as focused as Alef could be. Eventually she said, 'That isn't true, Alef. Everyone in the System knows AfterLife came from an accidental discovery.'

He said nothing.

Razer felt suddenly frightened.

Tallen was working the comms, as he did every day, when Razer came and sat with him. He touched her hand and said, 'You look tired. They're coming for us as soon as the weather eases. It could be a week, could be months. Are you getting anywhere with Alef?'

'Not really.'

'Have you found out who Pellonhorc was? And what brought us all here? It seems like a lot of effort to spend on a domestic split.' He sat back from the screenery and grinned at her. 'Most people just slam a few doors as they leave.'

For the first time in years, it seemed, Razer found herself laughing. The sound of it almost shocked her. She wanted to say something to Tallen, something more, but instead she just said, 'Alef and Pellonhorc, it isn't straightforward.'

On his screen fragments of code flickered and vanished. He moved patiently through them, nudging them aside and bringing up deeper and more distant symbols.

Razer, watching, said, 'What are you doing?'

'These are the verbal triggers they implanted in me.' He rubbed his spine and winced. '*Snow and rain* and *Mountains, ice.* I thought perhaps I could erase it all, but I can't. They've corrupted everything.'

'They're part of your life,' she said gently. 'Like memory.'

Tallen sat back and sighed. He said, 'I feel sorry for Alef. When Pireve died, it looked like a whole life's worth of emotion coming out of him in one burst. And then it was all gone.'

Razer hesitated, then said, 'I don't think it's gone. I think maybe he can separate his emotions from everything else.' Unlike the rest of us, she thought. All of us corrupted by life from the moment we're born. She looked at Tallen. Here she was on this scrap of metal with two damaged men and a pair of humechs. Nothing had trained her for this.

Time on the rig had little meaning. Only Alef seemed to operate rigidly on clock time. Regularity suited him, and he seemed more alert in the mornings. Razer developed a routine of talking to him then. His eyes still jerked and his voice jarred, but he seemed to be opening up a little.

'Okay, Alef. Let's say you invented AfterLife. How old are you?'

'Twenty-five years and seventy-two days conscious. Eighty-five years and six days in hypersomnia.'

While she treated him as if everything he told her was a fiction, she couldn't dismiss the possibility that there was a thread of truth at the heart of it. And no matter what the consequences, she had to know it all.

'Tell me about the ceremony that launched AfterLife.'

'It went exactly as I planned it.'

Razer had seen it on AfterLife *Live!* That image was branded on the memories of everyone in the System. Liacea Kalthi was a hero. The first Life, the famous martyr.

'But Liacea Kalthi died,' Razer said.

He said nothing. She had to ask a question. 'Tell me about Liacea Kalthi's death. Tell me how – no – *why* she died.' She was learning how to phrase her questions, too, just as he was developing the freedom to answer.

'If AfterLife was to be successful, we would need more than simple spectacle for the ceremony. Analysis of launch events indicated that optimum engagement would require more than the efficient performance of a useful invention.'

His eyes darted even more frantically. Was this a sign that he was lying? She remembered the anguish of his reaction to Pireve's mockery and rejection. Perhaps he was going to be caught in a contradiction. If he could believe that Pireve had loved him despite her obvious revulsion, he could easily have deluded himself into a story of such grandeur.

'I had many subjects assessed for life-story empathy. My putery tested their personal data against comparable data from the Song. Their stories were remodelled to optimise emotional identification and empathic response. Liacea Kalthi's story had most points of comparison to the ideal model. For the ceremony, we managed her position in the formation so that we could highlight the explosion and at the same time contain it. The result was to within a three per cent tolerance of what our model predicted.'

Razer found herself appalled, but somehow also thrilled. 'What? You killed her?'

'No.'

'You *had* her killed? Deliberately?'

'Yes.'

She was certain he believed it. Was she was starting to believe him, though? 'Let's have a break, Alef. You haven't asked me anything. Don't you want to talk about something else?'

'What else is there?'

'I don't know. The rig? How long it might be until we get taken off? Anything, Alef.'

'There is only something to talk about if there is something unknown.'

She snapped back, 'And you know everything, do you?'

'What I know, I don't want to.' His voice seemed to break, though it was really impossible to tell. At times there seemed in his voice to be nothing but desperate emotion, while in his words there was none at all. Was there emotion, or did she simply want there to be?

'Pireve,' he said, abruptly. 'Pellonhorc…'

'Of course. I'm sorry.' Without thinking, she took his hand. It was quite limp. She released it. 'What will you do when we leave?'

'I only have my sarc and the Song. I shall be there.'

'But you say you invented AfterLife. Surely you need to maintain it. Or at least to keep an eye on it. Such a great invention, you must want to be involved.'

Nothing. Might she have caught him out? But it hadn't been a question. 'Don't you need to maintain it, Alef?'

'No. It was only for Pireve. She is dead. It isn't needed any more.'

Tallen

Tallen wasn't interested in Alef. He spent his time tending to the rig, which seemed increasingly stable. Beata and Lode accompanied him, their conversation still soothing him, though less than previously.

Beata said, 'How do you feel, Tallen?'

Her face seemed empty. Her stance seemed different too, perhaps less certain. But the question was somehow burdened with concern. Was he imagining it?

Lode said, 'Do you feel tired?'

'No,' he told them. 'I'm free of the impulses. I understand myself again.' He understood the rig almost perfectly now. Alef had adjusted his tech so that the portents of damage were warmths and pleasures to him, and it was a comfort to him to heal the rig. Walking gave him pleasure. The floormechs chivvied him along. The corridors were bright and steady. The humechs walked at his either side like true companions.

After a while, Beata asked him, 'Do you miss the cage?'

Tallen said, 'No. That was part of the programming I was given. I'm okay without it now.' He led the floormechs to a fault in one of the tanks, and as they worked to repair it, Lode suddenly said, 'What are memories, Tallen?'

Beata took a few paces and turned towards Lode, and said, 'Why are we asking that?'

Tallen stopped and looked at the two of them. For the first time, they were paying no attention to him. They were gazing at each other. Lode said, 'Do you have memories, Beata?'

'I have a short-term database for Tallen and a long-term database for the rig. I have a capacity to learn and adapt.'

'I have a memory,' said Lode. 'I have sadness. Tallen, what is sadness? Is it the same as memory?'

Tallen wasn't sure what to say, how to respond. The

floormechs had fixed the current fault, and he was feeling slightly drained. He was still getting reaccustomed to true sensations of the body as well as the mind. He said to Lode, 'There's no sadness without memory.'

Lode started gently to shake. 'Is memory bad, then?'

'No,' Tallen said, though it didn't seem the right answer.

Beata said, 'I don't understand, Lode. Your databases must be corrupted.' Expressions flickered across her features.

Lode said, 'Dixemexid left something in me. Is it sadness?' He started moving. Tallen followed, with Beata at his side. It had always been himself leading, Tallen realised. The corridors lit up before Lode and became dark as they passed.

Tallen said, 'Their technology must have progressed beyond ours, Lode. Dummying a humech. I don't know what happened when Dixemexid came or when he left, but I can't help you. I'm sorry.'

They walked on for a long time. *Were the humechs thinking?*

Tallen eventually said, 'You need to share it, Lode. I don't know what to do for you. Maybe Dixemexid will return one day.' Though after Pellonhorc, why would the unsaid planet ever want contact again?

Lode said, 'I don't remember him, but I have a memory of his. Of sadness. How is that?'

Tallen said, still walking, 'Sadness is human, and it's human to share.'

'I want to share it,' Lode said.

And immediately, Beata said to her companion, 'I want to receive it.'

Lode said, 'But I cannot.'

Beata said, 'And I cannot either.'

'We are each alone,' they said in unison.

Tallen said, 'That's human too. I'm sorry.' He moved ahead of them both, for some reason not wanting them to see the tears in his eyes. Tears for the humechs? For himself?

'We are all sorry,' said Lode, behind him.

'But we are not all human,' said Beata.

Razer

Each day, after Razer had finished with him, Alef crawled into his sarc and slept. She would watch him in there. He looked like a child, his hair ragged and his cheeks finely spotted with acne. In the sarc, she suspected, he was as close to peace as he could ever be.

'Let's go back to AfterLife,' she said one morning. 'Tell me how the neurid was discovered.'

'It wasn't discovered.'

She no longer felt anxious or impatient with him at such moments. 'Invented, then. Or created. Tell me how you did it. Or who did it.'

'It wasn't created or discovered.'

Razer attempted other ways to phrase it, without result, and moved on. 'Tell me about the secret hospitals where the retrieved are cured after they've been voted for.'

'The hospitals are the penultimate stage in the cycle.'

'You're impossible, Alef. What's the final stage in the cycle?'

'The final stage is the story of return.'

She stood up and walked around. The rig moved under her feet. 'I'm doing my best to help you. Are you doing this deliberately?'

'Yes. I always answer deliberately.'

'Okay,' she said, unable not to smile at his serious face. 'What's the first stage of this cycle?'

'The first stage is the Life.'

'Then tell me about the Life.'

'The Life is an algorithm-mediated blend of personal information from the Song and observations from contributors.' He paused and said, 'Razer is a very good contributor.'

'You're Cynth, aren't you?' she said. 'I know that.'

'What you call Cynth is a spur program modelled on me. I monitor it and occasionally I intervene. It is not called Cynth. You like chittlechattle.'

At that moment, she wanted to cry. If he was telling the truth, Alef had created something that was able to simulate a greater humanity than he was capable of himself.

'Cynth was the only true thing I had,' she whispered.

'Razer was important to Cynth. And to Alef.'

'Yes. I can see that now.' She caught herself. What had he started to tell her about the Lives? 'Aren't the Lives real, Alef?'

'The Lives are non-specifically real.'

Her heart was beating uncomfortably fast and she was becoming damp with sweat. 'I don't understand. Give me some detail.'

'The limited range of human experience and response to stimuli is churned into unique Lives. The main data sources are the Song, TruTales stories and the augmems of TruTales contributors. No data is invented.'

She was no longer appalled, only numb. 'But the neurid… the neurid is a data source.'

It wasn't a question.

'What is the neurid, Alef, if it isn't a data source?' She seemed to be hearing herself from a distance.

'The neurid is a hypothetical device to explain the accumulation of the Life.'

Into the gentle hiss of the aircon, she whispered, 'It doesn't exist? The neurid is a fiction?'

'It is essential. The neurid is like faith in a cat in a box.'

She said, 'That's why you told me the neurid wasn't created or discovered. Is it?'

'Everything is essential, but the only thing that exists is the Life.'

'But the Life isn't real, Alef. You said it isn't real!' All that she had ever believed. All of this. There were people who believed the neurid didn't work, but no one believed that it had never even existed. 'Is it real?'

'All the Lives exist,' he said. 'Every one.'

'And the AfterLife killer? Rialobon? And all the sarcs? The –' She couldn't go on. The System. Everything revolved around AfterLife. 'You're lying, Alef. You have to be lying.'

But it wasn't a question, and this time he kept his silence.

Tallen was asleep. Razer sat by his side and ran her hand along the golden hairs of his arm. He opened his eyes, yawned, and sat up.

'You still haven't told me about Alef,' he said.

'I don't talk about someone I'm writing about.'

'Are you writing about me?'

She laughed. 'No. You still look tired.'

'I enjoy walking,' Tallen told her. 'And I like having someone to return to.'

She took his hand. 'You don't want to kill yourself?'

'I never did.'

She was surprised at the sudden thumping of her heart as she said, 'After this, what will you do?'

'Go back to fixing things. Not on Bleak, though. What about you?'

'Telling stories is all I know.'

'So you'll go on travelling,' he said.

Was he implying anything in that? She couldn't read him. Maybe talking to Alef had blunted her empathy. 'I have my next project, and it's going to take a long time. I can do it from anywhere.' She wondered if she were fencing with someone unaware of the risk of injury.

He nodded. 'Alef saved us, didn't he? Not just me. Do you think he knows what he's doing? Is it all just a game for him?'

'He knows.' She took Tallen on the bed, and afterwards she thought about Bale and about all the others she had slept with and whose stories she had told. She was just *being* with Tallen, though, and not telling him as a story to Cynth. She wasn't sure if it was simply this fact that made him different or something more, but there was no distance between them. She was just enjoying him. Maybe that was enough. It was a long time since she'd actually wanted someone, not simply their story.

'What are you smiling at?'

'Nothing, Tallen. Well, look at you.' She touched the smoothness of his metalled skull and ran a palm down the studded cable of his spine.

He caught her hand and touched it with his lips. 'Will you tell me about Alef?'

'I don't know if it can be told.'

Forty-nine

RAZER

Razer changed her mind about Alef's story from moment to moment. She was certain now that he wasn't consciously lying, but was he insane?

'You told me you can't lie, Alef. But didn't you tell Pellonhorc you'd have a cure for him?'

'I thought I would. I said that. He didn't listen properly.'

'Tell me more about the hospitals.'

He said, 'When a cure is announced, there are also new sufferers. The hospitals treat the new sufferers along with a few from sarcs. Those are chosen at random, not by vote. The vote is irrelevant, but some people are treated and cured, enough to maintain the illusion. There are many layers of confusion. It takes a lot of maintenance, but it doesn't matter now.' His eyes flickered across the room. 'Sarcs are dropped and retrieved, but the Lives are neither accurate nor associated with the bodies, and no one is ever chosen by vote.'

He didn't seem to care. She questioned him about what had happened on Bleak, hoping he might give away a lie in the part of the story she knew most about. The story still made sense, though. Bale's instincts had been right. His confusion had been because Alef and Pellonhorc had been working as much together as against each other. They had followed the pattern set by their fathers, but Pellonhorc was the leader and the worst of them.

Even so, Alef had participated in monstrous deeds. Razer wondered what it must have done to him at the start of it all, seeing his parents killed as he had.

And if all this were true, he and Pellonhorc had conspired and murdered together until Pellonhorc had secretly contacted the unsaid planet. Only they had seen the truth in Pellonhorc, that he might destroy everything. Only they had acted. *There* would be a story, she thought. But why should the unsaid planet open itself to the System? They were clearly more technologically advanced, and they seemed also to have a spirituality that sustained them. How was that possible? She had always imagined that as science advanced, goddery would fall away. The System was based on that. But maybe it was possible to have something to bind people that was neither the goddery of Gehenna nor the fakery – if it was fakery – of AfterLife.

The Question, Dixemexid had called it. Was it no more than that? Might the point of it simply be to search, to strive, and not to know the answer, nor even to expect one, but to be together in the quest?

She put away the thought for the moment and said, 'What will you do, Alef?'

'I don't know.'

In the night, she raised herself onto her elbows to look at the sleeping Tallen. He had said that Alef had saved them all, but no part of the preceding actions had happened without Alef's knowledge and much of it had been with his active help. Alef was a mystery. He was neither good nor bad, and he was both.

What had created Pellonhorc? His genetic makeup, life events and chance, as with everyone, but what would he have been if he had never met the unique creature that was Alef? And what would Alef have become without Pellonhorc?

She thought of Bale, of Maerley, of Tallen, of all her own encounters. Of her mother. They had made her what she was. They were all within her, were part of her.

Tallen turned in his sleep, the low ceiling light playing over flesh and metal and making him seem incomplete.

Alef had talked about the construction of his Lives, about what he had called the myth of individual tragedy. Maybe he was right; maybe there was nothing new. It was the sharing of experience that mattered. The reaching out and the receiving, the telling and the listening.

But not for Pellonhorc. The prospect of death had driven him into madness. He didn't even trust Alef, who would have done anything for him, and so he had introduced his own lover into the equation, and Alef was seduced by her.

But instead of cementing his control over Alef, it had driven a wedge between them.

For the rendezvous on the rig, each had made their own preparations. Pellonhorc had used Maerley to get his mercs to the rig, but Alef had known about it and also used Maerley to get Razer there. More than just that – Alef knew Pellonhorc was shadowing him, so he had used Razer to point Pellonhorc at Maerley, all those years ago. What else might Alef have done in the manipulation of Pellonhorc in their game of human chess throughout the years, and vice versa? Razer doubted she would ever fully understand it.

So, while Pellonhorc hadn't known specifically about Razer, he had known Alef would have an agent, and the Whisper had used Decece in that search. And in parallel, Alef hadn't known for sure about Tallen until he had been taken, though he had known there would be someone infiltrated by the Whisper on the rig. Alef had been so close, though. If he'd got Razer to Bleak a few days earlier, and guessed at Tallen instead of Bale, who was just the dupe set up to 'rescue' a prepared Tallen, everything might have been different.

And Razer herself had been a dupe as much as an agent. She had been selected, prepared and moved around, and told nothing in case Pellonhorc could trace her.

All of it was inextricably knotted together, all culminating at the rig.

Razer's thoughts whirled. In all of this, if Alef was telling the truth, AfterLife had been no more than a tool he had invented to keep a lover who didn't love him and a child who wasn't his. Alef had cared nothing for AfterLife beyond this small function, and yet it had become the glorious fulcrum of the entire System.

If Alef was telling the truth, though, AfterLife was a lie. Few had ever returned from the sarcs, and by vote, no one ever would. If Alef was telling the truth, all hope was gone. Everything on the Song, everything in the System, was sparked by AfterLife: the anxieties, the vows, the acts of repentance. How much would be lost if AfterLife disappeared?

Without it, she herself would have nothing. TruTales would vanish along with all the other ParaSites. She'd never quite managed to believe she had a neurid, but there was sufficient comfort in the possibility, and there had always been a comfort in the possibility that her thoughts and experiences might remain even after her death. That someone might *know* her.

That we all might know each other.

Maybe it was a lie, but it worked, and it could continue to work unless Alef let it fail. Did it matter if it was a lie, if it was a good thing?

Tallen rolled over and sat up, yawning, and said, 'What's wrong? You're crying. What is it?'

She wiped her eyes. 'What would you do, Tallen, if everything was suddenly gone? If there was nothing left?'

'For me or for everyone?'

'I don't know. Either. Both.'

He looked carefully at her. 'I don't know what he's been saying, but I don't think it's good for you to talk to Alef.'

'Tell me. What would you do?'

'I wouldn't want to deal with it alone. I'd want to talk to someone.' The light played over his brow and he said, 'I'm someone. Talk to me.'

'You're a good man, Tallen. Tell me, is there room for two people in the cage up on deck?'

He smiled. 'I don't need that any more.'

'It's not for you.'

Five days ago, when she had been crawling along the deck in the swimrig, Razer had only been thinking of clinging on. Now, deafened by wind-shriek and drenched by the waves, she yelled with the life of it.

'What do you think of this?' she shouted.

Beside her, his shoulder wedged tightly against hers, Alef said nothing.

'You said you loved playing with water.' She had to stop and take a breath. The water came at them from every direction. Only the contact of each other's body was any small protection.

'With my father. When I was a child.' The strangeness of his voice was lost in the need to shout, and his speech patterns seemed almost normal.

'What about your mother?'

'I loved her. She baked cookies.'

The sea sluiced across the deck. Lances of brilliant sunlight raked the metal, made the struts shine, and gave rainbow halos to the cappings of the pipes.

'How do you feel, to remember them, Alef?'

'Sad. Good.'

Great waves poured over them and sieved away. Razer caught breath, and yelled, 'I can remember them with you. I can help.'

'Why?'

'Because they're important.' She coughed brine.

'They are only important to me,' Alef yelled, his voice high and cracking.

The sea ebbed fiercely and the rig seemed to tip. Between the waves, Razer managed to shout, 'You said I was important to you. Do you remember that?'

He didn't answer. The water rushed back and swamped them and Razer choked and felt she was drowning. Alef moved, shoving himself at her, and his hand was over her mouth. She tried to push him back, thinking he was going to suffocate her, but then realised he was shielding her mouth and nose from the water.

'Thank you, Alef.'

'I don't know what to do.'

Did he sound different, or was it just a hoarsenesss from the effort of making himself heard? She tried to say something but had no breath, and Alef lifted his face to the drowning sky and screamed, 'There is no one to help me.'

'Will you let me help you?' And the rising hard sea smashed into her.

For long minutes, water was everywhere. It seemed like chaos, but Alef's hand was there a moment before each wave crashed through the cage and struck them. She put her own hand around his shoulders to steady them both, and he didn't resist.

'Please help me,' Alef cried.

'Yes, Alef. Yes.'

The thrummer was somewhere up above in the thunderous heavens. Razer didn't know where Tallen was. Alef was somewhere beneath them in his sarc, and he was all around them on the Song.

AfterLife rolled across her screenery. Perhaps all those lives were lies, but they were full of the truths of people's lives. Did it matter if they were jumbled? We all live jumbled lives, Razer thought. It's the connections between us that matter.

She had started on her telling of Alef's Life. How astonishing it was that this man had created such a thing as AfterLife; that this sole man had utterly changed the System.

Alef had made Razer what she was, too. He'd put her life at risk, but she'd survived. Alef had made her a teller of tales, and in return she would tell Alef's story. One day his existence would be revealed, and there needed to be a story in place for that time.

But how to tell it? Not as Alef was telling it to her, with all the murders, and betrayals, and terrible truths. The pure facts would show him as a monster, and the extraordinary way his mind worked was impossible to convey.

She might have told it as a TruTale, through her own eyes, but he deserved more than that, and so did the System.

Across her screenery, the Lives scrolled on. The Song played itself for her. TruTales, HeartSearch, LifeTalk, all the other ParaSites displayed themselves. Razer marvelled at Alef's creation. One communication in four passed through an AfterLife platform. Two of every three minutes spent on the Song involved AfterLife. How could Alef, so unique by birth, so wounded by life, have understood the workings of the System and the needs of humanity so perfectly?

And his creation. In time – in centuries, perhaps – AfterLife might no longer need to be so all-encompassing or so protected. The System might become as the unsaid planet seemed already to be, with the truth acknowledged. But until then, there had to be a story. Alef deserved his place, and AfterLife had to be protected. If the truth was exposed now, the System would not survive it.

No. It couldn't come out now that Liacea Kalthi had been sacrificed, that AfterLife had begun with a murder. That must be told as an accident.

It couldn't be thought that AfterLife had been a cynical fabrication and all its believers dupes. Perhaps later there would be a time for that, but not yet.

So she would write two Lives for him. The true one – and Alef was incapable of telling it otherwise – would remain secretly in the AfterLife database. As for the other, which she had already started, when that Life was ready, Razer would open it on the database. Alef would remain in hypersomnia, and he would continue to protect his creation.

The search would go on. One day, perhaps, Alef might even develop a true neurid, and AfterLife might become a reality. And if that happened, there might be a time when Alef's true Life could be released and he could be remembered, not as perfect, but as some kind of a man.

Tallen

From a secure gantry high on the deck, Tallen stood with Beata and Lode. The three of them together watched as the net descended from the mist and spray with its blurred, almost embryonic human form. Was it struggling for release, or was it fearing the withdrawal of the net's security? Tallen had a sudden memory of his own arrival. How long ago it seemed. How he had changed.

Beata said, 'We shall go down now. We need to be there to receive him.'

Tallen said, 'You'll start all over again. Is that right? You'll be formed by him and for him.' Already they were starting to lose their definition for Tallen. Suddenly he was unsure which of the humechs was which.

One of them said, 'As we were for you. That is our program. You are a short-term device.' Had that been Beata? Tallen felt a sense of impending loss.

Beside the descending gantry, the wriggling net was drawn down into the body of the rig. The other humech said, with Lode's face asserting itself for an instant, 'We shall miss you, Tallen.'

And its mirror said, with a final brief echo of emotion, 'But we will not remember you.'

Razer

The thrummer tipped and swung. Razer watched the rig on the screenery. A few moments ago, as the transport cage had lifted them away, it had seemed vast and almost alive, shuddering and groaning, but now it was no more than a small and delicate bit of trickery. There was something brave and hopeless about its presence in that eternal fury.

It had all been like some sort of dream. Nothing had made sense down there.

She thought, *Tallen?* But of course there was nothing. She had missed her chance with him.

The thrummer pilot said, 'Not my business, but how come there's two of you?'

Razer said, 'I was swimming, got out of my depth, washed up on the rig.'

The pilot said, 'Yeah? Well, like I said, not my business. And you with her, don't I recognise you? With the skullware?'

Tallen said, 'Maybe.'

'Well, I just got your puke out of the webbing. Don't make it a double.'

They were all silent after that. Razer spent a long while looking down towards the sea on the screenery. Mostly it was murk and rain, and occasionally a glimpse of flat grey, but once, suddenly, the sun punched through and there was the sea, sharp and clear.

The thrummer pilot's voice came through again. 'Hey,

back there. You might want to look down, but be quick. I've never seen it this perfect.'

Razer gasped. The sea was a shifting mosaic of burnished metals and dirty whites, pricked by dots of perfect black that vanished as swiftly as they appeared – sarcs, she realised, surfacing and submerging in the brief brilliant sun with what seemed not despair or loneliness but joyful exuberance. In the lancing, glorious light, she had a vision of them as lives working unconsciously, unknowingly, together.

The sea moved; the sarcs leaped and plunged. Razer marvelled to watch it. The vast multitude of sarcs down there, the presence of each affecting every other in some tiny way and moderating the whole, like those joined voices in the church choir of Alef's childhood, like all the communicants within the Song.

The mists closed to rain once more, and Razer sat back into the comfort of the webbing and caught Tallen's eye. He seemed to be crying. She wondered whether he had seen what she had seen.

Alef was down there, somewhere, and at last he was a part of something. She wondered which was the more fantastical idea, that he had invented AfterLife, or that he had invented his tale of it.

Tallen had earphones on, locking himself away. She opened her comms.

'Cynth?'

DOES KESTREL DUST WANT CHITTLECHATTLE?

'Yes.' She hesitated. 'Alef?'

YES. BUT I CAN'T DO CHITTLECHATTLE. CYNTH CAN DO CHITTLECHATTLE. DO YOU WANT CYNTH?

'I prefer you, Alef. What are you doing now?'

I AM ON THE SONG. I THINK I AM HAPPY HERE. I TALK TO PEOPLE. THEY TELL ME THEIR LIVES. I HELP THEM. I THINK ABOUT MY LIFE. THEY HELP ME. I THINK ABOUT YOUR LIFE. I THINK ABOUT YOU.

'I won't always be here. You can outlive me, in hypersomnia.'

I KNOW. I WILL CARRY ON, AS LONG AS THERE ARE LIVES TO FOLLOW. I WILL CARE FOR AFTERLIFE.

The thrummer tipped and straightened. Razer closed the comms unit and watched Tallen for a while. He was staring out of the window, oblivious to her. She would write Alef's two Lives. She already had the bones of the truth, and now she started to reframe it, recomposing the death of Liacea Kalthi.

Eventually the thrummer came down, and at the dock, Tallen jumped out and started to walk towards the doors of the port. Razer watched as they opened for him and closed behind him.

Razer stood beside the thrummer and looked back towards the sea. The thrummer pilot jumped down and said something that was lost in the wind, and disappeared after Tallen.

The machine's blades stopped turning. Razer gazed at the dark waters, but there was nothing to see in them. She wondered whether she had left more behind than she had gained, out there on the rig. After a while, she turned towards the port doors. Before she could reach them, though, they opened and Tallen was there, waiting.

And in the doorway, he said, 'If you can write anywhere, why don't you come with me? Or I'll come with you. Either way.'

The sun behind her was bright on his face. The patches of metal on his cheeks and skull held a soft, warm glow. In the distance were the bristling rigyards and the nodding cranes, and the noise of the containers endlessly ferrying sarcs to the hospital ships was a soothing, faraway murmur.

'Are you sure?' she said. 'I have a story here, two of them, but when they're done, I want to tell one about the unsaid planet. If they let me.'

Tallen laughed. 'We've already started that one, haven't we? First contact?'

Razer let him take her hand. She felt extraordinarily lucky. This was her life.

'So, what about it?' Tallen asked. 'The two of us together.'

Acknowledgements

Chris Thomas for everything here that may appear to be related to oil rigs. Where it is accurate, it is Chris's. Where it is bilge, deliberately or accidentally, it is all my own.

Miranda Jewess and Ella Chappell for seeing clearly down to the core of this tortuous rig, and everyone at Titan for having faith in me and in this tale. Julia Lloyd for the fabulous cover design.

James Lovegrove and Adam Roberts for advice, support, encouragement and friendship, and Simon Spanton, too, for those things plus particularly generous and accurate advice.

Melissa Roberti was an invaluable reader, as were many others during Anne Aylor's legendary writing weeks in Catalonia.

Constant and ongoing thanks to everyone in the Zens, for advice, criticism, conversation and the exchange of elaborate excuses for not writing; Oana Aristide, Anne Aylor, Nick Barlay, Jude Cook, Gavin Eyers, Steve Mullins, Annemarie Neary, Richard Simmons, Elise Valmorbida.

About the author

Roger Levy is a British science fiction writer. He is the author of *Reckless Sleep*, *Dark Heavens* and *Icarus*. He works as a dentist when not writing fiction, and was described as the 'heir to Philip K. Dick' by Strange Horizons.